Abergavenny Small Press.
publishing

1

2024

Abergavenny Small Press (ASP)

The Displaced

Produced and published in 2024
by Abergavenny Small Press (ASP)
Published by Draft2Digital
ISBN 978-1-7396520-9-8
Typeset by Nicholas Wilford, Scotland
Cover illustration:
By Danielle Farrington
asppublishing.co.uk
asppublishinghouse@gmail.com

ABOUT THE AUTHOR

Sharif Gemie is a retired history Professor who has lived in Wales for thirty years. He enjoys walking the still green spaces of the Monmouthshire-Brecon Canal, listening to trad-jazz and psychedelic-folk, and making his own ginger and apricot flapjacks. While a lecturer, he researched histories of marginalized and mobile peoples, such as refugees, migrants and travellers. After retirement, he fulfilled one of his lifelong ambitions: he took up Creative Writing.

The Displaced began with research into refugees during the Second World War, when Sharif noticed that some of the life histories of both refugees and UN aid-workers sounded like novels.

Sharif is writing a sequel to *The Displaced*.

Previous historical works

Sharif wrote eight full-length historical studies, plus about a hundred shorter essays and articles. The most successful of these was *The Hippy Trail: A History (1957—78)*, published in 2017, co-authored with Brian Ireland. He researched refugees and aid-workers in *Outcast Europe: Refugees and Relief Workers in an Age of Total War, 1936—48*, published in 2011, co-authored with Fiona Reid and Laure Humbert. Another work by Sharif which has attracted interest is *French Muslims: New Voices in Contemporary France* (2010).

Fictional works

'The Saved,' *The Quiet Reader*, 6 June 2022. https://thequietreader.com/magazine/the-saved-sharif-gemie/

'The Wrong Time to Die,' *The Quiet Reader* 4 (Sep 2021) https://thequietreader.com/magazine/the-wrong-time-to-die/

'A Problem with Sex,' *Storgy* (Sep 2021), https://storgy.com/2021/09/27/a-problem-with-sex-by-sharif-gemie/

'Leonardo and the Mad Girl,' *Magazine of History and Fiction* 1:4 (Winter 2019) https://magazineoftheoldwest.neocities.org/leonardomadgirl.html

'The Map and the Migrant,' in Emma Larking (ed), *We Refugees* (Raleigh, North Carolina: Pact Press 2019), pp. 69—73.

DEDICATION

To Angela Platt (1945—2020)

who taught me to write

Author's note:

For forty years, I wrote non-fiction. Changing to fiction has been an adventure, at once challenging, exhilarating and occasionally terrifying. I've been lucky to have many sources of advice, criticism, support and encouragement. Among the groups who've helped me have been: the Cwtch (Newport) Creative Writers, the Cardiff Writers' Circle, Newport Writers and the Renegade Writers Facebook page.

Many people took the time to read draft versions of this work. I'm grateful to everyone for their advice and insights. Thank you: Patricia Clark, John Crerar, Andrew Douch, Carmela Gianfagna, Karenne Griffin, Suzy Hobson, Brian Ireland, Nadia Lampis, Norry Laporte, Sarah Morgan, Dylan Moore, Jan Newton, Steve Pritchard, Fiona Reid, Gabriella Ross, Eryl Samuel, Susanna Schrafstetter, Paul Seligman, Dave Thomas, Alison Truesdale, Rhodri Williams and Jennifer Wilkinson.

Thank you to 'Dogs' for spotting an earlier story of my mine and deciding I looked convincing.

Above all, thank you Shirley McCully for sharing this journey.

The Displaced

'Without contraries is no progression.'

William Blake

'We're displaced persons too, when you come to think of it. But if you call another man a Displaced Person, it means he doesn't matter as much as you do, because he's destitute.'

Colin MacInnes

Part I...England

    Part II ....France

    Part III..Germany

    Part IV...Interlude

    Part V.....................................Darkest Germany

    Epilogue...To Eleanor

    Appendix...........................The Refugee's Lesson

    Sources cited

PART I
ENGLAND

'...as I walked home under an exquisite night sky that might be loaded with death, what I dug into and examined was my own mind.'

J.B. Priestley, 23 June 1940

'There has been no normalcy, no rest for any.'

Stafford Cripps, February 1943

1. Coming Home

I'm going the wrong way. At this time in the afternoon, everyone is leaving London—I'm in a half-empty carriage, trundling towards Waterloo station. The man opposite me, an officer in artillery or intelligence or something, gave up trying to chat soon after Dover, when I told him I wasn't in the forces. My uniform had confused him.

I look out the window. Signs of war are everywhere: smashed houses, craters in fields. But not like Neukirchen. Here, the smashed house is the exception—in Germany, whole streets were crushed into rubble and it was the odd undamaged building that stood out. Oh, but I'm sick of the whole thing, so sick of it all. I want to get away.

Will Muriel meet me at Waterloo? Of course she will, I can rely on her. But I wish she'd not be there, I wish I could just float past London, then drift away and leave everything behind. There's too much to think about. Muriel is sure to ask about Eleanor. What will I say? My hands tremble and half a sob slips from my mouth. I try to turn it into a cough. The artillery officer glances at me, then turns back to his paper. A nasty ache starts at the back of my neck—I know what this might mean, it might be the beginning of an attack. I breathe in slowly, then breathe out. Grey-green fields flicker past the window. The pain ebbs.

Eleanor. One more death in a world that's sick with death and destruction.

I ought to be grateful, shouldn't I? Muriel's arranged everything for me, at a few days' notice. Borrowed a little flat from a friend, just off the high street, so I don't have to go back to my house and all those memories of Eleanor.

The train judders and screeches: I check my watch. A quarter past six. We're late, of course, everything is late these days. Worse in Germany. Muriel will be waiting. If only Eleanor was there too—no, I must stop thinking that way.

***

There's something comforting about the vast iron-girded canopy of Waterloo station, which hasn't changed at all. I stare up at the rows of grey glass panes. You wouldn't see those in Germany! Not a single intact pane there, even a year after the war's end. I smile: I'm coming home, aren't I? Then crowds of commuters push past me. Their clothes seem odd—of course, no khaki. They wear grey, brown, blue and black, civilian colours, the men in their suits, the women with their coats. Khaki looks better. It suggests a common purpose, a resolve, while this crowd—they swarm and dart, dither and turn, with no real aim.

There's Muriel, damnit, at the barrier. Waving to me: round, cheerful face, smart coat, resolutely still while the crowd mill around her. It's starting, I've got to do this.

We stand close to each other, we don't hug, but she grips my elbow awkwardly and stares up at me.

'Poor Eleanor,' she says. 'I'll miss her so.'

There's a catch in her voice—is she about to cry? I turn my face away, I don't want her to see my tears.

'Was it—' she asks.

'It was very quick. They say she wouldn't have felt a thing.'

'And you, Edmund, are you—'

'I'm in a bloody awful state.'

We walk, she leads me to a bus stop. On the bus, she talks—she's kept my house properly, I needn't worry, she thinks I'll like the flat, I can stay as long as I like, she's moved some of my things into it, a change of clothes. I nod, say *yes* a couple of times, even remember to say *thank you*. It's not easy for either of us. Do I want to come round to eat tonight? No. A drink? Maybe. She drops a hint about her Graham—I don't respond, I never liked the sound of him, neither did Eleanor.

Stop. I mustn't treat Muriel like this, it's not her fault.

We find the old pub in the high street, which looks battered and filthy. I get a beer for me and a port and lemon for Muriel. I sip slowly: my beer tastes watery and there's a nasty metallic after-taste.

I've got to tell her my decision.

'Muriel,' I say. She looks up. 'I've decided—I've decided to sell the house.'

'No! You can't.'

'I've got to. It will never be a home for me, not without Eleanor.'

'No...'

I explain my plans: sell up, move back to Wales, set up a general store in Cardiff. She sighs, nods.

'Alright, but think about it carefully, Edmund. Don't rush into it. But—if you like, we could go to the house tomorrow.' She sips her drink. 'We could start sorting out stuff. All those books!'

'I don't want—'

'Let's meet for lunch first. One o'clock. The place down the road.'

I know where she means—the three of us went there a few times. It seems so long ago. But she doesn't see—doesn't see that I don't want to go back to the house. I *can't* go back. Maybe if we met for lunch, I could explain this to her?

Muriel looks at her watch.

'I've got to go.' She grins. 'Meeting Graham. Tomorrow?'

'Alright.'

***

The next morning, when I wake up, I need a few moments to remember where I am. Eleanor's absence aches inside me. I shake my head, get up, have a bath.

Muriel's brought over a couple of my suits. They look worn and grey, but I can't wear khaki anymore. I put on a suit and notice that

I'm thinner, despite all the wonderful food in Germany. Tall and gangly as ever. Sad and a bit grey today.

I need to get a grip. I sit at the kitchen table, try to think about the day's tasks. I've got a few precious hours of calm in this odd flat before I meet Muriel. For three weeks I haven't been able to think straight. Those last days in Germany were a tangled mess: Eleanor's awful, awful death, the formalities and the return of my epilepsy—they all blur into one dreadful, downward spiral. I keep thinking of those days as a story about someone else. No. It's my story, the story of Edmund and Eleanor, of me and you. It's got an ending: your death. But—is that *the* ending? Maybe it's the ending of a chapter, not the whole book. I don't know.

I spot a letter by the door. Muriel's round, regular writing is on the envelope: she must have slipped it under the door before I was up. Why's she written? I'll see her in a few hours—what can be so urgent? It must be about you. I can't face reading it, I don't want to know, not straight away, not now. Instead...

Breakfast. Breakfast first, then thinking. Looking round the kitchen, I find coffee and nothing else. I fill the kettle, put it on the ring, light a match, wait.

Sipping my coffee, I stare at the envelope, reach for it, stop, then pick it up. Muriel's note falls out. Her mother's ill, so she'll go back to Kent for a few days. She'll write again, before she returns.

My worries evaporate. No lunchtime meeting, no arranging, no explanations, no plans. I don't need to do anything. I have not just a few hours, but a few days of absolute freedom—no one's expecting anything from me, time's stopped.

I think again of breakfast and remember the café in the high street. Father would've said it was common, but my year in Germany has knocked all that out of me. I've learnt to muck in. Breakfast seems a good idea. Tea, bacon, fried eggs and toast. Maybe mushrooms and tomatoes as well. I can almost smell them.

***

The waitress looks surprised when I order, then surly.

'We could manage scrambled eggs on toast,' she says, as if doing me a favour.

After a few minutes she returns with a yellow mess that smells odd. Of course, *powdered* eggs. It's been a long time since I had powdered eggs. I eat a few mouthfuls. At least the toast is alright. Maybe some salt for the eggs? I check my table: no salt. I call to the girl. She gives me a dirty look and produces a salt-cellar from behind the counter. It's so battered that only a tiny trickle of salt drips out. The girl stands by the table, waiting for me to hand it back. I think about pepper, but decide not to risk it.

I remember our meals in Germany: we were lucky, weren't we? Thoughts of breakfasts with you fill my mind. I let the images linger as I eat, they take away the taste of the poisonous eggs. Your smile over a cup of coffee, the thoughtful look that crossed your face as we discussed the day's activities.

Sad. I can't recall any particular breakfast. None of them seemed important at the time. Thinking hard, I remember a day when we had a jar of the finest Spanish marmalade and you laughed at the sheer luxury of it: a whole jar, just for us, when there was so much starvation and poverty around us. You warned me not to get used to it.

Is that right? Is that what happened? But—so what? Does it help me?

I must pull myself together. I've got a stream of memories, a *storm* of memories, rising, churning round in my head. It's almost too much.

Looking out of the café window, I see a tired, nearly empty street: a milk cart going back to the depot, a man wobbling on a bicycle, a woman looking in a shop window, adjusting her hat. Then, no, I see a blur—*no*, not now, I mustn't, I can't have another fit, not here, not now, I can't become a gibbering wreck, falling to the café floor. I take a deep breath, look again, focusing carefully: it's just condensation on the window, nothing more. I'm safe, thank goodness.

I must do something today. I've got money. Catch a train up to town? See the big bookshops, lunch in Bloomsbury? Or walk to Crystal Palace Park? It might be good to stretch my legs. Or go back to the flat and read? I can't just sit and mope. I mustn't, I really mustn't.

What do I want to do? What do I want? I want you, but... So, instead, I want to understand. What happened between you and me? What does this jumble of thoughts and memories and feelings mean? It's strange: I've spent years of my life selling novels. Now I must create my own story and hang on to it. How else will I calm this storm in my mind? There's only one way to write that story: with the coin of daily life—words, images, thoughts, feelings. I could re-create you, you *and* me, that way. It won't be moping, no. I need to find some essence, some centre, some *thing*.

Reaching into my jacket pocket for my cigarettes, I find the house keys. How did they get there? I remember taking the flat keys, but I thought I'd left the other set on the kitchen table.

I could go—I could go to the house—by myself. An electric pulse races through me: it's like a thrill, a dare. I *could* do it. Muriel wouldn't know, nobody would. Go by the back alley, no one would see. I could, yes.

I puff on my cigarette, inhaling deeply. I want to find a centrepiece, around which I'll organise everything else. Six years of my life. Five and a half.

Yes. In the house, by myself, I'll find something, something of you. An earring? No. But some part of you, something private to me.

And—it'd be good to break the taboo, to prove I'm not scared of these memories.

I'll do it.

***

I don't give myself time to change my mind. I walk fast. Back up the high street. Over the hump of the railway bridge. Left into the backstreet and there's the alley. I glance round quickly, then catch my breath. It's okay, no one's looking. And anyway—it's *my* house. My father's one good decision: to buy a bookshop and a two-floor apartment in London. Not Charing Cross Road, of course. He wanted to be near a big Methodist congregation and so was drawn here.

The backdoor lock seems stiff: for a moment, I fear it's rusted. I try again and it creaks open. I ignore the door which leads to the bookshop and instead turn left, up the staircase. At the top, I open the door slowly, feeling more like an intruder than a house-owner: a thief in the night, returning after twelve months.

I glance round the first floor, looking with a stranger's eyes. This is Muriel's, we agreed that when we left: she's changed very little. I glimpse her bed through the half-open door of what used to be the spare room. The mess of boxes and unsold books has gone, and instead there's a green eiderdown folded neatly over a single bed. I won't go in. The kitchen looks the same: long, thin room with dark wooden fittings. There's still the same feel to the place. Bookish... Odd bookshelves along the walls and in corners, each crammed to bursting with books and pamphlets, and a couple of framed pictures—no, one's gone. The pen-drawing, a copy of that Renaissance picture from Italy. Spring, wasn't it? The Spirit of Spring? It's gone. Perhaps it reminded Muriel too much of you. Instead, there's a poster from a year or two ago. Bright, brash colours:

the United Nations advancing to victory, the flags of all the Allies
flying together. That sort of thing used to inspire us.

Oh. There—by the table. The crate. Your crate, all your worldly
goods, it got here before me. Who'd have thought it? For once, they
worked efficiently. It's open, Muriel must've done that. I feel a pang
of pain at the thought of her, alone, forcing it open to find—to find
so little, so very little. I want to see what's inside, what remains of
your thirty-one years. But I know what the crate contains, don't I? I
was there when Alma packed it. I was there, but not in a fit state to
think or act or help or do anything. That was a bad day.

I sit down, look round to see if anything else has changed. On
the wall is the collection of pictures we used to call the gallery. I
spot the framed photograph of you and Muriel, ambulance drivers.
Yes. There's that funny caption at the bottom of the frame: *Eleanor
and Muriel Save the World*. A surprise photograph as you started
your shift. Muriel, shorter than you, staring at the camera, a broad
grin lighting up her face, looking unexpectedly dashing. She used
to laugh about the photograph, saying it was the only time in her
entire service that she'd looked happy. Next to her, you: tall, posed,
hand on hip, looking down at the camera. Elegant, even in an
ambulance-driver's uniform. Dark hair tied back, but still spraying
round your head, intense dark eyes and some mischief, some
devilment in your look. That's the one. That's the one.

2. Blitz Outside, Blitz Inside

For six years, Eleanor and my sickness were the two poles of my life, the positive and negative. I'll never forget the day of my first fit. But had it visited me before, sneaked in, without calling attention to itself? I'm not sure.

It was the autumn of 1940. I was waiting for my call-up papers. As a 26-year-old unmarried bookshop-owner, I had no reason to refuse military service. My occupation wasn't vital to the war effort. Joining the army didn't scare me. I watched as my friends got their papers, left their shops and offices and travelled to little-known parts of the British Isles. They returned in their new uniforms for odd weekends of boozing and parties, looking strangely different: taller, maybe more determined or more cynical, certainly clearer about their lives and their place in society. Talking with them, I learnt something about modern warfare. Any man might be ordered to defend his country with a rifle or even a bayonet, but many were required for less exciting roles. There were clerks, translators, store-managers, accountants, technicians and engineers. As a grammar school boy, I was destined for one of those posts. It would be disruptive, but it couldn't be helped.

Meanwhile, the bookshop kept me busy. My father gave it to me in 1938, when he and mother decided to move to South Africa. I'd welcomed the chance to convert his drab religious store into a sophisticated literary salon, in which prestigious authors would drop in to discuss the latest literary trends and earnest but attractive young women would look up at me over their spectacles and say:

'Tell me more about modernist literature.'

Fat chance. I painted the interior white and I re-arranged the shelves so customers could walk round more easily. I converted half the basement into—if I say it myself—a really quite interesting second-hand bookstore. But Auden and Sitwell, Eliot and Woolf never visited. Soon, I faced a more pressing problem. The Methodist regulars deserted the shop and the local literary crowd weren't interested. In spring 1939 it was clear that I faced bankruptcy. What would I say to father? One afternoon, as I fretted in an empty bookshop, a girl came in and asked if I sold envelopes. I didn't, but she gave me an idea. It was risky, but I spent the last of my savings on some mid-range stationery: envelopes, writing-paper, fountain pens and bottles of ink. It worked, thank goodness. People would drop in for envelopes, then glance round the shelves, maybe buy a thriller or a romance.

After 1939, the post from South Africa got slower and more erratic. Early in 1940—was it February?—I had a letter from father, saying they'd move from Johannesburg into the bush. They had a calling to serve the natives and they'd revert to the old family trade of farming. They promised me a new address, but no further letters arrived. Their silence worried me, but I decided they were probably safer in the African bush than I was in the London suburbs.

But on that grim October morning in 1940... Previously, I'd sometimes sensed something odd as I opened the shop. My vision might be blurred, or there'd be a strange, flickering light in the sky outside and my pulse would pound. Sometimes I'd feel so dizzy that I needed to sit down by the cash till. Once a customer came into the shop and asked me something as I tried to catch my breath, and it was as if he was speaking from very far away or—more curious still—as if he wasn't really speaking to me at all. He must have thought I'd taken to the bottle. At that time, more and more people needed a drink or two to get them through the day. Whisky and gin could still be bought, if you knew the right people.

On that morning, I went outside to fix a heavy-duty shutter that had worked loose. When I came back, I sat by the till, contemplating the furled-up blackout curtains inside and the open shutters outside. The sunlight grew painfully bright, to the point that I raised my hand to cover my eyes. I felt the floor tremble. A day-time air-raid, I thought as I crumpled downwards.

Later—I've no idea how much later—I found myself lying on the floorboards between the bookshelves. My legs and ankles hurt: they were badly bruised. There was a ringing tone coming and going in my head, but the strangest thing was my left arm. It felt numb and I couldn't move it. I thought I'd stay there, on the floor, until I felt stronger, when a woman in an ambulance-driver's uniform walked by. Something made her glance in. I recognised her—Muriel, the sister of someone I knew from literary meetings before the war.

Within seconds, it seemed, she'd telephoned the ambulance service, locked up the shop and got me to a hospital, where my broken elbow was examined and my bruises checked. They said little that day. But the next day Muriel came by with a doctor—a tall Scotsman in a white coat, with gleaming steel specs, neat white beard and well-trimmed hair. A real old school type. He didn't actually intone *what seems to be the problem*, but I could tell he was thinking it. He looked at me for a few moments, then glanced at my notes.

'Has this ever happened before?'

'No!'

'No dizziness? Fainting spells?'

I shook my head.

'You just *fell*?'

'I don't even remember falling. One moment I was looking out the window, worried about the light—' He looked up at that point, so I rushed on before he could question me. '—then everything seemed to move.'

'And you found yourself on the floor?'

'Yes.' He was making me feel guilty, as if I was lying.

This seemed absurd. Why were they paying such attention to me? I'd had a nasty fall, nothing compared with the injuries suffered by people in air-raids.

'Tell me about the light,' he asked.

I knew he'd ask about that. There wasn't much to say.

'It was just—just bright. Too bright.'

'Still or moving?'

'Moving, I suppose. Flickering.'

'These are the classic symptoms of an epileptic seizure.'

I knew next-to-nothing about epilepsy. Wasn't it a sort of madness? I looked at Muriel and was embarrassed by the pity in her eyes.

'Have you ever had a head injury?'

'No. No, but...'

He looked up, an obvious question in his eyes.

'Well, once at school, I fell over on some steps. I hit my head and fainted.'

He nodded.

'But that was years ago!' I protested.

The doctor questioned me about my childhood and I recalled moments when I drifted away during classes, to the point where I didn't hear the teacher's words. And I fainted now and again. Doesn't that happen to all children? The doctor raised his eyebrows, then nodded.

'*Petit mal*,' he diagnosed. 'The standard pattern. I've checked your records. Have you received your call-up papers?'

I shook my head.

'No national service for you, I'm afraid.'

'No?'

'No. Can you imagine what would've happened if you'd been driving a tank?'

'But I could still do a desk-job!'

He shook his head. 'Arms-training is essential for all military posts.'

I glared at him. 'Everyone I know has been called up. Why—'

'Not you. You'll stay here.'

I felt a chasm growing, separating me from the great task that was demanded of us. I didn't want to be a shirker, I wanted to pull my weight. This doctor—he was saying that people wouldn't be able to trust me, that I couldn't work in a team. With my fall, I'd left one part of humanity, the reliable part, and joined another, inferior part. I was demoted, belittled, passed over.

I insisted on one point. There would be no mention of epilepsy in the doctor's report—the word alone frightened me. The doctor listened to me, thought for a few moments and then agreed he couldn't be certain. He recorded my *turns of indeterminate origin*.

***

They sent me home two days later. Muriel stayed around—it was difficult for her to travel into London from her mother's place in Kent. In those days, railways and stations were so damaged that people avoided train journeys. London was full of people sleeping on sofas and in spare rooms. I'd barely known Muriel before the war, although I could remember her asking a visiting speaker intense questions about Spanish republican novels. I knew her mother wanted to set her up with a nice young man who worked in a bank and Muriel was doing her best to find an unsuitable, disreputable alternative. To this end she attended no end of meetings about contentious political causes and I saw her grow more confident in asking questions. Other people wrote her off as a natural conservative dabbling in controversy—I had the impression she was genuinely interested.

After my fall, Muriel made herself useful in the bookshop.

'Edmund! You must take your pill this morning.'

'But they don't do me any good. They make me feel like I'm walking through fog.'

'Better fog than a seizure.'

'I need to write an important order today.'

'You need to avoid seizures first.'

And so on. She'd help me finish dressing while my elbow healed. A little later, when I felt steadier, she'd open the bookshop with me and give me a hand in running it, in exchange for a camp bed in the spare room. We argued over the pills I was prescribed. I was meant to take two a day, but I hated the soporific effect they had on me. So I'd split them in two and take half-doses. Muriel told me that this wasn't sufficient, but I'd ignore her.

Physically, I was recovering. My arm came out of plaster. Sometimes there'd be an odd twinge when I lifted a pile of books and Muriel would come along and insist on doing it for me. But something had changed in me. Sometimes I'd see that flickering light—or I thought I did. I'd get worried and look for my pills.

It felt strange having a woman in the bookshop, but so much was strange in London in those days. After my fall, I needed Muriel and she needed somewhere to stay in London. There wasn't a trace of romance between us—there was something horribly efficient about Muriel that reminded me of my father's Methodist friends and which I found unattractive. Anyway, I was coming to terms with my epilepsy and my new status as a non-combatant. While my contemporaries trained to fight Hitler, I was stuck in a bookshop. Just one fall! I felt cheated and wished I was doing something more useful.

One evening, Muriel brought Eleanor back with her. Eleanor's lodgings had been bombed and she needed somewhere to stay. It wasn't love at first sight. Eleanor looked tired and fed-up when she first arrived. Muriel told her she could sleep on my parents' old sofa.

'That'll be fine,' she said in a casual tone, but I thought I saw a flash of irritation in her eyes.

That evening, Eleanor's accent puzzled me: at times, I heard an echo of a debutante's cut-glass vowels. And there was something strange about the forceful, cutting gestures she made as she talked—a bit pretentious, I thought. But I didn't give her much consideration, assuming she was another example of social disorder in bomb-Blitzed London. A posh girl, slumming it as an ambulance-driver. She shared our fish cutlets and boiled potatoes and slept on the old sofa without a word of protest.

In November, the air raids got worse. Sometimes I felt brave: at least I hadn't fled the city like so many. More often, I felt scared. The three of us debated where we should shelter: in the Anderson shelter in my tiny garden or in the basement? The standard advice was that the shelters were safer, but Eleanor pointed out that the garden was surrounded by tall buildings. A falling chimney stack would go straight through the shelter. I preferred nestling down in the basement, next to my books. Muriel said that collapsing masonry might block us in there, turning the basement into a tomb, but I showed her the skylight that opened into the garden. We agreed: the basement it was. Muriel and Eleanor's shifts were wildly irregular, but when they stayed overnight, the three of us usually went down to the basement.

We soon learnt the pattern, like all Londoners. First a distant alert, a plaintive noise, something that might have been a creak from a passing truck—but then it spread, an animal-like cry of pain echoing across the sky, rising to a crescendo, taken up by borough after borough, growing closer. We'd look at each other, grab what we needed—a book, a bottle, a blanket—and head down the stairs. After the cry died away, we'd hear a throbbing in the night sky, a deadly, sinister sound, regular but unpredictable. Growing closer? Moving away? Passing over? Or coming for us? There was nothing worth bombing near my bookshop: no factories or docks. Just the railway line and station. But there was no rational pattern to the destruction. Any street might get smashed any night. The anti-aircraft guns would start. We'd recognise the crazy rhythm of the nearest one, a staccato waltz time, three beats and then a pause, with a stress of the last beat. The firing told us this really was a raid, not a false alarm. There really were German bombers up there and death really was close. If we were unlucky, we'd hear the *woosh* of falling bombs, then a *crump* and a vibration would rock the house. Sometimes I'd think that this Victorian building wasn't designed for this sort of treatment, mostly I lay still and unthinking, petrified by the noises outside.

The worst times were when the explosions grew closer, step by step. I could picture their route—the canal, the gas works, the library, the crossroads, the cinema, the high street and then...

One night, the inevitable happened. I remember a sensation like falling, although I lay on cushions. Muriel told me afterwards that it was a severe attack: they'd struggled to hold me down as I kicked and jerked. It went on for minutes as the bombers flew overhead. I couldn't remember anything about it, of course. I didn't hear the long note of the all-clear.

I came round in a strange calm filled with the smell of dust and smoke and the first grey traces of dawn seeping in from the skylight. My feet and ankles ached: they were severely bruised. I guessed what had happened, but lay unmoving, pretending to sleep. I couldn't face talking to Muriel or Eleanor. I'd have to apologise and I tried to think of the right words. My mind worked slowly and it took a few moments before I realised they were talking in tense, hushed tones.

'It's our duty! We must stay. Other people depend on us,' Muriel was saying. 'They'll say we're scared.'

'Of course we're scared. Everyone's scared. You'd have to be a lunatic not to be scared.'

Eleanor's voice had a tough, gritty tone that I hadn't heard before. The posh girl's accent had disappeared.

'I'm not a quitter,' said Muriel.

'This isn't quitting. We'd be doing valuable work. People need to eat, don't they? And what about him?' I guessed this meant me. 'Are you going to leave him to smash himself to bits on his precious bookshelves? Come back from the ambulances to find a bloody corpse?'

'If he'd take his pills...' said Muriel.

'It's not about pills. This is something bigger. His reaction's *logical*, don't you see?'

Muriel sighed, then began again: 'We're a team, in the ambulances.'

'It's not a team. It's another nasty little clique, rigged by those with money and power, sending the ones they don't like out into a nightly hell.'

'No, Eleanor, you can't say that.'

'This'll be the death of him.'

I was stunned. I'd thought of myself as a generous host, offering shelter to two poor females, victims of modern warfare. It seemed that I'd made a mistake: Muriel and Eleanor thought *they* were caring for *me*. What cheek! I took a deep breath, raised myself up on one elbow and spoke with as much dignity as I could muster.

'Thank you very much for your concerns. But, firstly, let me assure you, I'm quite capable of looking after myself and, secondly...'

Eleanor and Muriel never heard my invaluable second point. I collapsed back onto the cushions. Another seizure? No, just exhaustion and tension, but I couldn't say another word.

That evening, we held a formal house meeting. There was only one item on the agenda: Eleanor's proposal that we move to a farm owned by a friend of a friend in Somerset and help with the farm work. It was obvious that Eleanor wouldn't persuade us. I was determined to refuse any more assistance and the bookshop was my home. Muriel was committed to the ambulance service. Eleanor wedged herself into a corner of the sofa, ran her fingers through her hair and lit a cigarette. Then she spoke in a measured, lucid way, punctuating her words with that strange, downwards, chopping movement of her right hand. Sometimes she'd shoot a glance at me and I got an unexpected impression of a strength within her. Her eloquence impressed me.

'Fear is paralysing us here,' she began. 'We must leave this place to free ourselves from fear and hate.'

What did she mean? At first I was bewildered. But she spoke at length, telling us about how the war economy needed British-grown food, how women in a male-dominated society were denied positions of power (at that point, she had the grace to smile quickly at me), how we needed to stick together and how my needs as an epileptic affected us. She talked as if she was addressing a public meeting. Where had she learnt to do that? Occasionally, Muriel shifted forward, as if she wanted to interrupt, but Eleanor would glance at her and Muriel sat back.

'Look how unprepared London is!' said Eleanor. 'Thousands of shelters built without steel or cement. They collapse if a bomb falls near them, they're bloody death traps.'

Muriel got one sentence in. 'This is just what you'd expect from a red!'

Eleanor replied, 'I have never been a member of the Communist Party.'

I didn't speak. I was too tired after my seizure and—anyway—I enjoyed listening to Eleanor. She would've made a great preacher. She didn't speak with *hwyl*, that fiery passion that my father's Welsh family had admired in Sunday sermons in their chapels. But she had something else instead: a gritty, logical determination. She wouldn't stop, she beat us down with reason. It was rather fascinating and, for a moment, I wanted to know more about this strange visitor who occupied my sofa.

Eleanor easily defeated Muriel and me. Three days later, I locked the front door of the shop and patted it, as you might a favourite pet.

'I wonder if it'll be alright when we come back,' I said.

'I wonder if any of this street will be here,' retorted Muriel.

'I wonder if we'll ever come back,' said Eleanor.

***

Our new accommodation at the farm in Somerset was not as comfortable as Eleanor had hoped. The three of us were lodged in a huge medieval-looking barn, with enormous wooden beams holding up the roof. The owners had started to convert it into a house. There was a lavatory and running water—just one tap, supplied from a local stream. And that was it. Well, there was a sort of shed in one corner, which I think was the beginnings of a kitchen. It was bloody cold that winter, the roof leaked when it rained hard and the three of us pitched into that shed every night.

A work pattern was established. Eleanor and Muriel donned trousers and tunics at dawn and walked to the farm. I had expected to join them, but to my surprise I was considered *hors de combat*. At first, I was grateful. I had several seizures over the next months and I felt shattered for days after each one, when I'd hobble like a cripple, waiting for my bruises to heal. I couldn't have done farm work on those days. Often my fits came in the daytime, while the girls were away. I never told them, but they usually guessed. But by 1941 my seizures became less serious and less frequent, and I grew better at anticipating them. Every morning I'd do a quick check: blurred vision? twinges? If I sensed a tension inside me, starting at the back of my neck, it meant danger. I'd reach for the pill bottle and spend the rest of the day in an immobilizing fog.

The farmer was bringing old fields back into service. He set Eleanor and Muriel the most basic agricultural work: digging ditches and pulling up brambles. Some days an old labourer limped over to direct them, mostly they were left on their own. They found the work exhausting.

During the first days, I lay on an old carpet in that freezing shed, thinking. What sort of a man was I? Muriel and Eleanor came back every evening, sweaty, dirty, their arms and faces scratched by brambles and I did nothing. I decided to take a leaf out of Muriel's book: I made myself useful. I found some old bricks and made a fireplace in the middle of the barn, where it was least likely to set the old building on fire. I gathered dead wood and at sunset I warmed a large pail of water for Eleanor and Muriel, so they could wash. I boiled potatoes, I swept, I tried to make things tidy—a fool's task, in that filthy old barn. Muriel still fussed about my pills in the evenings, trying to identify the right quantity for me. Eleanor seemed distant. She didn't talk much and I didn't have much to say. I forgot about the fascinating woman who'd sat on my sofa and given a speech.

Some nights we heard an awful throbbing in the sky. If we looked out to the north-west, we might see an ominous red glow from Bristol, sometimes we even smelt smoke and dust. But no German bombers bothered the farm.

When spring came, I grew more adventurous. If I felt well, I'd walk a couple of miles to the nearest little town and get our rations of cigarettes, tea and maybe tinned peaches or a newspaper. Muriel and Eleanor came back from the farm with milk, eggs, butter, cheese and bread, but they still appreciated something extra. If the girls weren't too tired, we'd read the newspaper together. We had a shock in June 1941: Germany invaded Russia.

Muriel was distraught.

'This is it!' she wailed. 'Hitler will walk right in, like he did in France. He'll control the whole of Europe!'

Eleanor shook her head. 'I wonder. It'll be test, alright, a damn difficult one.'

I frowned. 'You think—you think Stalin can stop Hitler?'

'They stopped Napoleon, didn't they?' replied Eleanor.

We discussed the possible consequences for days afterwards and sometimes Eleanor would speak in her strange proclamatory style. I looked for newspapers more often after that.

In the summer, we developed a social life, of sorts. On quiet evenings, we'd go to the nearest pub, which had a curious clientele, part farm-labourers, part exiled city folk. I guessed they'd been told something about my condition. Sometimes when the regulars spoke to me, they adopted the irritating habit of using exaggeratedly simple words and talking very slowly. Muriel questioned whether I should be drinking, but Eleanor pointed out that the beer was so watered down that it probably wouldn't do me any harm. We'd join in the singing round the piano: it was a great time for sing-songs and sentimental ballads. After a few visits, I found that one city exile was an old English literature teacher and we'd talk about Bernard Shaw and Dickens. He surprised me one evening.

'You're doing okay!' he told me.

'Why? What do you mean?'

'A young fellow with two attractive ladies!'

I must have looked surprised, for he burst out laughing.

'You can't fool me!' he continued. 'It's obvious: the way the tall brunette looks at you! Good for you. Enjoy yourself while you can, lord knows there's enough misery in the world today.'

What was he talking about? I nursed my condition, Muriel and Eleanor battled with brambles and dug ditches. In the evening we ate cheese, bread and boiled potatoes, then went to sleep. That was the sum of our lives together.

***

Everything changed one warm afternoon in September 1941. I put the pail to heat on the fire, waiting for the girls' return. When they arrived, they were exhausted and I got out of the way to let them wash. Muriel had a rabbit that the farmer's son had caught in a trap and she talked happily about stewing it.

A little later, Eleanor came out of the barn, looked at me and suggested we go for a walk. We went up the hill, past the old churchyard, through the field with the sheep in it. Eleanor didn't seem as tired as usual and I think we both wanted to talk. Except for discussions about the relative strengths of the German and Russian armies, we hadn't said much in all those months.

'Rabbit,' she said gleefully. 'We haven't had a proper meal for ages.'

I nodded. In fact, I rather liked our simple diet, but a change would be nice. I tried to adapt to her happiness, but found I couldn't. Before I knew it, I was raging.

'What sort of life is this? The rest of the nation is straining every muscle to fight Hitler and I'm living like some idle hermit. I've been cursed by this—this *thing*, it's cut me off from everything valuable in the world.'

Eleanor gave me a long, cool look.

'You're doing your bit, Edmund. The barn's looking better since you've taken charge of it.'

'But I should be doing so much more! I look at you too going out to the farm every morning, and then I do domestic errands, like some skivvy.'

'We all do what we can. And there's nothing wonderful about pulling up brambles, believe me.'

'Other people are flying Spitfires or driving tanks through deserts,' I protested.

'And each of them depends on an army of support workers. This is a modern war, Edmund. Not everyone can be on the frontline. Would you have preferred to have stayed in London?'

I hesitated, but I knew the truth. Eleanor was right: without her, I probably would have kicked myself to death among my bookcases, just as she'd said.

Eleanor sat down on a rock by a little stream and watched the water gurgle past. I realised I was probably being unfair, expecting her to listen to my woes. After a few moments, she looked up.

'You've a medical condition, Edmund, not a curse. You're coping with it as best you can. Things may change sooner than you expect.' She looked back at the water.

We walked back. At one moment we crossed a stream and we held hands to steady ourselves. The smell of rabbit stew greeted us as we approached the barn. Nothing had been said—I mean nothing romantic—but everything had changed. I think it was the first time we'd talked together, without Muriel. There was something—something that felt *important*, but I wasn't sure what. She'd listened to me. At the beginning of the walk, we'd been two individuals, when we came back, somehow—we were a couple, or we were going to be a couple.

**

Me and women. I was caught between the puritanical Welsh Methodism drummed into me by my parents and the bohemian ethics of the literary set. I tried to reject Methodist moralism, but never quite succeeded and I tried to practice bohemianism, but never quite understood it. Often, the two forces just cancelled each other out. Before my parents left for South Africa, they'd set me up with Sarah, a large, bovine Methodist, with a permanently worried look on her face and her blonde hair tucked into a bun.

That's not fair to her. Sarah followed the creed of Social Methodism. One of her sayings was:

'First fill their stomachs with food and then fill their heads with prayer.'

The prayer evenings she organised included classes in basic literacy for children who'd failed in the state schools. She encouraged the girls to read out poems and the boys to tell stories. She was rather sweet, in a way.

But I was swept along by the literary crowd, who sneered at such do-gooding earnestness. And anyway—after two years of *stepping out*, as my parents called it, our sex lives consisted of a couple of confused clinches on the doorstep of her parents' house, and one alarming *Oh Edmund* which seemed to express shock, repulsion and female passion in a single, contradictory phrase. Poor Sarah, I never gave her a chance.

And after that? The terrifying daughters and sisters of the literary set didn't give me a second glance. I was the gloomy, gangly, awkward Methodist who ran that bookshop and spoke too passionately about the highly unfashionable H.G. Wells.

In 1941 I was a twenty-seven-year-old virgin with epilepsy, whose passions were stifled by a barbiturate fog. As unsexed a creature as you could possibly find.

3. A Wartime Romance

By autumn 1942 the Blitz was largely over, although there were still odd hit-and-run raids on unsuspecting targets. No one really felt safe. Many worried that our air-raids on Germany might provoke a furious German response.

The three of us held a formal barn-meeting one Sunday in December, when most of the local people went to church. This time there was a rank-and-file rebellion. Muriel was bored with farm work and I was unhappy. What was I doing here? My seizures had almost vanished: the last one had been a mere tremor, hardly anything. I held tight to an old chair we'd scrounged from the farmhouse, breathed deeply and slowly and then cautiously sat down. It was over in ten minutes. Not a medical crisis. Not even a bruised ankle! Maybe I was incapable of driving a tank—but I could run a bookshop.

Eleanor conceded that things had changed. But while Muriel and I spoke of the end of German air-raids, Eleanor talked about the entry of the Soviet Union and the United States into the war. Muriel and I said we couldn't spend a third winter in this cold, dirty old barn. Eleanor gave us a long stare and continued her evaluation of the respective strengths of the Allied and Axis forces.

'The war's not over!' she told us. 'Remember Singapore: eighty thousand of our soldiers captured by the Japanese. They're close to India now. And U-boats are stopping supplies getting through. Food is running short in the cities. Think of the advantages to working on a farm.'

'I'm sick of uprooting brambles and digging ditches,' said Muriel.

'But we're getting better at it,' insisted Eleanor. 'In those first weeks, we couldn't move after a day out in the fields. Now—'

'Yes, okay, we can go to the pub. But in London—'

'In London, we'd be queuing for every slice of bread and scrap of cheese. Do you want that?'

Finally, a compromise. We'd take soundings. Each of us contacted someone we trusted in London, asking how things were. Two Sundays later, we each had a reply. Eleanor imposed a formal structure on our discussion, even in that filthy, freezing barn. She and Muriel sat on rickety old chairs, I perched on an upturned bucket. Eleanor asked me and Muriel to report back.

I'd written to Gerald, an elderly Methodist colleague of my father's, one of the friendlier ones in that group. His letter was surprisingly warm—I'd been worried that he might have resented my transformation of father's pious bookstore.

I read out some passages of Gerald's letter. He warned us that there was no *getting back to normal*: that would take years, he predicted accurately. But the worst was over. He wrote at length about the voluntary services. He alluded delicately to *my condition*, but told me that this would not be an obstacle. Everyone was needed, he said.

I got the picture: the best young men had been conscripted, the most able middle-aged men had been sent to the factories and offices, and so the voluntary services had to take whoever was left. My God, this could be the chance I'd been looking for.

'He's saying there's a place for us.' I smiled at Eleanor and Muriel, delighted by the prospect of our return.

Next, it was Muriel's turn. She resisted that formal, intense style that Eleanor adopted: instead, she chatted about her correspondent, Daphne, as if she was a friend who wanted to meet us. Daphne ran a hostel for female Irish munition workers and for much of her letter complained about what a handful they were. She also threw in a few references to two romances she'd had with RAF officers—Muriel burst into giggles when she got to these sections and refused to read them out.

'So?' asked Eleanor. 'Is it safe to return to London?'

'Oh, yes.' Muriel nodded. 'Daphne sounds happy enough.'

We both turned to Eleanor, who then seemed curiously embarrassed. Her letter was type-written and looked very formal.

'Who wrote that?' I asked.

'Giuseppe,' she answered and I saw Muriel roll her eyes.

'What does he do?'

To my amazement, I learnt that he played jazz piano in a top London restaurant.

'He's a refugee and a—' said Eleanor.

'A red,' Muriel stated in a tone of weary tolerance.

Muriel and Eleanor stared at each other for a moment. They'd obviously discussed this before.

'Why on earth did you write to him?' asked Muriel. Eleanor didn't reply. 'Come on, share his insights with us.'

At Muriel's insistence, Eleanor read out some sentences: Giuseppe wrote of the balance of class forces, the difficult formation of a national-popular will and the hegemony of bourgeois culture. Muriel roared with laughter. Even Eleanor tutted at his vocabulary and muttered that Giuseppe took himself too seriously.

I didn't like Muriel's easy scorn. Although I didn't understand Giuseppe's observations, something about his letter touched me. I imagined a lonely, isolated man, far from his native land, trying to make sense of the world around him.

'He's happy, isn't he?' said Muriel. 'He's still playing piano, the Blitz hasn't stopped that.'

Eleanor nodded.

Muriel and I insisted that we would not spend another Christmas in that damn barn but, all the same, we were held back. The local railway services stopped for several weeks and it wasn't until January 1943 that we returned to my bookshop.

***

I talked with Eleanor about Giuseppe's letter, partly as an excuse to find out more about her and her ideas.

'Is he a Trotskyite?'

I had only the vaguest idea who Trotsky was and no idea what Trotskyism meant. But I'd learnt one thing: the most arcane, complex Marxist arguments were usually produced by Trotskyites. Eleanor answered absent-mindedly.

'No. He's Italian.'

What did that mean? No Italians were Trotskyites? No Trotskyites were Italian? Eleanor must have seen how puzzled I looked, because she explained further.

'He and his brother were imprisoned by the Fascists in 1926. They met Antonio Gramsci—a Communist MP—in prison. Gramsci never stopped writing and the two brothers adopted some of his thinking.

'Gramsci died in 1937, because of how he was treated in that Fascist prison. Giuseppe wants to edit and translate his unpublished papers, if ever he has the chance.'

She spoke in a still, flat voice, but I sensed some hidden emotion in her. I guessed there was more to this story. But how strange her world was! A place where pianists were really Marxist philosophers, where people lost their homes and freedom because of what they believed, where ideas had such importance—no, such a *presence* in people's lives.

'Giuseppe managed to get permission to stay here. Matteo, his brother, chose to go back to Italy, to work in the Resistance.'

I shook my head. I'd wanted to impress Eleanor and all I'd done was show my ignorance. As I recovered my strength and took fewer pills, I thought more and more about her. I saw the oddness of our life in that old barn. We lived so close together! During the winter, we all slept in that freezing shed, each wrapped in blankets, with our coats on top, shivering. A pattern had developed: Eleanor went to the back, Muriel to the right, by the wall, me to the left. At night, when I couldn't sleep, I'd hear Eleanor breathing. I'd see her walk to the farm in the morning, I'd wait for her return at sunset. I was obsessed with her, my eyes fixed on her movements. When I saw her standing, I'd imagine her naked, in that posture, her body proud, strong and handsome. I stared when she brushed her hair back from her face, I gazed at her hips as she walked. I wasn't sure what I wanted, but I knew what was happening. For the first time in my life, I felt desire. Not the vague, sibling-like companionship that I'd sometimes shared with Methodist Sarah. Not the helpless longing that I'd felt for the sophisticated females of the literary set. This was something stronger and more urgent.

But many things about Eleanor worried me. I knew little about her because she was so reluctant to talk about her past. I'd learnt from a form she completed that she was 18 months older than me: did that matter? I didn't understand her politics, but I wanted to learn more. And all the time, nothing happened: we were stuck in that damn barn. I hoped that if we'd return to London and my bookshop, we'd feel different, and then... It didn't make sense, but I was new to romance, I didn't know the rules.

***

I searched for a chance to talk to Muriel. One evening, while Eleanor washed herself, Muriel and I stood outside the barn.

'Muriel...' I began.

'I know what's happening.'

'But...'

'And I know what you want to ask.'

'You do?'

That was a surprise, as I didn't.

'I've no idea who she really is,' continued Muriel.

She and Eleanor had met in 1937 in an organisation that helped Spanish refugees. As Muriel told the story, there were two types of people in the group: reds, like Eleanor and *normal people* like her, people who just wanted to help. Muriel laughed.

'My mother was horrified! She kept asking me: Why do you want to mix with *those people*?'

The Spanish children were a wild lot, but friendly and very needy. Muriel and Eleanor hit it off straight away, as Eleanor always had the best ideas about how to raise money.

'The government insisted: they wouldn't give a penny! Not a penny. We had to find everything for them.'

I nodded, but I wanted Muriel to tell me more about Eleanor.

Muriel had never learnt where Eleanor came from: she'd always turn the conversation away from such topics. Still, they'd been friends for five years and Muriel had picked up some scraps of information.

Muriel thought that Eleanor was the illegitimate child of an old aristocratic family, who were probably Catholics, or maybe High Church Anglicans. As a child, Eleanor had enjoyed some luxury. She'd had a private tutor and went to a public school.

'Look at the way she talks!' said Muriel.

'What do you mean?'

'That confidence! She's so certain she's right. She's got public school written all over her.'

'She's clever, isn't she?'

'Oh, she's clever. Perhaps not as clever as she thinks, but she's clever.'

Something went wrong as Eleanor grew older: she'd argued with her mother. Eleanor had run away to London. She learnt to type and became a secretary, while searching out what Muriel called *the reddest of the reds*.

'Don't you know anything else?' I asked.

'No,' said Muriel. Then she spoke in a more confidential tone. 'She likes you, Edmund.'

'She does?'

'You know she's—she's been with other men, don't you?'

I nodded, unable to speak.

'Does that matter to you?'

I shook my head. In fact, I hadn't really thought about it. Was this something else to worry about?

'Muriel—she's older than me. By a year and a half, I think.'

'Yes?'

'Is that—is that important? Will she accept me?'

Muriel burst out laughing. 'Edmund! This isn't the Victorian Age. Of course she will, that's not important. You're right for each other, you really are.'

I nodded. Muriel's words should have comforted me: instead, I felt a sort of terror. If there weren't any obstacles, I'd have to act.

We moved back to London in January 1943. The bookshop was intact, thank goodness, although parts of the high street were terribly battered. London was like that in those days: next to a busy crossroads, packed with chattering pedestrians and rumbling buses, there'd be a spot of terrifying quietness, where weeds spread luxuriantly over the smashed remains of a wall, a roof and a window. If you looked in, you'd see remnants of someone's domestic life: yellow, streaked, flowery wallpaper, still visible, the trace of a mantelpiece, just a foot or two, even the remains of a picture or photograph, next to a jagged rent in the wall and the unexpected emptiness. There was something moving about such spaces, the way they evoked a lost domesticity and also the warning they gave: *this could happen to you.* It was a far more powerful image than those hectoring government posters.

On that first evening, the bookshop was damp and cold, and there was no chance of buying coal. I found some bits of wood in the back garden and got a little fire going in the sitting-room, enough to take the chill off, and I made tea.

I can remember the next scene very clearly. Eleanor went upstairs, and Muriel and I heard her footsteps as we drank our tea and looked at the fire. It was late and we were tired from our journey, but we still needed to sort out who'd sleep where. I imagined that I'd go to the bedroom, bring down a couple of blankets for the girls and then retire. In the past, Muriel had slept on the camp bed in the spare room, while Eleanor had taken the sofa.

Eleanor tripped down the stairs with a determined look in her eye. She'd made up her mind.

'Right,' she said. 'Muriel, you take the camp bed. Edmund and I will sleep upstairs.'

Muriel gasped. I was stunned. Upstairs, I found a set of striped flannel pyjamas and changed into them. They smelt a bit musty, but not too bad. Eleanor saw them and said she could do with some. I found another set. She was tall, for a woman—they fitted her, more or less.

There was a peculiar sort of cold in that bedroom. It wasn't the icy, penetrating cold of the barn, which could cut through any number of blankets and coats. It was more an old, stale feeling, a sense that the house had been longing for the warmth of a human presence. We lay next to each other in the bed and talked quietly about the train journey and our plans. Without clear movement, by some sort of molecular action, we grew closer, until our arms touched. Under the layers of blankets and eiderdowns, I could feel the warmth of Eleanor's body. We were tired and I guessed that this wasn't going to be a night of hot passion. At some point, just before we fell asleep, Eleanor reached out and grasped my hand. It was the first romantic gesture she'd made towards me. It was enough.

Things changed over the following nights. Of course, Eleanor wasn't a virgin. I'd guessed that, Muriel had told me as much. I wasn't shocked, I wasn't even surprised. I'd left that part of my father's Methodist moralism behind. Maybe, in truth, I was a little disappointed. The idea of a woman saving herself for her true love still appealed to me.

Eleanor followed a *take it slow* policy. We moved bit by bit, touching each other in ways that were new to me, Eleanor leading, me her keen disciple. We acquired a packet of what our American friends call *rubbers*, as Eleanor didn't want to get pregnant. Just as well, really: the last thing we needed was a baby. After a few nights, my virginity vanished and I laughed out loud as another wall of Methodist morality came tumbling down.

I learnt a lot. Some nights we used *rubbers*, but often we indulged in what my father would have called *unnatural practices*. With Eleanor, the more unnatural, the better, it seemed. We kept each other warm that winter and the house glowed back.

***

1943 was a good year for us. I re-opened the bookshop. Old customers returned. Some, like Celia, had awkward questions. Before 1939, she was one of the stalwarts of the literary set. She turned up in my bookshop in a military greatcoat and a Women's Voluntary Service hat, looking as if she'd commanded a battalion at Stalingrad.

'Not wearing khaki yet?' she asked.

'Medical exemption,' I mumbled.

'Oh, yes? What's that for?'

I couldn't tell her. Epilepsy—even the word terrified me. I pretended to be busy with the till. She stared at me for a few moments, snorted disapprovingly, then left.

But most customers were friendly. People generally welcomed the re-opening of my bookshop: it was a sign that normal life was returning. Lots of war work involved hanging round waiting for something to happen and some people wanted to read during those empty moments. They went for the old favourites: Trollope and Dickens, or Henry James for those who liked a challenge. Quite a few threw themselves into *War and Peace*: not many finished it, but they were left with an impression of the vastness of Russia. Above all, people wanted books that weren't about England in 1943. I felt a sense of obligation to my regulars, so I wrote and re-wrote to my suppliers, even telephoned them, trying to charm them and wheedle out their secret stores of favourite titles.

In February, I volunteered for the Fire Service and joined a seven-man unit of part-timers. The comments from people like Celia had hurt me. I wanted to prove to them and to myself that I could do my bit. Eleanor agreed with me, but warned me to be careful.

It wasn't like 1940 or 1941. I wasn't out fighting conflagrations every night. I attended courses in battered old schools and rubbed shoulders with those I thought of as *the regulars*: reliable men, who weren't going to turn into gibbering wrecks, writhing on the floor, at a moment's notice. To my immense surprise, they welcomed me. There was some predictable teasing. My impression was that the men of my unit were abnormally short: a gang of beetle-like men, all shoulders and grumpy faces. Curiously, they saw things differently: they considered me exceptionally tall. I was swiftly christened Little Ed and sometimes even 'Young'un'. Normally, I hate it when people abbreviate my name, but this time—well, it didn't seem worth making a fuss. They meant no harm.

Gerald had been right about the voluntary services. Everyone in the unit seemed to have an injury or chronic complaint, whether a limp, a badly-set arm or an appalling cough. It wasn't polite to ask questions. If I claimed dizziness for a moment or two and had to sit down, no one batted an eyelid. When they introduced assault courses as a compulsory part of our training, two of the less healthy ones left. The rules about physical fitness and the Fire Service were being tightened up, but as so often there seemed to be a grey area. One man who limped badly and another with a damaged hand stayed, and no one said anything. The Fire Service needed them.

I felt proud of my new blue tunic and tin hat, despite Eleanor's teasing, and enjoyed wearing them in the street. It wasn't khaki, not yet, but I felt closer to that active, reliable mass of the population.

In the unit, I was buddied up with Alf, an old East Ender who once ran a pub—a short, squat man with a coarse, salt-and-pepper moustache and a limp. He was old enough to have fought in the last war, but never spoke about it. He'd been in the Fire Service since 1940 and constantly told me that *things weren't as bad as they could be*. Alf and I were in charge of the hose: just basic stuff, making sure it didn't get tangled when it was reeled in or reeled out, for a kink could stop the water flowing.

In April, I was thrown into it: two big fires caused by hit-and-run bombers on successive nights. Our fire-engine rumbled along the blacked-out streets towards an ominous red glow. Soon I smelt thick smoke, although I couldn't see it. Then we turned a corner: my first thought at the sight of this pillar of fire, an enormous five-storey block engulfed in ferocious flames was utter bewilderment. What in damnation could we do?

'C'mon, Ed,' said Alf. 'You know the drill.'

There wasn't time to be scared. We carefully unreeled the great heavy hose, making sure it didn't catch on the debris. Our unit leader identified the best spot for us to stand and, as we prepared, another unit drew up. Thank God, we weren't alone in front of that gigantic blaze.

***

Eleanor and Muriel went to work in the hostel for Irish women munitions workers—the one that Muriel's friend, Daphne, ran. It caused our first argument. Eleanor and Muriel dealt with absurd problems at the hostel: endless disputes about wages, squabbles with the supervisor, girls fighting with each other.

One evening, I closed the bookshop and walked up the stairs to the flat. I could hear Eleanor and Muriel talking in low, tense tones—this was unusual. Normally after work they were either exhausted and I'd find them dozing on the sofa, or they'd be in a chatty, perky mood, drinking tea and swapping jokes about Daphne and the Irish girls' conspiracies. That evening, although I couldn't hear what they were saying, I guessed something wasn't right.

'What's up?' I asked.

'Oh, nothing,' said Muriel, unconvincingly. 'A problem, a problem at the hostel.'

I took one look at Eleanor and knew that Muriel wasn't telling the whole truth.

'Something difficult?' I asked.

Eleanor took a long drag on her cigarette. 'Maire—one of the girls—has got herself into trouble.'

'What—with the police? Black-marketing?' This had happened before.

Eleanor glanced at Muriel. 'No, not stealing. She's pregnant.'

Her voice had the taut, level tone that I now recognised. It meant she'd thought this over carefully.

'That's bad.' I shook my head, then guessed from Eleanor's expression that this probably wasn't the right thing to say. 'Is the father a GI?'

Eleanor shrugged. 'Seems to have been a nice, friendly, local Brit, as far as we can make out.'

'Where's he now?'

'Somewhere in the deserts of North Africa.'

'But there are—adoption agencies, aren't there?'

Eleanor glared at me. 'There are several Catholic agencies. Most of them have appalling reputations. Their mission seems to be to humiliate and crush the mother.'

'But what else—'

'If we send her to one of those, she's ruined for life. An outcast. She's only nineteen.'

'So...' My mind had stopped. What was Eleanor proposing?

'It's alright, Edmund,' said Muriel. 'We think we can arrange something.'

I nodded to hide my incomprehension. They clearly didn't want to talk. Maybe it was best that I said nothing else.

'What do you mean?' I couldn't stop myself.

Eleanor puffed on her cigarette, looking irritated. Then she sat up straight, looked me in the eyes. 'I'm arranging for her to have an abortion.'

'An abortion?'

'This may hurt her a lot. Muriel and I think it might be best if she stayed here to recover.'

'Here?'

'She could have the spare room. Muriel doesn't mind taking the sofa for a bit.'

'She'll stay *here*?'

Something about the physical presence of a girl who'd done—who'd done *that* terrified me.

'Do you object?' asked Eleanor.

I spoke without thinking. 'Yes, I bloody well do.'

Eleanor glared at me and I glared back at her. This was my house. I'd decide who stayed and who didn't.

'Look, we don't have to settle things now,' said Muriel.

'But we do,' said Eleanor. 'We need to get this sorted out as quickly as possible.' She puffed on her cigarette. 'Edmund, there's something you need to know about me.'

I stared at her, mesmerized, terrified about what she might say next.

'No, Eleanor,' said Muriel. 'You don't have to—'

'I'm going to. He needs to know. Edmund, I had an abortion. I was only seventeen. It hurt, it bloody hurt.'

I gasped. I'd never have thought... Memories of whispered conversations between my parents came into my head: talk of *that girl*, how she'd *ruined herself for life*. I had a sense that Eleanor was spoiling for a fight and I wasn't sure what I wanted. I turned round, grabbed my coat from the hook at the top of the stairs and walked out. In the high street, I asked myself where I was going. There was only one place: the pub.

The next morning, I woke up on the sofa. During the night, someone had thrown a blanket over me. Had it been Muriel or Eleanor? There was a clattering from the kitchen which hurt my head. Eleanor emerged, holding a cup of tea. She put it on a little table next to me.

'Shouldn't you be at work?' I asked.

'Shouldn't you be opening the bookshop?' She smiled.

I sat up, sipped my tea. It tasted good.

'Edmund, I need to tell you—'

'No, I don't want to hear.'

'I'm going to tell you anyway.'

Muriel's observation in Somerset had been correct: Eleanor didn't talk about her past. I'd told her about my parents and growing up in Wales, about the chapels and the valleys, but she didn't respond. I wanted to know more about her, but I guessed she'd talk when she ready. I hadn't expected it to happen like this. My head ached too much for a proper argument, so I thought I'd better listen.

She sat back in my father's easy chair, lit a cigarette, looked out the window. While I sipped my tea, she stayed still. Then she glanced at me.

'Where to begin?' she asked.

I shrugged.

She puffed on her cigarette. 'I can't tell you everything, I don't have time and, anyway...' She shrugged, then turned towards me. 'You know I ran away from home?'

'Yes.' I didn't really know, all I'd heard were Muriel's guesses.

Eleanor's usual eloquence deserted her. She started, stopped and then began again several times. In bits and fragments, a story emerged, taking me back to 1931, when Eleanor was 16. She'd lived with her mother in Whitby. Eleanor found this restricted little world frustrating. She went out as much as she could and spent long summer afternoons by the coast.

'I think that's the one thing I miss about that place,' she said. 'The sea and the swimming. I could swim for hours.'

Eleanor visited the local library and discovered the secrets kept in a second-hand bookshop, deliberately borrowing or buying the novels that were considered dangerous, using her schoolgirl French to discover a wider world. She was reading for herself: always a dangerous step, she told me, laughing. I nodded, knowing exactly what she meant. My real education had come through reading literature, not from school.

Then she had an argument with her mother.

Eleanor turned away from me, looking uncertain, almost guilty.

'I'll tell you about—about that later, I promise I will. There isn't time now.'

I frowned, but said nothing.

Eleanor had stolen money from her mother and spent most of it on a single third-class rail ticket to London. When she arrived at Kings Cross station, she only had a few pennies left. She saw a couple selling the Communist paper, the *Daily Worker*. Bold as brass, she walked up to them and said she had no money and needed somewhere to stay. Astonishingly, they gave her the address of a café in Soho that needed a serving-girl and told her how to get there. Two hours later, she was serving tables and being shouted at by the owner.

'His bark was worse than his bite.' She smiled. 'That's just the way they are in cafes and restaurants.'

She slept on a mattress in a store-cupboard above the café. It wasn't much of a life, but at least she'd escaped her mother. She wanted to find out more about politics, particularly about the left-wing groups that didn't exist in Whitby. The Labour Party held meetings above a pub in the next road. She went to them and there she met a tall thin boy who worked in a store. For a few months, they shared their free afternoons and evenings. He took her on walks in parks and heaths.

Eleanor smiled sadly at me. 'And, you know, we did what young people do.'

I laughed, more out of embarrassment than amusement.

'Then I got pregnant.'

It wasn't funny anymore. 'What did he do?'

'He deserted me. He didn't want to know. Out of his depth, I suppose. And as for me! I was lost, utterly lost and completely alone.'

She stopped for a moment and I thought she was going to cry. But instead she puffed on her cigarette, sat up straight and resumed her story.

There were two Italians who worked at the Soho café. Giuseppe and Matteo. Refugees. Matteo was the clever one. One day, he looked at her and guessed what had happened.

'Without them...' Eleanor said, then sighed.

They knew an Italian nurse, another refugee. She did the thing. What other option was there? Have the baby and give it to a religious charity?

'You see, Edmund, I'd been an unwanted child. I know what it's like. I couldn't have taken care of a baby, I really couldn't. I'm not going to say it was the right thing to do, just that it was the least wrong.'

She shook her head.

'It hurt, it bloody well hurt. I bled for ages afterwards and couldn't work.'

Giuseppe and Matteo took her in: maybe they felt guilty, as they'd introduced her to the Italian nurse.

'Their flat, Edmund, their whole flat wasn't even the size of this room. Two poky little rooms, one sink, one bed, two chairs. They gave me their bed and slept on the chairs.'

Giuseppe and Matteo spoke Italian to each other, but Eleanor could sometimes guess what they were saying.

'They were Communists, dissident Communists from the Italian Communist Party, anti-fascists and refugees.'

When they had money, they bought her food. When they didn't, they ganged up on the café-owner and insisted that he let her eat there. Reluctantly, he agreed, but only with the staff, before six o'clock. Late one afternoon, Giuseppe and Matteo took her to the café. They served her an enormous plate of pasta, telling her she had to eat, she had to get her strength back. Then, while waiting for the evening shift to begin, Giuseppe sat at the piano and began playing jazz. He wasn't a trained pianist—he'd played a bit at school. But after he'd arrived in England, something changed: he said it was as if the piano was talking to him.

'They were good people, Edmund, and I don't think I would've survived without them. It's why I'll always trust Giuseppe.'

'Why not Matteo?'

A shadow crossed Eleanor's face. 'He's gone. Back to Italy. Anti-fascist work. No one knows what's happened to him.'

She lit another cigarette, then looked me straight in the eyes.

'It looks different if you've been through it yourself, believe me. When you condemn a girl for having an abortion, do you really know what you're talking about?'

'But...' I began to say, but then stopped. A thought hit me. All I knew was what my father and mother had taught me, a vision of a world where sex was sin. Was that me? Was that who I was? I looked at Eleanor and felt an overwhelming sense of sorrow. How desperate, how lonely she must have been.

'You think you know, Edmund, but—'

'Eleanor: I don't. I don't know what I'm talking about. You're right.'

She looked up, bewilderment and surprise all over her face.

'You don't?' she said uncertainly.

'I don't. I really don't know anything about it. How could I? I'm a bookshop-owner and I didn't have a sex life until I met you.'

She laughed, quickly and lightly, confused. Then she nodded absent-mindedly, uncertain what to say next.

'A man who'll admit he's wrong,' she said, almost speaking to herself. 'Well—you don't meet many of them.'

She looked away for a moment and we heard a truck clatter by outside.

'It's what women do, Edmund. Sometimes when we can't control our own bodies, so we resort to desperate measures.'

I stared at her, not knowing what to say.

'So, this Irish girl,' she continued. 'It's not something any woman would choose to do if she didn't have to.'

'But—it's illegal...'

'Only because men make the laws.'

I finished my tea, stretched, then got up from the sofa. I had a pain in my back and didn't feel like opening the bookshop. I walked to the window, stared out at the pedestrians walking up the high street. I felt—I felt fear, real fear, like I was standing on the brink of a precipice. Who was Eleanor? What other secrets was she hiding? I was sure that there was still more she wasn't telling me. Did I really want her in my life?

What a story, what a sad, sad story. I could hear the condemnatory words of my parents—I didn't want to be like them, I was sure. I shook my head. A thought came to me: I could trust Eleanor, like she trusted Giuseppe. The way she'd told the story—it was a bad option, but I thought she was right: it was the least bad option. Her instincts were sound, she wasn't pontificating, she was trying to help someone in trouble. I felt more certain.

I turned back to her.

'Alright,' I said.

'You'll accept her?'

I nodded. 'It sounds like she needs all the help she can get.'

Eleanor smiled sadly and nodded.

In fact, Maire only stayed for two days: she was a short, slender, brown-haired girl with freckles, who looked very young. She was miserable on the first day, when Muriel and Eleanor left me alone with her. I made her a cup of tea, and to my intense embarrassment she burst into tears and clutched at me. I told her things would get better and hoped it was true. Eleanor and Muriel talked to her in the evening and on the second day she seemed more settled. The next day she went back to the munitions factory.

***

Something changed between me and Eleanor around that time. It puzzled me. There was a new intimacy between us: when we were apart, if only for an hour or two, we looked forward to seeing each other. We talked more to each other. I compared my feelings for Eleanor with my feelings for Methodist Sarah—they weren't the same, not at all. One morning a thought came as I opened up the bookshop: *we love each other*. Of course, that was it. Why hadn't I thought of that before? I didn't know the rules, I had no experience. That evening, I had to tell Eleanor I loved her. But I hesitated: Muriel was in the way and I was worried that Eleanor might laugh at me. When Muriel popped out to get some milk, I ran to Eleanor, seized her, but still wasn't sure what to say.

'What is it Edmund?'

'This is—this is *love*, isn't it?'

She laughed, happily, not laughing *at* me but laughing *with* me, then she looked at me. She nodded.

'Yes, I believe it is.'

A few weeks later, the topic of marriage came up, I don't remember how. I didn't get down on one knee and propose, there was none of that. It wasn't something we had to address immediately. During the war, plenty of couples lived *in sin*, as my father would have said, and plenty of settled marriages dissolved, pulled apart by the war economy, long-distance postings and those sad moments when two people realised they weren't the same any more. And then there were those American soldiers, voraciously hunting female flesh. They played their part in breaking up a fair few marriages.

All couples, all households in Blitzed London felt provisional. Eleanor and I could have stayed living together over the bookshop.

No one was bothered, the old 11th commandment, *What will the neighbours think*, no longer made sense. Everyone knew that any night a German bomb might mean the end of the neighbours and their thoughts. Curiously, Nazi bombing ignited a moral and sexual revolution in the English suburbs.

So, nothing *forced* us to get married: if anything, the tendency of the time was to leave things undecided. But I wanted to hang onto what we'd created and I guessed that marriage was the only way to do this.

'Let's do it,' said Eleanor one evening. 'There's too much that's unsettled and makeshift in the world today. Let's try to make something permanent.'

***

Three weeks later we were married. It was an odd little ceremony. A registry office, of course, and everything in it was worn out and patched-up—like the rest of London. Sometimes that lent a sort of charm to buildings and places, like the wild flowers that grew in bomb sites. We didn't have the time or money to organise anything grand and—if truth be told—we didn't want to. The clerk was an officious little man with slicked-back hair, but at one point he smiled at us so warmly that I thought he liked us. We invited a few friends to attend and then went for a meal in a restaurant that Muriel knew, which she swore still served proper food. It wasn't bad. There was a couple from the literary set, who came in their best clothes and out-shone us all, Gerald, the elderly Methodist, a few ambulance-drivers and hostel-workers who knew Muriel and Eleanor, a couple of firemen from my unit and Giuseppe, the jazz-playing Marxist. No one from Eleanor's family and nobody asked any questions about that. No one from my family. I'd lost contact with the Welsh contingent and there was still no news from mother and father in South Africa.

I'd been keen to meet Giuseppe, but found him disappointing at first. He wore a suit that was too big for him. He must have borrowed it for the day. He looked a bit like Groucho Marx and spoke an awkward, heavily-accented English. But, after our meal, I got to speak to him. There was a deep sadness in him. I asked him about the war.

'England, Russia and America will beat Hitler, that is certain. Maybe in three years. But, Edmund, there is the other war.'

I must have looked puzzled.

'Will we defeat the conditions that produced Hitler?'

He spoke with such feeling. I couldn't think what to say.

Gerald took Eleanor and I aside at one point and gave us a sort of private sermon. I'd dreaded this, but his words were unexpectedly friendly. I can't recall them now, but they reminded me of Blake's poems. Something about how warmth and companionship were precious gifts, and how we should treasure each other, particularly in these dark times. No mention of God. To my surprise, Eleanor listened to him quietly and seemed moved. He wished us well.

That was it. We were man and wife. The rest was up to us.

4. Coming Home

I get up. Even my father's easy chair, with its magic capacity to cure all backache, can't stop me feeling uncomfortable today. There's something I don't like about these thoughts. It feels like I'm reading someone else's story, it can't be about me. I'm as dull as ditch water, not the sort of man who travels to darkest Germany with his beautiful wife and then loses her.

But—it did happen, it all happened. I can't change the past: hell, I can't even understand it. Everything's confusing. If only I could find something clear, something certain.

I step to your cabinet of books by the table, the one with the glass front which survived the Blitz. For a year, these books have stayed unchanged, untouched, unread. You were the last person to touch them: the thought runs through me like an electric shock. Should I pick one up?

I hesitate and glance through the titles. I used to think that one day I might write a book. But what could I have written that might interest you? Look at these titles. Kafka, a chilling author who terrified me. I never read more than a few pages of him. Virginia Woolf, who sometimes I thought you loved more than me. I found her so difficult to understand. Proust, who you read in the original French. Honestly! Marx, of course, who you read and re-read and re-re-read. If I take down any of his works and flick through the pages, I'll see your spidery writing in the margins, entirely illegible. What did you see in that cold, mechanistic materialism?

I have never been a member of the Communist Party. How many times did I hear you say that? I found your politics so difficult to understand. If you weren't a Communist, you were damn close to one, weren't you? Perhaps not. There were all those arguments about the Spanish Civil War. You said the Communists betrayed the Left. But how could that be? I never understood it. And then—you hated, really hated, the bluff, belligerent, lying propaganda of the Reds. It wasn't your style. You were no friend of Russia: an admirer, maybe, but not a friend.

I come to the end of the row of books. Next to them, there's a cluster of pamphlets, held in place by a bookend. The last one is *UNRRA: Fifty Facts*.

Ah, UNRRA. The United Nations Relief and Rehabilitation Administration. That's part of our story, that's central.

5. Enter UNRRA

The months after our marriage were horrendously busy. Eleanor and Muriel worked at the hostel, I ran the bookshop and worked for the Fire Service. And yet—we enjoyed those months. We had that sense of being in the right place at the right time, of contributing something.

Married life suited us. We talked all the time, about everything, learning from each other. I showed Eleanor how a bookshop was run, she gave me ideas about authors I could stock. It was Eleanor who recommended J.B. Priestley to me: I read him and realised that he was one of those rare figures whose English patriotism did not blind him to England's faults. No wonder Churchill stopped him from broadcasting on the BBC! Eleanor and I discovered those new anthologies of short stories, created to evade the printing restrictions on magazines: odd combinations of jingoistic patriotism, escapism and half-comic, half-serious reflections on military life, which sometimes made me glad I'd never been conscripted. The great Russian authors, Tolstoy, Pushkin and Gorky, rose in popularity as the Russian tanks stormed westwards. While Muriel tried *War and Peace*, Eleanor and I shared volumes of Dostoyevsky.

Good news was coming through about the war, bit by bit. The Italians and Germans had been defeated in North Africa. The Russians were advancing. The U-boats were pushed back in the Atlantic, but the food situation remained dire. People said things like: *if I see another potato...* There was a new mood in the pubs and cafes, talk about how things would never be the same again. No going back to the old ways. People were impatient with the Allies' slow advance in Italy. Why weren't our soldiers in France? In Germany? Chalked graffiti regularly appeared by the station: SECOND FRONT NOW! It would be quickly washed down, but would re-appear a day or two later. People wanted to talk, to plan, even to dream: soldiers on leave, volunteer helpers, organisers of underground shelters, trade unionists and Christians all talked to each other.

The famine in Bengal seized Eleanor's attention and she went to meetings in central London which discussed it. The story finally appeared in the dailies in September 1943, after Eleanor had been talking about it for months.

'You've got to stock these pamphlets, Edmund, you've got to display them.'

'Why?'

'Because—this is *as* important as Pearl Harbour or Stalingrad, it will affect lives for generations.'

'Really?'

I wasn't sure, but I displayed a set of pamphlets in the bookshop window, with titles like *Famine, Politics and Empire*. Once those horrific pictures of starving villagers were published in the daily press, people saw what was so important, although there were always so many other things to worry about. Thank goodness Eleanor had told me about the famine—I was able to answer customers' questions.

Eleanor spoke with a new confidence, sometimes sounding as red as possible to provoke Muriel.

'It's the end of the corrupt old order, don't you see? They can't hang onto to India anymore, the Indians will go their own way. They see what the British offer of *self-government* really means and they'll reject it! Then the rest of the Empire will follow. No more grabbing and grasping, no more screwing the last penny out of the natives and then telling them it's for their own good, no more race ideology. It's all collapsing.'

'The Empire wasn't all bad,' protested Muriel.

I noticed she used the past tense, even though vast tracts of the world still remained under imperial control.

'And once that corrupt old layer falls away, then the rest will go. The old boy network.' Eleanor's eyes gleamed. 'There's no going back. It's going to be a new beginning.'

'Oh, Eleanor!'

Muriel refused to be provoked. I wasn't sure what to think, but I loved to listen to Eleanor talking that way. Like those fiery Methodist preachers I'd heard in Wales—but more intelligent, fiercer sometimes, but also... She carried a deep love in her heart, I knew that and I felt so proud of Eleanor as she spoke of the New World, *after the war*. How those three words inspired us!

***

There was one last crisis. The V1s, the doodlebugs as they were called. They hit London in June 1944. There'd be a mechanical droning in the sky, often in broad daylight. Even if they were shot down, they'd still crash into the streets and explode. A new wave of evacuations followed. We held a household meeting one night and unanimously resolved that we would stay. Muriel and I were more terrified of that old barn than we were of Hitler's new weapons.

The Fire Service were mobilised. Our units drove towards columns of smoke and fire, and played our hoses on the walls of burning buildings. Endless gallons splashed out, as we took it in turns to hold the heavy hose and its ice-cold nozzle, always keeping an ear open for another doodlebug. One night, our unit leader got hit on the head by falling bricks. His tin helmet may have saved his life, but blood streamed down his face. Two ambulance drivers took him away. Another member of our unit stepped up and directed the hose with a clear, calm voice. The usual stuff:

'Keep it steady. Direct it into the window above—no, the one to the right. Steady!'

He organised us to take turns with the hose, even shouted at the Red Cross to come over with cups of tea. He grew hoarse as we stood in smoke through the night. He had an odd voice: not the guttural shouts of the native Londoner, nor the clipped accent of the born-to-rule gentleman. His voice sounded particularly strange to my ears, because—he was me. *I* was giving orders. Little Ed. When our unit leader had been taken away, I'd looked round. His deputy seemed exhausted and bewildered: he sat on the blackened remnants of a brick wall, looking away from the fire. The others stood as if frozen. Someone had to do something, didn't they? They accepted my directions without question. By dawn, the blazes were dampened. We drove back to base, absolutely shattered. Alf patted me on the back as he left and muttered:

'Well done, lad.'

I'd done it. Despite epilepsy, despite my lack of experience in anything practical, I'd conquered myself and I'd gained respect. *I'd done it.*

***

Then—when was it? Sometime in 1944, before the invasion of France—no: after. Muriel noticed it first. The big leaders and the news broadcasts kept using this phrase, the *United Nations*. At first, it had been a modern, American alternative to Churchill's stuffy, backward-looking *Grand Alliance*. We laughed when we heard Churchill proclaim that on the wireless. The Grand Alliance? Like an alliance between a bicycle and a Sherman tank. One day, as we listened to the BBC news, Muriel pointed out how the words *United Nations* now seemed to mean something more than a coalition of wartime allies. They were planning for the world *after the war*. Muriel had heard about a report. The United Nations wanted to prevent widespread chaos at the end of the war. They'd learnt from what happened in 1918 and 1919: that dreadful flu epidemic. And there was something about *displaced persons*—a phrase which struck us as a strange euphemism. All these problems would be solved by a new, modern organisation, connected to the United Nations.

Eleanor said she'd investigate. Muriel switched the wireless to the American Forces Network and swing music floated through the house: warm, rhythmic, easy.

'Can't you find some proper jazz?' asked Eleanor.

Eleanor went to Westminster Central Library and then to an official bookshop that stocked the publications of the United Nations. They gave her a pamphlet: *UNRRA: Fifty Facts*. She read most of it on the train back.

She and Muriel were very taken with it.

'Look,' she said to Muriel, pointing to a passage. '*Professional standards*. For everyone. They're not do-gooding ladies.'

'Hmmm...' Muriel seemed sceptical. 'It certainly sounds like a different take on social work.'

'Of course it is. And here: *planning*. Using resources to prevent a disaster from happening, instead of waiting for it to hit, then getting in a flap.'

Muriel nodded.

'And the recruitment policy,' Eleanor continued. She read out a sentence. '*Without discrimination on the grounds of sex, race, nationality or creed, and recruited upon as wide a geographic basis as is compatible with efficient administration.*'

'Without discrimination...' repeated Muriel. 'That's a new one.'

'It doesn't sound like the old crowd. Do you think it means they'll choose women as unit leaders?'

Muriel shook her head.

Eleanor pointed to another section. 'They'll recruit teams of 10 or 15 in which all the different nationalities are represented. English and American and French and Danish...'

'Gosh! What language will they use?' asked Muriel.

I couldn't stop myself. 'Will they need booksellers?'

Eleanor paused and looked at me. 'No, but...'

A penny dropped. It would be like the army: they'd need accountants, organisers, store-managers. And if I could command a Fire Service Unit during a blaze, I could find a place in this new organisation.

'Let me see that pamphlet.'

The three of us sat on the sofa and read the pamphlet from beginning to end twice, considering each of the *Fifty Facts*. It was intriguing. Not always attractive. It sounded American: slick, streamlined, gleaming new and probably not very effective. The statistics irritated me. What about the human touch? But I could see what appealed to Muriel and Eleanor. This wasn't an old-fashioned, patronizing, do-gooding, religious charity. UNRRA thought in bigger terms: they wanted to change the world.

The problems would be immense: smashed roads and railways, devastated cities. Millions of displaced persons, or DPs, as UNRRA insisted on calling them, each with their own emotional and personal problems: injuries, traumas, separated families, orphans... New nations would emerge from the dust and rubble. In the middle of it all, there'd be a centre providing food, shelter, clothing, medical care, education, training the DPs, helping them work, caring for them, assisting their return. Dedicated, international teams, drawing together the best people in the world. Well-paid, as well.

We talked about UNRRA for the rest of that evening. Muriel stressed the practical, career-building points. She wanted to be a social worker *after the war*.

'It'll look good on a CV,' she said, several times. 'International experience.'

Eleanor nodded, but she and I were gripped by something bigger: we were entranced by the idea of a new international organisation which would heal the world. Of course, there were other factors. Eleanor, like Muriel, was considering a career in social work, and I still had a chip on my shoulder: what had I done during the war? UNRRA seemed to offer each of us so much.

***

There was a course of introductory lectures on UNRRA in central London and we attended when we could. We learnt to pick and choose between the lecturers: there were some Quakers who were very convincing. They spoke from their experience working with refugees, they cited examples and they clung to a basic principle: the DPs were people who deserved our respect. We liked those lectures. There was a thin Yorkshireman, a doctor, with a lung injury who would rasp and whisper for thirty minutes before giving up in a fit of coughing. We felt sorry for him. Some speakers were social workers, men and women. They were rather technical. And then the military and ex-military officials who turned up in their uniforms: some down-to-earth and practical, who we could appreciate, but also some who sounded more colonial. They spoke in the hard, clipped voices of the born-to-rule and were openly sceptical about UNRRA's internationalist ideals.

In March 1945 an UNRRA day school was organised in Reading, which included some practical exercises. It would be our opportunity to enrol in UNRRA. Eleanor and I went, but not Muriel. On the train, Eleanor explained.

'Graham.'

'Who's Graham?'

Eleanor sighed. 'Muriel's fallen for an RAF officer.'

'What's wrong with that?'

'He's married.'

'No!'

Eleanor nodded.

'She hasn't!'

I couldn't believe it. A *married* man. How had Muriel got into this mess? She seemed such a sensible, feet-on-the-ground sort of girl. But while Eleanor and I went to Reading, Muriel went off with Graham. Eleanor was certain that Muriel was fooling herself.

'Of course he'll never leave his wife. Why can't she see it?'

When the UNRRA training-day started, I missed Muriel. Her practical, down-to-earth nature restrained Eleanor's idealism and sometimes this was useful. But as the day progressed, I forgot Muriel and thought about how Eleanor and I could fit into UNRRA's programmes. We'd heard some of the lectures before, but the exercises got us thinking. Would we be able to do this? One of the lecturers mentioned that not only did they welcome married women (Eleanor muttered *at last!*), but they'd even accept married couples. That was the turning-point. I had a picture of Eleanor and I working together in some faraway place, helping to remake the world. I caught the gleam in Eleanor's eyes: she was thinking the same.

During lunch, I said to Eleanor:

'This is for us, isn't it?'

'They sound like good people.'

'Even without Muriel?'

Eleanor shrugged. 'I think we've lost her.'

'But what about the bookshop?'

'I know it'll be a break, but we'll just have to close it for a year or so.'

We got to talking to two Quakers who had just returned from Greece. In their stories, they miraculously converted human tragedies into logistical exercises about food supplies, clothing distribution and negotiating with guerrillas. They also corrected our pronunciation: instead of laboriously saying YOU-EN-ARE-ARE-AY, we were to pronounce UNRRA as a single word: *un-rah*.

At the end of the day school, we stayed to register our names. An efficient blonde woman with a gleaming smile talked to us before we filled out the forms. She wore the khaki that many UNRRA officials affected and had no less than five pens and propelling pencils in her breast pocket. There was one awkward moment. I needed to explain why I hadn't been conscripted. I was prepared. I had a new letter from the Scottish doctor who had diagnosed my epilepsy and a letter from the head of our Fire Service unit. The UNRRA woman barely glanced at them. I guessed the same rules applied in UNRRA as in the volunteer services: they couldn't afford to be fussy, they had to take the walking wounded—like me. But she was very interested in the Fire Service note and in my experience as a bookseller.

'You can do double-entry book-keeping?'

'Of course.'

She smiled. 'We're looking for people who could be Team Directors: you sound ideal.'

'And you...' she consulted Eleanor's notes. 'Let's see. You've been an ambulance driver and you've helped run a hostel.'

Eleanor nodded.

'Sounds like you've got the right experience for a Welfare Officer.'

This was wonderful. A couple of weeks later, we were officially accepted and we went for our inoculations. Europe was calling.

Afterwards, we talked with Muriel. Eleanor told her about the opportunities and assured her the UNRRA people seemed friendly. But Muriel just shook her head.

'I'm sorry, Eleanor, but I don't want to leave now.'

'Graham—he'll never get divorced, you know that Muriel.'

'That's what you think.'

The two stared at each other for a moment. Then Muriel spoke in a lighter tone.

'I can manage the bookshop while you're away. I probably won't be able to open it every day, but maybe weekends and a couple of afternoons a week.'

That cheered me up. I'd hated the thought of my bookshop staying closed for months on end.

**

In the last week of April 1945, Eleanor and I took a train to Southampton, with one small suitcase each, as the regulations insisted. We expected an overnight crossing and then a journey across France to the new UNRRA training centre in Normandy. But there were reports of U-boats in the Channel, so we were shunted into a creaky old boarding house for the night.

At first it was rather jolly: there were a dozen or so UNRRA workers, all excited about going to France. Eleanor knew one or two of them: reds, I supposed. We crowded into the landlady's tiny front parlour and called for tea, toast and cake. After what seemed ages, tea arrived. One of the reds produced a bottle of whisky and insisted that we each pour a few drops into our tea. A party started. Someone told a funny story about how Churchill had never spoken on the wireless, not once during the whole war. Instead, the BBC had used an actor to imitate him. This provoked a riot of Churchill imitations, each setting off waves of laughter. At first, I joined in, but the parlour seemed stuffy and the laughter too loud. I was tired after our journey and disappointed that we weren't going to France that night. I whispered to Eleanor that I'd go up to our room.

I had an idea that I'd read a few pages from my H.G. Wells omnibus: maybe the bit where the Martians' monstrous tripods arrive in Woking. I stretched out on the bed, picked up my book, but the light was so dim that I could barely read a word. And then—

Eleanor told me what happened afterwards. She'd heard a thud, followed by a repeated banging. She ran up the stairs and found me writhing on the floor, my legs hitting the side of the bed. She held me in her arms while the seizure ran through me, then calmed me, made me drink some water. With her help, I got into bed.

'Oh, Edmund,' she said, looking at me closely, 'that was a bad one. I thought they'd finished.'

I was utterly drained. My back ached, my vision was blurred, there was a ringing in my ears and red-hot jabs of pain were shooting up my legs. I felt hollow, empty of all energy and life.

'Poor Edmund.' She shook her head. 'We can't go to France, you know that.'

I wanted to protest, but hadn't the force. Eleanor reached for my pills, put one in my hand, then gave me a glass of water.

'You try to sleep. We'll go back to London tomorrow.'

Part II
FRANCE

'UNRRA... was like a Foreign Legion for peace instead of war.'
Francesca Wilson, UNRRA Welfare Officer
'I worked with many people who had risked everything and suffered much, and I saw their spirit flare up... in this multi-national community, co-operating in a constructive task involving the liberation of their own and other nationals, in a Europe that was quickly being freed from the invader.'
W. Arnold-Forster, Director of UNRRA Training Centre at Granville
'I think it was the unanimous opinion of everyone, regardless of nationality, that this [UNRRA] training centre was the most inefficiently operated undertaking they had ever seen anywhere at any time.'
Marvin Klemme, UNRRA worker

6. Leaving England

'Right,' said Eleanor. 'I'll go downstairs and scrounge some breakfast. You stay here.'

She expected we'd leave the boarding-house that morning and catch the train back to London. But I didn't want that. After a night's sleep, I felt stronger. My head had almost cleared, the ache in my back was just a dull throb. Re-opening the bookshop and working in the fire service hadn't cured my epilepsy, but I was tougher, I recovered faster after a seizure. We'd done those courses, got our inoculations and travelled to Southampton. Were we really going to turn back now? France seemed so close.

Eleanor returned with buttered toast and two cups of tea. She'd told the people downstairs that I'd had a nasty fall last night. There were some raised eyebrows and someone had muttered *too much whisky*. The main news was that the crossing had been delayed again: the boat would leave at noon, not 10 o'clock.

We ate quickly and then Eleanor packed our cases.

'Eleanor,' I said.

'Hmmm...' She didn't look up.

'I think we should get that boat.'

She turned round and stared at me.

'I'm not so bad, really,' I said. 'Look.'

I got up and attempted to stride vigorously to the window. I wobbled a little, but I made it. I turned round and smiled. 'See?'

She shook her head. 'You've just had one seizure, you could soon have another. You're in no fit state to travel.'

'It's different for you,' I said. 'You've travelled. You've been to France.'

'So?'

'I've never been further than Margate. I want to meet people from other countries.'

'UNRRA won't be a holiday, Edmund. You can't take a position of responsibility if you're going to have these dreadful—these dreadful fits.'

'I commanded a fire service unit in London.'

'In UNRRA you'll need to ready for anything, all the time.'

'I can do that.'

She looked at me. I could see she was surprised and was weighing up possibilities. I tried to change tone.

'This trip,' I told her. 'It's an opportunity, it's something we've been preparing for... It's something we both believe in.'

She went back to packing.

'We've wasted so many years,' I continued. 'Doing nothing. And now we've got a chance... It's not that I think I'm going to be a hero, but I want to do something useful. We're going to be there, as a new world is created on the ruins of the old. Think how you'll feel in a few years' time if we don't go.'

That was it. I had her attention. She stopped packing and gave me a long, hard look.

'Are you sure?'

I nodded.

She sighed. 'I don't know. It seems a shame to turn back now. I did think that later I might—I might go without you—'

'No!'

'No,' she shook her head. 'I thought about it and decided I don't want to go there alone. It wouldn't be the same. Now, if you're sure...'

She disappeared downstairs. Five minutes later she was back with a walking-stick she'd scrounged from the landlady and more news.

'The ferry's delayed until 1 o'clock.'

***

The old ferry wheezed its way across the English Channel, leaving slow, lazy ripples in its wake. The boat was battered from years of wartime service, its fittings bent and broken, the guard-rails warped into precarious angles. As we climbed the rickety stairs, Eleanor looked at the guard-rails and warned me:

'Don't hold onto those!'

There were no chairs or benches on the top deck, but Eleanor found a place to sit on the grey steel deck, out of the wind, with our backs against a funnel and our legs stretched out. Next to us a sea-grey inflatable lifeboat, tied to four rusty posts, rocked in time with the ferry's slow progress.

'Are you alright?' Eleanor asked as she placed my stick next to me.

I nodded. I'd taken double the maximum dose of barbiturates last night and another pill this morning. Around me, I saw a universe of grey: traces of grey mist floating over a grey sea, a weak, grey sun half-illuminating a grey boat. I moved my legs carefully and found that my ankles didn't ache so much.

The vibrations from the ferry's engine were strangely comforting, almost like they were massaging my back. The sun emerged from the clouds and I watched sparks of light twinkle on the rippling grey sea. Eleanor sat by me, smoking and reading a volume of Stendhal—she wanted to practice her French. Occasionally UNRRA people walked past, taking the air and Eleanor exchanged comments with them about the improving weather.

I wanted to experience this transition by myself, in silence, so I closed my eyes, although I didn't feel sleepy. It had been a bad fit, Eleanor was right. I'd lied to her. But something drove me on. I wanted to get out of England, to France, to UNRRA, to Europe. This beat-up old boat was taking me away from the bookshop, from the humdrum world of streets, shops and offices. At last, I was going to do my bit, I was going to live. I would join that other, dynamic world, I would be able-bodied. I had a strange sensation, as if I'd floated above the boat, then looked down at myself and Eleanor, two grey dots, inching our way from Blitzed England to battered Europe. We'd join something bigger, a great fraternal wave of reconstruction and reconciliation which would ensure that the world would never suffer another war.

***

There was a scream. I awoke with a start. U-boats? No, it was the ferry's engine: it had changed, no longer pulsing with a steady beat, it screeched and shuddered. I glanced round to Eleanor, but she wasn't looking at me.

'My God,' she whispered, dread in her voice. She was staring ahead.

I followed her gaze. There was Dieppe—or what was left of it. The town was just one mass of rubble: vast grey, yellow and brown piles of stones and bricks, with here and there a wall poking through, a girder sticking up, or a yard or two of road. As we drew closer, we spotted wrecks in the water: there were masts and funnels, stuck out at odd angles. The ferry picked its way through them.

'The ports always get hit bad,' I muttered, remembering the nights when my unit was sent to the Royal Victoria dock.

'Yes, but—*this*!' Eleanor waved her arm, encompassing the whole devastated horizon. 'I've never seen anything like this—this catastrophe. What can we do...'

'Welcome to Europe,' I said.

Eleanor shivered, as if she was cold. I reached out, put my arm round her and gave her a smile. She glanced at me, blinked and then looked back at the panorama of destruction. Together we looked up and down the shoreline, where there once must have been quays, trying to spot where we'd dock. The engine screeched again: the sound scared a few seagulls into flight—the only movement that disturbed that desolation. The boat swung round, slowly and painfully, and a dizzying view swept past our eyes: rubble, rubble, then more rubble... Finally, we saw it: one single, small, black square, some temporary military construction, a lonely solid point among the massed piles of destruction. Our destination.

**

We couldn't travel directly by train from Dieppe to Normandy, where UNRRA was based. The fighting had smashed the railways, so we had to go south to Paris, stay overnight and then come out again: another delay! The next day, the train to Normandy took us across improvised bridges and rickety railways, stopping frequently in bare countryside for no obvious reason. In the train, we saw French Prisoners of War or forced labourers, returning after years in Germany. They looked miserable: badly shaved, thin and tired, sometimes limping, in threadbare uniforms. They didn't want to talk. At each station, women crowded on the platforms and a few sad Frenchmen got out. We heard shouts from the waiting women. I saw a blonde girl hurl herself, open-armed, at one of the gaunt men.

'Papa!' she cried.

While they were returning home, we were travelling further from London, deeper into this strange land.

It was late when we arrived at the UNRRA centre in Granville and too dark to see anything. Men and women were separated and then shepherded into old trucks. Eleanor and I were both sleepy and we barely had time to say goodbye before a truck took her away, rumbling along narrow, curving lanes. I reassured myself that I'd see her tomorrow.

The men's quarters weren't as bad as I'd feared. They were on the upper floor of what once had been a grand hotel. There was no electricity and I stumbled up the dark stairs to a modest, bare room, illuminated by a flickering candle. There were two camp beds, one occupied by a half-asleep figure who grunted at me. On the beds were blankets, but no sheets. It was cold. After a moment's thought, I took off my coat, jacket, shirt and trousers, blew out the candle, then got into bed.

I stayed awake for a while, thinking over the day. We'd done it! Despite my epilepsy, despite everything, we'd got here. I'd had my first sight of my new world. It was chaotic and disorganised, barely functioning, just emerging from the dark shadow of war. We inhabited little squares of order in a mass of destruction. It was strangely exciting.

The next morning I found Eleanor queuing for breakfast in the hotel canteen. It was a long, low, steamy room, echoing with conversations in a dozen languages. The UNRRA personnel who'd been here a few days wore khaki. They picked up trays and strode confidently to the serving stands. The new ones, like us, marked out by their civilian clothes, looked round in confusion. The French canteen staff didn't speak much English, so questions and answers were expressed in a primitive sign language. But the food! Was the serving girl really offering us *two* fried eggs? Each? *Real* eggs, not that gritty mess made from egg-powder. I glanced at Eleanor: I couldn't believe this. As we progressed along the queue, there was a new surprise at each step. All the evaporated milk we wanted for our coffee, plus fruit juice, toast, marmalade and butter. Another serving-girl apologised for not being able to offer us tea—we laughed in amazement. We sat down and there was a full sugar bowl on the table. When had I last seen that? I dipped my spoon in, then let the little white crystals fall slowly into my coffee. I met Eleanor's eyes and took a second spoonful, smiling at her. I knew my coffee would be too sweet, but I couldn't stop myself. I sipped it, savouring each drop, while Eleanor grinned at me.

'Enjoying yourself?' she asked. 'A little luxury for the Team Director?'

'How's your room?' I said.

'Basic. Three of us, sleeping on canvas camp beds, with no sheets and no glass in the windows.'

'What are the others like?'

'A lively American and a subdued Pole.'

Before I could say anything else, a French girl holding a tray asked if she could join us. She looked about fourteen years old: thin, wiry and dark-eyed. She explained that she was Yvonne and wanted to practice her English. Within minutes we'd learnt that not only was she an UNRRA Welfare Officer, but she'd run a camp in southern France for Spanish refugee children. Eleanor looked up straight away.

'How many were there?' I asked.

She shrugged. 'Hundreds, at first. And—you know—they were *dérangé*, wild... Shouting, fighting, stealing...'

I shook my head. How had she coped?

She pouted. 'You have to try. You talk to them, you see them as people, you listen to them...'

'And that works?' asked Eleanor.

'Oh, yes. They become calmer. They learn they can trust you. But during the war... Many of them left.'

'Why?'

'Some went back to Spain. Some hid in the Pyrenees with the *passeurs*. Some joined the Resistance. And the older ones...'

She paused. We looked at her.

'Some were taken by the Germans. Mauthausen, you know...'

'A concentration camp?' asked Eleanor.

Yvonne nodded. I'd never heard of Mauthausen, but I felt a sudden chill. This was the world to which we were heading. Yvonne said goodbye, then left with her tray.

'My God!' I said to Eleanor. 'I thought she was fourteen! And she was in charge of hundreds of refugees. It seems unbelievable.'

'That'll be us in a few days.'

'Oh lord, you're right. How will we cope?'

Before Eleanor could reply, there was a shout from the canteen entrance: it was time to get our uniforms. In the foyer, we found an English UNRRA officer with a sandy moustache, round glasses and a podgy face. He was a short man and threw his chest out in order to shout. I guessed he was ex-military.

'Men's uniforms this side, women's uniforms over there.'

He pointed forcefully, as if addressing extremely dim children.

I approached him.

'When will we be sent to Germany?' I asked. 'We're expecting to be in the same team.'

He glanced at me, then Eleanor.

'Teams will be announced in a few days,' he said. 'Personnel will be assigned to teams according to need, not individual preferences.'

'But we were *told*, in Reading—' I began.

'They can say what they like in Reading. But *we* make the operational decisions.'

This wasn't what we'd signed up for. The idea of not working with Eleanor—it was unthinkable. But the officer had turned away from me and had gone back to shouting orders.

'Be back by the promenade, in uniform, at ten hundred hours *sharp*,' he called. 'Trucks will take you to the Training Centre. It is imperative that you are on time.'

Eleanor walked up to him.

'Now look here,' she told him. 'UNRRA's supposed to operate without discrimination.'

The officer blinked, staring at her with surprise.

'There's no marriage bar,' continued Eleanor. 'Married couples are meant to be welcome in—'

'Well, this takes the biscuit!' said the officer, looking round for an audience. 'Some do-gooding lady, fresh from the comforts of civvy street, telling me how to do my job.'

Eleanor stared at him a second.

'I'm an UNRRA Welfare officer,' she told him. 'I'm not some bloody jumped-up little squirt, who's been pushed out of the army for God knows what reason.'

The two glared at each other. It was funny, in a way. Eleanor towered over him.

'I could have you sent back—' began the officer.

'Eleanor!' I caught her arm. 'Let's get our uniforms. We'll deal with this later.'

I gave the officer a stern look, trying to shut him up.

I didn't like this. It wasn't a good start. The whole idea had been that we'd stay together.

The officer went back to barking instructions.

'Men's uniforms this side, women's uniforms over there.'

'I'll meet you outside afterwards,' I called to Eleanor.

7. In Search of UNRRA

When I came out of the hotel, I couldn't see Eleanor. There was only a slight, dark-haired young man, down by the battered promenade, dressed in the ubiquitous khaki of this place. With his hands in his pockets, he paced idly along the pathway, away from the hotel. I looked the other way, searching for Eleanor.

'Edmund!' a voice called.

I turned round: the young man! It was Eleanor. She'd tied her hair back.

'I didn't recognise you!' I laughed. 'In trousers!'

'Yes.' She shrugged. 'I didn't like the skirts and anyway they didn't have any in my size. Trousers will be more practical for where we're going.'

I looked at her again, from head to foot. Her clothes resembled mine: beret, dark green tie with a light green shirt, buttoned-up jacket, long khaki greatcoat, baggy trousers, shiny boots. At first sight, she looked masculine, but as I looked closer I saw that the effort to change sex hadn't quite worked and somehow the masculine uniform made her look more feminine. Attractive, in an odd way. Still my girl.

She stared at me, smiling, waiting for me to say something. I could guess: what would Edmund, the Methodist's son, have to say about a woman in trousers? But I wasn't shocked, the war had changed all that. I'd seen land-girls and bus conductresses, factory girls and female air wardens, all wearing trousers. Her uniform meant we were ready for service, it was a good sign.

'I've never seen you in trousers,' I said. 'Except at the farm...'

'Oh, that,' Eleanor snorted. 'And you—in khaki, at last.'

'Yes.' I grinned. Even that silly little officer couldn't take away the joy I felt about my uniform. Another step, away from epilepsy and towards the world of the healthy. 'We've joined UNRRA, at last.'

'Ready for Europe?'

'I hope so.'

We walked along the concrete promenade. Eleanor sighed.

'But,' she said, 'this place feels wrong.'

'I think that officer made a mistake,' I said. 'I'm sure they'll appoint us to the same team.'

'Are you? They've got their own priorities here.'

'But we're married!'

'So?'

Alongside the promenade, waves lapped onto a long beach.

'They've got to keep their word,' I said.

Eleanor shrugged. 'I suppose we'll find out soon enough. UNRRA—it's a big operation. Thousands of people. We don't count for much.' She sighed. 'I don't want to go to Germany without you. It's going to be difficult, bloody difficult. I need to know there's at least one person in my team I can trust.'

'Me too. Let's wait and hope for the best.'

'And all this—' She gestured towards the promenade, beach and sea. 'This isn't what we came for. It's like a holiday.'

'*Like* a holiday,' I said. 'But not really one. Remember what they told us about the beach?'

Eleanor nodded.

'Sun-bathing or paddling is strictly forbidden,' I repeated in the UNRRA officer's clipped accent. 'Because there are German mines buried in the sand.'

We both laughed. At that moment, the contrast between the seaside holiday atmosphere and the hidden landmines seemed absurd. This little port—Granville—hadn't fared badly. While other places had been smashed to smithereens by bombers and artillery, here there were only signs of wear and tear.

'That island.' Eleanor pointed out towards a grey-green bump on the horizon. 'That's Jersey, still occupied by the Germans. The war's not over... Everything feels *wrong* here.'

'Because it's a mess?'

'Of course it's a mess, we knew that. The whole damn continent is a mess. No, it's—it's UNRRA...'

'Not what you expected?'

'I don't know what I expected.'

We walked along the promenade, arm in arm, the sun on our faces, the sea air in our lungs.

'It's the set-up here. It's the people running it. That little squirt shouting out orders.' She mimicked his accent: 'Ten hundred hours *sharp.*

'And then the courses...' She groaned. 'We did those courses in Reading and many of them were pretty bloody pointless. And now yet more, while out there, in Germany, they need us, they need us *now...*'

I nodded. 'But, Eleanor—teams leave all the time, dozens each day... It won't be long...'

Two old French ladies approached us. They had brown, sea-blown faces, they clutched vast black shawls around themselves and their wooden clogs clattered on the concrete promenade.

'M'sieu'dame,' they said in chorus, in a tone suggesting that no further conversation was possible.

We nodded back.

'Those clogs...' said Eleanor, after they'd passed.

'I guess it was a wartime measure. I think the Germans seized all the leather.'

Eleanor nodded.

The promenade curved round the beach. Eleanor stopped and leant on the concrete barrier, looking out to the sea.

'Maybe we got the wrong idea about UNRRA. This place—it's not what we hoped for, is it?'

'It's not but... Let's meet the others first.'

Eleanor's words alarmed me. I knew what she meant: Granville was disappointing and that officer had been bloody annoying. But he was just one officer. We'd meet other people.

***

This was more like it, more like the UNRRA I'd been expecting. The lectures and classes were held in a strikingly modern three-storey building in Jullouville, the next village along the coast. It had been a school before the war, with gleaming windows and the slick, straight lines of an ocean liner. It was smashed about a bit after D-Day, but then it was requisitioned as Eisenhower's HQ and had been cleaned up. There was glass in most of the windows, intact furniture in the rooms and the taps usually worked. This was how I'd imagined UNRRA: futuristic, clean, international and efficient.

Today's lecture was on food and health. I needed to understand the basics, but it wasn't vital for me. We followed the khaki queue into the room. I could now distinguish the better-cut American uniforms from the stiff, scratchy, shoddy British khaki. Eleanor and I found a space on a bench towards the back of the hall. There was a buzz of conversation: people getting to know each other, checking details of the day's timetable, asking about who'd been sent to Germany.

'There's Helen,' said Eleanor. She pointed to a woman chatting and laughing a few rows ahead of us. 'She's one of my room-mates.'

In came the lecturer and my heart sank. It was the little squirt we'd seen at the hotel. Eleanor groaned: we knew he was going to be dull. He spent some minutes sticking enlarged photos of food parasites onto the blackboard.

I told myself to concentrate, but my heart wasn't in it. Sunshine streamed in and the room grew heavier and warmer. Statistics about the calorific value of various foodstuffs floated over me. I looked at the dust swirling in the sunbeams, at the patterns made by the cracks in the plaster along the walls, at the shades of khaki, green, brown and grey, in the rows in front, constantly shifting as people wriggled on the hard wooden benches. Next to me, Eleanor took notes, her pencil jerking in concentrated little scribbles. She was more professional than me: she cared about procedures and standards and, consequently, she expected more from the training. Would I get caught out when we got to Germany?

In the courtyard outside I heard one, then two trucks revving up and someone called out. I thought: they're off. Why couldn't that be us? I tried to imagine what an assembly centre for displaced persons would be like. The numbers we'd heard—camps of five thousand, ten thousand—were frightening. Could we be like Yvonne and talk to them, one at a time, so that the mass was transformed into approachable people?

All at once there was a clattering and a shaking. The lecture had finished, thank goodness, and people stood up, stretched, called out to each other, then followed the slow flow of khaki through the main door. Eleanor moved her head close to me.

'Not the world's most inspiring lecturer,' she whispered.

'No. Most of it went right over my head. Did you understand it?'

'We'd heard most of it before, in Reading. Still, it may be useful.'

***

'Dan.' He held out his hand.

I shook it and then introduced myself and Eleanor. Dan had arrived yesterday, like us. We'd expected a classroom exercise after lunch, but it was delayed and so the UNRRA people had spilled out into the courtyard. Some walked a little further, then sat on the grass and chatted. It was a fine, sunny afternoon. How happy my fellow students looked when they were left alone, with no lecturers or officers to bother them. Why couldn't we just stay here and talk? We'd learn plenty that way.

'You in 2C?' Dan asked, referring to the classroom to which we'd been assigned.

'That's right.'

'Me too. What d'you think of it so far?'

I thought for a second, not wanting to say anything provocative. Dan didn't wait.

'Bloody army officers. Colonial, pukka-sahib types.' His voice dripped sarcasm. 'I had to put up with them for five years. Thought it would be different here.'

'Shame there aren't any Quakers,' I replied. 'They're better. Surprisingly practical and they think about people first.'

Dan nodded. I offered him a cigarette. Eleanor took one. We exchanged details of our wartime experiences. Dan looked up when I said I was a bookseller.

'Almost my old line of business. Before the war, I was a printer.'

He had one of those East End voices: guttural, emphatic, rhythmic. After 1939, he was conscripted and worked in an enormous military workshop that churned out pamphlets for soldiers. Reluctantly, I explained that I'd been barred from military service for medical reasons. He shot me a glance and I feared he might turn scornful.

'Alright now?'

Thank goodness, he wasn't mocking me. I told him about my time in the Fire Service and how I'd re-opened my bookshop after the Blitz.

'Good for you,' he said. 'People need more than beer, skittles and movies.'

Eleanor puffed on her cigarette and glanced at an officer walking—no, *marching*—back to the main building, his back ramrod straight, a swagger-stick under one arm.

'Look at him!' she said. 'That's a tailor-made uniform, isn't it? He didn't get that from the piles in the hotel.'

'Just like bleedin' India,' murmured Dan.

I caught the smile crossing Eleanor's face. I knew what she was thinking: we weren't the only ones who didn't like this. A shout came from the main building. The exercises were starting. We finished our cigarettes and joined the khaki queue. Dan knew the way. Inside 2C was a blackboard and six assorted chairs, some more substantial than others. After a moment, an American woman with a big smile joined us.

'Eleanor!' she said, as if meeting an old friend.

It was Helen, her room-mate.

'Christ, that was a dull lecture,' she continued. 'Are all Brit teachers like that? I knew I might get killed by a German bomb, but I didn't expect to die of boredom.'

We laughed.

Two tall, thin, blonde figures came in: a man and a woman. Before a new round of introductions began, I stepped forward.

'Let's make this a bit more formal,' I suggested. 'I'm Edmund, Team Director.'

I caught the little start of surprise on Dan's face. He hadn't expected that. I looked round the room, wondering if anyone was going to challenge me. Helen smiled as if she was going to offer us home-made biscuits, then introduced herself as Deputy Director. The blonde man and woman were Poles: they were a doctor and a nurse. They shared the same long surname. I wondered if they were husband and wife or brother and sister. Dan was Messing Officer.

From outside, we heard other groups going through similar rituals. Then we waited. There was a distant hiss from the sea, a whistle of wind blowing through an empty window and a door slammed.

'When are they going to send us to Germany?' asked Helen.

There was a lot of nodding round the room.

'The Russians are about to take Berlin,' pointed out Dan.

'Yep,' said Helen. 'And our boys aren't far behind. Goddamn war is almost over.'

At that point we heard footsteps. It was the officer we'd seen marching across the courtyard. He had piercing blue eyes, streaked-back blonde hair and a born-to-rule look. He said nothing, but nodded at us. Then he went to the blackboard and laboriously wrote out an exercise, the chalk screeching each time he made a downward stroke.

We followed bit by bit, peering over his shoulder. The exercise required us to imagine we were running an Assembly Centre for five thousand Poles. (Those numbers! What could six people do in a camp for five thousand?) Six hundred Italians and six hundred Czechs would arrive in a station five kilometres away. Among them were fifty extremely sick people. How would we prepare for them? The chalk stopped screeching.

The blond officer stared at us, then barked: 'Who's Team Director?'

I raised a hand.

'Have your report ready in one hour *precisely*.'

'Of course,' I replied, trying to sound as if I prepared reports about the fate of thousands of DPs every day.

When the officer left, no one spoke. Five pairs of eyes looked at me. I had to say something, but my mind was blank. I reminded myself of Little Ed and the Fire Service. I could do this. I opened my mouth.

'It's essentially a logistical problem.'

Where had that come from? To my surprise, heads nodded round the room.

'Logistical,' said the Polish doctor. 'And medical.'

Somehow, those words did it. The six of us began to discuss procedures. Helen remembered that each Assembly Centre would have two three-ton trucks. How many people could they carry? How long would they take to make a 10-kilometre journey? Eleanor reminded us of the correct methods to transport the severely ill. Between us, we remembered things we'd heard from experienced relief workers, we dragged up points from lectures, we applied common sense. At one point, Eleanor gave me a look and nodded at my notebook. Of course. I picked it up and began scribbling notes.

At the end of the afternoon, we were back in the courtyard. The two Poles had gone, but the four of us—myself, Eleanor, Dan and Helen—were becoming friends, sharing a sense of achievement in passing the first test.

***

After dinner, Eleanor and I walked along the promenade towards a café at the edge of Granville. The sun was setting, the waves lapped on the shore and again we had that strange feeling we were on holiday.

'Our first day,' I said.

Eleanor seemed lost in thought. I wondered if she was unhappy.

'Thank goodness for people like Dan and Helen,' I continued.

Eleanor looked up. 'I like Dan—he's the sort you can trust. And Helen's wonderful. I hope they put us all in the same team.'

'She doesn't complain like some of the Americans do.'

'She told me something,' Eleanor said. 'She's leaving her husband. Coming here is the first step towards a divorce. She's determined to enjoy everything, she won't let anything get her down.'

'Why's she leaving him?'

'The usual: he drinks, he hits her...'

'No!' I couldn't imagine why any man would mistreat a woman as cheerful as Helen.

Eleanor sighed. 'Happens to so many. Thank God she's got the guts to get out.'

We walked on. I thought about what Eleanor had said—a nasty little story of violence, weaving its way through the bigger story of sieges, Blitzes and invasions. Could we change those little stories as well?

'But, anyway,' said Eleanor. 'These classes and these God-awful lecturers. What must we Brits look like to the Americans?'

I grinned. 'Underfed, underpaid, backward-looking primitives—'

'—who still think they have the right to rule half the world!'

We laughed.

'There's the café.' Dan had recommended it: the Café des Amis. He already knew his way round Granville. He was that type: if you met him on a desert island, in two minutes he'd be telling you where to fish and where to find fresh water.

The café was full of Allied personnel. I saw a few American officers, a couple of British engineers and some faces I recognised from the morning lecture. And there was Helen. Swing music was playing: I spotted a wireless in the corner.

'Two glasses of wine?' I asked Eleanor.

One of our fellow UNRRA workers heard us. 'Cider's the local tipple.'

It was served in bowls. I assumed that this was a wartime measure but, no, apparently that's how they drink cider in Normandy. I sipped it cautiously. It was cool, slightly bubbly and sweet with a savoury under taste.

Eleanor smiled. 'I could get to like this.'

'Now *you're* sounding like you're on holiday.'

She laughed.

Then there were cries to *hush*. The wireless was adjusted and turned up. An unmistakable voice entered the room.

'This is London.'

I smiled at the sound of clear, crisp BBC English. After only—what?—two days, London felt so far away. I listened with half an ear: the Russians were advancing in Berlin, the Americans and our forces were moving eastwards, another German general had been captured, another concentration camp had been liberated. The room went deathly quiet. But the details that followed were curiously anodyne and I realised that someone had decided to soften the report. Already, I had clearer ideas about concentration camps than most BBC listeners. I knew that, very soon, I might learn far more about them.

A little later, a Polish UNRRA worker was persuaded to sit at the café's piano. He was one of those pianists who could follow any song after hearing the first few bars. Each of us had to sing a song. When it came to our turn, I started on the first song I could remember, *Knocked Them in the Old Kent Road*. Eleanor burst out laughing: well, it was a strange choice. But after a few lines, she remembered the words and we sang in our best cockney English, dropping every H and swallowing every T, with the Polish pianist enthusiastically supporting us. Helen sang *Breadline Blues*, which she introduced as a ballad from the Great Depression. The other Americans found it funny: I think she exaggerated her Alabama accent for effect. I found it curiously moving. I hadn't realised that Americans sung songs like that.

That evening, we heard a sad Portuguese *fado*, a beautiful French ballad sung by a girl who really could sing, a Norwegian drinking song which—apparently—dated back to the Vikings, something utterly incomprehensible but extremely vigorous in Flemish and a couple of jazz numbers from the Americans, all accompanied by the Polish pianist. The whole world was there, in that one little Normandy cafe. We were an army of young people, carrying no weapons except our hopes and ideals. We'd remake the world, I was sure.

'This is it,' I said to Eleanor. 'This is UNRRA. This is what I wanted.'

She smiled at me, then sipped her cider.

'Yes,' she said. 'This is more like it.'

8. The Raid

Night-time: shouts in the dark, explosions outside. I knew the drill. Pulled on my trousers, grabbed my shoes, snatched a blanket, got to the stairs. I heard shots—something big, heavy—and glass shattering. On the stairs: dark shadows and no running—too many people and no lights. I clung onto the banister rail and followed carefully. All around me, shouts in foreign languages. I could sense fear, but this wasn't a mob in panic. My fellow UNRRA workers knew the dangers. They didn't push, didn't scuffle. Confusion, worry, impatience but nothing more. As I stepped down, the crowd grew thicker, my steps grew slower, but still—no pushing, no scuffling.

At last: a candle and an open door, leading to the hotel basement. Old wooden stairs, which creaked as each man stepped down. A long, dark room with deep shadows, a single flickering candle, a damp smell, a concrete floor, a few bottles in the rack which ran along one wall.

'Move to the end of the basement!' someone shouted from the stairs.

It wasn't an order, it wasn't a cry of panic: just sensible advice. We shouldn't crowd at the end of stairs, we had to make room for the others still coming down. We moved along, treading carefully on the rough concrete floor. People stationed themselves along the wall, some leant against it, some sat on the floor, some tough souls even lay down, pulled blankets under and over themselves, determined to get back to sleep. How many of us were there? Forty? Probably more. It was hard to see.

The talking started. Questions and answers, guesses and rumours. The Germans, obviously. Not an air-raid. But hadn't we heard firing? A counter-attack? They'd landed troops? By the promenade? I spotted Dan, coming down the stairs. He stayed on the second stair from the end and called out:

'German U-boat in the bay. It's got a heavy machine-gun, let's hope it's got nothing more.'

His words were immediately translated into French and Polish and God knows what else. He paused, waiting for these echoes to end.

'If it's only a machine-gun, then it can't hurt us. But it'll certainly sound bad.'

Again, the multi-lingual echoes.

'How long will this last?' An American voice, strained and worried.

Dan smiled grimly. 'It'll last as long as it lasts. We can't do anything to stop them. Until your boys arrive from the military base.'

'We're waiting for the cavalry?' Another American: tense, but cheeky.

A wave of laughter, then the quip was translated and new chuckles came from round the room. Dan waited for silence.

'Yes, that's about it. We're waiting for the cavalry.'

He noticed me, crossed the room, sat down.

'Alright?'

I nodded. 'I know the drill. Plenty of practice in the Blitz.'

He nodded and we looked round the room.

I think we both noticed the same thing, although we didn't say it out loud. The Americans were new to this. They were the ones who glanced round nervously, who jumped when something smashed outside, who whispered or spoke too loud. Us Brits and Continentals: we'd done it all before. It was nothing to feel proud of. I hadn't asked for four years intensive training in air-raid procedures. Someone near the candle produced a pack of cards, shuffled them and, without a word, dealt a hand to the man sitting next to him. My goodness, they really were prepared.

We heard more firing outside: repeated volleys, the machine-gunner was trying to hit something, I could hear crashing and breaking.

'The cars!' I whispered to Dan. 'He's aiming for the cars opposite the hotel.'

Dan listened for a second, then nodded. 'Sounds like it.'

The shooting sounded awful, but it wouldn't really harm us or damage UNRRA's operations. But the poor Americans: they jumped at each new bang.

Dan stood up. 'It's still just the machine-gun. It sounds bad, but it can't hurt us.'

I noticed he didn't look at anybody as he spoke. A nice touch: he wasn't accusing anyone of being scared.

After a few minutes, the machine-gunner got tired of smashing cars. The shots stopped. I felt myself relax, maybe it was over. Then the firing started again, hitting something more distant. I worked out what was happening. The gunner was firing at anything along the promenade: bathing chalets, cafes, houses, wrecking just for the sake of wrecking. I could picture it: an invisible giant, smashing down with its feet, step by step, growing closer... The candle flickered, the room seemed to lurch around me. I felt a stab of pain at the back of my neck. My God, no, I was going to have a fit, no. My back felt sweaty, my limbs grew tense and, without wanting to, I raised my trembling hands to my face.

'Edmund!' Dan leant over, grasped my shoulder. 'Edmund! It's alright, they can't hurt us.'

It was like a release of static electricity. I took a deep breath, I lowered my hands. But then a new volley started, growing closer to the hotel. When would it stop? I started to tremble again. No, no, *no*, not a fit, not here.

Outside, cars or trucks screeched along the road and firing started: first rifles, then—I think—two machine-guns.

Dan stood up and called out in his best showman's voice:
'Ladies and gentlemen! The cavalry have arrived.'

***

Dan and I were the last to leave. I told him I wanted to check on
Eleanor. Dan nodded in an absent-minded way and followed me
outside.

'I ain't married,' he said, as if answering a question I'd asked. 'Had
a girl back in Tunbridge Wells. But now—'

'Eleanor and I married two years ago.'

'Nice girl. Brave, I reckon.'

I nodded. We walked through the dark, empty streets.

'But what was that?' he said. 'What was going on in there, with
you? That wasn't nerves, I've seen nerves.'

My God, not much got past him. What was I do? Lie? Deny
everything? In a split second, I decided to trust him.

'Epilepsy. I felt I was close to a seizure.'

He stared at me. 'You don't say?'

'Don't breathe a word to Eleanor. She'll insist we go back to
England. Actually, don't tell anyone.'

He nodded. 'Epilepsy—should you be Team Director with that?'

'Probably not.'

'Epilepsy,' he repeated, thoughtfully. 'A mate of mine got that,
back at the printshop. Just came over him one day, out of the blue,
like.'

I said nothing.

'But his—it seemed different from what was happening to you
then.'

'I can control it—mostly.'

'Seen a doctor?'

'Back in 1940.'

'Bah,' Dan snorted. 'Don't believe a word those people tell you.'

We turned a corner.

'What causes it?'

This was awkward. I'd talked with Eleanor and Muriel about my condition, but no one else. Was it wise to confide in Dan? But—he seemed genuinely interested.

'Hard to say. Sometimes it just comes. There was something about that candle—the way it flickered. And being confined, underground, waiting for that bloody machine-gun to shoot its way along the promenade.' I shivered at the thought of it. 'I suppose it is nerves, in a way.'

'We all get that. If someone tells you he's without fear, then he's a liar.'

'I'm no better than those Yanks, am I?'

He laughed for a moment, then thought about it. 'That was our baptism of fire. You, me, them—everyone. It's no joke. People could've died.'

'But, Dan: not a word. Really. I don't want to be sent back to England.'

He nodded. 'You're here now. No point in turning back.'

I could see the women's dormitory: there were no signs of damage, thank goodness. But I still wanted to be sure Eleanor was safe.

Had I been right to insist on coming to France? I couldn't be a Team Director if I was subject to epileptic seizures. I couldn't be sure. Eleanor also had doubts. She wasn't certain about UNRRA as an organisation. It was annoying that we had so little time to ourselves: we weren't able to talk things over.

This place was dangerous. I was in a warzone. If the Germans had attacked once, they could do it again. They were close, very close to us. I glanced at Dan as we paced through the dark streets. He looked back.

'Nasty, eh?' he said. 'Those bastards—they're not all dead yet. Still, not long before we're in Germany.'

He began to whistle tunelessly.

9. Into Normandy

A couple of days later, they set us a different exercise. This time we had to drive a three-ton truck.

'They've run out of things for us to do,' I told Eleanor.

'Anything's better than one of those lectures! But this is pointless, you've already been trained to drive trucks. We're wasting time. When are we going to leave?'

'They'll announce who's in which teams first.'

Eleanor shook her head. 'They seem to make you wait until you've given up all hope.'

'Teams go to Germany every day.'

'Not us. Today, all we'll see are the verdant pastures of Normandy. I wonder if we'll be with those Poles?'

We'd noticed the same faces again and again in our exercises. Had some decision been made? Was this an UNRRA team in the making? Not knowing was so frustrating.

The day's exercise was simple enough: we were to load a truck with a week's supplies, then drive to Cherbourg and back. The UNRRA officer explained that for the long drive to Germany, we'd be supplied with trained drivers, but I could drive today.

We assembled at oh nine hundred hours in the courtyard at Jollouville. Dan was there, but there was no sign of the two Poles or Helen. Instead, we found Alma, a short, serious Danish nurse, Pierre, a thin, tall French doctor and Victor, a weasel-faced man with thick glasses.

'Where's Helen?' I asked Eleanor. 'We can't go without her.'

'Who's Helen?' asked Victor. I recognised his American accent.

'Our Deputy Team Director.'

Victor smiled. 'I'm the Deputy Team Director.'

I stared at him. What had happened to Helen? How could I be a proper Team Director if the team kept changing?

'This place, eh?' he continued. 'No one knows anything. Chaos. Everyone waiting in lines.'

Alma and Pierre loaded the truck, while I checked the items on the list.

'And those lectures! Ignoring all modern pedagogic theory. Dry as dust.'

While I agreed with Victor, I didn't want to show it. I pretended to concentrate on my list.

'That guy, the one in charge—what's his name?'

'Arnold-Forster,' said Dan. There was a slight stress in the way he pronounced the double-barrelled name.

'Yeah, that guy, Arlan,' said Victor. 'I mean, he's not so bad as a teacher. He speaks French, he tries to communicate. But so idealistic! He's like an old-time preacher. It's an indoctrination in the faith.'

Dan laughed. Eleanor looked at Victor, listening carefully. This was the last thing I needed: more reasons for Eleanor to doubt UNRRA. Why couldn't he shut up?

'And all the time, so many problems. No water in the taps, no glass in the windows and the food!'

'What's wrong with the food?' Dan was puzzled.

'Oh, come on,' Victor said. 'Don't you expect more than a slice of flavourless meat and two half-cooked potatoes for dinner?'

I felt a flash of anger at Victor's arrogance.

'There's a war on,' replied Dan. 'Everything's a bit rough-and-ready—you know, you scrounge here, you patch up there... They're doing their best.'

'Hah!' scoffed Victor.

Our truck was ready. I got in the driver's seat. Victor walked round to the passenger side and opened the door.

'No, Victor,' I called out.

He looked up, surprised.

'I'll drive with Eleanor on this trip.'

'That's not right,' he protested.

I gave him a stern look. Slowly, he stepped down.

'This ain't regular, not regular at all,' he grumbled, but he walked to the back of the truck.

Eleanor got in, smiling. 'I hope you haven't annoyed him.'

'He can't complain. The truck's been refitted: there's a new tarpaulin covering the back and the bench looks solid. Where's Helen?'

'Lost somewhere in UNRRA's bureaucracy, I suppose.'

'A shame, I liked her,' I said.

Eleanor nodded, then glanced at the gearstick, pedals, steering-wheel and dashboard.

'I could drive this. It's the same as an ambulance.'

'I know, but...'

I didn't say anything more, but I knew what Eleanor was thinking. There'd been a lecture on UNRRA *in the field*. The lecturer had been emphatic: UNRRA workers needed to be respected by the local people. This meant not flouting local traditions, which in turn meant that, under normal circumstances, women would not be appointed at Team Directors or as drivers. I'd heard Eleanor's intake of breath.

'Ridiculous!' she'd muttered.

Eleanor was probably a better driver than me, after her experience driving ambulances during the Blitz. What happened to UNRRA's promise to work *without discrimination*?

The truck started like a dream: someone must have serviced it. This wasn't one of the coughing, spluttering monsters that we saw limping out of the courtyard. We rolled away. Some UNRRA workers waved at us and shouted *good luck*, obviously thinking we were on our way to Germany. Eleanor waved back. She had a map and—more importantly—had scribbled a page in her notebook, listing broken bridges and new routes. She pointed out the route to me. We chugged through Granville and then we were out on the open road.

At first, it was beautiful. Rolling green fields, old stone walls, apple orchards decorated with pink and white blossom, gentle spring sunshine... I was reminded of Sunday afternoon drives with my father, out onto the Downs. It felt good to be with Eleanor. So often in Granville we were separated: sleeping in different buildings, attending different classes, talking to different people. But this was more like what I'd imagined: working with her, doing something we both believed in. Surely they'd choose us for the same team. For a moment, I allowed myself to think they would. I held onto the steering-wheel with one hand and gave Eleanor's arm a squeeze.

'Do you think that driving in Germany will be like this?' I asked, thinking maybe I should look forward to it, and that leading a team might be easy.

'No.'

We came to a crossroads, chugged along the Cherbourg road and then went up a slight incline. At the top—everything changed. The same landscape, but different features. We passed a tangled, burnt mass of metal, pushed off the road.

'What was that?' I said.

Eleanor shrugged. 'A tank? A personnel carrier?'

The fields were scarred with deep black craters, the orchards burnt and slashed open. Scorched, tangled lumps of metal lay rusting along the roadside, sometimes in clusters of two or three. Most were so distorted that we had no idea what they were or whether they were Allied or German. The wreckage of a plane lay in a field, its struts sticking up like the bones of a prehistoric monster.

The road led us through a little village, with twenty or twenty-five buildings in it. Each was comprehensively devastated: roofless and smashed open, their great thick grey bricks thrown about on the ground and only odd bits of walls left standing. I wiped my forehead, glanced at Eleanor. She stared out the window.

'That one was a tank,' she said, pointing to another twisted, burnt mass of metal. I heard the tension in her voice.

I felt a twinge at the back of my neck. I wasn't going to have a fit, I felt pretty sure of that, but it alarmed me. Maybe Eleanor was right, maybe I shouldn't be out here. Could I really direct anyone? But why were these sights so bad? I'd seen smashed streets in London. Yet that devastated village in Normandy seemed worse. Perhaps it was the background of the green fields and orchards, with their promise of spring and a new beginning for nature and mankind.

'This is one of the circles of hell,' I muttered.

I had to stop. We'd said that I would drive for an hour and then pull over, but I couldn't go on. I brought the truck to a halt just beyond the smashed village, without saying anything to Eleanor. We got out, then walked to the back of the truck. The other four were waiting. Perhaps they thought I had something to say, but I was speechless. We huddled in a little group at the back of the truck and exchanged brief phrases.

'I hadn't expected...'

'Terrible...'

'Destruction, on *this* scale...'

'It's the fighting—after D-Day...'

'It'll be like this for miles, all the way to Cherbourg...'

'What'll Germany be like?'

Birds twittered in an apple orchard and the sun shone on the fields. But the whole place had changed.

Victor brought us to our senses.

'D-Day was ten months ago! Why haven't they begun clearing up?'

Pierre looked up. '*You* did this. You clear it up.'

'Look, buddy, our boys crossed half the world to save you. At least you could *do* something after we defeated your enemy.'

'Our people...' Emotion was choking Pierre, who struggled for words. 'Our people, the French people suffered brutality... We had the Gestapo and the Nazis for four years, while you—'

'Victor!' Eleanor interrupted. 'Look at the scale of this. Look at it! Some of the heaviest fighting in the whole war happened here. It can't be cleaned up in a day.'

'And their menfolk,' added Dan. 'Still in Germany.'

'That's why we are here,' said Alma, brightly. 'It is the job of UNRRA to send them back.'

Victor wasn't satisfied. He shook his head. 'This is communism. They're all communists. They expect the state to do everything for them.'

Dan looked up, but Eleanor got in first.

'Communism?' she said. 'If you'd been through this, wouldn't you be a Communist?'

'No!' yelled Victor. 'I'd learn to stand on my own two feet.'

'Some people don't have that luxury, Victor. We're going to a land of cripples and shoeless children—'

'Oh, yes?' sneered Victor. 'The French people round here are well enough to steal our supplies and sell them on the black-market.'

'If you...' Pierre wanted to say something, but fell into silence.

Victor had raised another objection to UNRRA, as if we hadn't heard enough. Corruption. It was something Eleanor and I hadn't anticipated. I suppose it's a rule of human existence: if a well-stocked, idealistic organisation comes into contact with a half-starved, demoralised people, there will be corruption. The rackets that went on!

But I couldn't let this continue. Maybe the six of us were going to be a team. If so, we'd have to work with Victor and it was no good turning him into a minority of one. I needed to act as Team Director.

'Anyone who thought that working in Europe was going to be easy was a fool,' I told them. 'We're all keen as mustard, we all want to get out there—'

I looked round and saw agreement. Nods from Pierre and Dan, steady stares from Victor, Eleanor and Alma.

'We've been sent on this exercise for a reason.' I was making it up as I went along. 'They want us to know how bad it's going to be. Look at this wrecked village! Germany will be worse, the whole damn country is smashed to smithereens.'

'Good,' muttered Dan, but I silenced him with a look.

'Here we see ruins and wrecks, in Germany we'll see corpses.' I could see Dan had a retort, but I didn't give him time to speak. 'It won't be our job to reconstruct towns and villages. But we will help the people who suffered most and, by God, they'll need it.'

Somehow, that worked. No one disagreed.

'So no more arguments about who's to blame, alright?' I looked at Victor, Dan and Pierre. 'We can't solve all the world's problems, let's focus on what we can do.'

Five faces looked up at me. Maybe they expected more, but that was all I could say. This experience might have done some good: it could be called team-building. I'd rallied them, I'd prevented their talk from disintegrating into a vicious free-for-all. But when we got back in the truck, I felt less certain. Was that leadership? Was that *good* leadership? Saying some empty words in the middle of some ruins? There had to be more to it.

10. Sorrow at the Dance

Helen insisted. There was a dance at the American base and we were invited. She'd fixed things for us. There'd be music: a French band and some singers. Once she'd left, I looked at Eleanor.

'Might be fun,' she said.

'Yes.'

Anything that might make Eleanor feel happier seemed like a good idea.

That evening, instead of going to the Café des Amis, we walked to the American base. There were lines of barbed wire round the camp and even a couple of sentries at the gate, but nobody took security seriously. A queue had formed: a few UNRRA women, some British officers and plenty of American soldiers. I was relieved to see that no one had dressed for the occasion. In our khaki uniforms—Eleanor had at last found a skirt—we looked like everyone else. At the gate, we reached for our identity cards, but the sentry just drawled:

'Good evening, ma'am, sir.'

He waved us in, as if he knew us already. Music could be heard from a big building: the path towards it was decorated with fairy lights and bunting, blowing in the breeze. What about the blackout? Nobody seemed to care.

The hall was a rectangular, prefabricated military building, of the sort that were springing up across Europe in the wake of the Allies' advance. It wasn't a nightclub, but it was a pretty good imitation of one. As we walked through the door, we entered a warm, easy twilight. Coloured lights twinkled along the ceiling, and I could hear swing music. Comfortable chairs and little tables lined the back of the room. A stage, lit up by spotlights, dominated the space. It made me smile: after grim, Blitzed-out London, after the destruction we'd seen in the French countryside, at last we'd found somewhere friendly. This should cheer up Eleanor.

As we walked in, a large man wearing a cowboy hat—really! a cowboy hat!—greeted us as if he knew us. We learnt later that he was the base commander.

'UNRRA?' he asked.

We nodded.

'The first drink's on me.'

He signalled to the bartender, who nodded back.

We got two beers and sat at a table. After a few minutes I realised the swing music came from a jukebox. People had told me about them, but I'd never actually seen or heard one. It looked wonderful: a shimmering golden arch towered over it and showers of shining stars and dazzling buttons spilt over its front. A GI saw us admiring it.

'That's a real Wurlitzer,' he told us. 'Brought all the way from the States.'

The music was like the swing music we'd heard on the wireless in England, but faster, with more of a beat: music made for dancing. I felt a sudden admiration for these Americans. In the midst of the most savage war in history, they'd managed to create this haven of warmth and comfort. I wondered what a British military mess would look like and knew in my heart it would be amateurish, old-fashioned and cold. For the first time in days, Eleanor and I could really relax. I leant back in my chair and sipped my beer.

The man with the cowboy hat walked onto the stage and the music from the jukebox stopped.

'Good evening to y'all!' he bellowed.

It was obviously some sort of ritual, for every American in the hall shouted back:

'Good evening, uncle!'

Then there was a predictable exchange. He pretended he couldn't hear them and demanded that they shout louder. We laughed and joined in. After a few repetitions, 'Uncle' went through the evening's delights, promising hot jazz and wild jitter-bugging. The crowd cheered.

'But first—but first—' he struggled to get the audience's attention. 'From our friends from over the road... Some sweet, soulful sounds from the south.'

A small group of soldiers had assembled by the side of the stage. They were all coloured, something still new to me. The only coloured men I'd seen before had been American soldiers in London and a few dock-workers. There were eight of them and they arranged themselves in a semi-circle round the microphone. I looked for a band: there wasn't one. Then, without a word, they started singing.

I'd never heard singing like that. It had something of the warmth of the Welsh male voice choirs, but with a difference: while the Welsh choirs usually faced proudly outward, towards the audience, this group were more private, circled inwards, meeting each other's eyes as they sung, occasionally nodding. It was as if they'd allowed us to listen to a private singing session. I'd never heard any of their songs before, but I could sense their biblical origins. They weren't hymns, but they had phrases which echoed the Psalms. I'd thought that coloured men's singing would be—well, primitive or African, whatever that means. But this was clear and pure, beautiful and yet so, so sad.

I glanced at Eleanor as one song ended.

'They call them sorrowful songs,' she whispered to me. 'They're based on songs that slaves sang on the plantations.'

'They're—they're beautiful,' I replied.

How could a people who'd experienced such misery produce such beauty? They captivated this audience of impatient, war-weary young men, who wanted to drink and dance. I could have listened to them all night: the songs sounded so familiar yet so different.

Instead 'Uncle' climbed back on the stage and announced a short interval while a 12-piece French band set up.

In a few minutes, the band was playing loud, rhythmic music with a strong beat. The open area in front of the stage filled with couples. I don't know where the women came from: the base must have dragged in every available female for miles. They were French girls, wearing their prettiest dresses and brightest make-up, American women from the auxiliary services in their uniforms, UNRRA women in their khaki. The couples swung back and forth, separating and joining, their feet bouncing and tapping on the floor, their hips swinging, moving faster and faster. So, this was jitter-bugging. It was like swing, but more expressive and physical. We spotted Victor, dancing with a French girl.

'Isn't he married?' I asked Eleanor.

The GIs cheered as the band announced each new song. It was the ideal music for soldiers. Something loud and forceful that grabbed you, with a booming bass and a bang from the drums, with horns that blasted up and down. The sort of music that didn't give you time to feel miserable or lonely or concerned about what happened in the rest of the world. I loved its energy and exuberance.

By now we were drinking our third beer.

'Careful, Edmund,' Eleanor warned me.

I shrugged. For the moment, I didn't care about my fits or anything else: the war seemed a million miles away and I was sitting with my girl in something like a nightclub. I felt happy and I'd have another drink.

'Well, if you're not going to stop drinking, then I'll have to try something else.' Eleanor's eyes gleamed.

I frowned. What did she mean? She jumped up, then held out her hand.

'You want us to dance?' I asked. 'Jitterbugging? Do you think we can?'

'Course we can. And if you won't, I'll find a GI who will.'

That did it. If the GIs could do it, then so could I.

We hadn't been to many dances: they were rare occasions in wartime London. Sometimes in pubs, maybe on a Saturday night, instead of the usual singalong pianist, we'd find something extra: a bass-player or a drummer would join the pianist. A few couples would get up and demonstrate swing dances. We'd join in, carried away by the wave of excitement. Aside from what the American soldiers got up to with English girls in the dark backstreets, there weren't many public displays of affection in wartime London, so I'd enjoyed those rare Saturday nights. Eleanor was a wonderful dancer, skilled and flamboyant.

I grinned. This was going to be a night to remember! The music grew louder as we approached the stage. Eleanor grabbed me by the hand, I put my arm round her waist, she clasped my elbow and we stood facing each for a second, motionless, with the dancers swirling around us. Couples shouted to the band, calling them to play louder, faster... Then Eleanor pulled me, her feet started tapping and I knew what I had to do. I couldn't follow all her steps, but I could keep time. I was the base around which she pirouetted and swung. Her eyes twinkled and her hair unravelled. The floor itself seemed to be jumping in time with the music. Daring couples were doing stunts like flinging the girl over the man's shoulders. I knew we weren't going to do that, but Eleanor twirled round as she hung onto my hand, stretching my arm out to its fullest and then swinging back to me. I caught a brief glimpse of Helen, whirling vigorously. She waved, flashed a big smile, then turned back to her partner.

The band stopped for the interval and we regained our table, breathing deeply, laughing with the sheer joy of the moment.

'I'd never have thought...' I said.

'God bless the Americans!' said Eleanor. 'Without them...'

'Those were some fine steps,' I teased her.

'Couldn't have done them without you. That was fun.'

I raised my glass, she raised hers and we chinked glasses together. I gulped down my beer. In a few days we'd be in the middle of dreadful devastation, but for the moment... The American forces had given us a brief escape. Sometimes you just have to dance and laugh and shout.

'And tomorrow morning?' Eleanor said. 'Another of those lectures?'

'Let's skip it and stay here until it closes.'

'No, it's Arnold-Forster. He'll announce the teams, I know he will. We've got to be there.'

'So—' I was surprised. I thought Eleanor would want to stay.

'So we've got to go. The sooner we find out which team we're in, the sooner we leave.'

I nodded, pleased that Eleanor sounded so committed to UNRRA. The evening had been a success.

We got up and an idea hit me.

'Let's say goodbye to those coloured singers. They were so...'

I couldn't find the words. We looked round the hall, staring deep into the dark corners, but we couldn't see them. Suddenly I was aware that Eleanor was standing very straight and very still. Something was wrong. Inwardly, I cursed. A few moments ago, she'd been so happy. What had happened?

'Edmund,' she said. Her voice was flat and controlled. 'What do you notice about every man in this place?'

Absurd answers came into my mind: they were all soldiers, they were all drinking... I looked back at her. She had that look: her skin was very pale, her eyes small, sharp and dark. What was it?

'What do you notice?'

Then I realised. They were all white. There were no coloured men in the hall. But—what had happened to them? They'd been so moving. Who wouldn't have wanted to congratulate them?

'What's happened?' I wondered aloud. 'Where've they gone?'

'Let's ask Victor.'

There was an edge to her voice. Was she going to confront him? We found him at a table.

'Victor,' said Eleanor. 'We so enjoyed the coloured singers and we'd like to say thank you and goodbye to them, but we just can't see them.'

Victor looked embarrassed for a moment. 'I expect they've gone back to their base.'

'What? After that marvellous performance, didn't they stay for a drink?'

'I guess—I guess they prefer their base. They can get a drink there.'

'I see.'

We left and walked back to the town centre in the cool darkness. For a few moments the only sound was Eleanor's shoes rapping on the path. Then she began.

'We're fighting this war to build a better world, right? Isn't that what it's all about? And so we're fighting against the evils the Nazis have brought into the world. One of which is race-thinking.'

'Maybe Victor was right,' I replied. 'Maybe they've just gone back to their base...'

'Hah!' She didn't bother to argue. 'How can we oppose race-thinking if we practice it ourselves? These bloody Americans. They cruise over here, they create glittering dance halls for their soldiers, they steal jazz and jitter-bugging from the coloured people, and then... and then... They put them on show, just for fifteen minutes, just to demonstrate...'

'Eleanor: we'll do it bit by bit. We can't solve everything at once. And remember: we're UNRRA, we're not American soldiers.'

She was almost in tears. I put my arm round her shoulder. She shrugged it off.

'How many coloured people have you seen at Granville?' she asked.

'You know, there are one or two... UNRRA's different, it really is...'

'Is it? Are you sure? Are you really sure?'

Damnit. Just when everything had been going so well. For a moment, beer and jitterbugging had pulled us together and I'd thought that tomorrow we'd drive out to Germany and put the world to rights. But now—it wasn't so simple. We walked along the dark streets, in parallel but not together, not exchanging a word.

When we got to the women's dormitory, Eleanor turned, faced me, put her arms round me. We stood like that for a moment, the waves on the shore the only sound.

'Are you sure you want to do this, Edmund? UNRRA isn't what we expected, is it? We can go back, you know, no one can stop us. Others have gone.'

'We've got to go on. We've got to do something, we've got to try.'

She stared at me, but it was so dark that I couldn't see her face properly.

Then she nodded. 'Alright. We'll try.'

11. An Ugly Festival

Arnold-Forster spoke the next morning: he was as eloquent and passionate as ever, but there was no announcement about the teams. Eleanor and I were getting tired of him. Some of Victor's cynicism had rubbed off on us.

In the afternoon, we'd arranged a walk with Helen. We'd guessed she wasn't going to be in our team and we wanted to say goodbye. We met her outside the hotel and went on our usual stroll along the promenade.

The town felt different. At noon a train had brought a contingent of French forced labourers back from Germany, the first large group to return to Granville. Their homecoming sparked off celebrations. It was a bright, clear day and the streets were fuller than we'd ever seen them. Red, white and blue tricolours were displayed from windows, groups burst out in song at street corners, wine and cider splashed into glasses in the café verandas and passers-by were invited to drink a toast to France. We stopped once, raised our glasses and shouted *Vive la République, Vive la France,* long live the Republic, long live France. It was fun and made me think of how Londoners would celebrate the end of the war.

On the promenade, something struck me.

'It's odd that they all look so cheerful,' I said.

'Why?' asked Helen.

'Don't you remember those *returnees* we saw in the train from Paris? They weren't looking so good.'

'No,' said Eleanor. 'You're right. They had a hard time in Germany.'

'Not really an occasion for celebration,' I said. 'Seeing your husband or father come back like that.'

We stopped at a corner to let a group of Resistance fighters go by. They weren't in uniform, but you quickly got to recognise them. They were mostly young men in shirt-sleeves, sometimes with armbands. What made them stand out were their rifles: they still hadn't surrendered them to the Allies. These were a compact group of five or six, with serious, determined faces, so different from the cheerful passers-by who filled the streets. They strode purposefully, rifles in their hands or slung over their shoulders. People stopped to let them pass. Once or twice passers-by called out *Vive la France!* to them. The fighters ignored them.

'I wonder where they're going,' said Helen.

'Off for a drink,' joked Eleanor, but neither Helen or I laughed.

We'd intended to go to the Café des Amis, our usual haunt, but we guessed it would be crowded with cheering, boozy French people. Maybe we'd go there later, when the celebrations had died down. Instead, we found a bench on the promenade, by the beach with the German mines. We'd enjoyed Helen's company and we'd miss her. But first, I wanted to tease her.

'We saw you jitter-bugging. My goodness! You never told us that you were such a wonderful dancer.'

Helen laughed. 'Hell, those GIs. They sure wanted a good time. I danced for three hours straight.'

Eleanor smiled. 'And now you've left your husband...'

'I'll never again let any bastard tell me what I can or can't do.'

'If you meet someone nice here...' said Eleanor.

Helen grinned. 'No, no, no... I've just got out of one marriage, I'm not going to fall into another.'

There were loud shouts behind us and I had to lean forward to catch what she said.

'This place has done wonders for my foreign language skills,' Helen continued.

'Yes?' I said.

'I've learnt how to say *no* in six different languages.'

Eleanor and I laughed, and there were more shouts behind us. We turned to look. A crowd had formed on the street that ran from the promenade to the town hall. They were all staring in the same direction and shouting. I heard the same shouts, again and again, *tondez-la.*

'What does that mean?' I asked Eleanor.

She frowned. 'I can't remember. It's something agricultural, I think.'

'Agricultural?' said Helen. 'I don't think they're holding a cattle fair up there.'

The shouting had changed tone. The joy of *Vive la République* had gone. There was something more urgent, more threatening in the crowd's cries. We walked up the street to see more. It swarmed with people. Being tall, I saw the whole scene. On the pavements, rows of townsfolk stood: some cheered, some shouted angrily, some were silent and serious. In front of us, there was a middle-aged man in a threadbare suit and a woman in a faded floral dress, arm-in-arm. They stood on tiptoe, straining to see.

'*Tondez-la!*' he shouted.

I looked at Eleanor.

'I remember now,' she said. 'It's the word to shear. They're calling for something to be sheared.'

'What the hell's going on?' said Helen.

More people came down the street. A few Resistance fighters, with their guns and armbands. A group of three girls, wooden clogs clattering, each wearing a different-coloured handkerchief round their necks—one red, one white, one blue. They held hands, laughed and shouted. An older man, with a thin, drawn face, a dark corduroy jacket and a beret. What was happening? There was a solid knot of people: three Resistance fighters, one with a rifle over his shoulder, all looking round. A policeman, his arm round a woman. Helping her? No, pulling her along, almost dragging her. Two more Resistance fighters on the other side, sometimes stopping to pull her. I looked up and down the street, trying to see the centre of attention.

What were they all looking at? It was the policeman and the woman. But she looked so ordinary: a striped skirt, clogs, brown hair. Eyes darting up and down the street, trying to find a friend. Worried, unable to resist.

I didn't like this, I didn't like the mood of the crowd and these strange shouts. I felt this might turn into something nasty, I couldn't guess what. I wanted to turn back, but the pressure of the crowd carried us forward, up the main street to the town hall. We couldn't stop to discuss what to do, it was too noisy and the force of the crowd kept pushing us apart. I took hold of Eleanor's arm to keep her close, Helen grabbed me.

There was a little square in front of the town hall, with a statue commemorating the fallen of the First World War. Four chairs had been placed in front of it: on three of them sat scared, nervous women. The policeman forced the woman we'd seen onto the fourth chair. We were pushed onto a raised flowerbed and the three of us clung to each other for support. Who were these women? What was the crowd going to do?

A group of women standing under some trees burst into the *Marseillaise*. The first lines were taken up by everyone on that side of the square, but then faded away. Shouts erupted from all quarters, irregular and harsh, mostly incomprehensible. Everyone sounded angry. Eleanor caught one word, repeated again and again: *putain*, whore.

Then it began. There was no speech, no announcement, but everyone seemed to know what to expect. The resistance fighters and the policeman stood behind the chairs, occasionally grasping one of the women by the shoulder, as if to remind her there was no escape. The fighters' faces were mostly serious, but now and then they'd catch the eye of someone in the crowd and smile. A man in a white coat stepped forward: he carried a pair of scissors, a cut-throat razor and a bowl full of shaving-foam.

For a second I had the terrible thought that he was going to cut their throats and I gripped Eleanor's arm tighter. But it was Helen who understood it.

'He's a barber. He's going to—going to shave their heads!'

A thick silence descended on the crowd, all eyes concentrated on the barber's actions. The only sound was the clicking of his scissors, which echoed across the whole square. Someone muttered *oui*, but there was nothing else. The woman, held from behind, couldn't move, but her eyes jerked wildly. The scissors clicked and the woman's brown curls fell to the concrete steps. The barber worked calmly and methodically: there was no cruelty in his actions. When he finished cutting, he carefully spread foam over her head, shaved her, then wiped her head with a towel, leaving her as bald as a billiard ball. A young, smiling woman stepped forward—a friend of the Resistance fighters, I guessed from the way they looked at her. She had a tube of lipstick in her hand. She gripped the woman by her chin and carefully drew a red swastika on her forehead. When she stood back, the crowd cheered and shouted: there were more shouts of *putain* and a release of tension, something of a return to the holiday atmosphere of the morning.

'They're punishing these women,' said Eleanor, 'my God, they're punishing them because they slept with German soldiers.'

'He that is without sin, let him cast the first stone.' The words came to me unbidden.

I looked round at the smiling or angry faces of the crowd, and the grim faces of the Resistance fighters. What right did they have to make this judgement, to enact this dreadful punishment?

The barber turned to the second woman. She struggled a little and was held down by the men behind her. When the razor touched her head, she jerked and it caught her. A thin trickle of blood ran down her face. The barber stopped, tutted, wiped away the blood and then continued his work. When the woman with the lipstick approached her, the shaven-headed woman yelled a few words at the crowd. I looked at Eleanor, but she shrugged her shoulders.

A few moments later, there were four shaven-headed women in front of the statue. Two of them looked down, unwilling to even glance at the tormenting crowd. The third was in tears. But the fourth! She stared out, her face cold and defiant, as if etched in granite, throwing out a silent accusation at the crowd.

The resistance fighters led the people in cheering: *Vive la République! Vive la France!* The words were repeated, again and again. Then the poor women were half-dragged, half-pulled away, the Resistance fighters forcing them along the street.

'They're going to parade them across the whole town,' said Helen.

I wanted to collapse on the ground. I'd never seen anything so sad and so obviously wrong in my life.

The three of us went back to the bench overlooking the sea. For minutes, we said nothing. Now and again, we heard shouts and cheers from the streets behind us, as those poor women were paraded round the town. At last, Helen spoke.

'That,' she said, 'was like a lynching. We had them in the States, still do sometimes, I'm horrified to say. That holiday atmosphere, the celebration and the crowd revelling in—'

'Stop,' I said. 'I won't hear anymore. That—that horrific scene isn't why I joined UNRRA, this isn't why I came to Europe. It's over.'

I glanced at Eleanor: she hesitated, then nodded. She looked stunned.

'We don't want to be part of this. We'll catch a train back tomorrow,' I continued. 'Hell, we'll catch one tonight if we can. I don't want to spend another second here.'

Helen looked at me, then looked at Eleanor.

'Listen,' she said. 'You can't go. You're both good people. You chose to come to Europe at the end of the world's worst war. You're going to see some dreadful things, things which will make today's brutality seem like a flea-bite—'

I opened my mouth to protest.

'*Yes,*' Helen insisted. 'Believe me, Edmund, it's going to get far, far worse. And if good people run away every time they see something bad, then where are we? Hold on, hold on to each other. Don't turn away. You can do this, I know you can.'

'We don't even know if we'll be in the same team,' I said.

'Of course you will,' said Helen. 'Arnold-Forster isn't stupid. Anyone can see that you two need each other.'

Eleanor spoke, her voice trembling and uncertain. 'They were looking for scapegoats. I know they've all suffered and I suppose those women were no saints. But they all wanted—they wanted someone to blame. Men with guns. They always finally turn on women, don't they? That's what happens in war.'

Helen nodded. 'But you'll stay, won't you?'

'You're sure we'll be chosen for the same team?' I asked.

'I'd put money on it.' She smiled. 'But you have to be strong.'

'I never thought I'd see something like that,' said Eleanor. 'The—the hatred. The concentrated hatred of that crowd. And they weren't Nazis. It was—medieval. Like witch-burning.'

'But UNRRA? Europe?' I said.

Eleanor looked out at the sea, thinking. 'Helen's right. We'd be wrong to run away. But...' She sighed. 'As long as we're in the same team... I wish you were coming with us, Helen.'

'Arnold-Forster seems to have other plans.'

We stood up and hugged Helen goodbye. Such a shame: we never saw her again. I hope she coped in Germany, it wasn't easy for any of us.

12. Leaving

I needed to shave. I'd scrounged a bowl and filled it with hot water downstairs. I had a razor, a bit of soap and a small mirror, but now I was looking round my room for somewhere to rest the mirror and bowl. Images of the horrific scene from the day before went through my mind, unsettling me. A shout from the corridor made me jump. There was a clatter of feet on the stairs. For a second, I feared another German raid.

Someone outside shouted, 'The teams! The teams! There's a list in the lobby!'

That was it. I forgot about shaving, dropped my bowl on a chair and joined the pack of half-dressed, unshaven men running down the stairs. In the lobby about a hundred people struggled to read ten sheets of typed paper pinned on the wall. Women from Eleanor's dormitory were coming in—I spotted Eleanor. She began to push methodically through the khaki throng, getting closer to the wall. I followed her. Shouts echoed round the room:

'Waldeck! Leaving tomorrow!'

'*Moi aussi!*'

Being tall was an advantage: I could scan the first lines of each sheet. I spotted my name, to the left and I nudged Eleanor to push her way there. Was she in the same team? Was she? Someone pushed in front of me, I pushed back. There, fourth name down, Welfare Officer: Eleanor. Thank God. Thank God. We'd stay together.

I grabbed her and in the midst of that swirling, shouting khaki mass, I hugged her and I heard her laugh. I knew that whatever horrors Germany might have, I could face them if Eleanor was with me. We walked out of the lobby, still holding hands.

'But did you see?' she asked.

'What?'

'The rest of the team?'

I laughed. All I'd thought about was whether Eleanor's name was there. 'Tell me.'

'We'll be with Pierre, Alma and Dan, as expected. No Helen. And guess who else?'

'Not Victor!'

'Yes.'

'Damn. And where are we going?'

Eleanor hadn't got the name properly. It was something like Castle.

'Castle?' I said.

'And we leave in two days.'

We were back on the promenade. The sun was shining, the tide was coming in and Granville looked like a seaside resort. Eleanor and I walked along, hand in hand.

'Sometimes this place is really pretty,' I said.

'I've gone off it. The sooner we leave, the better.'

PART III
GERMANY

'I was thrilled to be functioning in a completely unstructured situation with near-total freedom from authority and restrictions, and to be able to draw to the fullest on my creativity and imagination. I found that almost nothing was impossible if I put my mind to it—that regulations were made by people and could be changed by people.'
Susan Pettiss, UNRRA Welfare Officer

'This cannot be the twentieth century, I think. I try to remember the redeeming attributes of man. None comes to mind.'
Marcus Smith, Medical Officer at Dachau concentration camp

13. To Germany

One bright, sunny morning in the first week of May, we set out in two trucks.

'About time,' grumbled Victor as the glass and concrete of the Jullouville centre faded behind us.

I had to agree. Our weeks at the UNRRA centre at Granville hadn't been useful, and we'd grown sceptical about the organisation. But I was sure we'd feel different when we were in a real DP camp.

We were heading for Germany, the epicentre of Europe's worst disaster. A thousand Russian DPs waited for us. We'd establish an Assembly Centre for them, we'd heal and repair. One of my father's pieces of Methodist wisdom floated into my mind: *God grant that I may never live to be useless.* For five years I'd been useless or, at best, semi-useless. Now, at last, I was joining the ranks of the useful.

UNRRA supplied us with two French drivers. They were like chalk and cheese. Marc was a short, thin, street-wise Parisian, dark, constantly smoking, his eyes darting left and right as he listened to you, a grin flashing across his face and quickly fading. According to the UNRRA authorities, he'd passed a test in spoken English, but I never heard him speak a word in our language. And there was Jacques, a blue-eyed, angel-faced Breton, with solid hands and a slow, steady way of walking. He readily spoke a ponderous and ungrammatical English.

Eleanor had the maps. She said that our destination in Germany was seven hundred miles away and it would take us a week to drive there.

Our two trucks rumbled along battered roads that wound between green fields and apple orchards. Few signposts were left standing. After about half an hour, we stopped at a sign-less crossroads. Eleanor got out, lit a cigarette, unfolded her map over the truck's bonnet and looked from map to landscape to road to map. Marc soon lost patience and fired off obscure French obscenities which Eleanor only half-understood. Jacques looked round to ask directions, but the surrounding fields were bare.

'I think,' said Eleanor, 'we go this way.'

We trooped back into the trucks, but twenty minutes later the appearance of the wrong church led Eleanor to call a halt. Again, she unfolded the map and searched the landscape. We were on the wrong road, and our two-truck convoy had to turn round awkwardly in the narrow country lanes. Half an hour later we met three enormous farm-carts drawn by plodding, white-haired horses, like pictures from a medieval manuscript. We couldn't pass them in the little lanes, so we trundled behind them at a moderate walking pace until the next crossroads.

But Marc's incomprehensible swearing and our slow, back-and-forth progress couldn't dampen my spirits. The sun shone, long stretches of roads had been cleared of the wrecks of tanks, lorries and personnel carriers, and the green crops swayed in the breeze. At last, we were heading in the right direction. I could wait another week if I had to.

In theory, our itinerary had been authorized by UNRRA, who had contacted the relevant local military authorities at each stage of the journey. This should have ensured our food and lodging each night.

'I'll believe it when I see it,' commented Victor and the rest of us nodded.

A pattern was set. Pierre and Marc travelled in one truck, drawn together by a common hatred of all things German. The rest of us piled into the Jacque's truck, squeezing ourselves between the apparently vital equipment and supplies that we had to take. We shared songs. Alma led with 'It's a Long Way to Tipperary'—singularly inappropriate, but it caught our mood and we all joined in. We passed villages and little rural towns, bright with the optimism of expected victory: bunting and flags fluttered in the breeze as if to welcome us. Sometimes we were cheered by locals sitting at a café or standing round a market. They must have thought that we were an Allied military unit. Once or twice pretty girls showered us with flowers. We stopped at midday, and Eleanor and Alma prepared lunch, as if we were on a picnic.

In Paris, Marc's truck led the way, for he knew the dull, long boulevards that curved round the northern suburbs. At one point, he pulled into a little side street and, without a word, strolled out of his truck, clutching a sack of—well, I never found out, but it was obviously some black-market deal. A few minutes later he returned with another sack and a satisfied expression.

'Typical,' commented Victor. 'They're all in it.'

I didn't like this: it confirmed my suspicions about Marc.

'Do you think I should...' I asked Eleanor.

She shook her head. 'If you report him, we'll lose a driver and you'll have to drive this truck all the way back to Granville. We've come this far. Let's keep going. He's probably doing nothing awful.'

I thought about her words, then agreed. Respecting the regulations was important, but turning back would have been more than I could bear.

The overnight stops were as chaotic as we'd expected. Near Verdun, we were lucky: the surprised military authorities directed us to a hotel and we slept in proper beds with sheets. There was even hot water. But normally, as the sun went down, we'd have a long, frustrating search for a military base, where we'd be greeted by the baffled stare of a Supplies Officer. Usually they found a tent for us, sometimes we slept in the open air.

After Paris, the roads got busier. We met returning Prisoners of War and labourers heading westwards: sometimes crammed into rickety vehicles, sometimes tramping along the way. Military vehicles, American, British and French, sped back and forth, hooting at us to get out of their way. After four or five days, we reached the end of French territory. We stopped to mark the moment.

The German border was marked by an empty sentry post and a large poster: 'YOU ARE NOW ENTERING ENEMY TERRITORY. DO NOT FRATERNISE.' Marc let out another incomprehensible oath and Pierre muttered:

'*Sales boches.*'

That was one French expression I had learnt: *filthy Huns*.

Dan nodded in agreement with Pierre. This surprised me and I glanced at him.

'Fascism,' he said. 'It's a sickness, it has to be destroyed.'

'Dan, you can't—' I began, but Eleanor interrupted me.

'Not all Germans are bad. What about the socialists and communists, the ones who tried to resist?'

'Precious little sign of resistance in Germany,' said Dan. 'The bastards all loved their *Führer*.'

I'd heard people talk this way before. Enter any pub in England and you could find someone sounding off, calling for our revenge on the bloody Huns. I understood this—just one look at the bombed houses along the high street taught everyone a lesson about German barbarism. But I agreed with Eleanor: there was another Germany, there had to be. The thought that an entire nation had been hypnotised by that little man with the Charlie Chaplin moustache was too horrible to contemplate. I thought that Dan, Pierre and Marc would change their minds once they met real Germans. It was something we'd have to talk about later. Anyway, UNRRA's rules prevented us from helping Germans. We were there for the nations that the Nazis had oppressed.

I looked again at the poster and thought about what it implied.

'Fraternise,' I said. 'It's such an odd term. What's everyone so worried about? The war's almost over.'

Dan replied. 'There's talk about German resistance to the Allies, remember? That underground group: the Werewolves. You can't trust anyone you meet, no matter how friendly or ordinary they seem.'

We stared at the poster for a few moments, then got back in the trucks.

***

Across the frontier was Saarbrücken, our first German town. It was a ghostly, devastated landscape, filled only by a deep sadness. I wanted to get through it as quickly as possible.

'In London,' I said to Eleanor, 'you'd see a house or two along a street which had been bombed. While here—

'—it's the whole street.' She nodded, twisting her head round to see better from the back of the truck.

'Street after street after street,' I said. 'I think the entire centre has been smashed to pieces.'

French soldiers waved to us: they pointed to the route we should follow.

The roads were different on the German side of the border: more damaged, patched with rough, temporary repairs. Sometimes gaping potholes took Marc or Jacques by surprise. We travelled slowly and cautiously, and I worried that these decrepit highways might damage our trucks. We'd been warned not to stray far from the roads, as there could be mines or booby-traps in the verges. I stared at the villages we passed, wondering what sort of people lived there and what they'd thought about Hitler and the Nazis. The houses were largely intact and some were picture-postcard pretty: white-washed walls with black beams and gables, some curled with age, hugging the side of a stream or a village green. How could Nazis have lived in such places? I didn't understand. But driving through Germany seemed rather pleasant, despite all the warnings we'd had.

We passed a number of churches and I saw that each one had a smashed steeple. I remarked on this.

'There were snipers in them,' explained Dan. 'Or observers, feeding information back to the German army. Sometimes it was the first thing our gunners did: take out the steeple.'

His words chilled me. I felt that a place of worship should be separate from the conflicts that divided men. What sort of world was this? But I was confused: should I be angry with the Germans for placing snipers in churches or with the Allies for expecting opposition in the most unlikely places? I comforted myself with the thought that we'd play no part in any destruction.

Without warning, there was a thump from the engine of Jacques's truck and then a nasty rattle. No! This was exactly what I'd feared. We could be stuck for ages in enemy territory. Jacques hooted to get Marc's attention, waved a hand out of the window and then drew into the side of the road. The two of them consulted, grabbed some tools and slid under Jacques's truck. The rest of us stood along the roadside. We heard banging as Marc attacked something and the inevitable string of oaths. To our surprise, Jacques then sang a hymn. Pierre walked up, took in the performance and commented:

'This truck is being repaired by a devil and an angel.'

That took away the tension. We lit cigarettes. Pierre told me about his sons: one training to be a doctor, the other a lawyer—the classic pattern.

'I don't know how I will afford the fees,' he said sadly.

His family had been ruined by the war and he expected little or no compensation.

Victor and Alma walked a few steps up the road, chatting about restaurants they'd visited: Alma had toured Germany in the 1930s, and still had fond memories about German cooking. Dan and Eleanor discussed the strengths of the Red Army. The delay was frustrating but, looking at the six of us by the roadside, I was pleased to see everyone getting on. Maybe incidents like this would form us into a proper team.

After about thirty minutes, the two drivers emerged from under the truck, their hands and faces black with oil and grease, Marc with a cocky smile on his face, Jacques as beatific as ever.

'All goes well,' he told us.

***

We filed back into the trucks and Eleanor directed us to a section of the *autobahn* that had been repaired. Our trucks raced along, sometimes reaching 50 mph, making up for lost time. We joined a stream of military vehicles and top-class German cars, usually driven by chauffeurs with American or British military officials sitting in the back. Their gleaming cars sped past us.

'It's unbelievable,' said Eleanor. 'The way this road curves through the countryside, the way it never stops. No crossroads: look!'

She pointed to a road joining the *autobahn*: the ancillary road grew closer and then merged with ours, seamlessly. It was like some magic trick. Looking backwards, we could see the regular curves and dips of this never-ending, off-white, four-lane highway, climbing hills, curving round mountains, held high by bridges over rivers and valleys.

I shook my head. 'What sort of people thought of roads like these?'

Alma spoke up. 'It was Hitler himself who ordered their construction. And no objections were allowed.'

'There's something menacing about them, isn't there?'

'If you want to move soldiers and tanks quickly from one end of the country to the other...' Dan didn't finish his sentence.

I knew what he meant. We were making good time, at last.

'I don't think we'll ever have them in England,' I continued. 'Well, part of the fun of driving in the countryside is seeing a village and choosing to stop. While this: it's relentless.'

'I think this is the future,' said Eleanor. 'Speed, at any price. People want to get somewhere fast and not to have to stop for villages and crossroads.'

Then we stopped. A bridge spanning a valley had been damaged by bombing and only one lane was safe. A single Military Policeman attempted to regulate the traffic, as various military big-wigs insisted that they had priority. We waited for at least two hours. UNRRA, it seemed, was less important than the rest of the traffic. This delay meant we were certain to be late.

We reached Frankfurt early in the evening. There followed our usual search for the military headquarters as we drove up and down smashed streets, past wrecked buildings, calling out to GIs for directions. The Americans had settled in a college which had survived the bombing. Eleanor and I looked for the Supply Officer, to see if there was anywhere for us to spend the night.

'Pointless, really,' I muttered as we tramped up some stairs. 'We'd be better off camping in those woods at the edge of town.'

I remembered a pretty river and some birch trees. It had looked rather attractive. Maybe we could drive back there if nothing had been arranged for us? It would make a change from a dingy military tent and we'd be able to wash.

We found the right office. The door was open, so we walked straight in. An American Supplies Officer at a desk turned to face us.

'UNRRA?' he asked.

Eleanor and I exchanged a glance. This was a surprise!

'Yes,' I answered. 'Is there accommodation—'

'There's been a change of plan. You're to stay here one night and leave at first light tomorrow morning for a new destination. Details here.'

He held out a couple of sheets of paper and a map.

'But—' said Eleanor.

'An emergency. We've had reports of DPs in the countryside. Greeks, who were held prisoner. A couple of hundred of them. In pretty bad shape.'

'Isn't anyone else available?' I asked. 'We're needed urgently to set up an Assembly Centre for a thousand Russians—'

'This is more urgent. A Red Cross and Quaker group are travelling from Holland, but they're delayed. You're the only suitable group in the area.'

'All this is quite unexpected,' I protested.

The officer shrugged his shoulders. 'Look, buddy, I don't make the rules. You've got your orders. If you don't like them, complain to Eisenhower.'

'Will we be issued with more supplies?' asked Eleanor.

The officer looked at her for a moment. 'We thought you were carrying supplies in your trucks.'

'Yes, but—these people may have specific needs.'

'You can put in a request for anything you think is necessary.' He paused and his tone softened. 'Look, ma'am, we'll do all we can to help you. We're sending a squad of GIs with you.'

'GIs?' I said. 'We're UNRRA, we operate without arms.'

He smiled. 'Wait and see. You don't know where you're going and we've heard of German resistance activities out there.'

Eleanor and I walked back down the stairs.

'What's going on?' I said. 'How can they just change our destination like this?'

'Maybe it really is an emergency,' said Eleanor.

'More urgent than a thousand Russian DPs?'

***

I convened a team meeting. I explained the new instructions as best I could, but I found it hard to disguise my own unease and frustration. Why were these Greeks so important?

Marc objected most strongly, claiming he had an important meeting in the next town. Pierre shut him up.

'We must go where we are needed. That's normal, in my opinion.'

Dan looked unhappy. 'The collapse of the Nazis—they've left behind some nasty stuff. Perhaps...'

Eleanor nodded. 'I know. This might be pretty tough.'

'But we've been trained!' Alma smiled. 'We know what to do.'

'Our opinions don't matter,' I told them. 'Orders are orders. My advice to all of you is to get some rest and be ready tomorrow morning.'

I looked round. I saw agreement, or at least acceptance, on their faces.

14. A Diversion

The next morning, we were ready at dawn. A lieutenant and six GIs joined us in their own truck. The GIs looked unhappy. Maybe they knew something we didn't. We left in a three-truck convoy. I made sure that our truck led the way, to show that we were an independent UNRRA team, not commanded by the US Army. Eleanor guided Jacques. We drove along quiet country lanes that ran between low, wooded hills. There were few signs of war here and I wondered if the Americans had made a mistake. Maybe these Greeks weren't badly hurt. We'd patch them up, call the Americans for more trucks and send them on their way. Maybe a day's delay, not too serious.

We got to the village marked on the map, then drove along a straight road in open country. It's all so clear in my mind: the green fields and the peace of the countryside. On the right was a little hamlet, just a couple of houses and some barns. We got out, and I heard a stream nearby and thought how pretty the place looked, before I noticed a strange smell which, at first, seemed almost sweet.

The Lieutenant and I led the way into a courtyard, bordered on three sides by barns, sheds and a house. Two German soldiers sat at a low table in front of the house. On the table, there was a knife, a loaf of bread, a sausage and two mugs of coffee. They'd been playing cards. I stared at them: these were the first enemy Germans I'd seen. Despite their uniforms, they looked terribly ordinary. I could see there was no fight left in them.

'They'll want to surrender,' the Lieutenant muttered to me. He'd seen this before.

One German looked like he was about 17, the other was older and fatter, and stared at us insolently. Behind me I heard some calls: something worried Pierre. He pointed to a larger barn, set back from the others. Alma, Eleanor and Dan followed him. Victor and I stayed with the lieutenant, who told the Germans to stand up. They gave us a bored, tired look and stood up slowly, laboriously buttoning their tunics. The older one moved with difficulty and needed to hold onto the table to stand upright. His leg was obviously hurt. Later, the lieutenant told me that he'd recognised they were SS by their uniforms: I didn't realise this at the time.

The younger one saluted, the older one reached into his pocket for some papers. He began to say something in slow, heavily-accented English: I caught the word *transfer*. I found it hard to concentrate, as Dan was shouting and for a second I wondered if Eleanor was alright. I saw the older soldier's eyes flash to the left, looking at something over my shoulder. I turned round and saw Dan march back from the barn, his face like thunder. He fumbled in his pocket. A second later, there was a revolver in his hand.

He moved so fast that neither the lieutenant nor I had time to react.

'You bastards!' he yelled at the two Germans. 'You murderous bastards!'

Holding the revolver backward, Dan swung it and caught the older German on the side of his face. He fell, clutching his cheek.

'You bastards!' Dan shouted again.

He gripped the revolver in both hands, aiming at the older German, who attempted to roll away, pushing with his good leg. The lieutenant and I rushed forward, grabbed Dan's arm, then pulled him back.

'No!' shouted the lieutenant.

'We're not here to kill people, Dan,' I cried.

Two GIs and Victor helped pull him away. Dan kicked and shouted, his face red with fury, but they restrained him. I looked back to the bigger barn. Eleanor was at the entrance. She was bent over, on her knees, vomiting onto the ground. Alma stood by her, white-faced, wiping tears from her eyes, while Pierre looked into the barn, unmoving. What was there? I checked that Dan was under control, then walked to the barn. Pierre noticed me and held out his arm to stop me. I brushed past.

It was dark inside and my eyes took a moment to adjust. But then... My God, oh my God, what a sight. The room was filled with still, grey objects—they were bodies. There must have been two hundred thin, pale figures crammed into that space, curled up on the ground, propped against the walls, even packed into the hayloft. My first impression was that they were corpses, but as I stared, I saw eyes flicker, hands move, heard rasping coughs. Their heads were mere skulls and they wore ragged, filthy pyjamas that didn't hide their sunken chests and bony ribs. Many were injured. I remembered the words of the officer in Frankfurt: *in pretty bad shape.* My God, oh my God. I felt Pierre's hand on my arm.

'You don't have to look,' he told me.

I couldn't stop. The dull brown patch over one man's ear: was that a cut? A bruise? A sore? The dirty, wrinkled toes of another, who shifted as I looked at him. The bloodied eye of a third, half-closed and continually blinking. There was an overpowering smell of rotting bodies, of blood, shit and piss. They must have been left there for days. Outside, the stream still trickled. How could this tragedy happen in the same world that produced food and houses, the world in which we danced and ate and laughed? I thought of Eleanor and stepped back to find her. She was in the courtyard, drinking from a water-bottle that a GI had given her. When she saw me, she stood up and breathed deeply. We held each other's hands, hugged each other. I looked into her eyes.

'Why?' I asked.

She shook her head.

***

A moment or two later, I came to my senses. We had to work as a team. I looked round, searching for somewhere to meet and talk. The house. I tried the door. It wouldn't open. I called a GI.

'Open it,' I said.

He looked puzzled. 'But—I don't have the key.'

'Open it! Use your rifle.'

His eyes met mine, he glanced at the lieutenant who was questioning the two Germans, then approached the door. He kicked out twice at the handle: there was a splintering sound and door opened.

I called out, 'Dan! Victor!'

Pierre and Alma heard the door smashing and came back from that dreadful barn. I remembered the lieutenant and called him. Inside, as I hoped, there was a table, with chairs round it. For a second, I gazed at a set of decorative cups hanging from the wall, at a clock with a floral pattern. How could these objects exist next to that horror?

Seven of us sat round the table: my UNRRA team and the lieutenant. We had to begin.

'It's a logistical problem,' I told them.

Victor snorted.

'Have you seen what's in that barn?' cried Dan. 'You call that *logistical*? It's murder, outright mass murder!'

'Edmund's right,' said Eleanor. 'We have to think calmly. We don't have time for emotion. *They*'—she pointed to the barn—'don't have time for *our* emotions.'

Pierre nodded. 'We have been taught the procedure for these emergencies.'

'What do you need?' I asked.

It was like one of the exercises at Granville. We all knew that Pierre was right and tried to remember the procedures we'd been taught. Pierre was gloomy.

'Already, I think, a tenth of them'—he shook his head—'or a fifth of them are dead. They are all weak, very weak. It is probable that they are infected with typhus and typhoid. More will die, it is not in our power to stop this.'

'We've been inoculated—' said Eleanor.

'Yes, yes,' said Pierre. 'We should be safe.'

'DDT.' Alma interrupted him. 'We need DDT.'

'But they need food!' said the lieutenant.

'And those two fat Germans,' said Dan, 'sitting there, eating their breakfast while...'

'We're not here for revenge,' I told him.

'Food's difficult,' said Eleanor. 'Their stomachs, their digestive systems will be damaged. They need—'

'They can only eat food that is very light. Soup. Very thin soup,' said Pierre. 'Anything else will hurt them.'

We talked, maybe for thirty minutes, maybe longer. After a while, we called for Marc and Jacques to join us. Looking back, I don't think either of them looked into that barn and I don't think Victor did. I don't hold this against them. The sight was awful, and—anyway—all three of them pulled their weight in the hours that followed. Without argument, we agreed on immediate priorities: DDT to disinfect; a large cauldron to make soup; bowls and spoons. We'd burn their clothes and then—

I realised that this was getting difficult.

'Where will we get these things?' I asked. 'We need a department store and a hardware shop.'

The lieutenant smiled grimly. 'Didn't you notice that village we passed? I think it's time they made a contribution.'

'What?' Eleanor was amazed. 'You're going to ask them to give—'

'I'm not going to ask them for anything. I'm going to tell them what I want. And I'll have six armed GIs behind me.'

'But that's—robbery,' Eleanor protested.

'We call it requisitioning.'

'They deserve it,' said Dan and Pierre nodded.

***

And that was how it was done. Marc drove one truck back to the American base for all the DDT they had. The lieutenant and the GIs went to the village and *requisitioned*. As well as food, bowls and spoons, they demanded that each house contribute a full set of men's clothes. Meanwhile, we investigated the farmhouse. There were some onions in the back of the larder, but nothing else. So: onion soup. We left Alma in the kitchen, and Eleanor, myself and Pierre returned to that barn.

It was worse the second time, knowing what was in there. Walking across the courtyard, I felt my chest tighten, noticed a spasm in the back of my neck and worried that my knees would give way. Pierre led, and Eleanor and I followed. It was one of those moments when I didn't want to remind people that I was Team Director. Eleanor reached out, gave my arm a little squeeze and whispered:

'Don't think too much.'

I knew what she meant: don't dwell on it, don't consider the meaning of what we saw. This is what I'd signed up for. I wanted to heal people. Now, I had to concentrate on the procedures and forget my emotions.

Pierre had talked about *triage*: I didn't know the term, but I understood that he wanted to identify the strongest ones. We each had a GI's water-flask.

Astonishingly, some of those poor souls were still alert. A few were even able to stand, with our assistance. Pierre gave one grey, thin figure a microscopic amount of water to drink, and then he and I helped him get up. As we moved, there was a rasping behind me. Someone was trying to speak. I heard:

'Ale... Ale...'

I turned round when I could and saw a thin, bony finger pointing at Eleanor. He was trying to say her name. I called her and she came over.

'Ale-len-nor.'

Eleanor stood stock still, rooted to the spot, her eyes wide, as if she'd seen a ghost. In a way she had. She stepped closer, taking care where she trod and knelt down.

'Matteo?'

15. Relief and Rehabilitation

At some point during the evening or the night I managed to talk to Eleanor.

'It's him!' she told me. 'Definitely him. He managed to say a few words. He got arrested in Italy in 1943 and then sent to Germany. Poor man, God knows what they've done to him.'

What a world! One brother, Giuseppe, was playing jazz piano in London. And the other was here.

On the morning of our second day, I remembered him. Matteo had responded well to the care we'd given him. He reached for the spoon as I fed him and I was delighted by this sign of improvement. He wasn't yet ready to walk from the barn, but Pierre had thought that maybe soon... I went to the corner where he'd been lying. Matteo wasn't there. I found Pierre.

'Has Matteo recovered?' I asked.

I saw a flicker cross Pierre's face. He shook his head.

'Too late,' he said.

I stepped back, stumbled. There was a weight in my chest, a spasm at the back of my neck. I'd so hoped that we'd have a spark of good news in this colossal tragedy.

Normally, if you have bad news to tell someone, you spend some time thinking about how to say it. But here—there was no time, there was no time for anything.

I found Eleanor in the house.

'It's Matteo,' I told her. 'He's...'

At first she looked up with hope in her eyes, but then she must have seen my expression. Her face fell.

'No,' she whispered.

There were two hundred men in that barn, but the death of someone specific, someone she knew, still hit with a particular force.

'He seemed so bright, so brave, so clear-thinking!' Eleanor said. 'He knew he was taking a risk when he went back to Italy, but he was certain it was worth it. And now!'

Tears welled in her eyes and she began to sob. I felt a sudden, acute sensation: life was so fragile and so precious. Why did we take it for granted? Why did we waste it? I tried to think of something to say, but I was exhausted and no words came to my mind. I hugged her, tried to comfort her.

Then we heard Dan in the next room, calling for Eleanor to help him with another poor soul. There was no time for our emotions.

***

My memories of those thirty-six hours are very confused. In the barn, I stepped between grey, damaged bodies with papery skin, looking for the ones who were still alert. I fed them lukewarm broth from a bowl with a spoon. I watched their faces, to see if their eyes followed the spoon, I listened to hear if they whispered anything.

About half the men in that barn were Italians, not Greek. A few hissed words. Pierre kept an eye on what we were doing and made snap judgements. The handful who could stand were half-led, half-carried to the other barn, where Alma and Dan waited with a hose, DDT and fresh clothes. Jacques and the GIs took their old clothes and burnt them.

For a day and a half, we concentrated single-mindedly on those two hundred men in that awful barn. I think that fourteen died while we were there and I'm sure that others died in the following days. They were too weak, they'd been treated too badly... It was heart-breaking, but there was nothing that anyone could have done for them. I don't remember sleeping—I think at one point I collapsed on a chair in the house and closed my eyes, only to be woken almost immediately by the lieutenant telling me that more DDT had arrived. The team of doctors, nurses and aid workers from the Quakers and Red Cross turned up late in the afternoon on the second day. They said we hadn't done a bad job.

Other than those moments, I remember only isolated incidents.

I remember Jacques arrived with an enormous iron cauldron, and he and one of the GIs made an improvised fireplace out of bricks, another GI found a stack of firewood at the back of the house, Alma and a third GI chopped up vegetables and gutted chickens… It all worked.

I remember a GI, in crumpled combat fatigues, carrying a bundle of filthy, ragged pyjamas from the poor souls in the barn. He nodded at me, then glanced at that barn.

'That ain't war,' he told me. 'I've seen war, in Africa and France. But that ain't war.'

I remember Pierre's calm: I hadn't realised he could be so strong. He explained to me later he'd been a doctor in the First World War and he'd learnt to work in such situations. As for Eleanor and me—we followed him. Without him… Maybe we would've turned round, refused the orders, walked out, resigned… Eleanor had been in some grim situations while an ambulance driver and I'd seen danger in the Fire Service, but neither of us had seen anything like that.

***

I didn't understand—I *couldn't* understand what we were doing, I just followed Pierre. It was only later that it became clearer. The lieutenant talked to us before we left, and then, over the next weeks, I talked to Dan and Eleanor. At the time, I thought I was seeing some sort of concentration camp. No, they told me. Concentration camps started as ruthlessly cruel prisons, became factories for killing people and then—by 1943 and 1944—were often converted into sites for slave labour. But they were vast places with specialised, fixed buildings. All sorts of people were sent to them: Jews and reds,

anyone who opposed the regime: Christians, liberals, pacifists...
Gypsies, Jehovah's Witnesses, criminals, sexual deviants or inverts,
people who got caught in the wrong place at the wrong time...

What we saw in that barn were the last convulsions of the Third
Reich. The rulers no longer knew what to do with the hundreds
of thousands of poor souls in the concentration camps. The Nazi
economy was breaking down, so they could no longer be used as
slave labour. Nazi leaders like Himmler, the head of the SS, thought
that some might serve as hostages in a last-ditch bargain with the
Allies. And finally, even among the most dedicated Nazis, some slow
awareness spread that this vast, industrial complex of exploitation,
torture and death might look bad to outsiders. They felt a
last-minute need to hide their traces. Not quite shame, I think, more
embarrassment. But that was *very* slow to emerge: the first thought
of the Nazi rulers was that these prisoners might be exploited for
some political purpose. Some Nazis thought that the Allies would
respect the men who'd organised the concentration camps for their
thoroughness and efficiency. Himmler even tried to open
negotiations with the Allies! His overtures were refused, of course.

Meanwhile, the captives in the last camps were dragooned into
columns and marched at gunpoint from the occupied lands in the
east into Germany itself. Maybe initially there was some plan, some
destination to reach, but as the Allies advanced, the whole project
broke down. Those poor souls were just dumped as the officers and
generals fled.

The actions of the SS by the barn were part of this bigger picture.
A 20-man SS unit had stayed in that hamlet until the day before
we arrived. Most of them fled: the two who stayed were uncle and
nephew. The older man had a smashed knee and could barely walk.
They remained because they couldn't flee and maybe because they
felt obliged to ensure an orderly transfer of responsibilities. But they
did nothing to help the two hundred prisoners who'd been marched

across half of Germany. God knows how many had died in that journey. The SS showed an evil neglect of anyone they didn't see as human. How many might have been saved if they'd distributed water from that stream, if they'd bought some bread in the village to share round? The two SS men were thrown into a Prisoner of War camp. I hope they died there.

16. Neukirchen: The Making of an UNRRA Assembly Centre

We spent the night at the American base in Frankfurt. In the morning, we heard the announcement of the German unconditional surrender. It seemed almost irrelevant, as now we knew what problems remained in Germany.

When we set off in our trucks, our mood was very different from two days ago. I knew that this time Alma wouldn't sing 'It's a Long Way to Tipperary'. Nobody wanted to talk. Alma, Pierre and Victor went in Marc's truck, Dan, Eleanor and I were with Jacques. We got to the *autobahn* in minutes and then roared along that endless concrete route. I hated those long smooth curves that tore through the countryside, for now I knew the evil they were hiding. Our lunch break was a brief, rushed affair. Eleanor and Alma made spam sandwiches and no one was hungry. I felt I had to say something about the last two days, although I had nothing prepared. When everyone had finished eating, I called them together. I noticed their glances: wary, worried about what I might say. Even Eleanor looked uncertain. They didn't want to hear anything more about those dreadful hours by the barn, but I had to show I could act as Team Director.

'I'm not going to thank you for the care you gave those poor souls,' I said.

Pierre frowned, Marc's eyes ceased flickering from the road to the trucks to the woods and he stared at me.

'I'm going to say something far more important: you all pulled your weight, you all did your bit. You worked under the most difficult circumstances and no one could ask more of you.'

Pierre nodded and a grin lit up briefly on Dan's face. I paused for a moment, searching for something else to tell them. Looking at the seven of them, all so different, a phrase of my father's came into my mind.

'We come from different nations, different religions, different traditions. Yesterday we proved that while we may have our differences, we are of one heart.'

Was that too chapel-like? Should I say more? I looked round.

'Yes, yes...' Jacques liked my words and he translated them to Marc.

It was the right moment to stop. As we climbed back into our truck, Eleanor put her head close to mine and whispered:

'Well done.'

That baffled me. I'd dragged one of my father's Methodist truisms from my memory: wasn't it utterly inadequate in the face of the tragedy we'd seen?

***

I was worried we were two days late, through no fault of our own. What would they say at the Assembly Centre? Would the Russian DPs have coped without us? Our destination was Neukirchen: a suburb on the north-western edge of the city. With Eleanor navigating, we ducked and dived through suburban streets, with fields and woods to our left. We got to the right place on the map and found—nothing. A series of comfortable-looking, detached suburban villas, but nothing resembling an UNRRA Assembly Centre. A few housewives were out walking, but when Eleanor or Jacques shouted *UNRRA* to them, they shrugged and continued on their way. We got out of our trucks and conferred. Of the eight of us, only Alma could speak German. She ran after another group of housewives. They were suspicious at first. They didn't understand her when she asked about UNRRA, but when she explained she was looking for a place with Russian DPs, they knew where she meant. They shook their heads and sighed, and told her that it was a bad, bad place, not right for any woman. When she insisted, they gave her directions.

A few minutes later, we drew up by a large estate of bungalows. At first sight, it looked good. The bungalows were long, white buildings set in regular rows round a central square, with lawns and even a children's playground. As I looked closer, I noticed piles of rubbish in the open areas and the remnants of bonfires. In the distance, a group of men in motley khaki stood talking. I guessed they were Russian DPs. My confidence returned: this would be our base.

We then met an unexpected problem: who was in charge? Where were they? We needed to explain our late arrival. When we questioned the Russians, they smiled but obviously didn't understand a word. Victor got impatient and said he'd drive to the local American military HQ. I agreed, and he and Marc left in one truck. Then Dan found a white-haired Russian officer in a worn-out uniform, who'd been a forced labourer. He spoke English and French, and introduced himself as Kotov. He'd never heard of UNRRA. He wasn't in command, but he knew the place and most of the Russians seemed to respect him. He chatted in an aimless way about the nature of war and the misfortunes of the world. I grew exasperated: we had a job to do. Whenever I asked him about accommodation and arrangements, he'd smile, nod and begin another lengthy anecdote.

A couple of hours later, Victor and Marc returned, followed by two jeeps. A tall American officer stepped out with an easy stride; four GIs, with rifles, stayed in the second jeep.

'Ah, there you are,' the officer greeted us. 'We were expecting you next week. Settling in okay?'

I heard Eleanor gasp. I was flabbergasted: we'd been so worried about being late.

The American introduced himself as Sam and we all shook hands.

'But where is everything?' I asked him. 'Where are our quarters? Our offices? The dispensary and the school?'

Sam smiled. 'I guess that's why you're here. There isn't anything. You're here to make it work.'

He explained. This estate had been used by foreign workers during the war. Many of them were Russian, most of them forced to come to Germany. The other nationalities had left, but the Russians had stayed. The estate had been built for German workers before the war, so the accommodation was reasonably comfortable.

'Look,' he said, taking in the square, the grassy open areas, the paths and trees. 'It's all been planned.'

'So, we'll be staying in one of those bungalows?' I asked.

Sam stared at me. 'Hell, no. The Russkies have wrecked them. They're—they're kinda over-enthusiastic at the moment. Sure, they suffered during the war, but... Oh, boy, the damage they do. I guess they see it as revenge.'

'Where will we stay?'

'Where d'you want to stay? See any places that caught your eye? Some of the villas in the next road look rather fine. Luckily, we never bombed this part of town.' Sam laughed.

'What?' said Eleanor. 'They're empty? We can take one?'

'They're not empty, but we can shift the Krauts out.'

'Of course,' said Dan.

'But—those are their homes,' protested Eleanor.

'Come now,' said Sam. 'Can't have you living in smashed bungalows. Clear out the Krauts and then you'll be comfortable.'

'And the dispensary? The school? The kindergarten?' asked Eleanor.

Sam nodded. 'They'll be a mite more difficult. But you're the experts. Choose which of those bungalows you want. We'll try and get you supplies, and we'll find some Krauts to clean them up for you. But don't worry about these Russkies.'

'Why not?' I asked.

'They'll be gone in a couple of weeks. Uncle Joe wants them back. No point in trying to rehabilitate them! All we gotta do is to try and stop them terrorizing the neighbours. If not, there'll be a goddamn diplomatic incident.'

'But...' I was speechless.

'We've just driven seven hundred miles for them!' said Eleanor.

'There'll be some Poles soon,' Sam said. 'In a couple of weeks.'

I felt crushed. The last few days had proved to me that UNRRA was inefficient, but I'd never expected this degree of confusion. We'd been told that we were needed urgently. I'd expected to be sitting in my office by the end of the day—instead, nothing. Just some smashed-up bungalows.

'This is ridiculous!' I muttered to Eleanor. 'Just one damn mess after another.'

She nodded. 'It's as if we have to do everything ourselves.'

'How can I be a Team Director if there's nothing to direct?'

'We're here now,' she said. 'Let's try and make the best of it.'

***

The next morning, we headed back to Neukirchen with Sam and a squad of GIs, plus a shabby-looking German that Sam introduced as the *Bürgermeister*. Apparently he was a local official, appointed by the Americans. I think he was meant to assist us, but he didn't say much. For a while, Sam sounded like a keen estate agent.

'Nice view from that one. You'd get the sun in the morning. Would you like a garden?'

I didn't want Sam to realise how lost I felt, so I tried to look as if I regularly claimed ownership of other people's houses. I whispered a word or two to Eleanor, who was as bewildered as me. Eventually, we picked two large, detached houses for us six UNRRA officers. They were solid, three-storey buildings that seemed to exude Victorian respectability, just one street away from the camp. Marc and Jacques would have a little cottage to the side. Sam walked up to the front door of the first house with two armed GIs behind him. A tall, grey-haired woman opened the door and turned pale at the sight of Sam. He barked orders at her in German. She burst into tears and was joined by two children, who clutched at her and stared at Sam with big, terrified eyes. I looked at Alma.

'He's telling them that they have three hours to leave.'

I pulled Eleanor to one side.

'We can't do this!' I whispered to her. 'It's not right. I know that requisitioning is permitted, but—like this? Throwing a mother and two children out of the street?'

'It doesn't seem fair, not fair at all. Let's see if we can't arrange something...'

I frowned, wondering what she meant. But there was no chance to talk further.

Sam called us to come in. The woman pulled herself together and showed us round her house. It was well-decorated and comfortable, with elegant wallpaper, paintings of landscapes and bits of pottery on display in glass-fronted cases. There was no obvious sign of Nazi affiliation—no photos of Hitler—but, if the woman had any sense, she'd have burnt those days ago. Looking more closely, I noticed some pale, rectangular patches on the walls. They must have been the marks left by Nazi pictures. The woman spoke some English. She explained that she'd lost her husband at Stalingrad and her oldest son had died in an air-raid. Her brother, his wife and their children had stayed for a while, but moved to the Ruhr in the last months of the war. She hadn't heard from them since.

'Don't ask to stay,' Sam warned her. 'These people are from England. They don't want to sleep under the same roof as a German.'

But when Sam left us alone, she turned to Eleanor and asked if she and her children could stay in the top floor. There was a scared look in her eyes. She'd be our cleaner and cook, her children would help.

Dan snorted and said, 'Out of the question!'

But Eleanor looked at me and I knew what she was thinking.

'Dan,' I said. 'Be reasonable. We're going to need someone to take care of us.'

***

After Sam and the GIs left, Hildegard—our new housekeeper—told us that there was almost no food in the marketplace. Those with money bought meat on the black market; those with cars went to farms in the countryside. Hildegard had no money and no car. The last time she'd walked to the market, she'd come back with five potatoes and had made them last two days. She stared at us, waiting for a response.

She didn't look like she was starving. Maybe a bit grey and obviously very frightened. I looked round this plush, well-kept drawing-room and guessed what had happened. Until just a few weeks ago, people like Hildegard had preserved most of their material comforts. Of course, she would have known shortages and inconveniences which grew worse in the last months, she would have been terrified by the air-raids, she would have grieved after the loss of her husband and son, but she'd have had savings or valuables she could sell and so her life continued. We'd seen signs of this everywhere: despite the massive Allied assault, the German economy continued to function until almost the last days of the regime.

Eleanor asked Hildegard some innocent-sounding questions. 'No air-raids here?'

'Not here,' said Hildegard, 'but the centre!' She shook her head. 'Two years ago. They came twice in two weeks. Very, very bad raids. Ten thousand dead. That was when—my son...'

We nodded. She didn't need to say anything more. I felt a sharp pang of sympathy for her, even if she was a German. This was awkward: much more difficult than I'd expected. What was I supposed to do? Celebrate the death of every German? I couldn't do that. I glanced at Dan, but he stayed stony-faced.

'Why did they bomb the centre?' asked Eleanor.

'Why? Why?' Hildegard shrugged. 'They came to all the cities. Maybe it was for the factories. And the old town!'

She explained that there had been a medieval quarter—*so beautiful! A thousand years old!*—but now all the old buildings had been burnt.

'Gone—gone forever. Because of the war.'

Eleanor looked at her. 'This is a big house. I expect you had someone to help you?'

Hildegard nodded. 'Of course, of course. First a Polish girl, but she was lazy and I sent her away. Then a French girl, but she went back. And then two Ukrainians, nice girls, but I had to watch them, watch them all the time.'

She looked at us again, waiting for us to say something. We exchanged glances—we were baffled by this new situation.

'There is no food,' Hildegard reminded us. 'I cannot feed you.'

Of course, that was it. The important issue. We had a week's worth of UNRRA field rations in our truck and the American base would be supplying us with more rations when we needed them. Monotonous food, yes, but substantial. We weren't going to starve. A few minutes later, Hildegard had three UNRRA ration packs in front of her.

'And cigarettes!' She held up a packet. 'Today, nobody pays with money, always cigarettes.'

Her eyes gleamed and she promised she'd have dinner ready in an hour.

After she closed the door, Dan pushed himself back in an armchair and gave an exaggerated smile. For a moment, all we heard was the ticking of the clock on the mantelpiece.

'Very nice,' Dan said sarcastically. 'Why didn't we ask her to show us the wine list?'

Eleanor shrugged.

'What do you propose?' I asked him.

'You can't trust these people. Look at her! Complaining about her servants. Those girls would've been forced labourers. What do you think happened to that Polish girl once she sent her away?'

'We can't avoid contact with every German in this city. We'll be here for months. The work's going to be tough—not as tough as with those poor souls in the barn, but difficult enough.'

'And as for the Allies bombing the *beautiful old medieval town*!' He mimicked her accent.

'Well?'

'This place was a centre of military production. There were factories making tanks. I don't believe a word she says.'

'She seems friendly to me.'

'And non-fraternization?'

'This isn't fraternization!' I protested. 'It's a business arrangement.'

But even as I spoke, I thought about Eleanor's questions and Hildegard's answers. Did that count as fraternization? It was so difficult. Dan's questions annoyed me.

'What do you want?' I continued. 'To shoot them all? Then you're as bad as them.'

'No—'

'And where did you get that revolver? At the barn?'

Dan looked away for a moment, then turned to face me.

'Those two bastards by the barn deserved shooting on the spot.'

'They were just little people, Dan,' Eleanor said. 'Cogs in the machine. Stupid, callous, thoughtless. Edmund's right: we can't shoot every German we don't like.'

'Shooting them wouldn't have helped the men in the barn,' I said. 'And if you can't respect UNRRA's rules, then you shouldn't be here.'

'But—' Dan began and then stopped. 'The sight of those poor sods in that barn... I saw red, I admit it. And I don't think I was wrong!'

His words reminded me of something else that had been bothering me for a couple of days: our different reactions to that awful sight. Pierre and I had been stunned, Alma had cried, Eleanor had vomited, but Dan had flown into a murderous rage.

'Why were you *so* angry, Dan?' asked Eleanor. 'Of course, we were all appalled by what was in that barn. But—you... It was something else. What was that?'

Dan looked at us, then sighed.

'Alright,' he said. 'I might as well tell you. Surprised you haven't guessed already.'

Eleanor and I looked at each other. What did he mean?

'I'm—I'm Jewish. Or at least, I was brought up as a Jew.'

I was astonished. My first thought was that he didn't look Jewish. He was stout, broad-shouldered, tough-looking. But that's ridiculous. I learnt in Germany that Jews come in all shapes and sizes. Then I remembered—

'Your surname: Ronson,' I said. 'That's not a Jewish name.'

'My grandfather was Issur Aaronson. He believed in assimilation. Staying Jewish, but becoming English as well.'

'And you?' asked Eleanor.

Dan smiled. 'I joined the Party.' He gave a little nod to Eleanor which I caught. 'All that synagogue and bar mitzvah stuff didn't mean anything to me. So: ten years working to build the printers' union and defeat fascism. I don't believe in the Promised Land or in recovering Jerusalem. I'm a class-conscious worker who speaks a few words of Yiddish.'

I tried to understand. 'So, you're not Jewish anymore?'

Dan gave a short, bitter laugh. 'It's not that simple.'

'And those people in the barn?' asked Eleanor.

Dan shook his head. 'They weren't Jewish. Politicals, I reckon. But when I saw them—I thought of the hundreds of thousands in the concentration camps...'

'And Hildegard?' I brought the conversation back to where we'd started. I wanted to get to a conclusion.

'She's not innocent,' insisted Dan. 'I don't feel sorry for her. She's not an anti-fascist fighter.'

'We don't know,' said Eleanor.

'Look at this place!' Dan waved his hand to indicate the room, the furniture, the pale patches on the walls. 'She enjoyed the benefits of the Nazi regime while it prospered. She should suffer now it falls.'

Eleanor nodded, but I could see the sadness in her eyes. Was Dan right? Was that how we would live? No sympathy for a widow, an eye for an eye, a tooth for a tooth? Couldn't we do better than that?

'We've got to live somewhere, Dan,' I said. 'And Hildegard seems reliable to me. You might get to like her more.'

'Never!'

***

The Russian DPs were a problem. A *big* problem. The Nazis' defeat meant the end of the horrific system that had regulated their lives. They seized every opportunity to take revenge for their years of hardship. Because they expected to go in two weeks, they didn't take us seriously. Instead, they did what they liked, terrorizing the people who had terrorized them. Gangs of Russians would walk into the countryside and intimidate German farmers. They'd come back with sheep or pigs, and bags of potatoes. Other Russians stalked the city streets, looking for loot and any alcohol. They'd turn up at the few remaining shops and demand drink with no intention to pay. Sometimes they'd spot something in the street—a bicycle, a wristwatch on a passer-by—and they'd just grab it. We heard of fights and, worse still, of rapes. One evening, Dan came back with a black eye. In the city, he'd spotted a Russian trying to drag off a fourteen-year-old girl, who screamed for help.

'She was German—but I couldn't ignore her.'

He'd waded in. Thankfully, none of the other Russians had joined in. But what surprised Dan was the attitude of the German passers-by.

'They didn't move. Like they were stunned.' He shook his head. 'And they were the master race!'

In the evenings the Russians would sit in the green spaces between the bungalows and roast whole pigs or sheep on open fires. Sometimes they'd sing together. Their rough, deep voices evoked some primitive life from long ago. They'd use anything as firewood: desks, chairs, musical instruments, books, bookcases... They were stripping the camp bare of all the resources that we needed: it made me furious. And their drinking! Some of them weren't just tipsy. They'd drink themselves stupid, comatose, even to the brink of death. Our contact, Kotov—the old Russian officer—alerted Pierre to this problem, who intervened. The Russians got to recognise Pierre, they'd even call for him. Pierre would load the worst cases into a truck and Jacques would drive them to the American base, where their stomachs were pumped. Three died from alcohol poisoning while we were there.

Victor took one look at the Russians and went back to the American base.

'Communism!' he said as he left.

I wanted to stop their senseless destruction of the camp's resources, but Dan and Kotov warned me not to.

'If we leave them alone, they'll leave us alone,' Dan said. 'Otherwise—leave it to the Yanks. They're the ones with guns.'

Eleanor and I tackled Kotov about the Russians' behaviour.

'You have no idea what it was like to live here,' he told us. 'The Germans—they didn't see us as human. You know about the air-raids?'

I nodded.

'There were big shelters made of thick concrete, tunnelled deep into the ground,' Kotov continued. 'Those were for the Germans. And we Soviets? We sheltered in trenches we'd scratched in the soil. Believe me: a little trench cannot protect you from an incendiary bomb.' He looked at us sternly. 'Many of our people died in those raids.'

'But now?' I asked.

'Now? The boys want to have their fun. I know they can be a bit rough—'

'A bit rough!' cried Eleanor. 'They're stealing, holding up pedestrians. And do you know how many German women they've raped?'

He sighed, looked sad and glanced down to the ground. Then he began again:

'Do you how many of us died in this city? How would you feel if you'd been a slave for four years? Would you still be a calm, liberal English gentleman and lady?'

His words made us smile. What would my father have said? Me: an English gentleman!

'But, Kotov, they're destroying the base and everything in it,' I said. 'We want to use this space, these buildings, to help people.'

'Think of it as a dialectical process, Edmund.'

He smiled at me, expecting a response, but whenever Eleanor used that word—*dialectical*—it just confused me. Didn't it mean something to do with change?

'First, the thesis: the Nazis and war,' continued Kotov. 'And then, antithesis: we Soviets and our counter-attack. Finally: synthesis.'

Eleanor nodded. Kotov smiled at me again. 'And who knows what that synthesis will be?'

He paused and glanced at a group of Russians building a bonfire. 'You should also consider what will happen when we return home.'

'Why?' said Eleanor. 'You'll be welcomed, won't you? Celebrated?'

'Perhaps, perhaps. But Comrade Stalin has declared that there were no Russian Prisoners of War, only traitors to the Motherland. You see?'

I can't say I agreed with Kotov. But after our talk, I saw the Russians in a different light. Their behaviour was certainly not excusable, but maybe it was understandable. Eleanor thought the same: there was nothing we could do. For the moment, our priority was to establish our Assembly Centre, even under these difficult circumstances.

***

With Kotov's help, we colonized two bungalows near the entrance of the camp and converted them into a reception area and offices. UNRRA had insisted that we carry a mass of kitchen equipment in our trucks, but this wasn't what we needed. Offices were our first priority: we needed type-writers, paper, folders, filing cabinets, pens and pencils. Nothing very exciting, but isn't this how any administration starts?

Victor contacted Sam and a couple of days later the Americans supplied us with some serviceable office equipment and a type-writer, obviously *requisitioned* from some unlucky German business. The Russians respected the two bungalows as our space. One afternoon, Eleanor, Dan and I pulled desks, chairs and filing cabinets around until they were in some sort of order. Dan found a few posters at the American base. I wanted it to be clear to everyone that we were not part of the Allied military, so I rejected ones which showed soldiers of different nations rallying to the cause of peace. But Eleanor and I rather liked a poster of the United Nations. It was a photomontage and showed children of different races holding hands to form a chain that stretched round the whole world. We liked the hope for the future it suggested. We also put up an UNRRA poster that showed trains and aeroplanes packed with supplies and proclaimed: HELPING THE PEOPLE HELP THEMSELVES. This was what we were working for. Eleanor, Dan and I looked at the spaces we'd created and we all felt the same thrill. Eleanor put her arm round me, smiled and said:

'This will be *our* base.'

I called a team meeting to inaugurate our presence. I made it clear: everyone was to attend. I prepared an agenda.

The meeting began badly. Jacques reported that Marc had gone.

'Gone?' I asked. 'Where's he gone? He didn't ask my permission.' Jacques shrugged his shoulders.

'It's no surprise,' said Victor. 'He was only here for one reason: the black market. Probably left with as much as he can carry from the American base.'

'He's done his job,' I said, impatient to get on. 'He got us here. We'll manage without him.'

I pulled the Team back to the agenda. I wanted to discuss the school, dispensary and kindergarten: all things that had to be ready before the Polish DPs arrived. We were drawing up lists of essential items we needed, which we gave to the Americans.

'The bungalows are absolutely disgusting,' commented Victor. 'Our Russian *friends* have left them in a dreadful condition.'

He looked at Dan, who refused to rise to the challenge.

Pierre spoke. 'I must agree with Victor. Before we consider which buildings can be used, they must all be thoroughly cleaned. It's a question of hygiene.'

Alma nodded. 'The rules are clear.'

'But,' I said, 'how will we get them cleaned in time for the Poles?'

'The usual way, I suppose.' Dan smiled.

'You don't mean...?'

'Yes,' he said. 'Make the Germans do it.'

'We cannot treat the local people as an inexhaustible supply of free labour.'

'Yes, we can,' Dan replied. 'Have you forgotten that barn? They deserve to pay.'

'The people here had nothing to do with that,' Eleanor said.

'No?' said Dan. 'They benefitted from *that* regime.'

'You're assuming that every German is guilty.'

'Damn right,' said Dan.

I thought of reminding him about the fourteen-year-old girl he'd rescued, but decided this wasn't the time for point-scoring. A lot of people felt like Dan. Pierre spoke often about the horrors of Nazi rule in Paris.

'I cannot see any other way of cleaning those buildings,' said Pierre.

'I'll talk to Sam,' said Victor.

'Wait!' I insisted. 'We haven't decided anything yet. And please—' I looked round the room. '—remember that we're trying to teach the local people the benefits of democracy.'

Pierre snorted. 'We're here to rule them and prevent another Hitler.'

'But—'

'It is essential that the bungalows be cleaned,' said Alma. 'The correct procedure must be followed.'

'They're an evil race,' said Pierre.

'Even the most evil are capable of redemption,' said Jacques.

Everyone in the room stared at him. He smiled back. Outside, a group of Russians walked from the bungalows, singing as they went.

Dan stared at Jacques. 'You could *forgive* the Germans?'

'It is my faith,' said Jacques.

Jacques's words left us all stunned and somehow ended the discussion. Reluctantly, I authorized Victor to contact the lieutenant and to *requisition* local housewives. It went against the grain, I've got to say, but I was learning. In order to do our work, we'd have to make some compromises.

***

Two days later, the Russians left. American trucks took them and their loot to the station: they carried tables, clocks, bicycles, tyres and two utterly incongruous portraits of German aristocrats in great gilded frames. Eleanor and I watched them squeeze into a train. While they waited at the station, they decorated their carriages. Improvised red flags, made with cloth torn from Nazi flags, were flown from the windows. Communist slogans were written in chalk on the outside of the carriages. Bundles of flowers adorned the engines. Singing erupted. Kotov spotted us and came over to say goodbye.

'Good luck, Kotov,' said Eleanor. 'I think you're wrong about Soviet policy: you'll be greeted as heroes.'

Kotov, looking very smart in a new tunic (where had he got that from?), said nothing, but saluted.

Once the Russians were gone, we turned to the bungalows. One hundred German housewives from the local streets were press-ganged into cleaning them. They protested loudly at first, but then realised that the longer they protested, the longer they would be forced to work. Their complaints changed: they cursed the primitives from the east who had defiled their town as they cleaned, washed and swept. Meanwhile, GIs cleared the open spaces of rubbish and even repainted some bungalows.

At last, I thought. The bungalows were ready, but under-equipped. We needed more supplies and I was having those fears that had haunted me in Granville. What could seven people do for a thousand disturbed, sick DPs? Eleanor agreed with me: it was frightening. We had less than a week to prepare.

***

Hildegard, our housekeeper, proved more resourceful than we'd expected. Once or twice a week, she'd set out into the countryside in a truck with Jacques, taking American cigarettes, candies and chewing-gum, and returning with smoked ham, sausages, fresh eggs, great round cheeses and bottles of wine. Soon, Dan and I were giving her two-thirds of our cigarette ration: we were only occasional smokers and we enjoyed smoked ham more than cigarettes. Eleanor tended to keep hers.

Our breakfasts were getting longer. They'd start with Hildegard asking whether we'd like scrambled eggs or fried eggs. After breakfast, Dan rushed to the camp, while Eleanor and I sat in easy chairs in the drawing-room and drank coffee, looking out through the French windows at Hildegard's garden. Little tips of red were emerging among the old rose bushes. At first, Hildegard served the dreadful *ersatz* coffee that the Germans had drunk in the last months of war—it really did taste like burnt acorns—but soon she gave us real coffee, from some black-market connection, I suppose. I liked these long, lazy moments with Eleanor in the comfort of the drawing-room. Above all, I liked to review the day's work with her.

'You know something?' I said one morning, after we'd sorted the day's priorities.

'What?'

'I was looking at that garden and thinking that if I had a broom and a rake...'

Eleanor burst out laughing. 'You are getting comfortable!'

'It's certainly better than that bloody barn in Somerset.'

'You didn't have to fight those giant brambles. Muriel and I were almost torn to pieces.'

A half-smile, then a shadow crossed Eleanor's face.

'What is it?' I asked her.

'It's as if we've travelled between two barns—the one in Somerset and that horror outside Frankfurt.'

'We've certainly travelled. But our journey's not over yet.'

We sipped our coffee.

'Is this what you wanted, Edmund?'

I smiled. 'I know it's the calm before the storm. The Russians have gone and the Poles will arrive in four days. We've still got so much to get ready.'

'We managed with those poor souls near Frankfurt—after that, we can do anything,' said Eleanor

It was a comforting thought. With Eleanor's help, I thought it would all be possible. I'd lay down the broad directions and she'd chivvy the team along. That was the way we worked. I smiled.

'I've a feeling that the team is coming together.'

Eleanor nodded. 'They're all good people, each useful in his or her own way. Victor's been helpful as a liaison with the American base.'

'Pierre was so impressive at that dreadful barn. So calm!'

'He really cares for his sons, you know. He talks about them all the time.'

'And Alma—'

'A stickler for the rules.' Eleanor smiled. 'But she's doing great work in preparing the dispensary and Jacques is helping her.'

'While Dan has been thinking about the logistics—'

'The right supplies for the right people. It's important.'

'But I wish Dan and Pierre would tone down their anti-Germanism,' I said. 'I know people have suffered—all of Europe has suffered—but we're a humanitarian organisation, we're not here for revenge.'

'I expect they'll change. The more you see the Germans today, the harder it is to hate them.'

We sat back in our chairs and sipped our coffee. I tutted.

'What?' said Eleanor.

'It's odd: Hildegard is serving these wonderful breakfasts, but she still can't find real sugar, only saccharine.'

'If that's all you've got to complain about—'

'It's not. How about a properly-equipped schoolroom?'

Eleanor laughed. 'That'll take a bit longer.'

Someone knocked at the front door and we heard Hildegard's footsteps trot along the hall and then walk back. She knocked at the drawing-room door. Before we could say anything, Victor burst in.

'The Poles!' he said. 'They're coming tomorrow.'

'What? Tomorrow? But the Commander said—'

'And there's fifteen hundred of them.'

'But this is absolutely impossible. You told me that—'

'The base Commander doesn't control everything, Edmund. He's just reacting to what other people do.'

'But we're not ready—'

17. In the City

Within minutes, I was in my office at the camp. I tried to telephone the base Commander to tell him to delay the arrival of the Poles. We weren't ready! Eventually I got through to a lieutenant, who said that the Commander wanted to see me and could I come over immediately. I asked if they'd send a jeep to collect me: there were none available.

'Edmund!' Eleanor had been watching me. 'Calm down! It doesn't matter if there are no jeeps. We can walk there. It's not far.'

'Walking will give the wrong impression,' I told her.

I shouted for Victor. He now drove a very sleek Mercedes that someone in the American base had found for him: he could lend it to me. But he was nowhere to be seen. Then I had an idea. Jacques could drive me. I went over to where the trucks were parked. Only one was there and there was no sign of Jacques.

'Right, I'll drive myself,' I muttered.

But when I got in, the engine was dead. Eleanor caught up with me.

'Edmund!'

'I'll give that Commander a piece of my mind, I will. He *promised* that we still had four days to prepare. Where's Jacques?'

'He's helping Alma.'

'Where's Alma?'

'The last time I saw her, she was going to the dispensary, on the other side of the camp...'

I banged my fist on the steering wheel of the truck. Everything was against me.

'Edmund! This won't do. We'll walk to the base. It won't take half an hour.'

I glared at Eleanor, feeling a flash of anger. Why wasn't she doing anything to help me? Then I realised that she was right: we'd have to walk. As I got out of the truck, she smiled.

'Poor old Edmund! Post-war Europe is a bit of a mess, didn't you know?'

Despite myself, I had to laugh.

'I'll tell Eisenhower about this, next time I see him,' she continued. 'He'll be furious when he learns that Neukirchen wasn't ready for the Team Director.'

We started out from the camp, along a long straight lane. I still hadn't seen the city centre. On the day we'd arrived, we'd skirted round the suburbs. Since then, Victor and Dan had been scurrying back and forth between our camp and the American base, and Eleanor had gone over a few times. I'd stayed in the camp, organising things.

Eleanor put her arm through mine.

'Edmund, pull yourself together. You've been sitting around and eating too much of Hildegard's cooking. A walk will do you good. It's about time you saw the city. And don't worry about the German resistance. There are no Werewolves.'

'No?'

'Not a trace of them. All the Germans look too tired and sad to do any resisting.'

I nodded and slowly my mood lifted. I'd be visiting a German city with my wife. Maybe we'd do some shopping on the way back. Get some proper sugar. I might buy a present for Eleanor as well, maybe get her some jewellery, something to contrast with Neukirchen's drabness.

'You know the way?' I asked.

'It's not difficult.'

We reached the end of the lane and turned a corner. From there, we looked down over the city centre: we could see for miles.

How stupid of me! I'd been concentrating so much on our offices, that I hadn't thought about the state of the city. Hildegard had talked of two bad air-raids. But—this! In front of me was a grim urban landscape, with grey, empty shells of buildings, stretching as far as the eye could see. In the centre, by some miracle, a single steeple remained, pointing upwards to the heavens. It was the only tall building left.

Eleanor pointed to the right. 'Over there. That's where the tank factories were.'

To be honest, that area looked no worse than the rest of the city. I knew that it had been essential to destroy the factories, I knew that most of the city's population had been Nazis—but all the same! The sight of so much destruction weighed on me. So many homes, so many families. I remembered that Hildegard's son had died in an air-raid and I thought of the others who had lost their lives. I couldn't be like Dan or Pierre and say that they all deserved it.

Eleanor led me along.

'What a sight—it's awful,' I said. My words sounded utterly inadequate.

'Yes,' she replied. 'It is. Absolutely awful. We must hope that something better replaces it.'

'It's a dead city.'

'Not quite dead, despite the best efforts of our bombers. You'll see. Come on.'

We walked down into an empty, grimy space. The big raids had hit the city two years ago, but a stale smell of dust and smoke still lingered in the air. Someone had cleared the roads and patched up the holes. There was a trickle of traffic: Americans in jeeps and trucks, Germans on old bicycles or pushing handcarts. Some one-horse carts, carrying produce from the countryside, I guessed. We followed a long, wide street, in which every building had been bombed to bits, leaving just the bare bones of walls and piles of bricks and mortar. Our shoes scratched the gritty pavement.

'So quiet, so empty,' I muttered, but even as I spoke, I caught sight of a movement from one of the smashed houses.

A woman in a shapeless coat emerged from behind a bare wall, clutching a bag.

'Where's she come from?' I wondered.

'The cellars,' said Eleanor. 'They've become a race of troglodytes. Sometimes, if it's safe, they repair a room or two on the ground floor. The Americans have got the water supply running, but there's still problems with electricity.'

'But where's she going?'

'Here.' Eleanor pointed.

We turned a corner. There was the wreck of what once must have been a large shop, now open to the sky. I saw a little knot of people gathered round a side wall. There were improvised stalls made of planks resting on rescued bricks, where people brought things to sell. Some were respectable housewives like Hildegard, selling off the family silver. I could see a green gramophone on one plank and on another some of that heavy, ornate pottery that Hildegard liked. A third stall had a few tins. Other sellers must have been farmers, or—more likely—people with gardens, selling vegetables.

'Hildegard said they don't use money any more,' I recalled.

'No,' said Eleanor. 'It's barter or cigarettes now.'

Was this sad imitation of a market a sign of hope? A green shoot, poking out of the dust and destruction? Maybe I was being naïve. The people here were desperate and perhaps this little corner was formed by some blind economic instinct, with no more meaning than a cloud pushed across the sky by the wind.

A group of children, dressed in ill-fitting, ragged clothes and mostly shoeless, spotted us. First one ran towards us, then three or four followed.

'*Zigaretten!*' they shouted. '*Zigaretten!*'

'Give them a couple, or we'll never get rid of them,' said Eleanor.

I pulled three cigarettes out of the pack in my inside pocket and flung them across the road. The children leapt at them, scrabbling, laughing, pushing at each other, almost like children playing anywhere in the world.

'That's no way to live,' I said.

Eleanor shook her head.

I could see why Eleanor said the city was safe. These people had no energy, no fight left in them. When we met Germans on the pavement, they automatically stood aside to let us pass, saying nothing. It was hard to look at them and see the enemy that had smashed their way through France and battered London. Harder still to see them as the people who had mistreated those poor souls in that dreadful barn. We strode through their streets and I felt uncomfortably like the representative of an advanced civilization, paying a visit to primitive savages.

We came to the station.

'People are always hanging round here, I don't know why,' said Eleanor. 'They can't afford to buy tickets.'

'Movement,' I said. Eleanor looked at me. 'Just—coming and going. Where there's movement, there's life, and where there's life, there's hope. Even if you can't travel, you can think about travelling.'

'Maybe,' said Eleanor.

We passed another imitation market, set up at a street corner, framed by the shells of smashed buildings. A back street led from it and I could see a row of girls with bleached blonde hair and bright lipstick, leaning against the remaining wall of a tenement. Two GIs stood in front of them. One was having an intense discussion with a blonde in a shabby blue coat.

'I don't have to tell you what they are,' said Eleanor.

I shook my head. Another economic activity was reviving. Eleanor stopped and stared at them. Then she tutted.

'Slaves trying to enslave other slaves,' she said.

I frowned. Weren't the girls to be pitied?

This strange promenade did me good. It put my worries in perspective: how could I get angry about the early arrival of the Polish DPs, when so close to me were people reduced to this desperate, hopeless life? Rather than arguing with the Commander, I would discuss options.

***

The American headquarters weren't far from the station. They'd taken over a school which had mostly survived the raids. An American flag fluttered outside: a rare splash of colour in this monochrome city of dust, debris and bricks. As we walked towards it, I looked forward to leaving the grubby wreck of the German city and finding somewhere more friendly. But I felt Eleanor grip my arm.

'Here we go,' she said in a tense voice.

What did she mean? I didn't have time to ask as we showed our papers to the sentries at the entrance and were directed towards the Commander's office. We entered a wide, walled space—the school playground. Clusters of American soldiers stood around: one group repaired a jeep, others shared papers, groups along a wall played those dice games that American soldiers loved, while some just walked and talked.

As we walked across the square, there was a sudden silence and then the noises started. First wolf-whistles, then shouts, laughs and whoops. Eleanor, of course, Eleanor.

'Men without women,' she muttered.

She didn't change her stance: she stayed upright, she didn't hurry her pace, she didn't look round.

'Goin' anywhere tonight?' was one shout I understood. Suddenly I wished I had Dan's revolver with me. Should I shout back? Or try to laugh it off? Or ignore them?

Thankfully, we quickly reached the main building.

Eleanor looked at me. 'Odd, isn't it? I can walk across a German city—an *enemy* city—and not a soul bothers me. But I enter an American headquarters, and I'm subject to—to *that*.'

'It happens—every time?' I asked.

'Of course it does!'

'These Americans.' I tutted.

'Edmund! It's not something special about American soldiers. This would happen anywhere, in a British or French base, in any military base.'

'But—'

'I suppose they think they're being funny. But you know what it really is?'

'What?'

'It's a way of telling a woman that she doesn't belong here, that this is a man's world.'

I felt awkward, but what could I do? I couldn't fight the entire American army single-handed. But it wasn't right, it wasn't right at all. I gripped Eleanor's arm, aware of her fragility and wanting to protect her.

***

We climbed some steps, up to the Commander's office. He was an experienced officer, who'd led his unit from the beaches of Normandy to here. Victor and Dan said he was cooperative and easy-going.

We turned a corner, where we met a soldier who said: 'UNRRA?'

Then we were in the Commander's office. He sat behind a fine mahogany desk (where had that come from?). The upholstered chairs in the office all matched: they were solid, well-crafted and properly polished. On the floor was a fine carpet, worn a little thin in places. I would've liked an office like this. The only discordant note was the view from the window, which was a wonderful vista of the bomb-wrecked city.

The Commander himself was in shirt-sleeves and a tie: his shirt had carefully-ironed creases. He had a fleshy, round face, close-cropped hair, broad shoulders and gold-rimmed spectacles. He walked round to shake our hands with that bone-crunching grip that some Americans like.

'Great to see ya, great to see ya,' he repeated.

Back in his chair, he asked: 'Coffee?'

We accepted his offer.

'Settled in okay? Finding all you need?'

'The Poles—' I began.

'Yeah, yeah,' he said. He ran his hand over his head. 'Earlier than we expected, I know, but what can ya do? They gotta go somewhere.'

'It's going to be difficult to give them—'

'Sure, it'll be difficult. But they're better off with you guys than staying in that goddamn wreck of a factory. No water, no food. Women and children too, y'see? The Army doesn't know what to do with them. So, we need you.'

'But they'll need rehabilitation—' said Eleanor.

'By God they will,' said the Commander. 'Rehabilitation, repair, recreation, repatriation and whatever else you can give them.'

'We need more equipment,' said Eleanor.

'We'll get you whatever we can, lady.'

'Schoolbooks, blackboards—'

'Schoolbooks?' The Commander frowned, thinking about it. '*Polish* schoolbooks?'

Eleanor nodded.

'Could be difficult,' he said. 'I'll get someone to look at it. Maybe the Red Cross can help.'

We talked in this fashion for another ten minutes. The picture was clear: the Commander was happy to off-load spare military supplies on us. Generous American rations would arrive and a fair amount of much-needed medical stocks. But anything more specialist was beyond him and he just kicked the problem away. UNRRA and Displaced Persons weren't at the top of his list of priorities.

'Okay?' he asked.

We looked at each other and then nodded.

'Seeya at the station tomorrow. Eleven hundred hours.'

***

As we walked back through the wrecked city, I let out a laugh.

'What is it, Edmund?'

'This morning I'd imagined that I might buy you a present in a shop!'

Eleanor chuckled. 'For the moment, we'll have to rely on the American army for our supplies.'

'What do you think of him, the Commander?'

'He seems a generous man,' said Eleanor.

'But?'

'But—all the military leaders see UNRRA as a way of closing a door on a problem. They're not interested in building a better world and they want the DPs shunted home as quickly as possible.'

I nodded. 'Would the British zone be any better?'

'It might be worse in the British zone. There's so many British officers who think they know how to run a foreign country. India, you know.'

We walked on, past the imitation market.

'At least the Commander is cooperating,' I said. 'We'll be able to run our camp.'

'If he doesn't see UNRRA as important, maybe he'll leave us alone to get on with things.'

'Maybe. But—'

'But what?' asked Eleanor.

'It would be nice if, just once, someone would recognise that what we're doing is important.'

We walked on a little further.

'Still—the Poles...' said Eleanor.

'We'll do our best. And he's right—whatever we give them will be better than what they can find in a ruined factory.'

18. The Rehabilitation of the Poles

Tymon's well-cut blue-grey tweed jacket was too small for him. As we talked, he'd reach to pull it closer round his wiry frame, forgetting that it would stretch no further. His trousers were vaguely brown and one knee had been badly darned.

'Tymon,' I said. 'A concert hall is out of the question.'

'But—'

'However, there's a space out there, beyond the bungalows, where the ground slopes. You could use that.'

It could make a fine amphitheatre, I thought.

'And in winter?' asked Tymon, turning his piercing blue eyes on me.

'Ah, winter. Winter's going to be difficult for all sorts of reasons. UNRRA wants us to *winterize* all bases.' I rolled my eyes and smiled, but Tymon didn't find it funny.

'But you know UNRRA's plan...' I continued, trying to get him to think more realistically. 'The Americans will find trains to take you back to Poland. There's no need for a concert hall.'

Tymon shook his head. 'Our people are too sick for a long train journey. They need more time to recover.'

'Winter here won't be pleasant.'

'Winter in Poland will be worse. And—' I guessed what was coming. The political questions. '—we cannot be sure about our security there. The Communists are—'

'They have sworn to respect the results of the next elections.'

'Hah!' snorted Tymon.

I looked at Tymon's thin, gaunt face and his pale blue eyes. God knows what he'd gone through in the last years. Hadn't Eleanor said he'd been a physics teacher before the war? He wasn't a concentration camp survivor—there were very few of them, for obvious reasons. A forced labourer, I guessed. I couldn't ask him outright. Questions about the past, about the war and before the war, were considered impolite.

Tymon started again. 'A hall would be good for us. We have a choir already, you know? And I think soon an orchestra.'

'An orchestra?'

'Yes, there are some fine musicians among us. Of course, they have not played for many years, because...'

I nodded. He didn't need to say anything. The more I learnt about how the Germans had treated the Poles, the angrier I got. Sometimes I sounded like Dan or Pierre. The Nazis had attempted to kill all Poland's intellectuals: all its musicians, artists, writers, teachers... What a crime!

'We have discussed this in our committee. We think a hall will be part of our *rehabilitation*,' Tymon continued. He stressed the word, hoping that it would have a special resonance for me. 'There is a large building in a street next to the camp. We think it would be suitable.'

'Tymon, we can't keep doing this. It's not possible to constantly take things from the local people.'

'Why not?'

'Because...'

Those bloody Americans and their *requisitioning*. Who could blame the Poles for thinking this way?

'Look, Tymon, I'll talk to the Base Commander. He might be able to think of something.'

'Thank you.'

Tymon got up slowly. I stood up and we shook hands, Tymon bowing slightly. He smiled at me and, as he left, I realised that this man really trusted me. Oh dear.

Eleanor came in, holding her portable typewriter. It was good to see her after my awkward meeting with Tymon. She'd be interested in what we'd discussed.

'Any luck?' she asked.

'Now they want a concert hall!'

'A concert hall? What ambitions!'

'Far too ambitious, if you ask me. We're meant to be helping them return to Poland.'

I packed my briefcase, took Eleanor by the arm and we walked out.

'And what did you tell him?'

'I said I'd consult the base Commander.'

Eleanor laughed. 'You kicked it into the long grass!'

'Exactly.' I sighed. 'I know it's not the best way to deal with issues, but—you know—I have to think about what's possible. What else can I do?'

Outside it was a bright, sunny afternoon. Opposite the office, an elderly Polish couple in the garden of their bungalow called out:

'Good afternoon, Team Director.'

I waved at them. They were on their knees, pulling out weeds from their vegetable patch.

'They're so hard-working,' whispered Eleanor.

I nodded. Each bungalow had its carefully tended garden. Sweet peas curled up trellises and tomatoes ripened.

'When you think of those Russians—' I began.

'Oh, the Poles aren't the same, not the same at all.'

The Polish DPs were keen and active. Many volunteered to help Alma in the dispensary and Eleanor with the schoolroom. They didn't stop there: Tymon's committee had organised the conversion of a bungalow into a church.

'They want to stage a concert, you know. That's why Tymon wants a hall,' Eleanor said. 'Their committee is so active.'

I smiled. 'But you had to insist—'

'Yes!' She laughed. 'They wouldn't have included a woman delegate if I hadn't made them.'

We walked back to our house.

'But—' I said.

'Yes, I know,' said Eleanor. 'It's wonderful to see this space being used and it's wonderful to see them looking so much healthier. This camp has even become a good place to bring up children, *but*—'

'Not much sign of repatriation.'

'Are they ever going back? What did Tymon say?'

'He was tight-lipped, as always. But he says two things: firstly, Poland isn't what it was.'

'We can't deny that. It's lost land in the east and gained it in the west, but it's not the same.'

'And then—they worry about Communism.'

We turned into our street.

'How are you getting on with your welfare report?' I asked.

Eleanor frowned. 'It's not easy. UNRRA seems to think that everything can be reduced to statistics. But some things can't be quantified! Look at that couple we've just seen—do I note them as gardeners (2) in garden (1)? But that doesn't capture what that patch of ground means to them. I want to address deeper issues.'

'When's the Zone Welfare meeting?'

'It's next week. I've still got time.'

***

Eleanor had done some *requisitioning* of her own. With the help of the Americans and the local *Bürgermeister*, she'd acquired a portable typewriter. As she'd trained as a typist, she was able to spot a good one: a lovely little model that folded up neatly into its own case. UNRRA was forever sending us twelve-page forms and demanding replies in triplicate within days. Dan, Victor and myself bashed out what we could on the typewriter in the main office. Pierre announced that he couldn't type and Eleanor introduced him to Lena, a delightful Polish girl who spoke French and English, and who typed beautifully. Pierre said that she'd improved his report immensely, so I immediately appointed her as my secretary.

Eleanor kept saying that welfare work was different. It was about healing, it was about *charity* in the true sense of the word, it was about UNRRA's real mission. Her report was more demanding. A proper welfare report needed to consider the *qualitative* as well as the *quantitative*, reviewing the entire camp and all the people in it. For these reasons, she needed her own typewriter. I wasn't happy with her approach.

'We must show UNRRA that we're efficient,' I told her. 'And that means completing reports on time.'

She gave me a long hard look. 'The Nazis were efficient. Look at their damn *autobahns*. We joined UNRRA for other reasons.'

'Eleanor! It's just a form. Fill out the boxes and have done with it.'

'I'm not working in a factory. I'm not just handing out toothbrushes and perambulators. I'm working with people, real people, Edmund—'

'We all are—'

'And my report will be about those people and their needs, not about supplies and statistics.'

'Is that what UNRRA wants?'

'It's what UNRRA's going to get. If they take welfare seriously, then they must start thinking differently.'

'But you can't write an analysis of the entire camp in the next week. Your report will be late, I know it will.'

Eleanor gave me a stubborn look, which meant that she wouldn't budge an inch. Every evening, after dinner, she'd retire to a small room on the first floor and I'd hear her typewriter tapping. She never let me see what she was writing.

***

Alma dropped into my office. She had an urgent request: barbiturates for a Polish DP who had developed epilepsy. I tried to hide my interest as I signed her form.

'Epilepsy? You're certain?'

'He shows the classic symptoms.'

'Which are?'

She looked at me for a moment, maybe puzzled by my curiosity.

'Sudden fits, often triggered by bright lights or moments of stress.'

I tried to look both surprised and sympathetic.

'The fits can be quite violent,' continued Alma. 'Upsetting for his children to see. And, you know—he soils himself.'

I must have looked baffled, because she gestured towards my trousers.

'Really? Every time?'

'No, not always. But it's one of the usual symptoms.' She sighed. 'It's a strange condition, it takes many forms.'

'What's the cause?' I asked.

Alma shook her head. 'It's not clear. Some research suggests it might be genetic.'

'And the barbiturates—'

'They help control the condition, they are not a cure.'

'Can it just—just go away?'

Alma smiled at me. 'Sometimes. You seem very interested, Edmund.'

'A friend of mine—he has epilepsy.'

She nodded, smiling. I don't know if I fooled her.

That evening, I told Eleanor what Alma had said. She listened quietly, nodding as I spoke.

'Have I really got epilepsy?' I asked. 'Do those pills do me any good?'

'Alma said it could take many forms. You've felt—alright, recently?'

'Yes. I still get the odd twinge at the back of my neck, but these days I sense it won't lead to a full-blown fit. That's not epilepsy, is it?'

'I don't know,' said Eleanor. 'I've seen you have fits. You've definitely got something.'

My mind raced. 'I could've joined the Army!'

'Not with those fits, Edmund. And after D-Day, Eisenhower managed to defeat the Germans without your assistance, extraordinary as it may seem.'

I laughed, then thought on. 'It was only because of my epilepsy—or whatever it is—that we met.'

'So something good came out of it.'

'Yes.'

We hugged, but I couldn't help thinking about the other Edmund, the one without epilepsy, who'd joined the Army in 1940. What might he have done?

**

Lena knocked and then put her head round my office door.

'Two UNRRA officers to see you, sir.'

I frowned. What was this? I hadn't expected anyone.

'Send them in.'

She came back with a large, sandy-coloured man who promptly sat in my best chair, and a thin, nervous-looking type, who stayed standing and whose eyes were never still. The large man introduced himself as Colonel Hilton and his thin colleague as Lieutenant-Colonel Moore.

'I expect you saw in the documentation—' he began.

'What documentation?' I interrupted.

He looked astonished. 'Why, it was sent to you a week ago. You need to check your post more often.'

'But—I assure you—'

'Colonel,' the thin man said. 'There've been problems with the postal service. We've seen this before.'

'I—' started Colonel Hilton and then stopped. But I caught his expression: he was furious with Moore for contradicting him in front of me.

Hilton sat back and began again in an irritated tone. 'We're British Army officers, seconded to UNRRA to conduct inspections of UNRRA Assembly Centres. We've driven a hundred miles to get here and we're not going to turn round just because you haven't read the documentation.'

'Inspections?' I was still getting over my surprise.

Moore looked at me. 'It's standard procedure. Nothing to be concerned about.'

Colonel Hilton glared at him. 'Except we've had some rather worrying reports about this Centre.'

'Really?' I was amazed. I had the impression that my camp was rather well-run.

'However...' began Moore. Hilton frowned. 'We've learnt not to accept rumours as facts. Most camps have their problems: it would be unusual if this one was working perfectly.'

'Still,' resumed Colonel Hilton, 'we intend to carry out an immediate inspection. Is your team assembled?'

'No,' I said. 'We've had no warning. The Deputy Director and Messing Officer are at the American base—'

Colonel Hilton's eyes lit up and he nodded in a knowing manner, as if to say *just as I suspected.*

'And the Welfare Officer?' he said. 'I believe she's your wife?'

'Yes...' He made me feel that I was confessing a guilty secret.

Colonel Hilton fired off a few more questions about the manner in which the Centre was run, which I answered as vaguely as possible, still wondering what on earth he could've heard. Moore intervened when Hilton's questions became almost offensive.

'Colonel, we've got a long drive back this afternoon. Maybe we should begin the inspection of the camp now and leave our interviews with the UNRRA team until later.'

With obvious reluctance, Colonel Hilton accepted the suggestion. We walked out of my office and to my amazement there were two armed soldiers in the foyer. They were sprawled out in the chairs, but jumped to attention when Hilton emerged.

'Our chauffeurs,' explained Moore. 'Regulations. They always come with us.'

Colonel Hilton beckoned Moore closer and said a few words *sotto voce*, while glancing at me. When they were finished, he barked:

'Sergeant Brown: you'll accompany me round the camp. Sergeant Pagden: remain here.'

Colonel Hilton marched off with his sergeant. With a discrete glance to me, Moore signalled that we should talk outside.

It was a bright, breezy day. Moore offered me a cigarette and I got out my lighter. We smoked in silence for a moment or two.

'Interesting operation, UNRRA,' said Moore.

'You think so? Generally the military don't approve.'

'We don't all think the same. UNRRA's looking at issues in a different way. After the war, the problems of the peace. We got that wrong in 1918 and we need to learn from our mistakes.'

I nodded, surprised to hear an officer talking this way.

'The Colonel's Old School, you understand,' Moore continued. 'You come in, you concentrate your forces, you defeat the enemy. Nothing more complicated than that.'

'You're based in the British Zone?' I asked.

'Of course.'

'Going well?'

He grinned. 'You know what the soldiers say?'

I shook my head.

'What does CCG stand for?' Moore asked.

I knew it stood for 'Control Commission for Germany,' but clearly Moore meant something else. 'Tell me.'

'Complete Chaos Guaranteed. Ha!' Moore chuckled. 'They're right. The war bled us dry. We don't have the equipment or the manpower to run a third of Germany. The problems are piling up. Whatever we think of them, we can't let the Germans starve. And the DPs! A lot of them have returned home, but so many are still here. We've heard the stories: Poles who go back to Poland on UNRRA trains, don't like it and then return to their UNRRA camp.'

'I know, I know. But, Colonel Hilton—'

'Don't worry.' Moore smiled. 'There's been some gossip. The Colonel will stomp round the camp, shout out orders, disturb a few innocent Poles and probably find something reprehensible.' He shook his head. 'Then tomorrow, we'll draw up a report and I'll ask him for proper evidence, and the whole thing will shrink to one nasty little story.'

'But what can he possibly find here?'

'He'll find something, believe me. He always does. You know the trouble with people like the Colonel?'

'What?'

'They want to create a new colony here. Maybe one to replace India after it goes.'

'Did he serve in India?'

'No. I think that's his problem. He's trying to make up for it.'

Moore looked over the estate, taking in the bungalows, the main square, the gardens and the green spaces. He nodded, apparently satisfied.

'Nice spot. Better than many Assembly Centres I've seen.' He paused and then grinned. 'Of course, the Colonel's terrified of what's coming.'

'What?' I couldn't imagine Colonel Hilton being scared of anything.

'Why, the General Election.'

'Really!' I'd lost touch of what was happening back in England.

'Don't you know? The red wave. The country's tired of the old lot. Churchill—fine as a military leader, I suppose, but would you want him running the country for another five years?'

'I see...'

Moore nodded: there was a keen, expectant look in his eyes. For a moment, he reminded me of Eleanor. 'Still, I'd better not stand here too long. The Old Man'll suspect something. I'll walk round and look busy.'

He stepped away and then paused. 'Keep your eye on Sergeant Pagden. He's—he's been a problem on some visits. You'd better go back inside.'

Moore's words calmed me, but I was still worried. I led a hard-working team. The Poles were obviously in better shape than when they'd arrived. What could anyone complain about?

Back in the bungalow, Sergeant Pagden lounged on a chair. I glanced at Lena and caught something in her look. Had Pagden upset her? Just to seem friendly, I got out my cigarettes and offered him one.

'American?' he said. 'Very nice.'

Soon he was telling the sort of stories that all soldiers tell. I only listened with half an ear, wondering all the time what Colonel Hilton was doing. I know our boys had a tough time after D-Day and they've every right to talk about it. But their stories! Pagden's first one was about a German sniper somewhere in the fields of north-east France, who'd shot a cigarette right out of his mouth.

'As sure as I'm sittin' here in front of you!'

I'd only heard that story three or four times before.

Then it was on to the fleshpots of Brussels, where—apparently—Belgian girls threw themselves on Sergeant Pagden. I didn't like the tone of this and I looked at Lena, but she made a great show of typing out a form. What with pretending to listen to Pagden, wondering what Hilton and Moore were getting up to and worrying about Lena, I barely noticed Eleanor coming through the other door. I thought about introducing her to Pagden, but decided it was better if she came and went as quickly as possible. She looked for a file in the filing cabinet. Pagden must have thought she was another secretary.

He was now reaching the climax of his story: the lesson, for the world to learn and admire.

'Y'see,' he told me, 'what yer ordinary soldier needs is three things. If y'like, it's the soldier's ABC.'

He puffed on his cigarette and began counting on one hand.

'A: alcohol. None better than what you get in Brussels!'

'B: baccy. Lucky Strikes, Yank baccy, will do nicely, thank you very much.'

He puffed on his cigarette again.

'And C—'

Here, he gave me a leer and I realised with horror what he was going to say.

'Cunt.'

In a flash, Eleanor turned round and slapped his face. The sound ricocheted round the office. Lena stared, her mouth open in amazement. For a second, Pagden was stunned.

Then he roared 'Hey!' and leapt out of his chair, pulling back his arm to punch Eleanor. I was on to him. With all my force, I grabbed his arm and pushed him back down into the chair. Who did this brute think he was? Speaking in front of my wife like that! Eleanor,

God bless her, seized his rifle and lifted it to hit him. With his free arm, Pagden punched me hard in the ribs. At that moment, Colonel Hilton and Lieutenant-Colonel Moore came back.

'What the—' said Hilton.

'Sir!' shouted Pagden. 'This woman attacked me, sir. And stole my rifle.'

I stood up, pulled my jacket back into place and glared at Pagden. My God, men like this were supposed to be liberating Germany. There was an ache in my ribs, where he'd hit me.

Once I'd got my breath back, I said: 'This man insulted my wife. I demand his removal from my office.'

The next few moments were rather tricky. Colonel Hilton threatened to have me and Eleanor court-martialled for attacking military personnel.

Moore intervened. 'I'm sure Sergeant Pagden doesn't want the whole of the regiment to know that he was attacked by an unarmed woman, who stole his rifle.'

Pagden visibly deflated.

Colonel Hilton didn't give up. He claimed that the camp was in a deplorable condition, absolutely deplorable. His criticisms centred on his discovery of an illegal still for a Polish drink called *bimber*, which was distilled from potatoes. Behind him, Moore rolled his eyes. *Bimber* from our camp was sold across the region, claimed Hilton. There was further evidence of black-market activities: a store of American cigarettes, a stack of tyres from military vehicles. I glanced at Eleanor and could see from her face that the accusations might be true.

On the way out, Moore had a quick word with me.

'I did warn you about Pagden. It's not the first time. He's always getting into scraps. Mind you, he usually picks on men. That's quite a wife you've got!'

He laughed, got into his car and told Sergeant Brown to drive off.

***

I sent a memo to all team members to report for an emergency meeting the next morning. But rather than waiting, I went on an immediate tour of the bungalows with Eleanor. I'd let things slip. I'd relied on reports from the others. I stayed in my office, waiting for the Poles to come to me. It had seemed sensible, as so many of them did seek me out. Most mornings, there'd be a queue waiting when I arrived, asking for everything from firewood to gramophones to visas for America. Someone had to talk to them. A large part of my job was repeating the words *sorry* and *no*.

But what if Hilton was right? Had Tymon been leading me up the garden path? Did all our work just provide a cover for some black-market scheme? I had to see the true state of the camp for myself, before finding another nasty surprise in Hilton's report.

'Edmund, I'm not sure if this is a good idea,' Eleanor said as we walked to the first bungalow.

'Why not? Aren't I Team Director? Don't I have a right to see what's going on in my camp?'

'But these people—they're families, they've got a sense of privacy.'

'And I've got a sense of responsibility. Did you know about the *bimber*?'

'It wasn't a surprise.'

'Why didn't you tell me?'

'Because these people—these people trust me.'

'Don't you trust me?'

'Yes, but—'

The more I heard her speak, the less I liked it.

We worked our way through the bungalows. It was a revelation. Some—mainly those for the single men—were relatively unchanged. They contained long rows of bunk beds, some lockers, tables and chairs, one or two bookshelves and not much else. But the family bungalows! They'd been converted into miniature suburbs. The Poles had partitioned off sections with wardrobes, stacks of luggage and khaki blankets which they'd pinned to the ceiling, creating elaborate labyrinths. Eleanor and I squeezed through improvised corridors. Within them, the range of activities was extraordinary: mothers changed babies' nappies, an old man worked on a sewing machine, a girl practiced on a guitar, two men played chess. Ducks, chickens and rabbits looked at us from cages. While the scenes changed, the smells lingered: nappies drying, fish being smoked, cabbage boiling, smoke from fires.

'What is this?' I asked Eleanor between two bungalows. 'What have they done?'

She looked at me. 'They're trying to re-create their homes. We haven't given them much, but they're doing what they can.'

'But these are like—like miniature cities! Why do they have to wall themselves in with khaki blankets?'

'Each family wants its own space.'

'And where have they got all this stuff? Those wardrobes? They didn't come from us.'

Eleanor shrugged. 'The black market, I suppose.'

'So it's all illegal?'

'Maybe. But they're showing initiative. How can they become economically active except through the black market?'

'The sooner they clear off back to Poland, the better.'

'They're not planning to go soon.'

***

The emergency Team meeting went worse than I feared. Pierre had the most serious revelation.

'I suspect that at least two women have had abortions. One of them may be seriously injured.'

'Abortions? Here?' I was stunned. How could such a thing happen in our camp? 'Why didn't you tell me before?'

Pierre wouldn't meet my eyes. 'I cannot be certain. But there are four or five people among the Polish DPs with the expertise to carry out such a procedure.'

Eleanor intervened. Cigarette in one hand, her voice taut and level, she insisted we listen.

'The majority of the Polish DPs are in broken families. The war has turned their domestic life upside down; it has separated husbands from wives, children from parents. During the war, all they thought about was survival. Now, in their first months of calm and stability, they naturally think of re-making families.'

'You mean—' I thought through what Eleanor was saying. 'You mean—the majority of those households we saw aren't married couples?'

'Of course they aren't! How could they be? They haven't been allowed to get married for five or six years.'

Dan had been listening, his face grim. 'And then—there's prostitution.'

Eleanor nodded.

'Prostitution? In our camp?' I said.

'It would be surprising if it wasn't there,' Dan replied.

'I have seen an increase in the number of cases of Venereal Disease,' added Pierre.

This was worse, so much worse than I'd believed possible. It was a betrayal, an absolute betrayal. They seemed such a polite, cooperative people. How could they...

Alma had been looking at me. 'Edmund, this is normal in a wartime situation. Bombs destroy buildings, they also destroy families. The process of reconstruction is not simple.'

'But what are we meant to do?'

'UNRRA's policy is to encourage the re-formation of family lives,' said Alma. 'But it will not be quick. Or easy.'

I had a thought. 'There's a priest! And a church.'

Pierre nodded.

'But,' said Eleanor, 'many wives who are separated from their husbands and husbands who've lost their wives, really don't know if their spouses are still alive. They don't know if they can remarry.'

'And now we've got that report from Hilton coming.' It just got worse and worse.

'Cheer up, buddy,' said Victor. 'After what we've heard today, illegal moonshine is the least of your worries.'

To my surprise, this phlegmatic approach was shared by most of the team.

Dan muttered, 'At least no one's been killed.'

I felt so disappointed. To think: Colonel Hilton had been right! He knew my camp better than I did. All our weeks of work—for nothing. And the rest of them knew all about it and never said a word to me. Not even Eleanor.

***

I stayed late in my office, drafting a report to persuade UNRRA that I was in control of the camp and that *rehabilitation* was taking place. I couldn't trust the others and I felt bloody furious with Eleanor. I'd have it out with her that evening: she was my wife and I had a right to expect her support.

These khaki labyrinths and makeshift families: that wasn't normal behaviour. I couldn't believe that the UNRRA leaders would shrug their shoulders and say: *what do you expect from DPs?* I feared that after Hilton's report they'd dismiss me and I would return to England, haunted by a sad story of failure and corruption. So I grappled with my report, drafting and re-drafting sections, wondering whether to highlight our achievements or to answer directly the criticisms I guessed Hilton would make.

I glanced at my watch: it was almost seven. I'd been working for over two hours! Hildegard would be serving dinner soon. I packed my briefcase and marched home. Rather than changing for dinner, I went straight to the dining room. From the hall, I could hear Eleanor and Dan arguing.

'No, Dan, no,' Eleanor was saying. 'You can't bring her here.'

'But, Eleanor—'

I walked in and they fell silent. What had they been quarrelling about? The last thing I wanted was another argument.

'What's going on? Can't we eat dinner in peace?' I said.

Eleanor puffed on her cigarette and then spat out: 'Dan has a proposal. About his *frat*.'

'Frat?' There were so many new words, mostly soldiers' slang, that I found it impossible to keep up.

'From *fraternisation*.' Eleanor spoke with that taut, level tone I'd learnt to mistrust. 'The soldiers use *frat* to mean a German girl or—'

'I've done nothing wrong!' insisted Dan. 'They're from a socialist family and they're desperate.'

'So it's an act of charity, is it? I thought you hated the Germans.'

'You can't hate them all. It makes no sense. These ones are anti-Nazi, and Elsa's brother—'

'*Elsa*,' Eleanor sneered.

'They're starving, they've no income—'

'How many cigarettes does she charge for a poke, Dan?'

Dan went red. For a moment, I thought he was going to hit Eleanor. Instead, he threw his napkin down on the table and walked out with tears in his eyes.

'Eleanor!' I said.

She ran her fingers through her hair, puffed on her cigarette, then turned to face me.

'Yes?'

'Dan—we need him. We have to work with him.'

'No, we don't. He's a hypocrite. We could find hundreds more like him.'

'But, in the team meeting— You were defending prostitution—'

She glared at me. 'I was not *defending* prostitution. I was saying that extra-marital affairs are inevitable in a displaced, shattered group like the Poles. Whereas Dan—I expected better from him. He ought to—'

But she stopped, gave me a dark look, puffed at her cigarette and then ground it out on one Hildegard's saucers.

'What's the point?' she said, not even looking at me. 'You wouldn't understand. And I've got that bloody report to finish.'

***

I had a horrible sense of things falling apart. First the camp, then our team, and finally—Eleanor and me. For the next few days she avoided me: getting up early and skipping breakfast, staying in the camp to eat. Dashing to her little room and typing in the evening, until I fell asleep. Leaving me alone in the bedroom. Avoiding me, not talking to me, not even looking at me.

I tried to understand what was worrying her and got to thinking about us, as man and wife, as a couple. I remembered that dance at the American base. Eleanor pirouetted and twirled, while I stayed steady. Wasn't that how our marriage worked? I was the solid base around which Eleanor orbited. Or was she going to spiral away?

One lonely evening I was thinking about our respective responsibilities, as Team Director and Welfare Officer, when a thought hit me. Eleanor would have made a better Team Director than me. The thought had all the weight of a self-evident truth. Of course, she would have to restrain her impatience and temper—but if she'd been Team Director, maybe she wouldn't have got impatient and angry in the first place. She would've inspired a Team in a way I never did. If only UNRRA had seen...

But women like Eleanor weren't ever appointed as leaders. There were a few women Team Directors in Germany, despite UNRRA's preferences. Sometimes bossy, sometimes charismatic—but I could see how difficult it would have been for any woman to be in command. Like walking a tightrope: not too bossy, not too friendly, not too lax, not too self-righteous... Could Eleanor have done it? Instead—Welfare Officer...

I grabbed Eleanor, in passing, in the corridor in Hildegard's house, as she walked by with her face turned away from me. I said we needed to talk. She stared at me, her eyes dark and deep, then she pulled her arm away and walked off without a word.

***

We didn't really talk until the evening Eleanor came back from the Welfare Officers' meeting in Frankfurt.

'I'm sorry, Edmund, I've been avoiding you.'

The tone of her voice sounded different. I said nothing, just waited. At least she wanted to talk.

'This place makes me sad sometimes. And that team meeting. All of you gathered round, citing those poor girls as examples of moral corruption.'

'I didn't—'

'You did.' She nodded grimly. 'You and Pierre see them as signs of moral decay, while Dan and Victor hunt for female flesh and Alma quotes from UNRRA's rulebook. Sometimes I wonder what I'm doing here. The only one who spares a thought for the poor girls, the *real* girls, is Jacques—'

'Jacques?'

'Yes, Jacques. He's got some Catholic obsession about redemption and forgiveness, but unlike most of them, he seems to mean it. I don't know.' She shook her head.

'Eleanor...'

'Yes?'

'This feels like a rough patch. Hilton's visit—it upset me.'

She nodded.

'I want us to get through this.' I had to say something more specific. 'I want our team to continue to run Neukirchen, I want us to stay in UNRRA and I want—'

'Yes?'

'—I want, I need you to stay by me to do this.'

She looked up, puzzled, concerned.

'Eleanor, I know you'd make a better Team Director than me.'

She blinked. 'What—'

'It's true, isn't it?'

'Edmund, I—I don't know what to say.'

'Not often that I hear you say that!'

She laughed, not minding that I was teasing her, clearly still thinking about what I'd said. She reached for her cigarettes, lit one, breathed in, then puffed out.

'I'd like to have tried,' she said finally. 'I'd like to have been given the chance. *Without discrimination*—remember that promise by UNRRA?'

I nodded, happy that we were talking again.

'I don't blame you,' she continued. 'It's not your fault that the world's built round powerful men. But—' She puffed on her cigarette. 'Let's use our time here wisely, let's make sure we—you and me—help those who need it most, alright?'

'You mean women?'

She nodded, then changed the subject.

The Welfare Officers' meeting had not been a success for her, but she'd come back curiously upbeat. Thirty-two people had been there, representing six nations: there were thirty women and two men.

'Why is that?' I asked. 'Don't men care about welfare?'

Eleanor snorted. 'UNRRA sees *welfare* as like playing happy families. It's for the girls. Most men aren't interested.'

Eleanor's long report wasn't welcomed. In fact, it was formally refused and she was told to produce another, quickly, following *exactly* the instructions given by UNRRA. I expected her to be disappointed or angry, but instead she rolled her eyes, puffed on her cigarette and muttered:

'UNRRA doesn't want original thinking. Maybe I shouldn't have quoted so much from *Das Kapital*.'

'Eleanor!'

'Only joking.'

She'd learnt a lot from the other Welfare officers. There were similar problems in all the camps. Eleanor had been discrete, hadn't given away much about Colonel Hilton's visit. She'd learnt that extra-marital affairs, wanted and unwanted pregnancies, and the unwelcome interest of British and American soldiers in DP girls were commonplace everywhere.

'Edmund: you don't need to worry so much. Our camp has its problems, but so does every camp. You can calm down.'

Something in the way she spoke made me believe her. So Hilton's report wouldn't be the body-blow I'd feared. I nodded, feeling calmer for the first time in days.

The meeting had cheered up Eleanor in another way.

'Those women, Edmund—the Welfare Officers—they haven't given up, you know. Some of them are do-gooding old women, better suited to charities and churches, but others—others are different. Hopeful about the future, but with their eyes open. Trained and intelligent. You know, we're seeing something important, here in Germany. Important for the DPs, obviously, but important for us, for UNRRA, for the United Nations, for the whole world. It's—it's a dynamic, and it's happening without anyone noticing.'

Her eyes gleamed. I always liked it when she spoke like this. I forgot the irritations and disappointment of the last few days and smiled at her. She coughed, then started again:

'What with the new socialist government back home and the end of the Empire coming in India—the old crew won't keep control over UNRRA for long, they won't last. Then we'll really see some changes.'

She got up and I knew she was going to type in her little room. I'd have liked us to talk some more, but I wasn't going to stop her. The distance between us had closed, that was enough. Eleanor had a strange look in her eyes.

'I also learnt something very useful,' she said, grinning.

'What?' I was curious now.

'How to get the Poles to go back to Poland.'

She vanished upstairs before I could ask for details.

I fell back into one of Hildegard's chairs and laughed to myself. Thank goodness we were talking again. I'd had the feeling that everything was falling apart. But now—I'd recovered some of my confidence. Our camp was sound and we could feel proud of our work. As for the Poles—even Eleanor couldn't solve the problem of Polish repatriation! She must've been teasing me. No, we'd tackle that problem later.

19. Poles and Poland

Tymon walked into my office early one morning, a broad grin on his face.

'I have something for you.' He placed an envelope on my desk.

It was gleaming white, quite different from the scratchy grey or brown envelopes used by UNRRA and the military. My name and Eleanor's name were beautifully written on the front, in a careful copperplate script. I looked up at Tymon.

'You may open it now,' he said.

Inside, a sheet of thick, white paper, with a finely-printed message.

The Polish Committee of the Neukirchen UNRRA Assembly Centre

invite you to a celebration of Polish culture.

Drinks reception

Chopin—Bartok—Dvorak

Mazurkas, Polkas and Waltzes

Of course! Eleanor had mentioned a concert. But this—this seemed so much more.

'It would be an honour if you and your wife would attend.'

'Tymon, we'd be delighted.'

***

It was a fine August evening, warm rather than hot, with a gentle breeze. We were greeted by smiling young women in white blouses, red waistcoats and multi-coloured skirts, with red beads round their necks and their blonde hair in long plaits braided with red and white ribbons. They pointed the way to follow.

'Where did those dresses come from?' I whispered to Eleanor.

'They've got sewing machines, they can do anything now,' she replied.

Bunting fluttered over the path. We walked arm-in-arm to where the concert would take place, stopping to say *good evening* to volunteer teachers and nurses Eleanor knew. The area had been transformed. Red and white Polish flags fluttered above us. We stopped at a long table with a spotless white linen tablecloth. Rows of champagne glasses stood ready: young men and women in Polish national dress filled glasses. We were given a glass each. We toasted them and then looked round. I couldn't help saying to Eleanor:

'I was right. It is a natural amphitheatre.'

She nodded. 'On a night like this, much better than a stuffy hall.'

At the bottom of the slope was a stout wooden stage, above which flew two enormous Polish flags. Families were walking down the slope, choosing spots to sit, then spreading out khaki blankets. Children in embroidered waistcoats ran back and forth, calling to each other. Tymon greeted us.

'You are our special guests—we have reserved places for you.'

Almost directly in front of the stage there was a row of ten or twelve chairs. Tymon led us down to them and insisted that we sit in the centre.

A thought struck me. 'Dan won't bring his *frat*, will he?'

Eleanor shook her head. 'He's got more sense. No German would be welcome here.'

I sipped my glass. 'Where did this champagne come from?'

'Don't ask,' hissed Eleanor.

The place was filling up. There was a buzz of expectation: people called out to each other, pointing to the places they'd reserved. All the UNRRA team were present, each in carefully ironed uniforms. A couple of American officers joined us in our row of chairs.

'This is good,' Eleanor whispered to me as she looked round. 'So good. They've done all this by themselves, starting with practically nothing. It's real *rehabilitation*.'

I squeezed her arm and nodded. I felt the same pride: we were running a fine camp, despite everything. This was why we'd joined UNRRA.

Eight musicians took their positions on the stage and then Tymon climbed up. Warm applause and shouts echoed round. I think they were crying *long live Poland*. Tymon spoke too long: his voice didn't carry and he chopped and changed between English and Polish in a confusing way. But when he ended, there was thunderous applause and whistles and cheers.

The music started. It was way over my head: harsh, intense, difficult sounds, the eight musicians playing with concentrated fury. After a few minutes, I sensed it told the story of the Poles' experiences during the war: destruction, destitution, separation, exile, persecution, slavery... I didn't try to follow, I sat back, let the sounds waft over me and felt the music's dark themes resonate within me. The two giant flags fluttered. The tone changed, bit by bit. I heard hope for the future, new beginnings, I heard joyful dance tunes emerge in the symphonic intensity.

I studied the others. The Poles looked on with rapt attention: they were determined to enjoy the concert. Pierre was gazing intently at the stage, nodding in time with the music, even raising his hand now and again to follow a particular flourish. Dan was more fascinated than comprehending. Like me, he looked round from the musicians to the audience, trying to grasp the experience. Alma sat still and quiet. The only one who looked relaxed was Victor, who sat back in an easy manner, as if the whole concert had been arranged specially for him.

The music ended. The crowd applauded and cheered. Many got to their feet, some whistled loudly. Bunches of flowers were thrown to the musicians. Tymon stepped onto the stage, holding his hands up for silence, grinning as the applause continued. Finally, he spoke:

the second half of the concert would be for dancing and he invited couples to come forward.

'Well!' I turned to Eleanor.

There were tears in her eyes.

'Oh, Edmund. It was beautiful, so beautiful. It wasn't perfect: they made mistakes with the stresses, the arrangements they used simplified the music—but what an achievement! If these people, having been through so much, can do this—then we must do better.'

She shook her head. When Tymon came to ask if we'd enjoyed the music, Eleanor clung to his arm and congratulated him again and again. It was Tymon's achievement, but both of us shared something of his sense of success. For a moment, we were like proud parents, congratulating their son on his triumph.

Tymon led us back up the slope to the table and offered us more champagne and little bowls of cut plums and redberries. Poles greeted us and chatted about the music. While we drank and ate and talked, the row of chairs was cleared. The sun was sinking and the children were whisked away, back to the bungalows. Young men and women in Polish national dress walked round, placing candles along the stage. Someone flicked a switch somewhere and fairy lights lit up all along the bunting. In a few minutes, we heard a waltz echoing up the hill.

Eleanor grinned at me. 'It's not jitterbugging.'

I looked at her and felt such joy that I was married to this woman.

'It's not—but would you like to dance?'

***

Insistent messages were coming through from the military leaders of the American Zone and from UNRRA HQ. We *must* do more to encourage the repatriation of the DPs. Forms arrived each week, asking how many had gone back. Sometimes telegrams followed, demanding immediate replies. UNRRA policy was clear: nobody could be forced to go somewhere they feared. UNRRA wasn't that sort of organisation. But we were expected to use all means to *persuade* the Poles to leave.

Eleanor said she knew what to do.

'What do they value more than anything else?' she asked me, with a strange smile.

I thought carefully. 'National independence?'

She laughed. 'More than that.'

I shook my head, baffled.

'Cigarettes,' she said.

'Cigarettes?'

'Cigarettes, chocolate, chewing gum, tinned fruit...'

'You mean—*bribe* them?'

She shrugged. 'I wouldn't call it bribery. I prefer to think of it as the provision of some material security to assist with their resettlement.'

It was an idea that had circulated at the Welfare Officers' meeting. We discussed it at a team meeting, then contacted the American base Commander and the Red Cross. The Commander was delighted with the proposal, the Red Cross willing to cooperate. I had posters printed, in English and Polish, offering eight weeks of ration packs for all who registered for the return journey. There was a promise of extra cigarettes for the first twenty-five. I considered holding a public meeting, down in the space by the slope, but Eleanor dissuaded me.

'Let them read the posters and talk among themselves. Give them time,' she said.

***

Two days later, when I arrived in my office, Tymon was waiting for me. I'd barely got behind my desk when he started.

'What are you doing?' His voice was urgent, thick with passion. 'Why? I thought I could trust you—but this!'

His words hurt me.

Tymon continued. 'Do you believe that my people—*my* people—will sell their motherland for a packet of American cigarettes?'

He flung a packet of Lucky Strikes on my desk and glared at me.

'Tymon, I've told you a thousand times: UNRRA policy is to encourage the repatriation of DPs to their native countries.'

'We have no country! It has been butchered, first by the Germans, now by the Russians. Our motherland has gone.'

'There is a space on the map called Poland. It has mines, schools, farms, industries. It is your duty'—he looked up at that point—'to return there and reconstruct your home.'

'I am telling you, no Pole will go back there, no matter how many cigarettes you offer.'

I smiled. 'Tymon, you are wrong.'

He stared at me.

'They are signing up, Tymon.'

'No!'

I pretended to search for a sheet of paper on my desk. In fact, I knew the exact figure.

'Yesterday—' I paused and pulled out a note. 'Yesterday, two hundred and forty-three accepted our offer.'

'No. This cannot be true.'

'It's true, believe me. I'd give you their names, if I didn't think you'd go round and abuse them. There'll be more today.'

'They cannot be Poles, not true Poles.'

'They have Polish identity cards.'

'No, no, no...'

He was absolutely crushed and I felt sorry for him. But what did he expect? That they'd stay forever in Germany, tending their gardens? True, some were too ill to travel: it would be a tough, ten-day journey. For this first trip, there were only basic boxcars, with no amenities at all. The old and sick would stay here, until they recovered their strength, or until UNRRA found better carriages.

I was right and Tymon was wrong. Despite his loud disapproval, more Poles signed up in the following days. Soon, there were over five hundred: enough to make UNRRA happy.

***

Eleanor wasn't as pleased as I'd expected.

'It's good they've signed up, don't get me wrong,' she told me over coffee in Hildegard's drawing-room. 'All things considered, Poland's probably the best place for them. But—' I waited as she puffed on her cigarette and then coughed briefly. '—it's a shame that it had to be done this way.'

'It was your idea.'

She ran her fingers through her hair. 'I know, I know. And it's better we're using the carrot rather than the stick. But—'

'What is it, Eleanor?'

'I wanted repatriation to be a voluntary choice, based on free will and consent. That's what the new Europe ought to be: democratic. Instead, we've bribed them. We're building a new society on stacks of American cigarettes.'

'But they can't stay here forever!'

'No, I suppose not.'

'And, as Welfare Officer—'

It was Eleanor's job to accompany the returning Poles to Poland.

She nodded. 'Yes, I've got to go with them. A shame: I would've liked a holiday, but this—'

I laughed. 'It's not going to be a holiday!' But her comment got me thinking of something else. 'We're due a holiday, you know.

We've been working hard for over five months, we've earnt it. Given the chance, where would you like to go?'

'I was thinking about London. Does it feel different with the new socialist government? And then seeing Muriel and the bookshop.'

I hadn't thought about the bookshop for weeks.

'Yes,' I said. 'That's an idea.'

The others had taken time off. Dan and Victor had gone to Paris for a fortnight and came back looking very smug but saying nothing. Pierre had a brief break in Vienna and Alma had visited relatives in Copenhagen. Eleanor and I had thought about going away, but there was too much happening in the camp, so we couldn't leave, not yet.

'And now,' I said, trying to cheer her up, 'you've a three-week round trip to Poland, all expenses paid by UNRRA.'

She sighed. 'Those boxcars are dreadful. They shake so much that it's impossible to write and difficult to read.'

'I'd thought you'd feel—well—happier or prouder. It's something that you've achieved.'

'Yes—but not the way I wanted.' She puffed on her cigarette again and then looked at me. 'Oh, Edmund, would you come as well? It would be less grim with you there.'

'Me? Leave the camp for three weeks? How could I?'

'Victor and Pierre could take over. And Tymon will still be here with his committee: they run half the camp anyway. I know it won't be a holiday, but at least it'll be a break. We'd get some time to ourselves.'

I sipped my coffee and thought about it. I'd been spending too long in that office and I was worried about Eleanor. She was working so hard and sometimes she looked exhausted. Too often we seemed on different sides. I was touched that she'd asked me. And I still felt proud that we'd persuaded five hundred Poles to go back. Maybe it was right that I should accompany them.

Eleanor looked at me, a smile on her lips. 'You said you wanted to see the world beyond Margate.'

I grinned and said I'd be delighted to join her.

***

The city station must once have been a fine, red-brick building, with its curved arches welcoming crowds for journeys across Germany. I could imagine newspaper kiosks and taxi cabs in the square in front. Commercial travellers, businessmen, commuters, families on holiday and foreign tourists would have crowded in here. Now, it was a battered wreck. Not a pane of glass remained in the windows of its upper-floor offices, its brickwork and plaster-work was smoke-blackened and scarred with great white gashes from bombing. In the square, children begged for cigarettes and—sadder still—a group of sickly-looking, idle adolescents hung around. They were dressed in ill-fitting, patched-up clothes and looked like they'd pinch anything from unwary travellers. Now and again, a German policeman would tell them to move on: they'd shift to the opposite corner of the square and then drift back towards the entrance. We'd seen such sights again and again, to the point where we'd learnt to ignore them, but something about that sad station touched me. Reconstruction was going to take a long, long time.

When we arrived, Eleanor was angry. 'He shouldn't have done it!'

'The American Commander was trying to be kind, Eleanor. And it'll make our journey more comfortable.'

'But the whole idea was to share the journey with the Poles. If it's going to be tough, let's show that we're with them. Instead—'

'Instead we'll sit on upholstered chairs in a proper carriage. Maybe we'll even be able to sleep! That's not so terrible.'

'We'll be like Victorian ladies. Or, worse still, like great-mama UNRRA, here to watch the suffering of others and pity them.'

Eleanor was always like this. A latter-day Puritan, suspicious of any perks or favours. I could see her point. It might have been a nice gesture to share the journey with the Poles. However, we weren't DPs. Our work for UNRRA gave us the right to a few comforts: we'd earnt our carriage.

The train was three hours late. It was enormous: thirty huge boxcars for the Poles and their possessions and one carriage for us. The Red Cross supplied a Swedish and a Norwegian nurse, and the American army lent us two GIs to guard the boxcar with the rations. The Polish DPs weren't like the Russians. They took no tables and no tyres, but they did have many prams, a few bicycles and countless packages: crammed into old suitcases, stuffed into shopping-bags, wrapped in brown paper and tied up with string, shoved into rucksacks. During the long wait before our departure, Eleanor walked up and down that endless train, making sure that each boxcar contained no fewer than fifteen people and no more than twenty. There were cries and protests whenever she moved people from one carriage to another. She tried to respect family groups and usually asked single adults to move, but it wasn't easy.

'They're vulnerable,' she explained to me. 'They've seen families smashed apart by war. Asking them to separate, even for a few days, terrifies them.'

While we waited, I strolled along the platform. The boxcars were basic, bloody basic: just empty wooden structures. When we'd been expecting to travel in one, Eleanor had been given some advice: find a boxcar that hasn't been used to transport horses or potatoes and one that doesn't smell. None seemed to meet all those criteria. But the Poles were happy. They showed the same home-making ability that we'd seen in the camp. Inside the boxcars, they banged nails into the walls to use as hooks for their bags and coats; they stretched bits of rope from one side to the other, on which they hung sheets and towels; they spread khaki blankets on the floor to cushion themselves during the journey. Most came with little stoves which they nailed down. These would keep their carriages warm and let them make tea or soup. The lavatory was a bucket in a corner, hidden behind a suspended blanket. The Poles decorated the outside of their carriages with branches from bushes, with red and white flags and with chalked slogans. A violinist began scratching out a tune and suddenly a boxcar turned into a choir: but whether their words were patriotic or romantic, I couldn't tell. Little flasks of something—*bimber*?—were passed round and sipped. Perhaps it would have been fun to share these unhomely homes with them, maybe Eleanor was right.

At last, the train whistle hooted and the sound echoed along the platform. Eleanor came running back.

'They need more nappies in that boxcar!' she shouted, pointing backwards.

I put my arm round her and shepherded her into our carriage.

'But—but...' she said.

'The train's about to leave. The nappies will have to wait.'

I made her sit down and told her to get her breath. I took out a bar of chocolate from my rucksack, broke it open and gave her a piece.

'I don't like American chocolate,' she said, but she bit on it and accepted another chunk.

The whistle went again, a long, impatient hoot. The train jolted and cheers rang out from the boxcars, full of hope and excitement. Eleanor jumped up, pushed down the window, stuck her head out and looked round. The wheels of the engine screeched and a great puff of black smoke floated past. Eleanor promptly closed the window. Another jolt rocked our carriage.

'We're moving!' she cried.

***

The nurses introduced themselves: Lili and Sidonie. I asked if they'd ever been on a journey like this. They smiled and said no. Eleanor explained that the spare seats in our carriage were for the sick and for anyone who had an accident. But at this point, everyone seemed well.

Over the next few days, the battered German railways tested the suspension of our carriage to its limits—it juddered and jerked in an alarming manner. God knows what it was like in the boxcars! Our carriage was immediately after the engine, so we kept the windows closed to keep out the soot. But the journey wasn't as bad as Eleanor feared. I'd wanted to take some UNRRA files with me, but Eleanor had put her foot down. Instead, I had my H.G. Wells anthology, which I hadn't read since that Southampton boarding-house. Within a couple of hours, I felt happy. No one was knocking at my door asking for visas or ironing boards. I started re-reading *The History of Mr Polly*, which made me miss London. If the train shook so much that I couldn't read, I snapped off a piece of chocolate and stared out the window. Germany must once have been a beautiful country. Sometimes Eleanor held protracted discussions with Lili and Sidonie about child welfare, but often she huddled up to me, put her head on my shoulder and fell asleep. Poor thing! The last few weeks had exhausted her. I'd doze off too and then we'd awake with a start as the train screeched and shuddered to a halt.

We had a rough idea of the train's route, but no idea about when and where it would stop. There were many, many stops, mostly with no warning, usually in open countryside, with empty fields stretching out for miles. Each halt was an opportunity for our travelling village to open its doors. Those boxcars weren't comfortable and everyone wanted to stretch their legs. There was often a more urgent reason—the men strode a few steps to the left of the train, the women a little further to the right and they'd relieve themselves in rows. During the stops, a few would make their way to the ration car and ask for things—bread, cigarettes or chocolate. Eleanor told the GIs to grant all small requests, but not to give complete ration packs to anyone. We soon had our first casualties: people who'd been making tea or soup when the train jerked and sent them crashing into their stoves. They came to us with nasty burns on their hands, even on their faces. Lili and Sidonie would administer creams and plasters, and tell them to be more careful. One or two mothers had concerns about their babies and Lili or Sidonie would walk along the line of boxcars, bringing pills and salves.

Towards sundown, the train would usually haul itself into a siding and shudder to a halt. People would queue at the ration car, take provisions back to their boxcars and the air would fill with the smell of stews and soups. I remember those evenings with great fondness. The Poles walked up and down the length of the train, exchanging greetings and jokes, sharing flasks of *bimber* and, as the sun went down, they lit lanterns which shone with a soft yellow glow and turned the bare boxcars into warm, cosy places. Violins and accordions came out and the evening air filled with song. Once again, I wondered if we should have refused the carriage and mucked in with a Polish family. It might have been good to really get to know them.

Less often, we stopped at stations. Here, travelling salesmen—the sort we'd call spivs in England—walked the length of the train, shouting out their wares in German or approximate English: schnapps, stockings, sausages, newspapers... They'd exchange them for cigarettes. Most stations had a water hydrant and a queue of half-dressed people would form for impromptu open-air showers. But there was tension in the air. The local Germans didn't like Poles and the Poles had scores to settle. This was their last chance and nearly always there'd be a scuffle. Our GIs would come running, sometimes with a Polish official from Tymon's committee. When there wasn't any trouble, Eleanor and I would stroll around. In some

German stations there were proper shops. In one, I wanted to buy some cheese and was surprised when the saleswoman asked to be paid with cash, not cigarettes. It was a small sign that economic normality was returning to Germany.

At night Eleanor and I would stretch out on two three-seater benches that faced each other. We'd drape blankets over ourselves and soon drift away. Normally I'd wake first in the grey morning light and I'd look at my wife. Look where she'd taken me! From lonely bookshop-owner to Team Director, on a train to Poland with five hundred Poles.

Eleanor's hair would be rough and tangled, her eyes half-closed and she'd pull her blanket up to keep the morning chill away. Sidonie would come with a mug of coffee and Eleanor would then drag herself upright, find her cigarettes and blow out great puffs of smoke. I'd cross over to her bench, give her a hug and feel the night-time warmth of her body. Sometimes I'd tease her.

'How did great-mama UNRRA sleep?'

She'd laugh and say next time she'd book a first-class carriage. Then one of the Poles would call for her from outside and Eleanor would get up to organise a hunt for a lost child or to reassure an old lady who had doubts about her return to the Motherland.

I felt close to Eleanor in those days. We had different expectations of UNRRA and different approaches to its work—sometimes we argued, but not often. That long train journey gave us time together and we filled it with our love for each other.

***

At the border into Czechoslovakia we were greeted by a ridiculously overlong customs check. All the DPs' documentation was carefully read and then vigorously stamped by a be-spectacled little man. That took hours. In Poland, the first station after the border had been decorated by a repatriation committee; red and white flags flew and patriotic music played over the loudspeakers. To my surprise, our Poles seemed shy. They stayed in their boxcars, peeking out from behind half-closed doors. Then an announcement came out over the loudspeakers: free coffee was available—meaning real coffee, not the *ersatz* coffee of Germany. The boxcars' doors opened and the Poles jumped out, in ones or twos at first, but soon whole families pushed along the platform. A few minutes later, hundreds were singing the Polish national anthem: the booming sounds of their patriotism echoed over the station platforms. Eleanor and I smiled at each other. We'd completed this stage of our mission.

Poland wasn't attractive. It was full of beggars and there was rubbish and stinking mud all along the tracks. Crowds of people camped out at the stations in the open air, waiting to get to their destinations. But there were proper shops. We visited them.

'Paperclips!' I said. 'I haven't had new paperclips for months. The Americans don't seem able to supply them.'

Eleanor bought pots and pans, scissors and thimbles, remarking she knew DP families could use these. Further down the road, we found a bookshop with a shelf of English-language works. But they were expensive and neither of us fancied odd volumes of Dickens. I was tempted by a Victorian edition of William Morris's poetry, but then I realised that I'd never have time to read it once we were back in Germany. We were saying goodbye to the bookshop owner, when Eleanor spotted something on the next shelf. It was an English translation of a German novel, *Steppenwolf*, which Eleanor said I had to try.

'German?' I said.

'Edmund, come on. Don't start sounding like Dan and Pierre. They're not a cursed race. Are you going to burn Beethoven and Marx as well?'

I bought it.

The plan was that our train would pick up a few hundred *volksdeutsche* and take them back to Germany. Neither of us liked the sound of this: these were people who had lived outside Germany, but who declared themselves to be German during Hitler's rise. Now, after his fall, they were beleaguered minorities in the newly-liberated countries. Eleanor and I talked to the nurses and GIs: we agreed that we six would occupy the carriage, where we'd store the remaining rations. In the event, none of the *volksdeutsche* arrived at the station.

'SNAFU,' I remarked to Eleanor.

'What?'

I was delighted that I'd picked up some military slang she didn't know.

'Situation Normal: All Fucked Up,' I told her.

She clapped her hands in delight and burst out laughing, then said all Europe was one big SNAFU.

Our great beast of a train was almost empty as it rattled its way back along the battered railways and devastated cities of Europe. Were we going home? Not exactly, but both of us felt better after that trip to Poland.

20. Decline and Fall

'But you're *married.*' I wasn't going to let Victor get away with it.

He looked away: his beady eyes, distorted and half-hidden by his thick, square spectacles, darted round my office, eventually settling on the view through the window. Eleanor struck a match, lit a cigarette and glared at him.

'Victor,' I began again, 'your private life is your concern, but I have to think about the team as a whole. We need to be sure—'

'—we need to be sure we can trust you,' interrupted Eleanor. 'There are many vulnerable young women among the DPs and—'

Victor looked shocked. 'Of course. I understand that. I'd never—'

He stopped and we sat in awkward silence for a moment. Eleanor offered him a cigarette. He sighed, then accepted it.

'So, your wife—' she began, speaking more softly and carefully.

'Mind your goddamn business!' he told her and puffed furiously on his cigarette.

I stared at him and waited. Eventually, he looked at me, then at Eleanor.

'It hasn't been a proper marriage for years.' He spoke uneasily. 'No children. I mean, six years ago, Rose seemed a nice girl and I had a good job.'

'You were a banker?' Eleanor asked.

He nodded. 'On the administrative side, not the financial. Thought I'd get drafted in '42, but the guys in Washington decided that banks were essential for the economy. I got seconded to a government department, pushing money around, making sure the war industries got financed, making sure they used the money properly. Basic stuff.'

'And Rose?' I asked.

'Stayed at home while I went to Washington.' He looked up, worried. 'There was no funny business, really. I missed her! Phoned her two or three times a week, when I could.'

He shook his head, looked down, sighed, puffed on his cigarette, then began again.

'Hell, I know to you people I must seem dull and conservative...'

Eleanor had the grace to shake her head.

'But you gotta understand what a thrill work in Washington seemed to a boy from small-town Missouri. This was under FDR—'

'Roosevelt?' I asked.

Victor nodded.

'He'll be missed,' I said.

'Sure he will. Mind you, he sure was sick in those last months—'

'And under Roosevelt...' prompted Eleanor.

Victor smiled. 'There was a social programme: taxing the rich, talking to organised labour, providing benefits for the returning GIs... Using money to help the whole nation, using it to build the nation. It made me think of things I'd never considered...'

'While Rose?' I asked.

'Still a small-town girl. Hell, she'd cross the road if she saw a coloured man coming towards her on a sidewalk.'

'Will you divorce her?' asked Eleanor.

'I...' Victor hesitated. 'I... It's difficult...'

'Because...' asked Eleanor.

'Hell, I don't know,' said Victor, stubbing out his cigarette in the ashtray on my desk. 'Here, everything seems different...'

'Everything is different,' I said. 'We're in Germany, for a start.'

'Sure, sure...' He paused, looked out of the window.

'What does Greta expect?' asked Eleanor.

Victor looked at her for a moment. 'She wants to leave this place, of course. Who wouldn't? She's not dumb.'

'And you?' I said.

'I kinda like it here, but I don't think it'll last.'

'No?' I said. 'What about the talk of permanent British and American bases here?'

Victor nodded absent-mindedly, staring out the window. We heard the sound of a truck drawing up to the camp entrance, stopping, then starting again. Victor pulled himself together and looked at Eleanor, then me.

'I guess I worry that if I took Greta back to the States—which would not be easy—I guess I might find that everything felt different. I might decide that I'd be happier with Rose. I don't know.'

'Victor!' Eleanor said. 'Women aren't—aren't coats that you put on or take off at will. You can't have one for Germany and one for America!'

'No?' said Victor quietly.

'No,' said Eleanor.

Victor and Eleanor glared at each other, then Eleanor coughed. Victor seemed to have nothing more to say.

'So,' I said, 'to return to the original topic. You *cannot* take Greta to tomorrow's cocktail party at the American commander's house—'

'But she so wants to come—'

'No. I will not allow it. Nor will I permit you to bring her into the camp anymore.'

Victor nodded sadly, looking out the window again.

'And I would prefer you not to invite her to your house, although I suppose I can't stop you.'

A grin flashed up on Victor's face, which he quickly hid.

'Is that clear?' I asked.

'Sure, sure, it's clear,' he said, avoiding my eyes.

He left a moment later.

'Well.' Eleanor looked at me.

I nodded. 'First Dan, now Victor. Must be something in the water.'

'Must be something that happens when you place young, well-paid men next to young, penniless women, more likely.'

'It's not—not prostitution,' I said.

'No?' Eleanor raised her eyebrows. 'Bloody close to it, if you ask me.'

'Still, he seemed to accept my conditions.'

'So everything's alright?'

'No, I'm not saying that, but...'

Eleanor ran her fingers through her hair, then looked round my office.

'Sometimes I wonder what UNRRA is for,' she said. 'What are we doing here?'

'We're helping people. We're helping the most vulnerable.'

'We seem to be doing many other things as well.'

'Such as?'

'Such as setting up a new ruling class in a new colony, with generous sexual privileges granted to all its male representatives.'

***

The Base Commander's cocktail party was held out of town, in his hillside villa. We drove out in a convoy of requisitioned cars. Victor, who knew the way, led in his silver-grey Mercedes. Dan went with him. Pierre and Alma were driven by Jacques in a well-polished black Daimler, its chrome bumpers gleaming in the sunshine. I drove Eleanor in our new bottle-green Daimler.

'I could drive, you know,' she said to me.

'I know, but think how it will look if I arrive at the Commander's villa driven by my wife.'

Eleanor tutted. We'd talked about this before: we didn't agree, but it wasn't worth arguing. Eleanor lit a cigarette and stared out of the window. The countryside was lovely, the trees still decorated with the orange leaves of autumn. The road snaked up a valley, taking us through shady forests and then, higher up, through terraced vineyards with lines and lines of the stumps of vines.

Victor's car led us round a long, wide curve and then, near the top of the valley, we were out into the open. It was impossible to miss the Commander's villa: an elegant white building, perched at the top of the valley, immediately suggesting good living and high culture.

'Gosh!' said Eleanor. 'These Americans—they know how to pick their prizes, don't they?'

I felt grateful that I'd refused Dan's suggestion that we all go in one of the three-ton trucks. This was an opportunity for us to get to know the Commander better. He was a useful connection and I thought we should be working more closely with him. I wanted to impress him.

There was a wide courtyard in the front of the villa. A white-jacketed assistant greeted us at the gate and pointed us towards a space to park. As we got out, we could hear music. A string quartet was playing on the veranda that overlooked the valley.

'Mozart?' said Eleanor. 'Yes, I think so. I suppose everyone considers him an acceptable German.'

None of us had any evening dress, so we all wore our khaki uniforms, but with freshly-pressed creases. As we walked towards the villa, I was relieved to see that most of the men were in uniform, but here and there, amidst the khaki and blue-grey throng, there were splashes of colour from glamorous red and green cocktail dresses. These were the first signs of the Occupation wives, as they were called. We hoped they would soften and reform the American presence. These women had bright lipstick, carefully-applied make-up and glowing hair. The more daring wore backless dresses.

'She'll catch her death in that,' said Eleanor, eyeing a sparkling blonde in a turquoise-blue dress that exposed all her shoulders and most of her bosom.

We walked up the white marble steps, through enormous double doors and into the entrance hall. Here, the throng was at its loudest: I heard American accents, English accents and a few French words. Two maids—German, I supposed—walked through the crowd, offering canapés from polished silver trays. I picked up two glasses of champagne and then we pushed our way through the hall, past the open French windows and onto the veranda. There were fewer people here—perhaps it was too chilly for backless dresses. The quartet were odd assortment: the lady cellist's black evening dress had definitely seen better days. German, I thought, looking at them. Their skin had that grey, unhealthy quality that came from a diet of bread, potatoes and thin soup. The view was spectacular: the setting sun illuminated the twists and angles of the valley's terraces.

'So this is how the other half lives,' muttered Eleanor.

'Where's the Commander? I wanted to talk to him about that hole in the road at our entrance.' I looked round, but could only see American officers and a few of their wives.

Eleanor coughed and said, 'He'll be holding court somewhere inside, I suppose.'

Pierre joined us, holding a champagne flute. 'It was good luck that the bombers did not reach here!'

'Lucky indeed,' I replied.

Pierre sipped his champagne and then smiled. 'This is too fine a place for UNRRA, of course. We have to live next to the DPs.'

Eleanor smiled back, but did not reply.

'But what is it? Who did it belong to?' I asked.

'This *château* was built in the eighteenth century,' said Pierre. 'During the war, it belonged to Hitler's favourite publisher, I believe.'

Eleanor looked away.

Pierre looked at me. 'What do you think, Edmund? Would you like to live here?'

'Here?' I was surprised by Pierre's question and took a few moments to consider the gleaming white walls and the high-ceilinged rooms. Then I shook my head.

'No. It'd need too many servants.'

Eleanor burst out laughing and Pierre smiled.

'That's Edmund for you!' said Eleanor. 'So down-to-earth. The Great Incorruptible.'

'But you have a servant in your house: Hildegard,' said Pierre.

'Yes,' I said. 'But there's just one of her and that's enough.'

'We're getting to like her,' added Eleanor. 'I suppose her husband was a Nazi, but—'

I knew that Pierre wouldn't want to hear that: he held to his hard line of implacable hostility to all Germans, without exceptions. I interrupted to change the subject.

'When you see a place like this—it gives a real impression of how long the Occupation will last. What do you think, Pierre? How long will the Americans, British and French be here?'

'A very long time, I hope. Long enough to make sure that there will never be another Hitler.'

I spotted Sam, the lieutenant who was our main contact with the American base. He made his way through the guests on the veranda and joined us at the balustrade.

'Cheers!' he said, raising his glass of champagne, and we chinked glasses with him.

'Getting ready for winter?' he asked.

'Yes: *winterization* continues,' I answered and we all groaned at UNRRA's assault on the English language.

'I hear they'll be needing some *winterization* in England as well,' said Sam, smiling.

I nodded vaguely, reminded once more that I wasn't keeping up with things in England. What had Muriel said in her last letter? Coal rationing was now stricter than during the war.

'Where do you live, Sam?' asked Eleanor.

'Nowhere as grand as this,' he said. 'I found a little house in the town.'

'The suburbs?' said Eleanor.

'Yeah, one of those parts that our bombers missed.'

'Thank God for the inefficiency of aerial bombardment!' I said, and everyone laughed. We exchanged a series of jokes about whether it had been the RAF or the USAF that had missed the street that Sam lived on. Pierre beat us all by declaring it was most probably the French, which made us all laugh again.

Our talk turned to a more serious topic: the *residue*, the DPs who refused to return to their homelands.

'Can't you guys do more?' asked Sam.

'We can't force anyone to go,' said Eleanor. 'Although we have our secret weapons to persuade them.'

Sam raised his eyebrows and waited.

Eleanor smiled. 'They're Lucky Strikes, Hershey bars, bubble gum, spam...'

Sam roared with laughter.

'And we've deployed them in all-out combat,' she continued. 'But still we can't move this entrenched enemy.'

'Sometimes I think this problem will get worse,' said Pierre.

We all looked at him, for he sounded so serious.

'At first, we thought it would be easy. We would help people return to their homes, yes? But what happens when people do not recognise their homes? The Jews—'

'Don't talk to me about the Jews!' said Sam. 'The problems those people are causing.'

I didn't like that, but I'd heard the military talk that way so often. To them, DPs were problems and obstacles, never people.

'But Sam,' I said. 'We can see the pattern now—there was an industrial slaughter—'

'Sure, sure,' he said. 'So let's find them a new home.'

'That would be best,' said Pierre.

Sam spotted someone at the other end of the veranda and moved away. He was replaced by another American officer, tall and broad-shouldered, with a big smile. We introduced ourselves and he told us to call him Mike, in that friendly, informal way that Americans often have. He insisted on returning to the topic of the *residue*.

'But they gotta leave. What else do they expect?' he said.

'We're UNRRA,' said Eleanor. 'We don't use coercion, we work *with* people.'

'But still—' Mike wasn't satisfied.

'And another of our roles is *rehabilitation*.' Eleanor spoke as she might to a rather dim child.

'Sure, but that's best done in their own country.'

'Their countries aren't ready. There's been a war: cities have been smashed, roads and railways destroyed.'

Mike shot Eleanor a look. I could see he was annoyed with her.

'So we just let them live here, doing nothing, living off other people's taxes?'

'They're not doing nothing. They learn trades and new languages, they perform concerts—'

'Very useful, I'm sure, but all things best done in their own countries—'

'But they have no country! Can't you see that?'

'I see their countries on the map.'

'What you see on the map doesn't exist on the ground.'

Mike paused to sip his champagne and began again. 'I think that you people are too soft on them. Sure, they've had a hard time—'

Now I was getting angry. 'Now look here. We've been slaving away, all of us, day and night to encourage repatriation. But we're not

the Army, thank goodness. We can't just issue them marching orders.'
How dare this man come in and tell us how we should do our jobs?

'More's the shame. This situation—it can't continue, it just can't
continue.'

'There's been a war,' Eleanor said.

'For Chrissake, I know there's been a war! I lost some damn fine
men in it. And now it's time—'

'—it's time for reconstruction and that's going to take at least as
long as the war,' I told him.

Mike shook his head. 'There's a limit to what America can do
here. You know that?'

Thankfully, he left a few minutes later. Carrie joined us. She was
an Occupation wife, dressed in a glittering green cocktail dress. She
asked about schools and activities for her children. She wanted to
learn German and even hoped to write a couple of newspaper articles
about her time here. I rather liked her: maybe these women would
reform their menfolk. I hoped something similar might happen in
the British zone.

I never got to speak to the Commander about the problem with
our road. He always seemed to be on the other side of the room. It
was frustrating. Instead of getting closer to him, I had the sense that
we were pushed further to the margins. For these people, UNRRA
was just a stopgap and perhaps one that had served its purpose. They
weren't interested in what we'd achieved with the Poles.

The more we looked at the *château*, the more we were surprised.

'The Commander seems such a practical, feet-on-the-ground
type,' I whispered to Eleanor. 'Who would've thought?'

'He must think he's forming a new elite,' she replied. 'I expect it's
the same in the British zone. Look at those new Officers' Clubs.'

We had a surprise when we left. Pierre asked if he could travel
back in our car: he had something important to tell us. I looked at

Eleanor, she nodded and so he joined us, sitting in the back of the Daimler with Eleanor.

'I heard you coughing this evening,' he said to her.

'I've got some bug,' she replied. 'The DPs, you know...'

'I fear it is not a *bug*. I have heard you coughing this way before. I think you have tuberculosis.'

'No!'

'I think it may be so. You must have an X-Ray at the American military hospital.'

***

Pierre's suspicions seemed correct: there was a shadow, thankfully only a slight one, in Eleanor's right lung. Pierre insisted she stop working, ordered her to give up smoking and prescribed an immediate holiday. He spoke in a small, quiet voice, in oddly-accented English, but in those moments he possessed an unanswerable authority. Eleanor didn't argue—she didn't even protest about giving up smoking.

As soon as I'd heard this news, it made sense to me. Thank goodness Pierre had spotted it. Eleanor had been working too hard: rushing back and forth across the camp, searching for every object under the sun, contacting the American base, liaising with the Polish Committee... It was too much. We talked after breakfast and agreed that we missed London. We felt guilty, as Muriel wrote us long, detailed letters and days later we sent her short, rushed notes. The journey to London would be difficult: another rail-based odyssey, but thankfully the trains westwards were quicker and more comfortable than the ones to Poland. It would take two days. We'd stay in London for a few weeks, maybe even until Christmas. There were doctors we knew who'd make sure that Eleanor had recovered before we returned.

We told Pierre our plans later that morning. He frowned.

'London?' he said.

Eleanor laughed and then coughed a little. 'Pierre, you're like all Frenchmen. You think of London as a city where it rains all the time and it's constantly foggy. I remember beautiful, crisp, clear winter mornings.'

Pierre shook his head.

The next morning, after breakfast, he returned to our house. He met us in the drawing-room and took coffee with us. He spoke in the same calm, firm tone: he'd arranged a trip to Morocco. We were stunned.

'Morocco?' I said. 'But that's hundreds of miles away. I've never—'

'We've decided to go to London!' protested Eleanor.

'It will be dry and warm, which is what you need most. You can fly there in less than 24 hours. You change at Marseilles.'

'An aeroplane? I've never flown—' said Eleanor.

Pierre looked her in the eye. 'This could be very serious. I believe that staying in London during the winter will not help you and could harm you. I have a friend in Casablanca, a doctor. She will look after you.'

PART IV
INTERLUDE

'It's a time of contrasts.'
Elsie Culver, ecumenical representative of American churches,
visitor to Europe in October—December 1945
'A country without a guide-book.'
Edith Wharton, visitor to Morocco, 1927

21. Gratified Desire

I screwed up my eyes and scanned the horizon. Sparks of golden sunlight, peacock-blue sea, azure-blue sky. Eleanor had transformed herself into some fabulous amphibious creature: she was somewhere out there. She'd given up smoking and, after just three weeks away from Neukirchen, her constant coughing had ended. Each day she grew stronger, each day she swum out further. Soon she'd swim back, glistening and glowing. This break was doing us both good. I felt better, more settled after the chaos of Germany. I'd brought my pills, just in case, but I hadn't taken one for ages.

It was too bright to scan the horizon. I looked down, where a ripple of water gurgled in over a ridge of golden sand. Flickers of sunlight sparkled on its crest, then faded away. Salty sea smells floated on the breeze. I smiled, but pulled my ankle in, under the shade of the umbrella—I hadn't forgotten last week's nasty sunburn. The water trickled back, over the little sandy ridge. This was one of the world's greatest pleasures: watching the tide flow in and then watching it go out. Who needed more?

It wasn't that hot. The mid-70s, perhaps. But hotter than late autumn in Germany: hotter, brighter, sunnier, quieter... And in this little suntrap, our own secret beach, hotter still. Eleanor loved the sea and sun. After our first days in Morocco, she refused the sticky sunscreen lotion that Dr Thérèse had given us. I still used it. The early mornings weren't bad: I'd walk in gentle yellow sunshine to the dock-workers' café and buy coffee and bread. And in the evenings, we'd walk round the promontory, maybe two or three times, watching the sky turn pink, then purple. But midday remained risky for me. Either I stayed under the umbrella or I applied the sunscreen.

I spotted something in the waves: Eleanor's arm? Her head? No... Just a foam on a wave. Further out, a steamer chugged along to the French port at Casablanca. At first, I worried when Eleanor swum out, further and further, until she merged with the waves. But now... She'd proved her point. Nothing touched her.

Would Amira cook tonight? She hadn't come last night. Dr Thérèse had warned us: she wasn't reliable. When she did come, she cooked us endless variants of the same basic dish of lamb and this strange, half-sweet, half-savoury Moroccan rice, prepared on an age-old stove in the corner of our one-room cottage. Amira's cooking filled the air with warm, spicy smells. Sometimes she added raisins and apricots, sometimes peppers and onions, sometimes parsley and paprika, concocting wonderful flavours I'd never tasted before. Eleanor tried to talk with her, but Amira's Arabic-inflected French and Eleanor's schoolgirl French weren't well-matched.

When the meal was ready, Amira would rap on the old iron saucepan, smile at us, utter a few words in Arabic and then leave. We'd grab the cracked dinner-plates, the bent old forks and fall on her food. Each day, we walked and swam; each day, we were hungrier for her cooking. If Amira didn't come, I went to the café and scrounged beer, bread, butter and cheese. But before Amira arrived, there'd be time to...

There! I spotted an arm and a head, high on an incoming wave. Eleanor, my mermaid, coming closer, her head and shoulders visible, rising from the rippling sea. For a second, three perfect, pure colours met: the peacock-blue sea, the glistening wet-black of her swimming costume and the warm golden-brown of her skin. She shook the water from her long black hair, then spotted me. She took another step, then stopped, an arm on her hip, leg thrust forward, grinning at me. I felt a shiver of frustration: the black costume hid the curves and slopes I knew so well. Images flashed through my mind: a mermaid—one of those busty eighteenth-century marble statues; an Oriental water-goddess; a Hollywood starlet... She was none of those things, she was lovelier than all of them.

Seconds later, she was under the umbrella, shaking her hair so that drops of cold seawater fell on me. She laughed at my yelps. Then she towelled her hair dry, humming to herself.

'Think I'll have a cigarette,' I said, to tease her.

'No, you won't.'

'What'll you do to stop me?'

'I'll think of something.'

We both laughed.

She rolled up the towels and packed them in her basket. I pulled down the umbrella and put it over my shoulder. We walked from our sandy cove, hand in hand, following the track between the jagged rocks, to the cottage and its old brass bed. Eleanor smelt fresh and salty.

'This place,' I said, 'it's just—perfect.'

'You don't want much, do you Edmund? A tiny, rundown holiday cottage, ten yards of beach and an old Arab woman who'll cook for you most evenings.'

'Who needs more?' I smiled. 'And yet—there is something else.'

We stopped, kissed quickly, then walked on.

'That old bed!' said Eleanor. 'It's hard to believe the noises it makes: all those creaks, jingles and rattles. It's like some weird symphony.'

'A symphony that plays twice a day.'

She chuckled, then gripped my hand tighter. The cottage wasn't far.

22. The Colonial City

'We can't stay here all the time!'

Eleanor shrugged. 'Why not? I have to go to Casablanca once a week to see Dr Thérèse, but apart from that... I thought you liked it here.'

'We're in Morocco! We can't stay in this tiny cottage for weeks on end.'

'Casablanca's just another post-war city, Edmund. We've seen them all.'

'It's not like a European city, it's different—it hasn't been smashed to pieces, for a start.'

'I'm not interested in touring the sights: seeing the picturesque statue, admiring the pretty mosque, strolling along the magnificent boulevard... And as for all that nonsense about how "far-sighted" General Lyautey created a new form of "humanitarian colonialism".'

Eleanor did have a point. We'd found a guidebook, in French, which she'd translated to me. The eulogies it offered to Lyautey, who'd run Morocco in the 1910s, were unbelievable and rather sickening. I certainly didn't want to follow some sort of pilgrimage to his memory. But weren't there other places to see?

'We could go to the Arab quarter,' I suggested.

'Hah!'

The expression on Eleanor's face was unreadable. I didn't understand. She was normally so brave, so independent: of the two of us, she was usually the one who wanted to try new things.

'Aren't you feeling well?'

She looked up. 'I'm fine. Giving up smoking wasn't easy, but I can feel the difference in my lungs. So much stronger! Apart from that—you know, I'm not sure that Pierre's diagnosis was correct. Dr Thérèse couldn't see any trace of TB in the X-ray photographs.'

'So...' I said.

'So what?'

'So why don't you want to explore a bit? We won't get this chance again. How many English people can say they've been *to Morocco*?'

She shrugged and looked away.

I wouldn't give up. 'Next time you go to Dr Thérèse—'

'Alright, we'll get the bus together and then I'll leave you at the square.'

'You won't come with me?'

She shook her head. It was very strange.

***

On Tuesday, we walked to the bus-stop, joining the queue of dock-workers. Eleanor had seen Dr Thérèse several times: we were fairly sure that her next visits were just formalities. Sitting next to Eleanor on the bus, I stared out the window, but my first impressions confirmed what she'd said about Casablanca. Just another city. Four-storey, five-storey blocks, mostly white, along wide, straight streets. American jeeps and trucks, a few cars, a few carts with their horses, lots of bicycles. No bombing, no shattered houses.

'You see,' Eleanor said. 'Nothing special. French cafés, American soldiers.'

'But the Arab quarter—' I began.

She laughed. 'Haven't you seen a slum before?'

Her words shut me up. But what was she trying to hide? The more she tried to discourage me, the more I wanted to explore. I liked our secret beach, but I wanted more. Maybe I'd find something extraordinary and then I'd persuade Eleanor to see it. I'd be her guide.

As we'd agreed, we separated in the square. She went to Dr Thérèse, I strolled along the boulevard, looking at the people coming towards me. Wartime drabness marked their clothes: coats frayed thin, trousers darned at the knees, faded dresses with ragged hems, well-polished shoes worn at the heels. The Americans stood out: taller, better-dressed, usually walking with a sense of purpose, even when they were only soldiers looking for a bar. I turned a corner and slipped into the Arab quarter.

Something felt different straight away, but I wasn't sure what it was. Maybe the smell: blocked drains? Or the roads and buildings—I'd left the wide, straight boulevards and moved into a zone of narrow, winding streets and low, two-storey buildings. Arches spanned the streets, their plaster cracked and discoloured. No, it was something else, something deeper, that puzzled me. I looked around. No more polished shoes. Slippers, old sandals, bare feet. Boys with dark skin, big eyes, shaven heads, clutching sheets of paper—schoolboys? A woman opposite, enveloped in layers of voluminous white cloth that floated around her. Islam? Men wearing loose clothes, like night-dresses, off-white, beige, striped, patched, baggy hoods over their heads. A man in worn blue dungarees, carrying a box of tools. A girl in a loose white skirt, with a straw basket, running, weaving her way through the pedestrians. A crowded café, full of tubby men in grubby suits, all gathered round a little table where two of them played dominos. A sudden cheer: had one of them won? A boy pointed at me. Should I be worried? No, no, he was curious, not hostile. Others glanced at me and then turned their eyes away. Besides—I wasn't alone: there were two American soldiers, like me, uncertain where to go. Like me. *Like me.* When had I ever thought of Americans as *like me*? But here we were: white men in the Arab quarter.

I came to a crossroads. Where to go? I wasn't sure. Was it dangerous to look lost?

There was nothing memorable in the Arab quarter. No picturesque sights. Yet it was different because—because of the sheer density of the population. There were more people on the pavements, more people crowded in the cafes, more people queuing outside the small, dark shops.

A muffled cheer echoed from a nearby street and I decided to walk towards it. After a few steps, I found an open, sandy space, where people gathered: old men sitting in the shade, their backs against a wall, younger people, men and women, standing, some pulling hoods over their heads to protect them from the sunshine. In the centre, a single figure. Tall, straight, in a thick beige night-dress, a gleaming white turban on his head. Sharp eyes, sharp nose, high cheekbones. He was—he was holding a violin, not pushing it under his chin, but holding it vertically, against his chest, scraping it with a bow: a busker, in front of a crowd of passers-by. I decided to stay. The streets didn't feel dangerous, but I was less exposed here, as everyone stared at someone else. Here I was, exploring the Arab quarter by myself.

The music sounded strange. I suppose I didn't know the scales or keys or however music is organised. The crowd were in a patient, good-natured mood, willing to cheer anything the violinist did. I relaxed, my fingers in my pocket, feeling the coins I'd throw him. His performance was fragmentary and changed without warning. There were wild sections of what must have been improvisation, with notes echoing back from the walls (wild cheers from the crowd), then more regular tunes (the crowd clapping and whooping), then a fragment of a song they all knew (enthusiastic singing).

I wondered why this cheering, smiling crowd were so easy to please and then it struck me: these people were starved of amusement. What I was seeing was the entertainment of the poor. And that was the difference that I'd been searching for, that was what made these crowded, labyrinthine streets with their constant smell of bad drains different from the wide, straight boulevards of the French quarters: it was poverty and wealth. Just that, nothing more complicated. Despite all the rhetoric about great General Lyautey spreading civilization, all the talk about schools and railways and docks, this is what Empire boiled down to: the ragged crowd in the Arab quarter. I began to feel uncomfortable: not because anyone was threatening me, or even looking at me. But what was I doing here? They hadn't got much, couldn't I leave them alone? Maybe this was why Eleanor hadn't wanted to come.

I went back to the square to wait for Eleanor. Soon, she stepped out from the door to the doctor's office. She looked happy but, all the same...

'Everything alright?'

'Yes, thanks, yes. Dr Thérèse thinks I did have a problem. There's still a trace of something, but it's nothing of concern. Just one more visit, she says. But she was very clear about one thing.'

'Yes?'

'No more smoking. They all seem to be saying that now.' She sighed.

'Odd, isn't it?' I said. 'There's something so relaxing about lighting a cigarette, then breathing in that—'

'Edmund! Stop it. I mustn't.'

'Sorry. I wasn't thinking.'

'Maybe you should give up as well.' Eleanor grinned. She was teasing me.

I thought about it for a moment, then shrugged my shoulders. 'If that's what you want.'

'It's so easy for you!'

'Of course. They're just cigarettes. What's the problem?'

Eleanor took my arm and we walked to the bus-stop.

'Thank goodness you're alright,' I said. 'I was so worried by Pierre's diagnosis.'

Eleanor frowned. 'This feels strange.'

'What?'

'You being worried about my health. It's always been the other way round. For—what?—five years I've constantly thought about your epilepsy, or whatever it is. But now—'

'I've been too busy to have a seizure,' I joked.

She nodded, thinking about my words. 'Maybe that's the truth.'

'Some days I miss those pills. They made everything foggy, yet I felt safer, somehow, after taking one. But in Neukirchen there's always something to do and I forget about them.'

'UNRRA certainly kept us busy,' said Eleanor.

'But I feel—I feel UNRRA's right for me. I know I make mistakes.'

'You do better than most.'

'And I think that's why the seizures have stopped: I'm in the right place. You don't need to worry about me anymore.'

'So now...' she stopped.

'What?'

'You'll be worrying about me?'

'Maybe I will.'

We got to the bus-stop.

'How was the Arab quarter?' asked Eleanor.

'Interesting.'

'Picturesque? A place filled with colourful spectacle and exotic, mysterious females?'

'No. It smells of blocked drains.'

Eleanor laughed.

'But the people seem friendly enough,' I continued. 'Big eyes, wide smiles.'

'Like happy children?' There was an edge to Eleanor's voice.

I thought about her words, then shook my head. 'There were some happy children, but also some sad ones. But—well, they're people, like anywhere, I suppose. But poorer, definitely poorer than most.'

Her hand gripped my arm a little tighter and she nodded. Why did I feel that I'd just passed a test?

'Actually, Edmund, I think I agree with you about something.'

'Yes?'

'We shouldn't stay by that beach forever, nice as it is. We've probably only got one week left, so let's get out a bit.'

'But I thought—'

'Dr Thérèse gave me an idea. We got talking, you see, as my lungs aren't a problem anymore.'

In a few days, there'd be a concert in a nearby town by an Arab musician who'd been in the French army. He'd picked up jazz techniques from American soldiers in Algeria.

'Apparently, he can play anything. Guitar, violin, piano and an Arab instrument called an *oud*.'

'Really?' I remembered the busker I'd seen: I'd tell Eleanor about him later. 'Alright, let's go to this concert.'

Looking along the street, I caught sight of a brown-skinned man, pushing a two-wheeled cart piled high with firewood. I saw the muscles in his legs stretch as he twisted it round a corner. On the other side of the road, an Arab street-cleaner swept the gutter with a broom made of branches.

'That's odd,' I muttered.

'What?'

And there: in front of a fashionable café, whose glittering golden lettering advertised the finest coffee in Casablanca, sat an Arab boot-black, huddled in a sad little crumple of limbs.

'Well, before, when we walked to your doctor, I didn't notice...'

'You didn't notice what?' asked Eleanor.

'There are—there are Arabs everywhere.'

'Aren't there just?'

'And all of them—in the lowest trades. Doing the pushing, pulling and hauling, the menial work.'

'After thirty-five years of General Lyautey's enlightened and humanitarian rule, the Arabs have been taught how to clean a street-gutter with a broom. How grateful they must feel!'

I laughed, but then realised it wasn't funny.

23. After the Concert

I didn't like the way he looked at us. Fortunately, he stayed on the other side of the station waiting-room, he and his wife—or whoever that woman was. They muttered to each other in Arabic. I checked my watch: thank goodness, the train was due in ten minutes.

Eleanor, sitting beside me, had stopped talking. I didn't know if she shared my worries about the couple opposite, or if she was thinking about the concert, or if she was just tired. I couldn't stop myself from glancing again at them and I met the Arab's cold, clear stare. It disturbed me. When I'd wandered round Casablanca's Arab quarter by myself, I'd felt safe, but here, at night, alone in this shadowy waiting-room, in this strange town, I felt uneasy. Maybe we'd been silly to come out here. Only seven minutes until the train.

The concert had been interesting. I think Eleanor enjoyed it more than me, but it was good to see more of Morocco, to leave our beach and travel across the plains to a different town. When the performance ended, a multi-coloured crowd, chattering cheerfully in at least three languages, had dispersed across the dark streets. There'd been American officers, French officials and their wives, middle-class Arabs in suits, poorer Arabs in those night-dresses. This was the sort of world I wanted to live in: one where all the races and all the peoples attended the same events, brought together by a common love of the arts, where they'd mix as equals. We'd had the impression that we were leading the way back to the station but, in the event, it was just us and this odd couple who walked there. They seized the best chair in the waiting-room: an upholstered settee in one corner. Eleanor and I perched on two hard wooden chairs which had seen better days.

The man was definitely looking at us. Could he understand English? Had he been listening to us? He sat upright in a crumpled white linen suit, occasionally stroking his neat, black moustache. The woman sat back in the shadows, but leaned towards him when they spoke. What were they saying? Was this a trap?

Only four minutes until the train. It was a tiny station, just two lines. When we'd arrived, five hours ago, we'd been with commuters from Casablanca and the station had been bustling. There were loud-speaker announcements and uniformed staff, who gave us directions in French to the café where the concert was held. But now: nothing. No staff and even the lights were off. The waiting-room was only lit by the streetlamps across the road, which left half the room in deep shadows.

'Let's go out to the platform,' I said to Eleanor.

She roused herself: maybe she'd been dozing. The Arab couple followed us. I'd hoped they were waiting for another train.

It was a relief to leave behind the smell of stale cigarette smoke and step into the quiet, cool night air. I checked my watch: it was time for the train. I listened. Someone shouted in a nearby street, heels clicked along a pavement, a dog barked, a door banged shut. No sound of a train. I saw the Arab glance at his watch and then look along the track. Had he seen something?

The train could still come, maybe it was just delayed. Eleanor and I took a few steps away from the Arab couple, then a few steps back.

'I don't like the look of them,' I whispered to her.

'What?' she said, frowning.

We waited. The train was now eight minutes late. I strained my ears, hoping for a sound, for a way out. Nothing.

'Oh, damn,' said Eleanor.

The Arab couple walked towards us. Were they going to talk to us? It was a trap, I was sure of it. Whatever they said, we mustn't follow them back into the dark town. We had to stay here. I'd make sure that Eleanor was safe.

'I'm afraid the Casablanca train will not arrive tonight,' said the Arab man. He spoke English clearly and precisely, with almost no accent. In fact, it was only the neutral quality of his English—the lack of any identifiable accent—that gave him away as a non-native speaker.

'It's the last train of the evening,' he continued. 'It's often cancelled without warning.'

I couldn't help myself. 'But you speak English!'

Eleanor squeezed my arm: a little warning signal. I ignored it.

He smiled coolly, with no warmth in his eyes. 'I had the benefit of five years' training in an accountancy school run by a British firm.'

The woman with him tutted, as if to tell him to stop teasing me.

'And now? What should we do?' I asked. I expected him to propose some suspicious-sounding journey into the town.

He shrugged. 'We have access to the waiting-room and its facilities. If my memory is correct, the first train in the morning will arrive shortly after five o'clock. We will have to make ourselves as comfortable as possible until then.'

***

Back in the waiting-room, introductions were made. Our fellow-travellers were Tawfeek and Nafah. They lived in Rabat, further up the coast and had friends in Casablanca. We chatted about the war. I suppose Eleanor thought it was a neutral subject, but I wished she hadn't mentioned it. God knows who these people were. They might be German agents! Hadn't some Arabs backed Hitler?

The Arab couple explained that Morocco had seen little fighting—*thanks be to God*, added Nafah—but it had been affected in other ways.

'Trade almost ceased,' Tawfeek told us. 'Agriculture went into a sharp decline and the workless flocked to the cities.'

He spoke in precise, measured English phrases which reminded me of an accountant's report. Nafah spoke less grammatically, but with greater passion and accompanied her words with extravagant hand gestures. There was something striking about her: her dark eyes, her rhythmic speech and the flash of her white teeth when she smiled.

At some point, Eleanor said *you Moroccans* and the two of them exchanged a glance.

'I have to tell you—' began Tawfeek.

'We're Palestinians,' interrupted Nafah. 'Exiles. Refugees.'

'Palestinians?' said Eleanor. 'When did you leave—'

'We were *expelled*,' said Tawfeek with a new firmness, 'from our homeland in 1938.'

'So, you were expelled by—' I began.

'—by the British Mandate authorities.'

The penny dropped. This explained the coldness that I'd felt in his look, as soon as he'd heard us speaking English. Curiously, it made me feel less uncomfortable. At least now I had an idea of where he came from and who he was. Next to me, Eleanor was thinking fast.

'Were you part of the disturbances—' she said.

'I was an active participant in the Palestinian Revolt.' Again, there was that determination in the way he spoke. His voice, now strong and clear, echoed round the dingy waiting-room, as if he was addressing an audience.

'My husband was a leader,' added Nafah. 'He will return to Palestine, one day soon, God willing.'

A few minutes later, Eleanor mentioned her activism publicizing the Bengal famine during the war and explained that I'd stocked the relevant pamphlets in my bookshop. Tawfeek's eyes met hers; I thought I saw him give a little nod and relax slightly. I suppose they understood we were no friends of the British Empire. Certainly, the tone of the conversation changed at that point.

It was a long night. They wanted to talk and I grew interested in their story. I'd never heard someone speak with such deep hatred for the Empire—Eleanor opposed imperialism, but her speech was always warm and compassionate, full of sympathy for the underdog. Tawfeek and Nafah were bitter: they'd been forced out of their family home. They'd had to bribe officials to get the visas to travel. England had been their destination, but by the time they'd arrived in Morocco, one of their visas was no longer valid.

'And then there was the war!' said Nafah.

I could hear the frustration in her voice.

They were stuck in Casablanca, with no friends. They'd been reduced to begging for assistance, before Tawfeek found work with a French firm in Rabat. In a way, they were still stuck: unsure about whether to renew their applications to travel to England or to try to return to Palestine.

At times I sensed a malicious undertone, as if Eleanor and I were personally responsible for their distress. But I no longer felt threatened: I was sure that we could trust Tawfeek, at least for this one night. I tried to talk about UNRRA and our work, but Tawfeek raised his eyes to the ceiling and looked bored. He said he had no faith in new international ventures.

Tawfeek told us that the world had forgotten Palestine and the Palestinians: all were mesmerized by the legend of the *Holy Land*. He stressed those words, looking right at me.

I found the politics of the place confusing and I think Eleanor did as well.

'But the radical Jews, the Zionists,' she said. 'Aren't they basically idealists, or socialists? Their *kibbutz*, their agricultural farms—they're cooperatives, they're modern, aren't they? Won't this be good for Palestine?'

Tawfeek stared at her.

'Socialism?' said Nafah. I got the impression that she wasn't really familiar with the word. 'How can you build socialism by taking another people's land?'

'But—' began Eleanor and then her voice died away.

Tawfeek laughed. 'You British! You thought you were so clever! You conquered an exotic land, the home of *your* Bible.' His stress on *your* hit me in the heart. 'You obtained permission to run it from the League of Nations, for the purposes of spreading civilization and enlightenment, of course. And then you used Zionist money to fund your plans. Magnificent! A new colony with no cost to the British tax-payer.

'And the result?' He paused, looking at us. 'Where once there was a land with one people, now there are three—Jewish, Palestinian and British—all fighting for the same place.'

His voice rose and fell, his words had a rhythm that echoed round the dusty waiting-room. Something in the way he spoke made me feel the gravity of Palestine's problems. I'd heard Eleanor adopt the rhetorical style of a public meeting, even when only talking to Muriel and me, but she was an amateur compared to Tawfeek. This man could inspire crowds and lead people.

'There will be fighting, there will be blood.' Tawfeek made a cutting gesture with his hand, as if to dismiss the suffering. 'Our enemies will fight hard, we know that. But we will win, because our cause is just.'

I can't say that I liked him, but I admired him. But why couldn't I be more like him?

24. Behind the Curtains

We stopped at the dock-workers' café and bought coffee and croissants. Our near-sleepless night had left us shattered and the morning sunshine was too bright, too unsteady for my tired eyes. Somewhere deep in my mind a warning-bell sounded: I knew what might happen next. I hadn't had a fit for months, but I still had to be careful.

'We ought to rest,' I told Eleanor, 'out of the sun.'

Back in the cottage, we pulled the curtains shut, undressed, then lay down in bed. Outside, we heard waves fall on the shore and gulls squawk. Sunbeams sparkled through the frayed curtains and played on the walls. I was sure that I'd sleep for hours, but as soon as my head touched the pillow, I felt unsettled. After a few minutes, Eleanor turned on her side and faced me.

'Can't sleep?' she asked.

'No.'

'What's wrong?'

'Nothing. I just—just don't feel comfortable.'

'Tawfeek upset you?'

'No, of course not. If I was Palestinian, I'd follow him, no doubt about it. But...'

'But what?'

'It was that idea that I was responsible for something, or that something was being done in my name—when...'

'What?'

'Well, I agree with you. The great empires are sure to collapse soon, thank goodness. There are still a few English people who talk about the white man's burden and how the natives ought to feel grateful for all we've done for them. But most people see the Empire for what it is: a racket.' Eleanor nodded. 'But—it feels different when you meet someone like Tawfeek. You have that sense of something being done in your name, something bad. I don't like that feeling of—of responsibility. Why on earth did we seize Palestine? I know it's the land of the Bible, but that's not a reason, is it?'

'No.'

'Don't you feel the same? Almost—ashamed?'

Eleanor gave a short laugh and turned to lie on her back.

'Don't you?' I repeated.

'No, not really.'

I frowned. I didn't understand. 'But you're against the Empire, Eleanor, you've always said that. You must feel ashamed of what's been done in your name.'

'I don't.'

'Why not?'

Again, that short, dry laugh. Then she grabbed one of the pillows, doubled it up and put it under her head.

'Wish I could have a cigarette,' she said.

'That's not an answer.'

'No, it's not.' She sighed. 'Edmund—Edmund I need to tell you something, I owe it to you. An explanation, I suppose.'

'What?'

She sighed again. 'Alright, if this was a political meeting, I could tell you that, as a woman, I have no country. I've no reason to feel ashamed of what the British Empire has been doing for centuries.'

'Really?'

'Yes, *really*. Women didn't decide that it'd be a good idea to seize Palestine or run India. Why should I feel responsible for what men have done?'

I'd heard her talk this way before. It made me feel uncomfortable, but it was hard to argue against her. It was always hard to argue against Eleanor about anything.

'I can't even join UNRRA on the same terms as you,' she continued. 'No women as Team Directors. Not suitable. I know that a few have slipped through the net, and good luck to them, but they don't change the fundamentals. In UNRRA, women become Welfare Officers, who are—well, glorified mothers. Or something like that. I'm pushed in with the typists and tea-makers. And when you want sandwiches—'

'Alright, alright. I see the point you're making. But—'

'I'm not dismissing UNRRA. Work in UNRRA is still a damn sight better than most other jobs. Welfare work *is* important, whatever men think. I'd even say that I've enjoyed it, despite all the problems. I've helped some of the most deserving people in the world.' She sighed, then her voice softened and grew more hesitant. 'But I'm avoiding the important point, aren't I? I'm still not being honest with you.'

'So what is—the important point?' I was baffled.

'It's me, Edmund.'

'You?'

She pushed herself up in the bed. 'Do you want a glass of water?'

'Alright.'

A few minutes later, she was propped up in the bed, staring at the cracked plaster wall opposite.

'It's time I told you. I should've told you ages ago. But—I don't really know the story myself.'

I sipped my water, but said nothing. What could she be hinting at? It had to be about her past.

'How can I make this simple?' she said.

'Begin at the beginning,' I told her. 'Then go on until you come to the end and then stop.'

She laughed. 'But I don't know the beginning! And this story hasn't reached its end.' She shook her head. 'I don't *know* anything for certain, that's why it's all so difficult. But—maybe. Yes. Let's start with Muriel.'

'Muriel?'

'What did she tell you about me? I know she'll have said something, she always does.'

I searched my memory and then repeated Muriel's speculations: Eleanor was the illegitimate child of a Catholic aristocrat.

'Oh, that silly woman!' exclaimed Eleanor. 'Don't get me wrong, she's a good friend, but she does romanticize. What a fairy story!'

'So you're not—'

'No! They weren't aristocrats, they weren't Catholics. Alright, yes, I was illegitimate, but mother came from a quite ordinary, middle-class Yorkshire family. Well, with a family tradition of service in India—'

'Ah.' I thought I'd grasped something. 'And in India, they were able to have servants and live in a grand style. To play at being aristocrats.'

I'd met families like this, who'd returned to England from India and complained constantly about their problems with servants.

'Yes, I suppose so. But that doesn't make them special, does it? And they certainly weren't great aristocrats.'

'And you went to public school?'

'A prep school. And that, obviously, was just to get me out of the way: a girls' boarding school, way up on the moors. That's where I got my accent. Now I think about it, I suppose half the girls there were bastards.'

'Eleanor!'

'That's the word, isn't it? No point in being frightened of it.'

At last, Eleanor was talking about her past. I waited for the jigsaw pieces to be joined together.

***

Her mother. A difficult figure, crippled by guilt, imprisoned by convention. Blue eyes and faded blonde hair, drawn back into as tight a bun as possible. When she wasn't being watched: attractive, regular features, a pleasant, warm smile, a stocky, round body. But when someone looked at her! Transformed into a stumbling, stuttering fool, her eyes to the ground.

'Have you a photograph of her?' I asked.

Eleanor shook her head. 'I've nothing.'

A church-goer, who searched for redemption for her sin and found only more guilt. Someone who repeated moralistic platitudes as if they were holy scriptures.

Muriel had been right about one thing. As Eleanor got older, her mother had less and less money. After the prep school, there was no chance of her going to a proper school, so Eleanor lived with her mother in a little cottage outside Whitby. Her formal education was limited to occasional visits by eccentric tutors. Her mother grew less active: incapable of working, unwilling to meet people, uninterested in going out, except for church, utterly reliant on the declining allowance her parents sent her. Eleanor began to take charge. She persuaded her mother to let her keep chickens in the yard.

A late afternoon in September. Eleanor in the backyard, by the hen coop, reading a volume of Balzac she'd scrounged from a second-hand bookshop.

'That man was a revelation! What a vision. The whole world revealed, its passions and tensions—'

'Eleanor! Now's not the time for literary appreciation.'

There was a sudden shower and Eleanor took her book inside. To her surprise, her mother had lit a fire—it wasn't cold and they had to be careful with coal and firewood. Her mother sat in front of the fire, concentrating on something, unaware of Eleanor's presence. Unobserved, Eleanor looked at her mother. The warm light of the flames brought out a tenderness in her face. She'd undone her hair, which hung, long, thick and yellow, over her shoulders. Her blue eyes shone in a way that Eleanor had rarely seen. What was she doing? The flames in the fire leapt up: her mother had thrown in a piece of paper—a letter. Eleanor crept closer. Her mother had a photograph in her hand—old, sepia-brown, crumpled. Eleanor caught a glimpse of a tall man, upright, wearing a smart suit.

'Like Tawfeek—clothes absolutely correct, but still, somehow, foreign—'

She had time to see his dark eyes, his dark hair, his white teeth and then she watched her mother, with tears in her eyes and sighing softly, rip the photograph in two. There was a signature at the bottom. She never caught the name, but only saw the last three letters: -jee.

'You mean—' I was trying to understand.

'How many English surnames end in -jee, Edmund?'

Eleanor cried *Mother!* as the photograph was consumed by the flames. Her mother turned round, guilt and shame stamped across her face. Eleanor stared at her.

'Who was that? That photograph? Was that—'

Her mother nodded.

***

I turned and gripped Eleanor's arm.

'He was your father? You're Indian? But—'

I was going to say: *but you don't look Indian.* I stopped, thinking, while Eleanor gazed at me. Of course. Yes, of course. Dark skin, no sunburn. Dark eyes. Dark hair. Brown nipples. I pictured her dressed as a Hindu goddess—yes, of course.

Eleanor smiled patiently.

'It's a little lesson in identity, I suppose,' she said. 'If you dress like an English girl, have an English name and speak with some sort of public-school English accent, people will think you're English. And—' She sighed. 'My skin's not really dark, is it? Tea-coloured, I suppose, not coffee-coloured. In India, the colonials would be a bit more suspicious. A touch of the tarbrush, they might say. But in

England, it doesn't come up as a question, so nobody asks it. But what a world! Tea-coloured or coffee-coloured? As if that's all that matters. Apparently in India, they examine your fingernails to find definitive proof of your race.' She paused and held her hand up, looking at her nails. 'I wonder what they'd make of mine.

'But it explains the shame felt by my mother,' she continued. 'Not just sex outside marriage, not just an illegitimate pregnancy, but sex with one of *them*. Her family must've made her feel awful. Put the fear of God into her. Crushed her. A shame, because I think that once she was a bright, pretty girl.'

***

Eleanor had felt an immediate fury.

'Why didn't you tell me?' she'd shouted at her mother.

There was no response. Her mother wept a little and then refused to talk. There were no letters left: she'd burnt them all.

Eleanor had stomped out of the house and walked as far as she could, fuelled by fury. This explained everything! Why hadn't her mother said anything? She immediately decided to leave.

When Eleanor returned, she said nothing to her mother. They ate in silence, her mother with tears in her eyes. At one moment her mother had said:

'I know I was wrong not to tell you about—'

But Eleanor had given her such a fierce look that she fell silent. At night, Eleanor went to her room and waited for her mother to go to hers. When the cottage was quiet, she crept to the drawer where her mother kept her savings—a few pounds. She pocketed these, then left at first light, before her mother was up. She caught the train to London.

'And afterwards? Did you ever speak to her again?' I asked.

'There was no afterwards. I suppose I ought to feel sorry for her, but she'd betrayed me by not telling me the truth. And what life would I have had there? The dumb woman's bastard daughter? I had to start anew.'

'But—you're Indian?' I had to come back to this.

Eleanor sighed. 'Look, Edmund, I don't know. I don't know what I am. Maybe I'm half-Indian. Probably. I certainly don't look like the daughter of a short, stocky, blue-eyed blonde Yorkshire woman, but—well, biology is complex.

'Think about what I've told you, Edmund. Nothing is certain. I don't know who was in that photograph. I don't know that he was my father, I don't know what happened to him and I can't even be sure if he was Indian.'

'His name!'

'In a shadowy room, I caught a glimpse of a signature. I thought I saw a name ending in -jee.'

I shook my head, baffled and disturbed. 'But what do you think happened?'

'I don't know,' she said. 'If there's one thing those colonials hate, it's Indian influences in their families. They want their children to grow up pale-skinned, they correct their accents, they even send them to English boarding-schools rather than risk them absorbing *degenerate* Indian influences. They watch their Indian servants like hawks. But somehow—maybe, somehow my mother grew close to an Indian. She must've been brave, in a way.'

I smiled. 'Maybe that's what you inherited from her.'

'Maybe.'

Eleanor's first years had been in India, hidden in a lodge up in the hills, alone with her mother and an old Indian servant.

'I'm sure the family wanted to send me to England as quickly as possible, but—you know—it was the war. No ferries.'

I nodded. It was something we shared: being born during that dreadful conflict. 'We're both children of war, aren't we?'

'Children of war and empire,' she replied.

She and her mother had made the crossing to England when she was five and Eleanor was sent to the prep school.

A thought struck me. 'Have you ever told this story to anyone else?'

She shook her head.

'Never?' Only me, I thought. Only ever to me.

She looked away. 'I met some Indian nationalists in London. I think—I think one or two of them might've guessed something. Sometimes I thought they were dropping hints. But nothing clear.'

'Why now? Why are you telling me this now?'

'I had to tell you sometime. And here—'

'In Morocco?'

She nodded. 'In a colony, like India. I didn't want to come here. One day, I'd like to explore the East, but I'll do it on my own terms. Just travel with a rucksack, at my own speed. Certainly, I'd like to visit an independent India. But now, in colonial Morocco—it's not something I can enjoy.'

'It was quite a shock, I have to say—my walk through the Arab quarter.'

'I know and—Edmund—I loved you for that.'

'For what?'

'Because you didn't blame the Arabs for their poverty or their smelly streets. Because you saw them as people.'

I stared at her, still trying to understand all that she'd said. It was almost too much.

'Do you think of yourself as Indian?' I asked.

'No,' she said. 'Well, sometimes, maybe. When I hear colonials complaining about the *lazy wogs*, I feel hurt—I mean, personally hurt. And then, sometimes—well, you feel things, you hear things, that other people don't seem to notice and you think: is this *because...*'

***

'But then—,' I said. 'London.'

She nodded. 'Yes. London. Matteo and Giuseppe. And the abortion.'

She paused for a moment, looking sad.

'Matteo.' I guessed she was thinking of him.

'Yes,' she said. 'One of the best. And what a way to die—in that bloody German barn.'

'We tried, we tried our hardest.'

'We were too late.' There were tears in her eyes. 'Such a shame, such a crying shame.'

She stared at the wall, where the sunbeams played. Then she gave a deep sigh, wiped her eyes and started again.

'That was the turning-point, Edmund. Meeting Matteo and Giuseppe. It suddenly became clear to me: these two men had been in jail, they'd fled their country, they were working all hours—and still they took care of me. I asked them what Communism was.

'I needed to make sense of what had happened to me. Of everything—India, my mother, that prep school, working in London, my abortion. Matteo listened, tried to explain what he could. You see, Marxism attempts to grasp the world as a whole, it attempts to understand things in relation to each other.'

I smiled.

'What?' she asked.

'You've reminded me of something.' And I recited those lines by Blake:

To see a World in a Grain of Sand

And a Heaven in a Wild Flower,

Hold Infinity in the palm of your hand

And Eternity in an hour.

'Blake wrote that?' asked Eleanor. I nodded. 'Well, yes, that's it, in a way. I wanted to understand what had happened to me, I wanted to connect my life to the bigger picture. That's what I wanted from Marxism. Now—well, I'm not sure.'

'Because of the Russian DPs?'

Eleanor shook her head. 'No, they were simply brutalized men. People don't come out of four years' captivity and act like angels. But—watching the Soviet policies—it's all about power, it's not about liberation.'

With Giuseppe and Matteo's help, Eleanor got back on her feet. She went back to working in the café and enrolled on a secretarial course, where she learnt to type. She attended concerts when she could, taught herself about music.

There was another question I wanted to ask. I wasn't sure how to phrase it. I didn't want to sound jealous—I wasn't, I was just curious.

'And—men? Boyfriends? After that?'

Eleanor smiled. 'Oh, men. Well, I wanted to prove I wasn't scared of them.' That made us both laugh. But then Eleanor's face fell.

'For a while it seemed like a game, one that I could win. Outwitting men, guessing what they wanted, seeing how shocked they were if I gave it to them, or how disappointed they were if I refused. Going with them to grubby hotel rooms. But then...'

She sighed.

'What happened?'

'One morning, I woke up to find my latest catch had left before me. And there were two pound notes left by the bed. He'd *paid* me. That made me stop and think. What was I becoming?

'After that, I concentrated more on meetings and politics, less on men. I taught myself how to address angry crowds in crowded rooms, I taught myself to appear confident, even when I felt terrified. I wanted to find out who was in control of all of this, why dreadful things kept happening—I wanted to stop fascism. And I wanted to help others, to make sure they had happy lives, whoever they were. That's why I worked with those Spanish refugees.'

'With Muriel?' I asked.

'Yes, that's how we met. But then—'

She stopped, looked me in the eye.

'Yes?'

'The war,' she said. 'Everything was thrown upside down. And, by accident, I met a man who wasn't a threat, who wasn't ever a threat... After a while, I realised I could trust him.'

She stopped, looked round the room, then looked back at me. My mouth was dry—I couldn't say a word.

'I'm not sure what love is,' she continued. 'Not in an absolute sense. Many people have told me that it's a bourgeois illusion.' I grinned. 'But I know what it means for me. Someone I can trust. Always.'

***

I got up from the bed, stepped to the window and pushed the curtains back a little. Outside, it was bright and sunny, and I could see the sea. We'd have to go out soon, it was too good to waste.

But what a story! It answered so many questions. Eleanor had always seemed so—*different*. Was it because she was Indian? I ran through her story in my mind, wondering if I could have coped.

Had she lied to me? Not exactly. She hadn't told me the whole truth. But what was the truth? I was gripped by a strange sensation. Around me I sensed complex webs and connections, the vast institutions of the British Empire, the industries and organisations of the war, the United Nations, all pulling crowds of unwilling people back and forth across the globe, letting two people meet in India, decades ago, letting another run away to London, and then finally pushing Eleanor and me to Morocco, to this crumbling holiday cottage and the tiny beach. It was as if we'd inherited the twisted legacy of hundreds of years of history and now we had to untangle it and repair all the damage it had done.

Behind me, I heard Eleanor's breathing. I needed to say something—she was waiting for me. She'd shared her secrets with me. I had to say something. I had no idea what to say, but I had to speak.

I turned round and looked her in the eye.

'I'm not going to say that this makes no difference.'

Her face fell.

'Of course, it makes a difference,' I continued. 'It changes everything. I know who you are now. But—but it doesn't matter. As far as I'm concerned, you're Eleanor and that's what really matters.'

***

Later, we got to talk about UNRRA.

'Haven't we done enough?' said Eleanor. 'More than six months hard labour.'

'It's tough going. What did Pierre say in his last letter?'

'The Poles have gone. Tymon and his committee held out to the end and they've been *consolidated*.'

'What does that mean?' UNRRA's continual assault on the English language infuriated me.

'UNRRA's got this idea of using the camps more efficiently. They're trying to identify specific groups and then gather them together. The Poles have all been pushed into other camps. I think because Neukirchen is a small camp—'

'They'll think of it as inefficient?'

Eleanor nodded. 'Don't you want to go back home? See Muriel and the bookshop? We could be in Socialist England for Christmas.'

It was a tempting thought. After all, we'd done our bit. Maybe accompanying those Poles on the train would be my greatest contribution to post-war reconstruction.

'Don't you miss your bookshop, Edmund?'

I did. And the first Christmas after the war was bound to be special. But then—

'The coal ration,' I said. 'What did Muriel say in her last letter? They were cutting back again?'

'I think that was it.'

'While Hildegard—'

'Yes.' Eleanor nodded. 'If anyone is going to find coal in Germany, it will be Hildegard and Jacques.'

I thought about Hildegard's house: the fine wallpaper, the well-decorated rooms. To my surprise, it seemed more attractive than my bookshop.

'Hildegard's got a nice house,' I said. 'While that bookshop in winter, with no coal, will be bloody freezing. Might not be good for you. You need to stay warm and dry.'

She nodded, looking a little sad.

'Who's going to replace the Poles?' I asked.

'Pierre said they were sending us Jews next,' said Eleanor. 'The ones who are refusing repatriation.'

'That's not going to be easy.'

I thought about Pierre, Victor, Dan, Jacques and Alma. How would they manage?

'Do you think we could help these new DPs?' I asked Eleanor.

'Of course we could do something for the Jewish DPs. We managed with those people in that awful barn. And we did alright with the Poles.'

'Eventually.'

She laughed. 'Eventually.'

'We like a challenge, don't we?'

Eleanor grinned. 'We do. We can't leave it all to the others.'

'Let's stay for a full year—until April or May, until the spring. Then London will be safer for you.

'Alright.'

The worst decision of my life. If only I'd known.

25. Coming Home

Sitting in my father's armchair, in my bookshop, I smile. Those few weeks in Morocco—those were the happiest times we had together. It was supposed to be a cure for your TB. Instead, it was our one holiday. It did us so much good: the sun, the swimming, the fresh air, our walks around the promontory and that old brass bed. I haven't got any postcards, photographs or tourist knick-knacks from those days. I didn't need them. The important things—they're all in my mind, they'll always be there.

In Morocco, I was no longer your Team Director. And there was that strange reversal: I was caring for you, not the other way round. You complained about not being able to smoke, while I tried to distract you. Your illness brought us together, it made me look at you anew. So we found each other again, or perhaps we truly found each other for the first time. Thank heaven you told me your story, because only then could I know who you truly were. How long does it take to really know someone? Perhaps only five minutes. I think it took you and me five years.

And to think—I was the only one who knew your story. *Only me.* You trusted me with it. That thought fills me, anchors me, makes me feel complete. It tells me that our years together achieved something.

There was one question I never asked. Children. I wonder if you would have wanted a son or daughter. Maybe you'd have said your career came first. Maybe you'd have been one of those single-minded, militant women who dedicated themselves to a cause. Or maybe you'd have replied, *after the war...* I sigh and imagine a baby playing on the floor, here, in front of the window. Maybe.

In Morocco, we were like children. A boy and a girl, mongrel off-spring of war and empire, of England, India and Wales. That little beach in Morocco was our blessed playground, for a few weeks. At least I've known that, at least I can say we had that: real happiness.

Some couples never find it. They stay miserably married for decades, until their graves. At least...

Oh dear. If only, if only, if only...

PART V
DARKEST GERMANY

'...under present conditions, I think one year in Germany is
enough for anyone.'
UNRRA official requesting a transfer, July 1946
'As I drove through ruined Cologne at late dusk, with terror of
the world and of men and of myself in my heart, for a moment I just
couldn't believe that we were deliberately... adding further ruin to
this unspeakable desolation.'
Victor Gollancz, *Darkest Germany*

30. Return to Neukirchen

The warm smell of a coal fire greeted us when we opened the door of the drawing-room. Dan lounged in an easy chair, a cigarette in his mouth, a newspaper on his lap. Behind him, Hildegard put some spare cutlery into a drawer. There was something different about Dan that I couldn't quite put my finger on. He grinned as we came in and this provoked Eleanor. She went on the attack.

'You've been seeing that German tart, haven't you? You've been bringing her here.'

That again. Sometimes, Eleanor just didn't know when to stop. Of course, we had to think of UNRRA's position and what people might say, but there was a time and a place for everything.

Dan puffed slowly on his cigarette, then sank back into his chair. 'You mean Elsa?' he said.

'Yes, *Elsa*.' There was venom in Eleanor's voice.

Hildegard clattered cutlery into place.

'Well, no.' Dan shook his head. 'No. Haven't seen her for a while.'

'So who is it now? Some other blonde tart you bought with cigarettes and stockings? You've had her round here, haven't you?'

'Blonde tarts?' Dan was obviously enjoying himself, playing the innocent. 'Can't say that I know any. Have you seen one, Hildegard?'

Hildegard didn't turn round, but replied awkwardly, 'No, I have not.'

Eleanor wasn't having any of this. 'Whoever you're seeing, it'll stop now. You can do what you like outside this house, but you're not bringing her back here.'

'Really.' Dan puffed again on his cigarette and nodded, making a great play of carefully considering Eleanor's words like some over-enthusiastic am-dram player. 'Not round here, eh?'

'No. No *frats* here.'

'You might find it difficult to enforce that rule.'

'Why?'

'It would make this house tricky to manage. Don't you think so, Hilde?'

Hildegard finished with the cutlery. She turned round and hesitantly held her hand out towards Dan. Still sitting down, he reached out and grasped her hand, all the time staring at Eleanor. This little gesture astonished me. Eleanor gasped.

'*Blonde tart*,' Dan said. 'Now, that's not a nice way to refer to our housekeeper, is it?'

I said the first thing that came into my mind. 'But you said you hated Germans, *all* Germans.'

'I've revised my position.' Dan grinned. 'There's good and bad among them, like with everyone.'

'But what about your politics? Hildegard's no red, is she?'

'We've both learnt a lot during war. I reckon it's time I moved on. There's a lot you could do with a house like this, once reconstruction begins. Of course, it'll need some repairs, but—'

Eleanor was still getting over her shock. 'Hildegard... What...'

Hildegard smiled in an innocent, happy way and it struck me that in all the months we'd lived there, I'd never once seen her smile. 'There is no one to look after me now. What will happen when you leave? This house needs much work.'

I was trying to understand. 'Do you talk to each other in English?'

They burst out laughing. Dan looked at me ruefully.

'Never thought I'd say it, but it was one of the few good things my old dad did for me.'

'What?'

'Taught me Yiddish.'

'So?'

He looked up, clearly surprised that I didn't grasp what he was saying.

'Yiddish,' he repeated. 'It's basically German.'

'Well...' Hildegard protested. 'It is certainly *similar* to German in some ways.'

They looked at each other and laughed again. This was clearly an old joke between them.

'He thinks he can speak German, but sometimes I help him,' Hildegard explained.

Dan looked at Eleanor and spoke in a different tone, firmer and clearer.

'Now, you're not going to ban Hildegard from her own house, are you?'

Eleanor shook her head slowly.

Hildegard said something to Dan in German. He nodded, smiled and they left.

***

'Eleanor,' I said.

'Hmm...' She didn't look up from her book.

'Eleanor: you're going to have to say something to Dan.'

This time she looked up. 'What?'

'You were rude to him—and Hildegard. You need to apologise.'

'Apologise?'

'Yes, apologise. We've got to work with him, remember?'

She looked puzzled for a moment, then shrugged. 'So Dan's found himself another *frat*. What have I got to apologise for? If anything, it should be—'

'Eleanor! Didn't you see the way they were looking at each other? It's not some fly-by-night affair. I'd never have believed that a stout German house-matron could look like a schoolgirl in love.'

'It's not love, it's just another form of prostitution. He might as well have gone to the girls by the street market.'

'He didn't. He chose a widow.'

'Who just happens to own a substantial property. Probably her most attractive asset.'

'You can't reduce all emotions and feelings to—to economic transactions!'

'Can't I?'

I glared at her. 'And what about us? Did I buy you two years ago?'

'No! I'd never let anyone treat me like that!'

'Eleanor: give them a chance. That was the first time I've seen Hildegard smile. The first time in eight months.'

That point seemed to hit home. She fell silent, then looked away, irritation, disgust and uncertainty crossing her face. I waited. The ticking of the clock on the mantelpiece filled the room.

'Eleanor: you've got to apologise. We need to work with them. And you shouldn't be so cynical about everyone you meet.'

Slowly, reluctantly, she spoke. 'I suppose I was—I was a little harsh with him. It's just—it's just that everything here seems so revolting. Starving German girls with no chance in life and hordes of English and American soldiers, their pockets full of cigarettes and chocolates, lording it over them—their new masters. And they call this Liberation!'

'Dan and Hildegard don't seem like that, do they?'

Bewilderment crossed Eleanor's face. 'Perhaps not.'

'Definitely not.'

She nodded.

***

To be fair to Eleanor, she didn't wait. The next day, at dinner, while we were waiting for Hildegard, she turned to Dan.

'Dan, I owe you an apology.'

Dan looked up, utterly surprised.

'I shouldn't have spoken to you like that yesterday. I—I was wrong.'

Dan nodded thoughtfully, but stayed silent.

'Hildegard's a fine woman and I think you both deserve—'

At that point Hildegard entered, bearing a beef pie covered with sizzling onions.

'Hildegard!' said Eleanor, as if seeing her for the first time. 'It's time you ate with us. We can't carry on with you eating the left-overs in the kitchen after our dinner, like some skivvy.'

Hildegard stared at Eleanor as if she'd heard something extraordinary. I have to confess, I was surprised. Allied personnel were making all sorts of arrangements with Germans about housing. Non-fraternization was breaking down left, right and centre. However, in most cases, Allied officials requisitioning houses still insisted on their German owners leaving. Only a few made arrangements like ours, which were practical, if a little tense. But sharing meals? I knew that most Allied personnel would see this as a step too far. On the other hand—we were leaving in four months and I was tired of this endless circle of separation and hatred. Maybe Eleanor was right: it was time for some fraternization.

Hildegard was speechless.

'Are you sure?' Dan looked sceptical. 'I think that might be—might be tricky for Hildegard, what with cooking and serving the meal, and all the time looking after her children.'

Hildegard nodded.

'Oh, she'll manage, I'm sure she will,' said Eleanor.

At that point, Hildegard looked terrified.

'Hildegard,' I said, 'if you don't feel comfortable eating with us, then you don't have to.'

Eleanor shot me a glance.

'I think it would not be right,' said Hildegard. She made a curious little movement, almost a half-curtsey, then turned and left.

For a moment, Eleanor occupied herself with cutting the pie and serving myself and Dan. We heard Hildegard closing the kitchen door.

'Did I go too far?' Eleanor asked me.

'Yes!' said Dan. 'It was a nice thought, but—'

'Only eight months ago,' I said, 'Brit's and Germans were knocking bits out of each other. It's going to take more time.'

***

Despite the failure of Eleanor's offer, the mood in the house changed for the better. It increasingly felt like we were living in Dan and Hildegard's house. Hildegard continued to cook and care for us—if anything, her meals got better, even in that harsh, difficult winter. During the weekends, Dan walked round the house with a hammer in his hand and a screw-driver in his back pocket. Hildegard would point out the door that didn't close properly, the smashed windows where glass was replaced with bits of plywood, the wobbly step on the stairs and he'd get to it. Her German was soft and precise; his replies, half-Yiddish, half-German I guessed, were more hesitant, jumping from an easy phrase to a difficult word. He often stopped, looked puzzled, then started a sentence again. She'd laugh and pronounce the word he'd been looking for.

I knew what I was seeing. They were a proper couple, like we'd been in Morocco. It touched me to see this. It was another side to war and reconstruction, different from the heroics, destruction and prostitution that everyone talked about. The whole house felt more comfortable.

***

In those first weeks back in Neukirchen, I didn't want to resume my official duties. We'd had such wonderful freedom in Morocco!

There was a pile of papers waiting for me in the office, I didn't know where to begin. I wanted to hide myself away from the DPs and their problems.

Rather than face the world outside, I turned to the accounts, which Victor had kept while I was away. How hard everyone had been working. Orders from Dan for the new DPs: herrings and goulash. Pierre, visiting the American base almost every week for medical supplies. But then—a nasty shock. The figures didn't add up. It had to be Victor's fault: no one else was involved. Was it evidence of corruption? I spent a whole week going through the books and checking some points with the American base. Finally I spotted it: an accounting error. Victor, despite all his banking experience, was a poor mathematician—it was that simple. While checking the accounts and writing long overdue replies to letters, I turned away from the camp. I delayed calling a team meeting. No one seemed to notice as I hid in my office and ignored the niggle of guilt at the back of my mind.

The weather didn't help: it was cold, really cold. Sleety rain whipped across the camp most days. It made such a miserable change from the Moroccan sun. There was a tiny coal fire in my office—enough to fill the room with smoke, but not to warm it. Some days, there was very little coal, despite Jacques's best (or worst?) efforts. I wore two sweaters and stomped round my office every fifteen minutes, but it did no good. Sometimes it was too cold to think and the pages of accounts seemed to swim in front of my eyes.

My thoughts turned to London and I thought of the crowds round Piccadilly, the cafes in Bloomsbury, the pubs in Soho, the chatter, the singing, the boozing. Maybe we should have gone back to England.

It was Eleanor who jogged my memory. One cold morning when snow threatened, we sat over cups of Hildegard's coffee, putting off the evil hour when we'd walk to the camp.

'Isn't it time we had a team meeting?' she said.

'What's the point?'

'Well, there's Christmas, for a start.'

'Christmas?'

I'd forgotten about that. Of course, it would be up to us to organise something for the DPs.

***

'Edmund, you're forgetting: they're Jewish.'

Victor's voice was relaxed and confident. I couldn't help feeling that there was an undercurrent to it, as if he were laughing at me.

'Yes, but—even Jews can celebrate Christmas, can't they?'

Victor laughed. 'You're too late, *old chap*.' He did a poor imitation of an English accent. 'They celebrated Hanukkah just before you got back from Morocco.'

Was it my imagination, or did he stress the word *Morocco*? Was he implying something?

I stopped myself from asking what Hanukkah was, but glanced at Dan. He looked irritated, but explained it was a traditional Jewish festival to celebrate the re-taking of Jerusalem in ancient times.

'Look, I'm not proposing a church service,' I said. 'But couldn't we have a tree? Sing some carols?'

To my surprise, there was a ripple of laughter in the group.

Pierre shook his head, smiling. 'Edmund, you have to understand: Christians are Christians and Jews are Jews.'

Even Alma smiled. 'And these are people who are now very proud of being Jewish. They have something they want to prove.'

Knowing nods followed her words. There was clearly something I was missing.

'But this is the first Christmas after the war!' I said. 'There's so much to celebrate, isn't there?' Words of a carol slipped into my mind and I couldn't help repeating them: *The hopes and fears of all the years are met in thee tonight.*

Again, chuckles went round the room. They were laughing at me, I realised.

'Plenty of fears,' muttered Victor.

'Isn't anyone going to do anything?' I asked.

'The American commander wanted to have a cocktail party at his villa, but he's not sure the roads will be safe,' said Victor. 'He'll probably hold something in town. And there'll be concerts and dances for the GIs.'

I looked at Eleanor. 'We could have a cocktail party of our own.'

She looked back, but said nothing. There was definitely an undercurrent in the room. My old doubts returned: was I really fit to be a Team Director? I couldn't even persuade my team to celebrate Christmas.

Victor weighed up my words.

'We could try holding a cocktail party,' he said eventually, as if granting me a favour.

'And we could invite the Jewish DP committee,' I continued.

Glances flashed across the room: from Victor to Pierre, from Pierre to Dan. Eventually, Victor said:

'Possibly.'

***

The certainty in Victor's tone unnerved me. I would have preferred to have gone home at that point, and maybe to have talked about the meeting with Eleanor. Instead, Dan and Alma had something they wanted to discuss. Eleanor stayed as well.

'You don't understand, Edmund,' began Dan. 'A lot's changed while you were away.'

I smiled, thinking of him and Hildegard, but of course he didn't mean that.

'These Jewish DPs,' Dan continued. 'Well, they're—different.'

Alma nodded. 'Excellent, in many ways. They have created their own committees, their own welfare service and police service. There are two schools and many evening classes.' She smiled. 'And, Eleanor—'

Eleanor looked at her, puzzled.

'They even chose a woman to serve on their committee. Hanke. I did not say anything to them!'

Eleanor blinked. 'Well, that is a surprise.'

Alma gave one of her warm, bland smiles. 'They do everything.'

'But that's—that's almost a problem in itself,' said Dan. 'It's as if they don't need us.'

Eleanor sat up. 'But—after all they've been through! The concentration camps... They must need so much. How can they...?'

Dan nodded. 'Some of them are survivors from the camps. Incredible people, I take my hat off to them. But many of them got through the war in other ways. Some were disguised, some hid underground during the Third Reich. A lot of them—I'm not sure how many—survived by getting out to Russia. And now they've returned—'

'But they must be traumatised or injured after such experiences,' said Eleanor.

'They are, they are indeed,' said Alma. 'But—there's not one pattern. Some of them have experienced, well—demoralisation.'

'There's a criminal element,' explained Dan. 'A small one. After all, some only survived through trickery and theft. The black market here—it's too much of a temptation. It's hard for them to unlearn those habits.'

'But what's the big issue?' I asked. I was getting impatient. 'We were told all this back in Granville. We've never idealised the DPs.

That's why we're here: to help, to rehabilitate. It's a moral task as well, we've always known that.'

Eleanor nodded. I had her attention now.

'Remember the Russians!' I added. 'They can't be that bad.'

Dan gave a short laugh. 'Yes, I won't forget them. Putting aside the criminal element, these people aren't like the Russians. When you meet these people, what first strikes you is what a mixture they are. They're all sorts—civil servants, teachers, fishermen, rabbis, engineers, students. They come from different countries. They speak Romanian, Russian, Polish, Greek... Yiddish is their common language, but they speak it in different ways. Even their food!' Dan grinned. 'The Poles want herrings and potatoes, the Hungarians want goulash, the Russians want cabbage, the Greeks want aubergines—'

'But now,' interrupted Alma, 'they want to be one nation. A Jewish nation.'

'Ah,' I said. I thought I understood. 'It's a grammatical problem.'

'What?' Dan frowned.

'Is a man a Jewish Pole or a Polish Jew?'

Eleanor and Dan laughed and even Alma smiled.

'Yes,' said Dan, grinning. 'That's it. A grammatical question.'

I'd been joking, but—in a way—it was that simple. Which was the adjective and which the noun? One implied a range of nationalities in our camp and the other implied just one nation, even if it was a nation in the process of formation. And this new nation was definitely not Christian.

'But why don't they go back to the countries they come from?' I asked. 'The war's over. Why stay here?'

'The Jewish Poles have gone back,' said Dan. 'The ones remaining have decided they're Jewish first, Polish second.'

'If at all,' added Eleanor.

Dan nodded. 'And they want a Jewish nation. Even here, in a DP camp, they want the trappings of nationhood.'

Once Alma had left, I tackled Dan about another question.

'Have they worked out that you—that you're from a Jewish background?' I wasn't sure what were the right terms to use.

'No, at least not yet. But they know about me and Hilde.'

'So?'

'As far as they're concerned, there are no good Germans. They don't feel they can trust me.'

'They don't know you speak Yiddish?'

He smiled. 'No. That's been awkward. Sometimes I find it difficult to keep a straight face when I hear what they're saying.'

'That might be useful.'

'I'm not going to spy on them!'

'No, no, of course not. But, all the same...'

27. Negotiations

Joel was a large, affable man. His tweed jacket and matching waistcoat were too big for him, as if he had yet to grow into them. He had an easy sense of authority that I envied. His eyes would twinkle during disagreements, but he'd always stay calm, even chuckle in a genial manner, like an uncle indulging a favourite nephew. I could see why he'd become the chairman of the Jewish DPs' committee: he must have been the obvious choice.

Joel happily talked about his background. He'd been born in Romania, then studied law in London in the 1920s. He was an Anglophile and delighted in sharing his memories of student life in Shaftsbury Lane, Hyde Park and Hampstead Heath. His story changed after that. He'd moved into commerce, set up an investment company in Palestine and supervised trade with Poland. In September 1939 he'd been in the wrong place at the wrong time: Warsaw, just as the Germans entered. He'd had the wits and good fortune to get out to the Soviet-occupied zone, then into Russia, where he'd survived for six years, working as a bookkeeper for a large military restaurant.

'Communism!' he said, rolling his eyes. 'What people!'

I thought about the Russian DPs and nodded. 'They can be rough, I know. But, in the war...'

Joel nodded. 'Yes, of course. Their tanks got to Berlin first.'

I was embarrassed when he asked about my military experience. But this was what men did when they met: exchange war stories. I thought back to those wasted years in England. That barn and re-opening a bookshop. I couldn't mention my epilepsy. So what could I say to Joel? I told him about the Fire Service and tried to hint at a family commitment which had taken up my time. He didn't look convinced. He shot me a long, hard stare at one point and I could see he was calculating something—maybe wondering what sort of man avoided the army.

'Still: to business,' he said, smiling.

I was glad he'd changed the subject—but it had been an awkward start to what I guessed would be a difficult negotiation.

'A hall.' I sighed. 'This has come up before, you know? The Polish DPs found they could use the grassy area beyond the bungalows. It's a sort of natural amphitheatre.'

'A pleasant spot, to be sure. But in this weather!'

'I can't authorize a major new construction project on this site, Joel.'

'Of course not. Times are hard and even UNRRA is short of funds. But—'

I was getting to understand Joel's negotiating technique. He'd stay polite, give a point or two, but stick to his central demand.

'I know there are many buildings nearby which seem suitable,' I said, 'but I can't permit you to raid the surroundings like that. I suggest that you wait until the fine weather returns and then use the grounds here. You'll find there's plenty of space. And, of course, you might be gone in a few months.'

'You think so, Edmund? It's possible, but I doubt it.' He sighed and I sensed the deep sadness within him. 'Speaking for myself, I'd be willing to wait until summer for the hall. But there are many voices on my committee, and... You know, Hanke...'

I nodded, although for a moment I was confused. Who was she? Then I remembered: the sole female delegate on the new DPs' Committee.

Joel began again. 'The young ones, the hotheads, demand that this matter be resolved with some urgency.'

I shrugged. I was tired of this issue. Of course, I wanted to help—we all wanted to see the rehabilitation of the DPs. But they had to be realistic. What next? A swimming pool? A skating rink?

Joel looked at me, waiting for a response. 'The young, eh? Always impatient.'

'Just tell them that, in a few months, they'll be able to put on all the performances they want.'

'Edmund, forgive me, but I can't help noticing that you give much consideration to the welfare of our *German* neighbours'—Joel stressed the word *German*, wincing as he pronounced it, almost as if it was an obscenity—'and little weight to the needs of their victims. While the *Germans* enjoyed a full range of pleasures, concerts and entertainments, almost until the end of the war, my people—'

I couldn't let him get on to that, for I knew I'd lose the argument.

'Joel, I can't right the wrongs that have been done to you. That will take a long, long time. But, in the meantime, you must respect the law.'

He stared at me. 'I think there is a higher moral code which *we* must respect.'

'I will not allow you to seize German property.'

'You may not, but we're asking for your cooperation, not your permission. After all, this is not a matter for your jurisdiction.'

'What?'

Joel smiled. 'The American commander has given us permission to requisition the hall near the camp entrance.'

'He's done *what*?'

'Of course, the building is in poor condition, but he will arrange for the supply of building materials and, among us, there are some of the finest builders in Europe, and so...'

Joel must have seen that I was furious.

'I realize that this has come as a surprise, Edmund, but your colleague, Victor—'

'He authorized this?'

'No, no, not exactly. But let's say he assisted in our negotiations.'

***

At dinner with Eleanor and Dan, I could not contain myself.

'Do you know what that bloody American commander's gone and done?'

They weren't as annoyed as I was.

Some of Dan's old anti-German feelings came back. 'Why shouldn't the DPs use what they can find? It's time for the Germans to give them something back, after what they stole from other people,' he said. 'And, anyway, all reconstruction is to be welcomed, isn't it? At the moment, that hall's just a wreck.'

'But this is the law of the jungle!' I protested. 'It's not much better than theft.'

Eleanor was as unperturbed as Dan. 'They're very active, these Jewish DPs. They have so many plans and ideas. We should help them all we can.'

'Why's a hall so important to them? Will they perform Shakespeare throughout the winter?'

Eleanor smiled. 'No, Edmund, it's not that. They're planning meetings and rallies.'

'Rallies?' I was suspicious straight away. I couldn't help thinking of Hitler's Nuremburg rallies: a stupid comparison, I know.

'You must meet Hanke,' said Eleanor. 'I think you'll like her. And after listening to her, you'll understand more.'

Eleanor was clearly very taken with Hanke. As we ate, she told me more. Hanke had a remarkable biography. A Polish dentist's daughter, she'd been separated from her family when she was 15 and then sent to the Warsaw Ghetto. *Ghetto!* What a dreadful word! Those awful places had re-appeared on European soil. Hanke had lived in that dirty, crowded space with its starving inmates for two years, but had got out just before the end, before that desperate rising of April 1943. For the next two years, she hid in attics, cellars and tunnels. Eleanor and Dan both thought that Hanke felt guilty for having left the Ghetto and its fighters to their fate, and her new militancy repaid the debt she felt she owed them.

The oddest thing was that Hanke didn't have any religious faith. Her father had converted to Catholicism. She told Eleanor that she only believed in one god: living man. And woman, she'd added promptly. But she followed every traditional Jewish ritual, explaining that these were the customs of her people which had guided them through their centuries of wandering. She thought she had no right to question them.

Eleanor was thinking. 'Why don't we invite Hanke for dinner?'

Dan looked sceptical. 'Do you think she'll come to a German's house?'

'She will if we invite her!'

***

I had a lot to think about. These Jewish DPs were certainly different from the Russians and Poles. Would they cause problems? But Eleanor sounded so positive about them. If she felt happy with them, then our last four months wouldn't be so bad. She could negotiate with Hanke and the radicals, and I'd deal with Joel and the moderates. It'd be teamwork, once again. In this way, we'd last the winter, and then we'd leave, proud to have stayed a full year in Germany.

28. Hanke

Dan was right. Hanke wouldn't come to a German's house. She wasn't interested in a Christmas cocktail party, either. But she wanted to discuss a project with me, so one afternoon after Christmas, she and Eleanor came to my office.

Hanke surprised me. I'd expected somebody flamboyant, but my first impression was that she looked like an assistant schoolmistress: a short, soft-spoken, big-eyed girl with round spectacles and dark hair, parted in the middle and tied back in a bun. She had a precise, neat way of walking and sitting down, arranging herself carefully in the best of my office chairs, before turning to look at me. Like so many of the younger DPs, Hanke seemed strangely ageless. These poor souls had missed out on their youth and had already acquired some of the habits of old people. The one discordant note was her clothes. Instead of a dress, she wore faded blue overalls—the sort a mechanic might wear. Couldn't Dan or Eleanor have found her something better? After a few moments, I realised this wasn't a mistake in supplies. Hanke's clothing was a statement of her beliefs.

'Thank you for assisting us with our hall. It'll make such a difference!' she said, before I could say anything.

Had Joel told her the true story? Or was she just being diplomatic? Before I could reply, Eleanor spoke.

'One of UNRRA's tasks is rehabilitation and so helping with the hall is part of our job. We're delighted to see that you're all so active, after...' Eleanor paused, lost for words.

Hanke nodded, sat up and looked at us. 'Exactly: *after*. After all those dreadful, empty years. After leaving behind our old lives, the ghetto and the *shtetl*.'

I must have frowned, for she turned to me.

'Forgive me: it's a Yiddish word. One of many we're trying to forget!' She laughed and her face came alive for a second. 'It refers to the sad lives we were granted by the old Russian authorities: when we were permitted to be shoe-makers, tailors and money-lenders.'

Her English wasn't perfect, but she spoke with such force and passion that there was never any problem understanding her. Apparently, she knew five languages. Without prompting, she launched into a speech.

'The last years have been years of silence for us. We hid from Europe's Nazi masters, we disguised ourselves, we threw away anything that might mark us as different, we closed our mouths. We tried to be like *them*. And now, we who have survived, we few, the last remnants of a great people, we will speak. This hall, this shattered, bombed relic of a hall in an enemy town, it will be the start of something great, a great beginning, a great revival, you will see.'

I couldn't help myself. Despite Eleanor's warning look, I leant forward.

'But tell me: now Hitler's dead and the Nazis are gone, why don't you return to your homes?'

She started as I said the word *home*. She looked up, her muscles tensed and I thought she was going to shout at me. But then, she sat back in her chair and thought for a moment, obviously weighing up her words.

'We *are* trying to return to our *home*.'

I frowned, puzzled. 'But you've refused all offers of transport to Poland. The journey's not so bad: Eleanor and I have done it.' I glanced at Eleanor, but she was looking at Hanke, waiting for her to speak.

'We cannot live in Poland,' said Hanke. 'Or anywhere in this old continent, stained with the blood of our people. I tried: believe me, I did. Without my parents, without my sister, I went back to our old flat in Warsaw. It was occupied by a civil servant and his family, who said they had no intention of moving out. I told him what had happened to my family. He said everyone had suffered in the war. His last words to me were that if I wanted my flat back, he'd see me in court.'

She shook her head. 'When we left the death camps, the cellars and the tunnels, we thought the world would welcome us as heroes. Instead, we find we're an inconvenience: we remind the world that the war has not ended, that blood still flows from Europe's wounds. It's not a message anyone wants to hear.'

'Of course, I was lucky.' Hanke laughed: a short, sharp, bitter sound. 'Do you know that there are still mobs in Polish marketplaces who shout to people not to buy from Jews? And there are still Polish policemen who'll give Jews a sound beating and ignore the mob who's baying for their blood? That civil servant only threatened me with a court case.'

She looked me straight in the eye. 'So what home is waiting for us in Poland? In Romania? Or do you suggest we should settle in Germany?'

'But you have come here,' I said. 'You've chosen to stay in Germany.'

'A temporary residence, while we prepare for something better. The last time a choice is forced on us, I hope.'

'And now—' I wanted to bring her back to the topic we had to discuss.

'Yes, now, we must prepare ourselves. We need more.'

'But, Hanke, you have to understand that UNRRA's resources are very limited.'

She shrugged. 'You can find trains to deliver us to the Jew-hating mobs of Poland. You can even find cigarettes to bribe us to go there. I'm sure that you can find one tractor and someone to train us.'

'But the land you want to farm—it's not our land, I can't give it to you.'

'Then we will take it.'

'Joel said—'

A light flickered in her eyes and she raised her hand, palm outwards, as if to push something away.

'Ah, Joel,' she said. She paused, then looked at me. 'Joel has not—has not really left the *shtetl*. He's a businessman, he thinks in terms of deals to be struck. Of course, I respect him: he found his own way to survive the murder of our people and he works tirelessly for us, tirelessly. I respect him, but—' She paused, weighing her words again. 'His way is not our way, let me say that. We seek the spiritual transformation of our people, he looks to balance the books.'

I had to laugh. Now I could see Joel's problem.

'But Hanke,' I said. 'I still don't understand. You want to create a farm? Here? Why?'

'It's not because we wish to contribute to the German economy, believe me. If I have my way, our farm and all its land and produce will be burnt when we leave. I wouldn't leave a single seed.

'But we must prepare ourselves for our ascent,' she continued. 'When we arrive in our home—'

'Your home?' I interrupted her.

'Our *home*,' she repeated. 'The one established by my people five thousand years ago, the one which is rightfully ours.'

'You mean Palestine?'

'Where else?'

'But—'

'Europe has been our graveyard. America closes its doors to us. England will not take us. We must return to our true home and end our long wandering. And before we travel, we must make ourselves ready, we must be worthy, we must be able to give something to this new nation. Our persecution has made us a strong people, strong as steel, but we must also be productive. We will return to the land, that is the answer.'

'You'll be farmers?'

'We will share the land. Each of us will give what he or she can, each of us will take what he or she needs. In our language, we call this a *kibbutz*. There are other useful professions, but the land is the basis of them all.'

'But—the British authorities...'

A crafty look flashed over Hanke's face.

'You British!' she said in pitying tones. 'Still clutching to your Empire when everything else has been destroyed. How much longer do you think your flag will fly over our land?'

Something else occurred to me. 'But Hanke—Palestine isn't empty. There are other people already there.'

It was the first comment I'd made that really surprised her. For a moment, she looked uncertain.

'There are some, I know,' she said. 'Some peasants, some villages—'

I thought of Tawfeek and his accountancy. 'They're more than that!'

'We won't come to exploit, but to share. We will share this land with all who will work with us.'

'What if they don't want to work with you?'

'We will bring the best minds in Europe, we will bring all that was good in the old Europe and we will bring our passion, our ideals. Who would not want to share this?'

I shook my head. 'Hanke, all this is beyond me. But I cannot help you create a training college for agrarian communists.'

She smiled: a big, broad, generous smile. 'Fine. Then we'll do it ourselves.'

***

After Hanke left, Eleanor turned to me. 'You handled her well. But maybe you could've given her a bit more.'

'Maybe.' I shrugged. The heady idealism that Hanke lived and breathed left me feeling old and jaded. And I wasn't sure that Eleanor was right: should we be giving *more* to Hanke? Wasn't our job to persuade Hanke to be realistic and ask for *less*?

'But do you believe her?' I asked Eleanor.

'Believe her?' replied Eleanor. 'What's there to doubt?'

'Are conditions in Poland as bad as she says?'

'I think they may be. Hanke's reminded me of something.'

'Yes?'

'You remember our Polish DPs?'

'Of course. Nice people. Cooperative. Polite, mostly.' I smiled. The Poles had become pleasant memories.

'Yes, yes. How many of them were Jewish?'

'Jewish? Why—none. Weren't they all Catholics?'

'Apparently, in 1939 one-tenth of the Polish population was Jewish. What happened to them? Do you think Tymon would've accepted Jews onto his committee?'

'Yes, of course he would.' But even as I spoke, I doubted my words. There'd been something all-encompassing about the Poles' Catholicism. Not much room left for other faiths.

'Well, where were the Polish Jews? Did we ever meet any?'

When I said nothing, Eleanor continued: 'I think she's right. Anti-Semitism is still a danger in Poland. Borders are closing everywhere, despite reconstruction and the need for workers. And these people need a home *now*. Where else can they go except Palestine?'

'But—Tawfeek—'

Eleanor tutted. 'I think he exaggerated. Look at Hanke. She wouldn't hurt a fly, she and her group are pacifists. And it's part of a dialectical process.'

There was that word again. I was lost.

'She's bringing to Marxism something it's never had,' said Eleanor. 'She—and the people like her—they're creating a socialist *ethic*, based on the communal labour.' She nodded, as if this was something very important.

I thought back to our night in the waiting-room in Morocco.

'Remember Nafah's words?' I asked Eleanor. I had a brief memory of Nafah dramatically waving her hands and looking right at me.

Eleanor shook her head.

'She asked: how can you create socialism by taking another people's land?'

'Hanke and her friends won't *take* anything,' said Eleanor patiently. 'They'll just farm the empty land that's not being used and they'll form cooperatives. They'll train the Arabs in modern, scientific farming techniques.'

'Palestine's not a big place,' I told her. I remembered something that my father had said. 'It's about the size of Wales. And UNRRA—'

'UNRRA's confused about this,' said Eleanor. 'No one imagined that there'd be so many DPs who didn't want to return home. And their numbers are growing all the time.'

'And as for Palestine—'

'The Mandate authorities don't want new arrivals, it's true. But that makes me suspicious.'

'Why?'

'The last excuse they use to stay in India is that they're needed to protect the Muslims,' said Eleanor. 'They seem to be trying the same trick in Palestine.'

'What do you think should happen?'

Eleanor shrugged her shoulders. 'British forces should get out, I suppose. Let the Jews and Arabs sort out their differences between themselves. But, in the meantime—'

'Hanke isn't going to wait, is she?'

Eleanor shook her head. 'There are attempts to smuggle Jews from Europe into Palestine.'

'We can't assist in that!'

'No, of course not. But we can't stop it either.'

I was confused by Hanke. On the one hand, who would've thought that such a bright flower would grow in the debris of Europe's bombed cities? On the other hand, I'd met people like her before, among my father's Methodists. Full of righteous zeal. Well-meaning, for the most part. I remembered one of my father's warnings: *Light yourself on fire with passion and people will come for miles to watch you burn.* Eleanor was moved, even inspired, by Hanke's idealism. I was more sceptical: she was harmless, I supposed. And, yes, her activities and meetings did constitute a sort of rehabilitation. But where was it leading?

It was odd to disagree with Eleanor about politics. Normally Eleanor was so sharp-thinking about world events—throughout the war, she'd been the one who'd accurately predicted what would come next. What did she see in Hanke that I'd missed?

29. The UNRRA Conference

Snow fell almost every day in January. It lay *deep and crisp and even*. Each bungalow was covered in a thick white blanket and the shattered city had some of its wounds covered. The cellar-dwelling troglodytes and stall-holders at the imitation markets shivered and froze. Travel became difficult: thick icy patches covered the roads and that nasty, treacherous hole grew deeper at the entrance of our camp. It was about a yard deep and a yard wide, and caused problems for anyone who drove in or out. We trudged back and forth from our houses to the camp, hoping each day that an American truck would bring more coal and that it would be proper coal, the sort that produced some heat and not just a nasty, sooty smell.

But the snow brought some blessings. Under its blanket, Hanke and her disciples were less active. The hall hadn't been reconstructed: even the American commander couldn't produce building materials as fast as Hanke wanted. Dan reported that fervent meetings continued in the walled-off suburbs of the bungalows: there were classes in Hebrew and on Jewish history, even an attempt to teach agriculture. Pierre muttered suspiciously about strange new faces coming and going. But all seemed calm. I checked the accounts and sent them to UNRRA's central office. Eleanor, Dan and Alma produced lists of items that our DPs needed and I went through them and deleted everything I thought was superfluous. There was a limit to the number of sewing-machines and type-writers that UNRRA could supply.

In February, UNRRA arranged a two-day conference for teams in the American zone. It was a stupid time for a conference. Although much of the *autobahns* were repaired, snow and ice made travel difficult, even dangerous. We'd need to drive a hundred miles to Frankfurt. Our team discussed the conference in a meeting and I said I didn't expect everyone to attend. Victor was openly dismissive: he was growing more critical of UNRRA and talked of transferring to the American military government. Alma and Pierre had sick DPs to care for and Pierre was so annoyed with UNRRA's questionnaires that he wasn't in the right mood for a conference. In the end, Eleanor, Dan and I decided to go. We all had criticisms of UNRRA, but we thought it was worth talking about our experiences.

Thankfully it wasn't snowing on the day of the conference. In fact, it was one of those bright, crisp February days with a sky so blue that you could almost think it was summer. Jacques checked my Daimler and declared it road-worthy. Just as we were about to go, Alma ran into my office. She needed morphine for an elderly man with an emergency kidney problem. I signed the form while Dan and Eleanor waited.

Once Alma had left, I said, 'She's probably being over-careful. Pierre makes sure the surgery's well-stocked.'

Eleanor smiled. 'That sounds like Alma!'

We wrapped ourselves in our greatcoats and scarves, grabbed our sandwiches and thermos flasks and set out, Eleanor with the map. We agreed that Dan and I would share the driving. Dan sat in the back as Eleanor directed me to the *autobahn*.

'Have you heard the latest joke?' Dan asked after a few minutes.

He was always picking up jokes: people liked to talk to him, they saw him as a ready audience. These days, he was even chatting to Germans.

'No,' said Eleanor.

That was all the encouragement that Dan needed and off he started.

In a ruined German city, a thin man in a ragged coat lolls against a wall. He watches a street-cleaner with a broom, a shovel and a dust-trolley slowly advance along a battered street. It's obvious that the street-cleaner doesn't know his job: his trolley catches on the potholes and he can't use the broom and shovel properly. The thin man watches. When the street-cleaner reaches him, the thin man calls out:

'Alright?'

The street-cleaner stops and wipes his brow.

'Can't say I am,' he replies. 'Tough work, this. Of course, I'm not used to it. I used to work for the government.'

'Under the Führer?' asks the thin man.

'Yes. They gave me a huge office: great polished wooden desk, pretty secretary, magnificent car. I had a wonderful house, a beautiful wife, three children and a couple of cute girls on the side. Oh, I've known some good times. But now...' The street-cleaner sighs.

'What happened?' asks the thin man.

'De-nazification. I lost everything.'

'How terrible.'

'No point grumbling,' says the street-cleaner.

He picks up his broom and shovel, grabs the handles of his trolley and is about to move off, when a thought occurs to him.

'What about you?' he asks the thin man.

'A bit like you. I lost everything after de-nazification.'

'Really?' The street-cleaner is interested. Maybe this thin man is an old comrade. 'Why, what were you?'

The thin man gives him a long, hard look and then says, 'I used to be a street-cleaner.'

Eleanor and I roared with laughter.

'I used to be a street-cleaner!' repeated Eleanor, before warning me to keep my eyes on the road.

'Oh dear,' I said. 'Is it really that bad? Aren't the Allies doing anything useful?'

'They rely so much on that bloody form,' said Dan.

'The dreaded *fragebogen*?' I asked. Everyone in Germany knew that word.

'That's the one: six pages long, one hundred and thirty-one questions, and over thirteen million of them distributed.'

'And the idea is?'

Dan sighed. 'Who knows? Can you really tell a good German from a bad Nazi by their answers on a form? Look at Hildegard. If she filled out that form, it'd show that she was linked to the Party, to its charities—she had to be. Does that make her a Nazi?'

'What do you think should happen?' I asked Dan.

'The Soviets have the right idea. You know what they say: first food, then morality. Radical social reform. Abolish the ruling class, put the workers in power, that'll make sure that no Hitler ever comes back.'

'But—' Eleanor and I said together. We glanced at each other and she continued:

'Their methods are so brutal, Dan. Sometimes the Soviet cure seems as bad as the German disease. And I don't see much sign of working-class power in the Soviet zone.'

'And those Russians—the ones we first met in the camp,' I added.

'They were a rough lot,' conceded Dan. 'But remember what they'd been through.'

'Aren't we in UNRRA managing better than the Allies and the Military Governments?' I asked. 'We're trying to help people.'

'*Helping the people to help themselves*,' intoned Eleanor, making it sound like a pious line from a catechism.

'Looking at our current lot, I'd say some of them don't want to be helped,' Dan said.

'We're doing good,' I insisted. 'We're making things better.'

'It's interesting,' said Dan. 'I'll say that. After five years in that military printshop, I had to get out. I wanted to see Germany, to see what we're doing here.'

'And now you know!' said Eleanor. 'We've distributed millions of *fragebogen* while the population starves and freezes. And UNRRA keeps telling us that we can only care for the DPs, it's not our job to help Germans.'

She pointed to a turning on the right and I pulled the wheel round.

'I'll take care of Hilde,' Dan said, almost as if he was talking to himself. 'I'll make sure she and her kids are alright.'

In a way, I envied Dan. At that moment, he could say he was helping the Germans. What were Eleanor and I doing for them? Sometimes UNRRA seemed very self-satisfied.

We were on the *autobahn* now. The snow had melted in the sunshine and the Daimler sped along, reaching 60 mph.

'This is the way to travel,' I said.

'Careful, Edmund,' said Eleanor. 'There are patches of ice on the road.'

Eleanor turned the wireless on and found some jazz music: proper jazz, played by black musicians, not the syrupy stuff churned out by the swing orchestras. It was good to get away from the camp, good to drive this luxury car along the straight, grey highway in the glittering sunshine, through valleys and round hills, whizzing past the military trucks that lumbered along in the slow lane. We got to Frankfurt in record time: I'd have happily driven further.

***

'Not this again,' groaned Dan.

I knew what he meant. It was like being back in Granville—but worse, for now we had nine months experience of running DP camps. We'd hoped this conference would be a chance to exchange notes with other teams, to evaluate successes and failures, maybe to learn something useful. But, no, UNRRA had other ideas. There was a long table on a raised platform at one end of the room. One by one they filed in and sat along it, the colonels and majors, nodding to each other and exchanging polite whispers.

'Not a single woman,' hissed Eleanor.

I didn't catch the name of the first speaker, but it didn't really matter. He was a tall, thin, weasel-like fellow with square glasses, obviously used to giving orders, but trying to sound welcoming.

'And so,' he said, 'repatriation must begin again in the spring. Teams must try harder to persuade Displaced Persons to return to their rightful homes. This residue, this hard core, cannot be permitted to stay in the camps, and—above all—their numbers *must not grow.*'

I heard Dan snort next to me. In fact, all around there were ripples of annoyance: people shifted in their chairs, tutted, shook their heads.

As soon as I'd heard the speaker's English accent, my heart had sunk. What was wrong with us Brits? I'd seen plenty of American incompetence and bullying in the last nine months. I knew the Russians could be brutal, but maybe Dan had a point: at least they had a strategy for de-nazifying Germany. As for the French—they had no real power. But us Brits! To my shame, I knew we specialized in a splendid blend of ineffectual gestures and old-fashioned colonial arrogance.

Another ripple of annoyance went through the audience. Behind me someone said *no* in a quiet, clear voice.

'Further resources will be provided,' said the speaker hurriedly. His eyes glanced back and forth across the hall. 'More rations, a subsidy—'

'Nonsense!' said a woman to my left.

The speaker stopped for a moment and looked along the rows of listeners, like a teacher trying to spot a disruptive pupil. Next to me, Eleanor was shifting in her chair. No, she wasn't: she'd stood up. All the great and good on the platform stared at her.

'You seem unaware of some basic facts—' she began.

'There'll be time for questions from the floor at the end of my paper,' interrupted the speaker.

'Madam, I remind you we have a lengthy agenda to get through today,' said the chairman, giving Eleanor a stern look.

That would be it, I thought. She'd sit down now.

'Let her speak!' It was a woman, the same one who'd called out *nonsense* earlier.

'Yes, let her speak!' An American, sitting somewhere to the front.

The cry was taken up across the hall. The speaker looked at the chairman, who shrugged his shoulders. With obvious reluctance, the speaker sat down and the hall fell silent. All eyes were on Eleanor.

She spoke in that measured, taut tone that I knew so well.

'You seem unaware of some basic facts about the Displaced Persons. You speak of *returning home*. Many of those you call the *residue*, have no homes to return to.'

'Exactly!' called out the woman to the left, while others muttered *yes* or nodded.

'In some cases, their homes have been bombed or destroyed by military action. But in other cases, the problem is still more serious. Nations have been twisted by these long years of conflict and by the evil presence of Nazism.'

The audience was silent, hanging on Eleanor's every word. Her voice rose, echoing round that cold hall.

'Do you realise that anti-Semitic, Jew-baiting violence continues in Eastern Europe? Have you not heard the polite, discrete anti-Semitism in the committee rooms and cocktail parties of western capitals? Under these circumstances, how can you expect a Jewish DP to *return* to his home?'

The speaker moved to stand up, but was restrained by the man sitting next to him.

'We talk of rehabilitation and reconstruction,' continued Eleanor. 'We must apply these words more consistently, we must apply them to nations themselves. Each nation must be *rehabilitated*, each must become a home for *all* its people: for the Jews, and also for the coloured people, the gypsies, the religious minorities: for all the down-trodden and forgotten victims of the conflict.'

The speaker abruptly stood up. 'Now look here! I've heard quite enough from you. We're here to discuss UNRRA camps, not the whole of Europe.'

Immediately, I knew what to do. I saw it, I just saw it. Without thinking, I was on my feet.

'How many UNRRA camps have you been to?' I shouted.

His face went white. He opened his mouth, but said nothing. My words were taken up across the hall. *How many?* people shouted. *How many?*

'I've visited...' he began, then his voice trailed away.

'How long have you spent in an UNRRA camp?' I called out.

The hall fell silent.

'I've made official visits to three—'

There was a great wave of jeers and catcalls. People laughed at him and there were shouts of *sit down*.

When silence returned, I was still standing next to Eleanor.

'We've been running an UNRRA camp for nine months,' I said. 'And, let me tell you, it hasn't been easy.'

To my astonishment, my words were greeted with prolonged applause from across the hall. I'd stated what everyone in the audience had been thinking: we were the experts on UNRRA camps, not the speakers on the platform.

***

The Conference had to be changed. Dan helped, using the skills he'd picked up in his rabble-rousing days as a trade unionist. Instead of the hoi polloi listening to the wisdom of the great and good, each UNRRA worker who wanted to report on their camps spoke for fifteen minutes and then took questions. Dan made himself chairman and chose who was to speak next. Eleanor nudged him occasionally and made him select female speakers. It was a varied tapestry: an American Welfare Officer obsessed with counting calories and making sure that DPs ate fresh vegetables; an aristocratic-sounding Pole who spoke with tears in his eyes about the DPs' stories of suffering; a Quaker who found evidence of a new spirituality among the DPs; a ferocious Frenchman who warned that tough Allied policies were only provoking a nostalgia for Hitler's regime among the Germans. Surprisingly, only one or two of the UNRRA big-wigs walked out. The others stayed, maybe thinking that eventually they'd take back control of the proceedings, but I think some grew interested in what we were saying.

Yes, it probably sounded incoherent—but all these people knew what they were talking about. And within it all, there was that core, the point which had originally attracted Eleanor and me to UNRRA: these were people who wanted to make the world a better place.

At the end of that long afternoon, Dan stepped between Eleanor and me, put an arm round each of us, looked us both in the eye, grinned and said:

'Your finest hour.'

35. Confrontations

After several attempts, I managed to get an appointment with the Commander at the American base. He was as affable as ever: offering me coffee, congratulating me on our camp's successes. But when it came to the main issue...

'A hole? In the road?'

'It's because of the ice. It's right at the entrance, it's becoming dangerous, it can't be filled in.'

He laughed. 'Hell, can't you just drive round it?'

'No, not for much longer. Soon the trucks won't be able to get in.'

'We'll sort it out then.' He smiled at me.

I gave up, exchanged a few pleasantries, then stomped out.

Outside, I saw Pierre, in the road leading to the back of the base. He was loading a large box into the back of his car. He shot me an odd glance—I guessed he was embarrassed about his new Daimler.

'Nice car, Pierre.' It was: large, black and glossy. I felt a pang of jealousy, then told myself to stop being petty. 'Ideal for your medical supplies.'

He nodded. 'Exactly. But you must excuse me—Alma needs these.'

He left without another word—my second failed conversation of the morning. Didn't anyone want to talk to me? Pierre always had a lot on his plate.

I drove back to the camp to meet my secretary, Lena. Her typing was so beautiful that I couldn't let her go. Only a few Poles were allowed to migrate to England and Lena hoped to be one of them. I hoped she would be too, but not yet. That afternoon, we were checking and revising a list of required items from Dan: blackboards, desks and inkpots. Half-way through we stopped for a coffee. I mentioned that I'd bumped into Pierre at the American base and said how much I admired him and Alma, dealing with constant emergencies.

Lena frowned. 'I think the surgery is almost empty now.'

'Then why does he always want more supplies?'

Before Lena could answer, there was a strange crackling noise outside. She jumped.

'A car?' I said.

She shook her head and looked scared. 'No, I know that sound. That's gunfire.'

'Gunfire?'

Without a thought, I put down my coffee and walked out.

'Be careful!' called Lena.

I felt sure that I wouldn't get hurt. Maybe it was stupidity or innocence: after all, I'd never been in an armed conflict. Outside, I heard shouts coming from the DPs' bungalows.

'*Deutsche raus!*'

I'd picked up enough German to understand this: *Germans, out!* What did it mean? I ran to the square in front of the bungalows. There was another crackle of shots. They were coming from the bungalows. A bullet whizzed past me. I kept running. I noticed Dan at the door of the stores. He dashed after me.

But then—my God—on the ground, a crumpled figure, lying in a way that looked wrong. A red stain flowed from his chest.

'Get Pierre!' I shouted to Dan as I ran towards the body.

A few more steps and I fell to my knees, sliding in the snow. I feared there might be more shots. I shouted towards the DPs in the bungalows:

'Stop! Stop! He's hurt.'

Stupid really. If they'd been shooting at him, they wanted to hurt him, didn't they?

I didn't move him: somewhere I'd heard that this could make any wound worse. But I lowered myself to look at the man's face, half-covered by his cap and scarf. He was an old man, with deep wrinkles round his eyes and a yellowing moustache. His face was twisted with pain. He smelt of cheap tobacco, the sort the Germans smoked. I brushed some snow off him, it was the least I could do and recognised the grey uniform. A policeman! He looked up at me, tears filling his eyes. The blood from his chest was flowing onto the ground, it was staining my trousers. He croaked something in German that I didn't understand.

'Pierre! Where's Pierre?' I shouted.

As I watched, he gave a little cough, and some drops of blood trickled down his mouth. Then his face grew greyer and the tension left him.

'No...' I said.

I felt that I knelt there for hours, panting at first from my running, sweat dripping down my back, my legs growing stiffer, wetter and colder, the policeman's blood flowing into the white snow. The camp was very quiet: there were a few faces at the doors and windows of the bungalows, and I noticed another policeman, a younger man, crouched at the corner of a bungalow. I felt I was at the very centre of the camp, quite still, while all around me, people moved in a slow, quiet, circular fashion. This shouldn't have happened, by God this shouldn't have happened. A death, here, in a camp that was meant to repair the damage of the war and to preserve life, not to kill people.

'Pierre!' I yelled. Where was he?

He was by me in seconds. He knelt down and his hands flew over the policeman's body, his long fingers touched him gently at the neck and then carefully unbuttoned the man's patched greatcoat. Pierre sighed as more blood oozed out and then tutted.

'Too late,' was all he said.

I looked up at the cast-iron sky and suddenly, in that crowded camp with hundreds of people, I felt utterly alone.

At that moment, there was a swirl of movement behind me. I turned as Eleanor threw herself on me.

'Edmund!' she cried. 'Are you alright?'

She clutched me tight, staring at me.

'I'm fine, but...' I gestured to the dead policeman. She gasped.

A door opened in one of the bungalows and Joel stepped out. Without thinking, I shook Eleanor off and marched towards him.

'What do you call this?' I shouted at the top of my voice, pointing to the body in the square.

Joel looked confused. I wanted to get close to him, I wanted—I don't know what I wanted. But in some strange reversal of the scene by that terrible barn, Dan caught up with me and grabbed my arm.

'Edmund, stop!'

I looked at him, puzzled. Eleanor grabbed my other arm. Did they think I was going to attack Joel?

Some other DPs stood beside Joel. One held a rifle. And there was Hanke. Joel looked around him, took a deep breath and said:

'We will not permit the intrusion of German police into this camp.'

I lunged at him, but Dan and Eleanor held me back.

***

We met in my office—Alma was the last to arrive, she'd been talking to an expectant mother. Dan, Pierre and Eleanor seemed to know something about the causes of the incident. A story emerged. There'd been reports of black-market activity at our base, involving the smuggling of medicines. Two German policemen came to investigate. The younger one had fallen to the ground at the first sound of gunfire: he was unharmed. The older one had walked forward.

I couldn't contain myself anymore.

'What's going on here? This isn't why we joined UNRRA. We wanted to help the people who'd suffered during the war. Now there's been a death, a murder—a tragedy.

'Some of you say that black-market activities are inevitable, that any economic initiative by DPs will involve the black-market.' Eleanor signalled with her hand: she wanted me to stop. I ignored her. 'So it's not to be taken too seriously—even, that we should tolerate it.'

I looked round, furious. Now Dan wanted to speak, but I wouldn't stop.

'Look where it's got us. A murder. There must be armed gangs of black-marketeers among the DPs. This is unacceptable, absolutely unacceptable. UNRRA's regulations are there for a reason and must be obeyed *to the letter.*'

I looked round the room. A minute ago they'd been trying to stop me talking, but now there was silence. My words echoed in my mind and I thought how inadequate they sounded. Everyone looked shocked. Pierre had a face like thunder, Alma was close to crying.

'Where did those shots come from?' I said. 'Who's got weapons in this camp? There was more than one person shooting, wasn't there?'

Dan nodded.

'With the assistance of the American forces,' I continued, 'we will institute a meticulous search for weapons—'

'Edmund.' It was Eleanor, again. What did she have to say? 'Edmund. The shots. I don't think they were from criminals or black-marketeers.'

'No?'

'I believe—I think they were from the DP police force.'

'The police force! But I never gave permission that they could be armed!'

I looked at Victor.

'Don't look at me, buddy,' he said. 'Nobody asked me either.'

'The German police should've known,' said Eleanor. 'After all, they're not armed. The Allied forces won't allow it.'

I frowned. 'Those policemen came to investigate criminal activities. What should they have known?'

Eleanor looked at Dan.

He sighed. 'It's something the Jewish DPs insist on. No German policemen or officials in their camps. Now, I'm not going to excuse them, but—'

'—but there is a reason for it,' said Eleanor.

To my surprise, Alma nodded. 'It's a trauma,' she said. 'They've been left with a fear of all Germans, particularly those in uniforms.'

'But they know they're safe here,' I said.

'It's not that simple,' said Dan. 'It's something they learnt in those long, bad years.'

'Like those who starved,' added Alma. 'They can't stop themselves from hoarding tins. Even though they know that more rations will arrive tomorrow. They can't stop.'

'Deep down, they're still frightened,' said Eleanor. 'They can't forget what men in German uniforms did to them.'

'But...' I lost track of what I wanted to say.

Pierre signalled that he wanted to speak. 'I think we must see this in a bigger context. There has been massive violence in Europe. It didn't stop with Hitler's death and it may continue. While I do not condone the shooting of a policeman, even a *German* policeman, I remember the millions of deaths that regime caused.'

'But that doesn't solve the problem!' I shouted. 'It just makes everything worse.'

Pierre nodded, looking calm. 'Exactly. So how do we cure the disease? It's time to face the bigger issues.'

We were all looking at him now. What was he going to suggest?

'There must never be another Hitler,' he said and most of us nodded. 'And there are two ways to ensure this. Firstly, Germany must be kept weak. Call it de-Nazification, call it what you will, but she must never again be allowed her own army. Secondly, the other nations of Europe must arise from the ruins stronger and more united than ever.'

I frowned. None of this seemed relevant.

'What are you suggesting, Pierre?' I asked.

'It's very simple. I am a Frenchman and I say: France for the French, Palestine for the Jews. Let each race have their own nation.'

'What?'

'The Jews are not happy here, in Europe. They have never mixed with other people...'

'Pierre!' Dan interrupted. 'This is ridiculous. Jews have thrived in Europe.'

'They have always kept to themselves,' answered Pierre. 'And there is a reason for this: they are different. It's biological.'

Laughs and disagreement burst out at his words.

'Biological!' sneered Dan.

'Do not misunderstand me,' said Pierre. 'I am no Nazi. I am a doctor: I heal and prevent pain. The true solution to the Jewish Question is not extermination, but foundation of their own home. It is a matter of biology.'

Dan snorted. 'You really believe that being Jewish is a matter of biology?'

'Of course,' said Pierre.

'Next you'll be saying that you can recognise a Jew by the shape of his nose!'

'No, it is more complicated than that. Each race has its own distinctive culture.'

Dan looked at me and Eleanor, and then laughed.

I wanted to call the meeting to order, but I was so shocked by Pierre's words that I had to respond. I looked round me: I saw Eleanor, half-Indian and half-English. I saw Dan, a Jew who was as English as anyone I knew. I thought of myself: born in Wales, but living in London. What was Pierre suggesting?

'But, Pierre,' I said. 'What you're saying would mean the end of any fusions between peoples: what of exchanges, of dialogues?'

'Of course, these are permitted, but to be authentic, they must be between properly formed racial groups.'

'So a Jew can't convert to Catholicism?'

'Not if he is true to himself. Look at Hanke: her father converted and now she tries with all her strength to renew her Jewish roots.'

'This is nonsense,' said Eleanor. 'And not just nonsense: it's poisonous nonsense. There's only one race and we all belong to it, we all *fully* belong to it: that's the human race. That's the only one that matters.'

I nodded. As always, Eleanor spoke with an eloquence that escaped me.

'I disagree,' said Pierre.

Victor smiled. 'While I don't follow my French friend in his cloudy racial mysticism, at least he's got an answer. What do we do with the Jewish DPs who won't repatriate? Make a place for them in Palestine.'

'But there are already Palestinians in Palestine!' I said.

'The less evolved races must make way for the superior races, and—' said Pierre, but shouts from Dan, Eleanor and Alma stopped him from continuing.

I called the meeting to order.

'None of this is relevant.' I glared at Pierre. 'We're here to run a camp for displaced persons. Let's stick to practical issues.'

'But it *is* relevant,' said Victor. 'It is practical. Activists like Hanke are working for a Jewish Palestine. They want to leave as soon as possible. They're creating illegal, underground routes, through Italy, across the Mediterranean. For them, it's a very practical issue. Hanke has already contacted Palestinian Jews.'

Pierre nodded.

'Well, we can't help them,' I said. 'And UNRRA can't help them. We don't control the borders of Palestine, which are currently closed to further immigration.'

'Palestine!' said Victor. He shook his head. 'That's the root of the problem.'

I looked at him, puzzled.

'You Brit's want to preserve your empire at any cost,' continued Victor. 'Why don't you just let the Jews in?'

His words annoyed me. It wasn't as if I personally ran Palestine. But I answered carelessly, adopting his terms.

'If you Americans care so much about it,' I asked, 'why don't you open up your borders to refugees from Europe?'

Dan laughed, which annoyed me. There wasn't anything funny in what we were discussing. But then he spoke:

'He's got a point, Victor. You used to welcome the *huddled masses*. Can't you take a few more?'

'For Chrissake.' Victor looked uncomfortable. 'This war was your problem: you Europeans. First we sent you trucks, planes and tanks. And then we sent you GIs. Many of them will be staying here, in their graves—'

'—not as many as the Russians,' interrupted Dan.

'Plenty of them,' insisted Victor. 'Too many. We've done enough. Now sort out your own problems. Dismantle your empires, reform your governments, build your economies. Can't you do that by yourselves?'

This had gone on too long. We weren't a team anymore, just a group of people scoring points. I thought of that policeman, dying in front of me. I'd seen a few corpses in the last months, but I'd never actually seen someone die. I couldn't forget it. I wanted this meeting to achieve something, we owed the dead man that much. I took a deep breath and tried to bring some gravity back to our discussion.

'A man was murdered, just a couple of hours ago. A man going about his legitimate business. *In our camp*. What are we going to do about it?'

I hoped this memory might make the discussion change tone but, no, the mood had been ruined. Pierre had dragged us away with his pseudo-biology and Victor was smarting from the comments by Dan and me.

'Hell, we'll clear it up for you,' Victor said.

'What do you mean?' I asked.

'Our Military Police will hold some investigation, for the sake of form.'

'Will they prosecute the Jewish DPs?' asked Dan.

Victor thought about it for a moment. 'Probably not. Our government respects *the legitimate aspirations of the Jewish people*.' He spoke as if quoting from a government document. 'We can't muddy the waters, we want to stay friends with them. So—there'll be an investigation and I guess they'll conclude that there was an accident.'

'An accident!' I was astonished. 'But there was a volley of shots from the bungalows.'

Eleanor looked up. 'We don't *know* that the DPs were firing.'

'Of course they were. Who else could it have been?'

She shrugged. 'Other people might've infiltrated the camp.'

'You weren't there!' I shouted. 'I *saw* the shooting, hell, the shots whizzed past me. And I saw Joel and Hanke there.'

'I'm just saying—' Eleanor began.

'You're not saying anything worth listening to,' I told her.

Eleanor stared at me: my words shocked her. She pointed at me, opened her mouth to speak—then stopped. We waited, but she looked away. Good, I thought. If she won't support me, then she shouldn't speak at all. The others were silent: they'd never heard me and Eleanor disagreeing like this.

Lena continued typing next door and Dan lit a cigarette.

'I guess this policeman made a mistake,' said Victor. 'He should've known better than to enter a Jewish DP Camp.'

'We're an *UNRRA* camp,' I corrected him.

'If you say so.'

Something else occurred to me. 'The black-market activities: the dealing in medicines. Is that really going on here?'

Dan looked at Eleanor and Pierre. 'Doubt it,' he said. 'Our DPs deal mainly in cigarettes and canned fruit. They make a tidy profit from them.'

Pierre looked away, Victor nodded.

'So—it was all—' I said.

'All for nothing,' Victor said.

'A turf war, I reckon,' said Dan. 'The coppers trying to prove a point. Show they could come in, if they wanted.'

Victor nodded. He was looking bored. 'Are we finished now? Because I have a meeting with the American commander.'

'No, wait,' I said. Victor glared at me. 'What about the funeral?'

'Do you want our boys to do that as well?' he said.

'Edmund,' said Dan patiently. 'The German police will have their own ideas about when and where to bury him. It's not for us to decide.'

My God, that was the worst meeting ever. After such a terrible event, no one said anything useful and Eleanor let me down.

31. Losing Eleanor

'What were you playing at in that meeting?' I asked Eleanor.

We were back in Hildegard's house and had the drawing-room to ourselves.

'It was a bloody difficult meeting, right after that murder,' I continued. 'Can't I expect *my wife* to support me at such moments?'

'I've a right to my own views!'

I stared at her. 'What views? What else is there to say about it? A policeman was murdered in our camp.'

'Edmund—the political situation here, it's not as simple as you think.'

'Yes, it is!'

'Those police. Some of them served under Hitler.'

'They've been de-Nazified.'

Eleanor shrugged. 'There isn't a stock of trained, anti-fascist policemen to recruit, don't you see?'

'So?'

'So—some police are still suspicious of any Jewish organisation. And now—if they can pin a murder on Hanke and her group—'

'So that's it!'

'What?'

'You want to defend Hanke, at any cost.'

'And you want to attack her, whatever happens. She wasn't involved, Edmund.'

'She was there in the square, I saw her.'

'She wouldn't shoot someone.'

'Somebody did. Maybe one of her disciples.'

'It wasn't Hanke,' insisted Eleanor. 'Or any of the DPs who work with her. People always blame Hanke for anything that goes wrong. Joel, or one of the others, will use this against her.'

'She's been inflaming the DPs, making them believe that they're above the law. Something like this was bound to happen.'

'They've got a right to be angry after what they've been through!'

'You're condoning murder, are you?'

'No—but... There's a bigger context and you don't want to see it.'

'Eleanor: I've been here for ten months, just like you, and I've seen plenty. I'm capable of making up my own mind after witnessing a murder.'

'But you don't see—what Hanke believes in—what she's trying to do—you don't understand how she inspires—'

'Are you saying I don't understand my own camp?'

'No, it's not that Edmund, it's just that...'

More thoughts welled up inside me. I didn't stop to think. 'You don't trust me, you've been using me! I've been just a—just a front, a puppet for you to direct—'

Eleanor glared at me. 'How dare you! You're the one who's exploiting me. In your eyes, I'm just a glorified sandwich-maker.'

'When have you ever listened to me? To my ideas?'

'When have you ever had any?'

'I've got responsibility for this whole bloody camp. When do I have time to think?'

I sensed a gap between us, a deep gap that could grow wider. Should I push further? Should I stop? I didn't want this to get out of hand. I took a deep breath and tried to remember what we shared.

'We came here because we wanted to help people,' I said. Eleanor nodded, looking at me suspiciously. 'We wanted to do our bit—to help make the world a better place after the destruction.'

'And Hanke's farm—it's the best example of that!'

I shook my head. 'No! They're a bunch of backward-looking zealots. A dentist's daughter, dressing up like a worker and pretending to be a farmer.'

'Edmund! That's a horrible thing to say.'

'Is it?'

'She's lost her family, she's got no one. She's trying to re-make her life.'

'That's exactly the point. We should help her find a home and have a new family here in Europe, not let her chase some utopia in the East.'

'That's never going to happen. I heard a lecture on the wireless the other night, talking about the war that Hitler won. There's race-thinking everywhere, even now. People can be so stupid. They hit out against the minorities to make themselves feel big. It hasn't stopped.'

'Why do you admire Hanke so much, Eleanor?'

'Don't you see? She'll bring socialism to the Orient. It's a way of joining East and West.'

'And Tawfeek?'

Eleanor made an angry, contemptuous gesture. 'Tawfeek! A minor son of some outdated Muslim aristocracy. They're the backward-looking ones. What have his sort ever done for the people?'

'At the UNRRA conference you talked about nations becoming homes for all their people.'

'I'm sure Hanke will make Palestine into a home for all its people.'

Another pause. I thought of reaching out to her, telling her I understood, even if I disagreed. But I was still angry. Couldn't she see how difficult Hanke made it for me to run the camp? And how could I direct the Team if she attacked me in front of the others?

We stopped arguing when Hildegard called us for dinner.

***

Afterwards, we went to our bedroom and talked some more. I didn't repeat my accusation that she'd been manipulating me, but I thought about it over the next few days. All those words of advice, all those little signals during the meetings. In the end, I decided there was what the police might call *circumstantial evidence*. If I wanted to make a case against Eleanor, I could. On the other hand—I didn't want to. I had to acknowledge that, usually, I was grateful for her advice. It was just that now—I really thought she was wrong about Hanke.

I didn't like it, not at all. I wondered if Eleanor wanted to leave me. Life without Eleanor seemed impossible, but I could see that life with her came at a cost. Maybe it had been a mistake to think we could work as a husband-and-wife team.

Both of us were surprised by the force of our argument and, after a few days, both of us decided that we didn't want a separation. We worked at a compromise. I agreed that Eleanor had the right to her own views and that I'd listen to them. She agreed not to challenge me in Team meetings. She accepted that I'd learnt something as well, that being a Team Director wasn't easy, and that perhaps she was romanticizing Hanke and her disciples. I agreed to help Hanke more in future. Was this enough?

'We've only got one more month here,' I reminded her, trying to speak more softly.

She looked at me, nodded, but said nothing.

There remained a distance between us. A page had been turned and we couldn't un-say what had been said. We talked less in the mornings, after breakfast: there was always something urgent that needed doing instead. In the evenings, Eleanor would type in her little room and sometimes stay there overnight. She'd say that she'd fallen asleep over her typewriter. Maybe it was better that we stayed apart for a while.

32. The Enemy Within

'Wait, Eleanor, this is important.'

'I've got a class to arrange.'

'It's about Pierre.'

We'd finished breakfast and she wanted to leave straight away. But when I mentioned Pierre's name she stopped.

'Pierre!' she said. 'That man's got some strange ideas. Has he been causing trouble with Hanke's group?'

'No, it's not that. It's the accounts.'

She lost interest straight away.

'There's something that doesn't add up,' I continued.

'Accounts! I can't make head nor tail of them. That's your job, Edmund, you've got to sort them out.'

'He's ordering medical supplies, every week, but the surgery's almost empty now, isn't it?'

Eleanor stopped and thought. 'It was very busy in November and December. But now—the serious cases go to the American hospital. Alma's moved on to preventative work, giving advice.'

'So why's Pierre—'

'Look, Edmund, I think you're too suspicious. The incident with the policeman—it's unsettled you. It was awful, I know. But Pierre—well, I don't like him as much as I used to, now I know how he thinks, but you saw him at that awful barn! And with the policeman.'

'Yes, I know—'

'Could anyone have been more professional?'

'No, but—'

'So you've got to trust his judgement, alright? Asking questions is only going to upset people and we need Pierre.'

She left without another word.

***

Later that morning I reviewed the problem. The thought of publicly criticizing Pierre made me nervous: accusing him of corruption seemed impossible. I thought about my own lifestyle. I lived very comfortably in Germany. In London, I'd never have stayed in somewhere as plush as Hildegard's house, I'd never have driven a bottle-green Daimler, I'd never have had an efficient, friendly secretary like Lena. And while nine-tenths of Germany starved in that freezing winter, we lived like kings off the fat of the land. Well, if not kings, then certainly pretty well-heeled minor aristocrats.

Wasn't this corruption, really, wasn't it? I was corrupt, I was corrupted. I had the usual defences: look what the others got up to! Even Victor's silver-grey Mercedes out-classed my bottle-green Daimler. Hadn't I earnt my house, my car, my office, my generous rations and my secretary? So many Allied personnel grasped these prizes without a second thought. But these privileges weren't good for us: it was so easy to take them for granted. And now—maybe the atmosphere had got to Pierre as well. What could I do?

Obviously, Eleanor wasn't going to help me. Who else could I contact? Dan? Dan might be interested, but he'd charge in. Alma and Victor would be unwilling to challenge Pierre directly. Jacques was too nice. Was there anyone in the American base? This was about their supplies, after all. What about our main contact, Sam?

I met Sam in his office. It wasn't like the Commander's office—just a little box room with a grimy window. He didn't offer me coffee or tell me that I was doing a great job. But he was interested in what I said.

'Morphine,' he said, nodding. 'There's a lot of it on the black-market. Hell, you can get anything on the black-market these days.'

'Why morphine?'

He shrugged. 'Two reasons. There are people with acute problems with pain—after the war. They can't get anything from their normal doctors.'

I smiled grimly. 'In many places, there aren't any doctors.'

'Exactly.' Sam nodded. 'But also—addicts.'

'Addicts?'

'Yep. People take morphine for the kick and then find they can't get through the day without it.'

'Just like that?'

'It might take a few weeks.'

I nodded, relieved that someone took me seriously. 'But, Sam: what can we do now?'

I looked at him closely when I said *we*. To my relief, he met my gaze.

'We want to leave Europe in better shape than when we came,' he said. 'Encouraging dope addicts and drug-running isn't part of our mission.'

We talked for an hour, considering options.

***

Pierre's next scheduled visit to the American base was at 11 o'clock on Wednesday. The store he visited was at the back of the base: a large, brick, three-storey building, with a reception just inside the entrance. Sam had called in a couple of Military Policemen or MPs to meet us in a wrecked building opposite the store, at half past ten. It had no windows, but the door had been smashed about: we could see through it and observe the store. Inside, it was dark and dusty. The back wall was smashed, allowing us an exit that couldn't be seen from the store. The two MPs were tough, wary men, used to giving orders: an older one, with round glasses, willing to talk; the younger one more restless, constantly looking round the building and through the door.

The older one looked at me. 'UNRRA?'

'Yes.'

'We know something's going on—but your man... Well, his connection—it doesn't look likely.'

'It's Lieutenant Lerner in there today, at the stores,' explained Sam. 'Now, he's a good man.'

'Decorated after D-Day. Solid,' continued the older MP. 'You know what I'm saying?'

'On the other hand—' said Sam.

'Morphine, penicillin: it's all been going,' said the MP. He sighed.

'So—' I said.

'We watch and wait.'

Sam nodded. We stood quietly, listening to the sounds from the street at the front of the base: cars coming and going, GIs chatting, a horse neighing. The younger MP lit a cigarette and stayed close to the door.

'What's this?' he said.

We clustered round. A GI had arrived and was talking to Lerner. The GI pointed to front of the base and Lerner walked off in that direction.

'I'll check,' said the younger MP, leaving from the back of our building.

The GI walked into the store and sat down at the entrance.

'Well, I'll be...' said Sam.

Almost immediately, Pierre's car drew up. He got out, walked up the street with an easy stride, wearing a smart blue-grey greatcoat. As I looked at him, I knew I must be wrong. Pierre exuded confidence and reliability—how could I doubt him? He turned into the store entrance.

'What will he leave with?' whispered Sam. 'A small parcel or a box?'

Pierre came out, looked quickly to his left and right, then walked to his car. He carried a box under one arm—it was almost too big for him to hold. The sort of box he'd been carrying last time I saw him.

The older MP moved fast. He was through the door in a second. 'Just a second, sir.'

'Oldest trick in the book,' said Sam.

'What do you mean?'

'He goes in with a legitimate request for five vials of morphine, he signs for them, gives the guy at reception a few bucks, then leaves with fifty vials.'

***

A meeting was called in the Commander's office an hour later. I telephoned the Camp: Dan and Victor were away in Frankfurt, Alma was needed at the dispensary, but Eleanor would come. I waited for her at the entrance to the base, so I'd be with her when she faced the catcalls and shouts from the American soldiers. I spotted her walking. She stood out from the ragged Germans: tall and purposeful, striding along in her khaki trousers, her greatcoat open, flapping behind her. She seemed lost in thought. I felt something move deep inside me: Eleanor and I, we had to reconcile properly, I didn't want this tension between us to continue. Maybe when we got back to London... She looked up.

'Edmund!' she smiled. 'So you were right.'

'I'm afraid so.'

She stared into my eyes, nodding. 'But—Pierre?'

'It's an open-and-shut case. He must've thought that no one would check the accounts.'

She laughed. 'He reckoned without you!'

She shook her head, then looked at me again.

'Edmund—Edmund, I'm sorry I didn't believe you, I know I should've helped. It's just that—'

'—suspecting your colleagues isn't a nice thing to do?'

'No, it's not. And I would never have thought...'

'Neither would I. But shall we go in? I thought you might like me with you, when you...'

Eleanor looked at the courtyard. 'Oh, that. No, they've changed. I don't know whether someone had a word with them, or they got bored, or they've all found *frats*—but it's safe for a woman to enter here now.'

'Good.' At least there was one sign of progress in Germany.

***

There were six of us in the Commander's office: Eleanor and myself, the older MP, Sam, Pierre and the Commander himself. As always, he offered us coffee, but his attempt to put us at our ease was spoilt by the sight of Pierre in handcuffs, sitting awkwardly. He stared at the floor, refusing to look at us.

'Is that really necessary?' the Commander asked the MP, pointing to Pierre's handcuffs.

'Regulations,' said the MP.

'So...' said the Commander, drawing out the word into one long sigh. He glared at Pierre, as if blaming him for spoiling the comfort of his office. 'What have we here? Black-marketeering. Morphine.'

'And penicillin, sir,' said the MP.

'We've caught one,' continued the Commander. 'God knows how many others are out there. Good work, Sam, I'll make sure—'

'Sir,' said Sam, 'I can't take credit for this, sir. It was our colleagues from UNRRA who alerted me.'

'Really?' The Commander raised his eyebrows, looking at Eleanor and me.

Eleanor coughed. 'It was Edmund who spotted what was happening.'

'OK,' said the Commander, looking more closely at me. 'You came to see me about that hole in the road, outside your camp, right?'

I nodded.

'We'll get something done about that.' He scribbled a note, then faced Pierre. His face hardened. 'What did you think you were doing? You're a doctor, right? You know how valuable that stuff is?'

Pierre looked up for the first time. His face was grey, but his eyes were defiant. 'I had no choice.'

'You had no choice! What—someone made you steal morphine?'

'My son—he wants to go to medical school. And—'

'What?' asked the Commander.

'We have no money left, after the war. It has ruined us.'

'For Chrissake,' muttered the Commander. 'Was it really worth it?'

He stared at Pierre for a few moments, then said to the MP, 'Take him away.'

Pierre glared at me as he left.

***

Eleanor and I walked back to the camp.

'You must be feeling proud,' she said.

I didn't. I felt confused. What had I done? Ruined Pierre's career? And maybe blocked his son's chances as well. Black-marketeering would continue, the Commander had been right.

'I knew we couldn't trust Pierre after what he said at that meeting, I knew it,' continued Eleanor. 'And, you know, our trip to Morocco?'

'Yes?'

'I wonder if that wasn't all a set-up. Dr Thérèse couldn't see anything wrong with my lungs. Alright, I smoked too much...'

'He invented that?'

'He wanted you out of the way.'

We turned a corner, walked past the shattered buildings.

'I don't feel proud, not at all,' I said. 'We've lost a good colleague. Maybe I should've tried to talk to him instead...'

'He'd never have accepted that! He'd have exploded if you accused him of anything.'

'I wanted to be in a team of people that I could trust, all working together...' I said.

'I know. But—still, I don't understand. Why did he...'

'I think all the different elements came together.'

I explained: Pierre wanted to see a stronger France and came to believe that his family had to contribute to its re-building. 'Almost as if it was their destiny.'

Eleanor nodded. 'Nationalism. We're seeing it everywhere. But what Europe needs, what the world needs is—'

'Internationalism,' I said.

Eleanor slipped her arm through mine. 'You did the right thing.'

38. Birth and Death

The weather improved in March and, at first, April seemed positively balmy. The roads were safer and deliveries to the camp came frequently, if unpredictably. We wrote to Muriel and sometimes her reply came back the same week. The Americans had these new 10-ton trucks, great monsters that thundered along the roads, putting our battered 3-tonners to shame. The Americans seemed particularly proud of these giants and would drive them out to our camp to deliver a sack of potatoes or a hundred packets of cigarettes. Just showing off, I thought.

As the weather improved, the DPs grew more active. The hall was repaired and redecorated, and used for fervent meetings. I sent Dan to observe some of them, though he hated pretending not to understand Yiddish. One thing surprised me: I'd understood that there were two tendencies among the DPs—the moderates, like Joel, who wanted to work with us where possible, and the radicals, led by Hanke, burning with righteousness, who wanted to strike out on their own. But Dan told me it was more complicated than that. A religious revival had started among the DPs: some truly believed that Palestine was the Promised Land. Religious Jews controlled one of the schools and were rivals with the other school, which was secular. Parents were forced to choose. There were arguments about the correct rituals to follow at each date on the religious calendar. Then there were the DPs who were loyal to both Moscow and the new Jerusalem: true communists, they argued that Zionism in Palestine would modernize and industrialize the country, so transforming the Arabs into an industrial working-class, organised into trade unions. There were long debates about socialism and Zionism: were they compatible? Which was more important? Under other circumstances, I might have found all this rather interesting. It reminded me of arguments my father had with Methodists who joined the Labour Party.

Hanke got her tractor. She led her disciples in ploughing up a large patch of waste ground near the camp. But I noticed something. The DPs certainly admired her vision of agrarian communism and always listened to her passionate, idealistic speeches, but most of them showed no interest in working the land.

***

I had an interesting meeting with a DP and his wife. When I heard what they wanted to talk about, I mentioned it to Dan and he said he'd come along. Normally, I would have invited Eleanor, but in those days we weren't talking much.

Uri had been a tailor before the war. His skills in restoring and adapting old clothes were highly valued among the DPs. He was one of the few French Jews in the camp. Uri and his family had been picked up by the Nazis in 1943: he'd been sent to one concentration camp and his wife, Tova, to another. They'd lost contact with their son and they thought they'd never see him again. By some lucky chance, Uri and Tova found each other in Frankfurt after the war and made their way to our camp. They weren't happy. I think that one problem was they didn't speak Yiddish. Uri spoke a little German and some English, while Tova could express herself in reasonably effective English. They had one request: they wanted to go back to France.

'But why now?' I asked. 'There were plenty of trains to France last autumn.'

They spoke in general terms about changing their minds, but—as politely as I could—I kept pressing them. I wanted to know more. Eventually it came out: the turning-point was a planned parade in the camp to mark the first anniversary of the Liberation of Buchenwald concentration camp.

'Why do you object to this?' I asked.

I should have guessed. Uri was the camp's best tailor: they wanted him to make the uniforms for the parade.

'They plan to have a hundred DPs dressed in the striped pyjamas of the concentration camps. Can you imagine?'

I nodded. This was exactly the sort of theatrical event that Hanke would want.

They exchanged a few words and then Tova elaborated. 'It was our greatest tragedy. The worst humiliation of the Jewish people in history. It should be mourned in synagogues and churches, maybe commemorated in museums. But it is not something to be made into a public spectacle.'

Uri wanted to begin his life again.

'What will you do in France?' I asked.

'I will be a Frenchman. I will change my surname to one of those French names—Lavigne or Blanchet.'

'But—' Dan interrupted. 'That's stupid. You can be French and Jewish, can't you? There's no need to change your name. That's going too far.'

'You know the old saying?' asked Tova. 'We will be *French patriots outdoors, Jews indoors*. We will stay Jews, but we will look and act and talk like the French. That was our mistake, we were too visible.'

'No.' Dan shook his head vigorously. 'There was only one mistake: that was not fighting Hitler soon enough. The world's changed since 1939: there's room for everyone in a nation.'

They both laughed and then looked sadly at Dan.

'The world is not going to change,' said Tova. 'So we must change, so we can live.'

'But don't you want to go to Palestine with Hanke and her—' I stopped myself from saying *disciples*—'her followers?'

They looked at each other.

'Hanke,' said Tova. 'She is a great fighter. She's very brave. But we don't want to make our living by digging the earth. We're modern people. We miss Paris. France is our home.'

Uri said something in French. Tova nodded and then translated. 'We would go to America, if we could. But...'

I nodded. Closed doors everywhere. A shame, as he really was a good tailor: he could have worked anywhere.

I thought of Pierre and his insistence that Jews could never belong to France and wondered what he would think. I disagreed with almost every word Uri and Tova said, but I had to help them, that was my job. It seemed so wrong that they return to France and then, well, almost disguise themselves. But they were doing what UNRRA wanted, they were going home.

***

Hanke came to my office more often, two or three times a week, sometimes with Joel in tow. My heart sank each time Lena told me that she'd made an appointment. Hanke's demands grew more extravagant and she threatened to hold noisy demonstrations outside my office if I refused them. She was planning a big meeting in the hall, with Zionist speakers from Palestine. She demanded that I authorize it, always with the threat that it would happen anyway, if I didn't. It worried me. Things could get out of hand and a noisy, rowdy demonstration could become a full-blown riot. I hadn't forgotten the policeman's murder.

Some DPs thought like me about Hanke. They came to see me quietly, in ones and twos, complaining about how the communal areas in their bungalows had been converted into sites for militant Zionist propaganda and how their gardens had been ploughed up by Hanke's tractor. Eleanor said not to confront Hanke, or there really would be a riot. I didn't like this. Hanke was always getting what she wanted, but I reminded myself that in a few weeks, it would be someone else's problem.

One Wednesday I had a spare hour before another difficult meeting. I had to complete a report, but my mind kept wandering. Spring was coming and I longed to be outside, maybe walking with Eleanor, instead of thinking about the DPs. Sunbeams sparkled through the window, reflecting on the desk that Lena had polished. It was bright for April. My office was warm and I loosened my tie. The sunbeams flickered over my desk, on the top of my fountain pen, the base of my desk-lamp, the rim of my coffee cup, almost too bright to look at. There was something wrong with my chair. I tried to get comfortable. The sunbeams danced and shimmered on my desk, my fountain-pen, my coffee cup, they sparkled, how they sparkled, they didn't stop. The sun—that sunlight, it was too strong, too bright...

Lena came in straight away and found me lying on the floor, my legs flailing. Apparently, I'd yelled as I fell. She said she'd get Alma, but I stopped her. I asked for a glass of water and said I wanted Eleanor. I insisted Lena spoke to no one else. She got me up and into my best chair. Her voice sounded too loud. My ankles ached, my back hurt, an insistent pulse pounded painfully at the back of my neck. Lena went to find Eleanor, which seemed to take hours. I sipped the glass of water, trying to pull myself together. Eventually, Eleanor rushed in, her hair wild, concern written all over her face.

'Oh, Edmund,' she said. 'I thought...'

'You smell of tobacco,' I said. 'You've been smoking.'

***

'We're leaving tomorrow,' she insisted.

'We can't. We said we'd stay for another two weeks.'

'You're not well. This isn't good for either of us.'

'We won't be able to travel at such short notice.'

'There are trains!'

'There's going to be storms.'

'We've got to get out.'

'We can't. I feel better, I really do. It wasn't a bad one. Why are you smoking?'

'It's none of your business.'

'I worry about you.'

We stayed, unfortunately.

That was our last real conversation. I can't remember exactly where or when it took place. We did speak again, but it was just administrative stuff.

***

I'd never seen Alma look like that: grey, all the colour gone from her face. She and an American doctor had been up all night, working in shifts, caring for a mother who was ready to give birth. It was a long, difficult labour and the mother had a dangerous infection. They'd used the last of their penicillin earlier in the week. Alma spoke in a tense, agitated tone.

'More should have come, yesterday,' she said. 'But—nothing came. I know what Pierre did, but I need penicillin—I need it *now*, Edmund. It's essential. Without it—without it, both mother and child will die. She can only last another two or three hours.'

She was sure the American hospital had supplies. Normally, it would have only needed a telephone call. But the predicted storm had arrived: icy sleet was falling like bullets. I told Lena to ring the base, but she had trouble getting through: the line kept cutting out.

I was worried about the visit by the Zionist speakers from Palestine. I'd met them in the morning: tall, big-shouldered men, who'd glanced round my office with something like contempt. I couldn't help comparing them with Joel and Hanke. Joel's strong point was his easy-going geniality: it might have been a front, but it was a front he used well, it made him easy to talk to. Hanke had a passionate sincerity about her. She wore her heart on her sleeve and even when I disagreed with her, I still felt reluctant to say it, as her beliefs were so precious to her. Despite everything, I wanted to protect her. These two Zionists weren't anything like Hanke or Joel: they gave off a sense of raw power.

I'd told Dan that he was to observe the meeting in the hall. He refused at first, but I was worried about possible disturbances in the camp. If the DPs were going to demonstrate in large numbers, we'd have to call the American base for Military Policemen or even soldiers and I wanted as much warning as possible. Dan was reluctant, but I insisted that he went and, with bad grace, he agreed.

Our team was dangerously dispersed. Victor and Jacques had taken one of our trucks: they were in Frankfurt to pick up supplies for Hanke. Alma was with the sick mother, Dan at the meeting. Eleanor was at one of the schools, but she'd join me later. I stayed in my office, watching over the camp and waiting. I asked Lena to check again when the Americans would send the penicillin.

Eleanor arrived, but I was too tense to talk. She smoked three cigarettes, one after another.

Dan came back, looking grim. It had been an emotional meeting, he said. Two very forceful speakers and a receptive audience. They'd painted an alluring picture of the Palestine that awaited the DPs: deserts would be made to bloom, bright new towns would be created, modern agriculture, technology and industry would flourish in their new home. At the end, there'd been a mass singing of Hatikvah, Hope, the Zionist anthem. Dan admitted he'd been moved by it.

'Did they mention the Arabs in Palestine?'

Dan stopped, thought for a moment. 'No. Not a word.'

I shot Eleanor a glance. She looked away.

'And afterwards?' I asked. 'Any trouble?'

'The sleet was keeping people indoors,' he said. 'But it's stopped now and they're gathering in the square. Some of them have placards with slogans like *To Palestine* or *Open the Gates of Palestine.* They're waving blue and white flags.'

I looked at Eleanor.

'Where's Hanke?' I said.

Dan frowned. 'She was at the meeting. But, afterwards...'

I didn't like the sound of this. 'She's up to something.'

'Honestly, Edmund,' said Eleanor. 'What do you think she's going to do? Blow up the bungalows?'

'We can't have a riot here,' I said. Dan nodded.

We walked out and looked at the crowd gathering in the square. More people were joining every minute. I judged them to be boisterous, but not hostile. Still, I asked if Dan had his revolver with him. He nodded. Eleanor laughed at us and said there was nothing to worry about.

'Let us go to Palestine!' one or two shouted, but most waved and smiled when they saw us.

Hanke was nowhere to be seen.

'Let's try the hall,' I said.

The hall had been transformed with fiery posters in Yiddish and Hebrew, and blue and white flags. It looked empty, but just as Eleanor and Dan turned round to go, I thought I heard someone.

'Wait!' I called to them and went to investigate.

I walked down an aisle and there was Hanke, curled up on one of the chairs. As I approached, she shot me a poisonous look: her face was twisted, her eyes puffy, her lips trembling.

'Hanke?' I said. 'What's happened?'

Dan and Eleanor came back. We all sat down round her. Eleanor clutched her shoulder. I couldn't believe it: this strong, fearless woman had become a blubbering schoolgirl.

'Hanke?' I asked again.

She shrugged off Eleanor's hand, then made an effort to pull herself together.

***

Bit by bit, Hanke told us what had happened. She'd gone to the meeting with great hopes: finally, Palestinian Jews had arrived—this was a vital contact, joining the old Jewry of Europe with the new Jews of the Promised Land. As Dan had reported, their speeches had been effective. Hanke's heart had been filled with faith. At last, there would be a home for the Jews. They would leave the continent that had tried to annihilate them, they would begin again. The speakers had stressed how they needed every person: every Jew had to be ready to fight in this struggle. They spoke of leaving behind the parasitic, empty lives of the *shtetl*, marching from dependency into freedom. Hanke had seen—she swore that she really had *seen*—a vision of her future: she was driving a tractor across her people's land. She'd sung 'Hope' with heart-felt fervour, forcing her voice up high, proud that everyone was looking at her.

At the end of the meeting she'd left with the others, full of exuberance. But when she'd got to the doors of the hall, a thought occurred to her. She wanted to thank the speakers for the faith they'd communicated, she wanted to tell them, on behalf of *her* Jews, how grateful she was. She turned round in the foyer, walked back into the hall, where the speakers laughed as they tidied up their papers and pamphlets.

She looked up at us, her mouth trembling. I worried she would burst into tears.

The speakers hadn't seen her.

'Do you know what they were saying?'

Of course not, we said.

'More *sabon* for the nation.' She looked grim.

We had to ask her to translate.

There was a bad story, a nasty story about the fate of Jews killed in the concentration camps. It was said that their flesh was boiled down to make soap for the Germans. Apparently it wasn't true, but the word *sabon*, meaning soap, had entered the Zionist vocabulary to refer to the Jews of the concentration camps and then it became a general expression of contempt for the victims of the Nazis who had failed to resist.

'They see us as—as rags, tatters, rubbish!' shouted Hanke. 'They think we did nothing for six years! They use us to publicize the cause of Holy Israel, but they don't believe we're worthy of it. I have dreamt of this moment during all those years I spent in hiding, I have prepared for it for months and months in this filthy camp. *I* got the tractor, *I* started the farm on this cursed land. All to make myself worthy for *them*: myself and my comrades.'

'You're making a lot of just one word,' said Dan.

Hanke looked at him. 'They *laughed*. It was an old joke, one they'd told before. One they share!'

She spoke with absolute certainty.

'I was wrong,' she continued. 'There will be no ascent to our rightful land.'

'You mean—you won't go to Palestine?' asked Eleanor.

Hanke looked at her, shocked. 'Of course I'll go. Where else is there for us?' Her voice recovered some of its confidence and I recognised the words she spoke next. 'Europe has been our graveyard. America has closed its doors to us. England does not want us. We must return to our true home and end our long wandering. Of course I will go and as quickly as I can.'

She stood up, composed herself, adjusted her coat, looked thoughtful.

'But...' something occurred to her. 'I pity the Arabs of Palestine.'

'Why?' I asked.

'Those men do not want to share anything.'

She walked out quickly.

***

Dan, Eleanor and myself exchanged glances.

'I never thought I'd hear Hanke say—' said Eleanor.

'We can't stay here,' I interrupted. 'We need to check the camp: what are the protestors doing? And has that penicillin arrived?'

Outside, the sleet had returned. There were still a few people in the square and some chanted *Let us go to Palestine* as we crossed from the hall to our offices. They didn't look dangerous. But, if the sleet lessened...

Back inside, we shook the sleet off our greatcoats. I shouted to Lena: 'Has the penicillin arrived?'

She shook her head.

'Call them again,' I told her.

Alma burst through the door, her face red.

'Where is the penicillin?' she shouted. 'We need it, we need it *now*!'

I looked at Lena, who was on the telephone, looking surprised.

'What has happened?' yelled Alma.

Lena covered the telephone with her hand and looked at us. 'They say they know nothing about it. But I called them—I called them three times this morning.'

'No,' said Alma.

'This can't be,' I said. 'We'll have to drive to the American hospital.'

I looked round the room: Alma needed to stay with the mother. I needed to watch the protestors. I wanted Dan with me, as he had his revolver. That left—

'Eleanor,' I said.

'Yes,' she answered. 'Do you want some sandwiches?'

'You'll have to drive! Take a truck, it'll be safer than one of the cars.'

Alma looked surprised. 'You can drive?'

'I was an ambulance-driver for two years in London. They were the same as our trucks.'

Alma looked sceptical, but Eleanor was already buttoning up her greatcoat.

'Be careful,' said Dan, looking at the sleet outside. Eleanor nodded.

***

Outside my office, I heard Eleanor start the 3-ton truck. A moment later, through my office window, I saw her pull out past the camp entrance, carefully taking the left-hand side of the road to avoid the hole. She stayed on the left-hand side as she accelerated. Then I heard an American 10-ton truck approaching fast, as if driven by someone carrying urgent medical supplies.

I had time to think *no*.

***

Alma told me later that it would have been very quick. Eleanor wouldn't have suffered. The bigger truck smashed into the little one. My God, it almost smashed through it. We all ran out there, but I was so full of despair and agony that I could barely stumble and when I got to the smashed trucks, Dan pulled me back. It was over, I knew it was over.

The American driver was bruised, but otherwise uninjured. Alma got the penicillin.

My memories of the next hours are confused. Volunteer DP nurses guided me to a dark little room and made me drink something. They absolutely refused to let me leave. After a while,

Alma and Lena arrived with my greatcoat and they took me to Alma's house. Again, Alma made me drink something and I suppose I must have slept.

At some point I remembered the baby and the penicillin.

Alma looked sad. 'The baby died. The mother is healthy, she will live.'

Most of the time, I felt nothing. Maybe it was because of the drugs they were giving me. It was like a sort of seizure, a slow one that lasted days. I sat up in bed, stared at the walls, found patterns in the plasterwork, listened to the sleet and rain. I don't remember sleeping, although I suppose I must have. Could I live without Eleanor? I thought not. I expected to go mad, I expected to die, I couldn't understand why I was still breathing.

***

They came to see me, one by one. Or was that after the funeral? I'm not sure.

Alma told me it wasn't my fault. The road was slippery, the sleet made it difficult to see. I'd sent repeated requests to the Americans for someone to repair the hole outside the camp entrance.

'It was bad luck, Edmund, just terrible bad luck. You must not blame yourself.'

But I knew it was my fault. If I had let her drive earlier in our stay, she would have been more used to the roads. If I had agreed to go back to England, like she wanted, or if Dan or I had driven the truck to the American base...

Victor told me that Eleanor was a fine, fine woman, really one in a million. It was a privilege to have known her, something he'd always treasure. I realised he fancied her. I wasn't surprised. She was very attractive, too good for me.

Jacques came in and looked at me. I expected him to tell me that Eleanor was in heaven, as if that would be any comfort. I tensed myself, waiting for him to speak.

'This world is not the world we want, Edmund.' He spoke slowly, struggling with English, even after working with us for a year. 'Our task, while we are here, is to make it better. Eleanor did that.'

He shook my hand, grasped my arm.

But why is she not here with me, I thought.

Dan came in, looking awkward. 'She was a good comrade,' he said after a moment. Normally, I hated that word, with its resonances of closed ranks and closed minds. But he pronounced it with such gravity it had a spiritual quality.

'She chose to ally herself with the working-class,' he continued. 'Her ideas were sometimes misguided, but she was always on the side of truth and justice.'

A communist obituary for Red Eleanor. It might have been true, but it was no comfort.

***

I could have arranged for her body to be sent to London, but the idea of Eleanor being jolted in trains across half the continent was too horrible. I refused the suggestion and Alma arranged a funeral in a little German churchyard.

In those days, I was unable to follow a timetable or understand an appointment. One afternoon Alma and Dan turned up in my room. I was confused, not really understanding what they wanted. They got me dressed in my smartest uniform, newly pressed and then Victor drove us to the church. I was surprised so many people were there—all the UNRRA team, most of the DP Committee, many American officers from the base. I wondered what had attracted them.

An American pastor took the service. When he spoke the eulogy, I didn't recognise who he was speaking about. Then Dan and Alma stood next to me by the graveside and it all became clear. I would never see my dearest Eleanor again. I fell to the ground, convulsed with sobs. Dan and Alma lifted me up and got me back to Victor's car.

She'd gone.

34. Return Journey

Alma said she'd booked my train tickets for London and soon I'd be back in my bookshop. I shouted:

'No!'

She looked surprised.

'I can't go back there, Alma. It's the home I shared with—with Eleanor. I'll never set foot in that place again.'

'But you cannot stay here.'

We talked and Alma said she'd send Muriel a telegram and ask her to find somewhere temporary for me.

I can't remember if I thanked her. Probably not.

***

It was a slow, difficult journey back to England. On the train, I began to wake up from the nightmare of my last days in Neukirchen. I sat and thought and dreamt, instead of reading. My mind played tricks on me. I was haunted by this feeling that I'd lost something and I kept checking for my passport and my wallet, and looking to see if my case was in the rack above. Of course, all those things were in their proper places. I'd lost something else, something deeper and bigger. I'd lost Eleanor. I'd go through the scene of the crash as if it was something I'd seen in a film and I had to keep reminding myself that it *really* had happened and I, Edmund, was the one left alone at the end of it. It was difficult to understand.

I tried to pull myself together. The train stopped at a station and I got a coffee at a kiosk on the platform. I smoked a cigarette. It was strange to be doing such normal things, they just didn't feel real.

Back in the train, I looked at the green, lush countryside of Germany and thought that this was probably the last time I'd see it. A shame, it was a beautiful country and I'd never got to know it. Apart from Hildegard, I hadn't really spoken to any Germans. We'd lived in a bubble of UNRRA workers, DPs, soldiers and military government officials. Still, all that was behind me. That got me wondering about what to do next.

I was sure of one thing: I couldn't go back to the bookshop. Even the thought of it gave me a headache. Could I face friends and neighbours and tell them what happened? Of course I couldn't. I needed a clean break. After twelve months in Germany, I'd saved a lot of money. It wasn't that I'd been so well paid, it was just that there'd been nothing to buy. I could do anything I wanted.

As the train juddered through Germany and France, through one day and one night, I made plans. I'd sell the bookshop and flat. If possible, I wouldn't step inside it. I'd ask Muriel to clear it out, or I'd pay someone to do it. With the money from the bookshop, I'd buy a store in Wales, probably in Cardiff. A general store, the old-fashioned sort, the sort that sold almost everything. Focusing on this cleared my mind and made me feel stronger. I stomped up and down the carriage a bit, just to move my legs. A couple of squaddies offered me a drink: I shook my head.

With any luck, I'd be back in Wales in a fortnight. A month at most. I'd give up my ambitions. I'd seen France, Germany, Morocco and Poland. That was enough. Travelling hadn't worked for me. I'd been a failed leader in a failing organisation. I'd expected so much from UNRRA and I'd got nothing in return. Hell, I'd lost the most precious part of my life.

Would I ever marry again? Probably not. But I'd have my shop in Cardiff, my assistants, maybe I'd join a local church. I wouldn't be alone.

35. Home

So that's it. End of story. I shift in my father's easy-chair, suddenly uncomfortable. Is it the end? It's certainly *an* ending. But maybe not *the* end: my story will continue, without you. I look round the room. I still haven't found the object I was searching for: the thing to remember you by. I glance at the pictures, books and furniture. There's so much of you here. And while it's disturbing, it's also comforting. How can that be? I whisper *Eleanor*. There's no reply.

We were very different people. Sometimes we argued and it hurts so much that we never had a true reconciliation after that last argument. If we'd got back here... But no. That didn't happen.

A phrase of Blake's comes into my mind. *Without contraries there is no progression.* No, that's not it. He used that strange, contracted eighteenth-century speech. *Without contraries is no progression.* That's it. Between us there were all the contraries anyone could wish for. But that never stopped us from loving each other. It didn't separate us. I feel certain of that. In fact—it was those differences that made our marriage, I see that now. It meant I could give something to you and you could give something to me. So was there *progression*? I'm a different man from who I was six years ago. A better man, I think. A wiser man, probably. In part, because of you. But also—because of what we did together. I still don't understand it all but—that doesn't matter. I've got plenty of time to think about it.

And in Germany: contraries everywhere. We came at the end of the battle of the century. Opposing forces smashing against each other, all the time. That's what Kotov tried to tell me. I see now: that's what *dialectics* means. History progresses in ways we don't understand. UNRRA didn't achieve what we hoped for. But it was part of a bigger cycle of world history: fascism and communism, democracy and capitalism... And UNRRA played a part in this cycle, even if none of us were truly aware of it. Even UNRRA's failure achieved something. Our efforts countered some of the hatred and destruction of the Nazis; we stood for something good, we helped people find their homes, we saved lives and that's never to be dismissed. I hope we laid the foundations for something better and we showed History a new path, maybe we even took a few steps along it.

***

My mood has changed. I look at this room with new eyes and I realise: *it's home*. This is my home. Alright, it reminds me of you, but is that a bad thing? I won't ever be able to stop thinking about you: every time I light a cigarette or drink a coffee or read a book, whether I'm in London or Cardiff or anywhere, I'll think of you. Am I going to give up those things because they remind me of you? Of course not: it would be like giving up life. So I'll think of you, I'll think of you every day and maybe it'll make me sad or maybe it'll make me happy—or maybe both—but I'll still do it, because I want to live. My story hasn't ended.

As for this flat and bookshop. I mustn't sell everything and move on, that'd be a mistake, an attempt to wipe the slate clean that would never work. I'll change them, I'll adapt them. That's not denying our story here, but I'll move on to a new chapter. I'm right to do that. Out of these swirling emotions in my mind, there'll come *progression*. I think I've already started. I'm a bookshop-owner, that's who I am, that's who I'll be. I'll try to be a good bookshop-owner.

I think of Muriel for a second: she'll be so happy to hear I'm keeping the bookshop.

I smile and whisper, *Eleanor*. You'd be pleased, I'm sure of that.

Then I know it. Of course. That's what I was looking for. How silly people are when they look for something that will last forever. I think of the chatter I've heard about marble gravestones with engraved letters, always with the idea of creating something that will endure for eternity. Ridiculous. Just walk round a graveyard, any graveyard and look at the tombstones. They're weathered, the sun, wind and rain corrupt and deface them. Leave them for a few decades and they'll crack. Is that a bad thing? Do we need stronger, bigger gravestones and better marble to resist time? No, no, a thousand times, no. This is our condition, our human condition, we ebb and flow like the tides, this is part of our *progression*. It's the big-wigs and the *führers* who build pyramids and towers and walls to defy the times and eventually they're always defeated, thank God.

I've been trying to clutch onto a solid object that will last forever. Nothing in this house that belonged to you can do that: jewellery would corrode or get lost, paper would rot, clothes would fade. But there are some things that last—at least as long as a lifetime and that's long enough. My thoughts, my memories of you will never fade—or, if they fade, it will be the trivial incidents that I forget, the important memories will never, never go. I don't need an object to help me keep those.

And now I know it: there is one thing of yours I can take and which will stay with me for all my life, unaffected by wind, rain and time. I smile and whisper once more, *Eleanor*. That's it. I can take your name.

My parents never gave me a middle name. I think there were too many arguments between the family clans and my father eventually decided to refuse all suggestions. So I'll take your name: wherever I live, however hot the sun or cold the rain, in wartime or in peace, whatever job I'm doing, you'll be there with me.

I feel a sudden doubt. Can a man have a woman's name? But most of the time, it'd just be an initial. Edmund E. Jenkins. It's got a certain ring to it, I like it. But what about forms and passports? Won't people laugh? Ah, hell, I'll tell them it's an old Welsh spelling of Alan.

Epilogue: To Eleanor

I pick up my fountain pen, pause, then begin writing.

14 April 1950

Dear Eleanor,

Someone recommended that I do this. Apparently, it's therapeutic. But it still seems a strange thing to

I put down my pen. This is stupid, just plain stupid. I can't do it, I can't think of anything to say. What's the point of writing a letter to someone who's been dead for four years? All because of some strange man. He just appeared, in that pub in Bloomsbury. When I sat down, I was sure that nobody else was there—and then, there he was. Interesting fellow. An academic or student, researching in the British Museum. Easy to talk to. Dark, a bit like you. Could almost have been your brother. No, he was English, definitely English. Turned out he was a widower too—well, happened to lots of us in the war. Said writing a letter to his late wife had helped—a way of focusing thoughts. Maybe it worked for him.

This week, my evenings stretch out, long and anxious. A difficult moment, a worrying moment. What would you think of me now? I think you'd be pleased. After all, I've managed. You wouldn't have wanted me to stay lonely and miserable for the rest of my life, would you? No. It's better this way, I'm sure.

My seizures have gone. Some bad moments, back in 1946. Dark times. I was lost, let's face it. Tried everything. Even went to see Methodist Sarah. Would you believe it? She's married, with two children. Seems happy. Still a Methodist, of course, but I felt it had become almost a convention for her, not a matter of faith. But she's a socialist! Never expected that, although she said she always had been. Husband has a shop, seems a pleasant fellow. She still does charity work.

I even—I even tried to re-join the Methodists. Gerald interviewed me and gave it to me straight. Told me that I wasn't moved by faith, but by circumstance. He was right.

Lots of lost, lonely people after the war. Plenty of widowed and divorced women—for a while, I searched for them. But it never felt right. Obviously, they weren't you, they couldn't be you. I felt that they'd never understand. Bumped along with Abby—Abigail—from the literary set for a few months. Widowed, of course, and a painter. Dark, gloomy canvases. After a while, decided she was making me feel worse.

The literary scene wasn't bright. Lots of officers writing their memoirs: How I Defeated Hitler. But where were the great novels? Our *War and Peace*? No one seemed capable of expressing what we'd been through.

The best that could be said was that things were settling down, people were going home, or at least trying to. News trickled in. Dan wrote regularly—I think he was worried about me. He's converted Hildegard's house into three flats: they let out two of them and live off the rents. Does odd jobs for extra money. They sound happy. Alma and Jacques got married: we didn't see that coming, did we? Jacques moved to Denmark, his only worry being the scarcity of Catholic churches. He finds Danish difficult, so they still communicate in English. He works in a garage, she's still a nurse. Pierre avoided prosecution! He must've pulled some strings. He went back to France and got a university job. Hope he isn't teaching his students that Jews are biologically different from Frenchmen. Victor had the hardest time. He went back to America, found he barely recognised his wife. So he returned to Germany and spent three months searching for Greta. Never found her. He works for an American firm in Frankfurt. Muriel's sorted herself out. Cut ties with Graham and found Brian, an unattached RAF officer. She pops round now and again. Giuseppe has his own jazz trio: piano plus bass and drums. Plays a difficult, complicated sort of jazz, not really my sort of thing, though I think you'd like it. He still wants to edit the manuscripts of that Italian Communist.

I finally got a letter from father and mother. They had sent me long letters in the first years of the war, but none of them arrived. They guessed what was happening and then limited themselves to sending a card every Christmas. The 1943 card arrived in 1947. It's a story you hear all the time: lost mail, letters turning up, years out of date.

They sound well. They've set up a chapel for the natives. Surprised by my news, obviously, and disappointed that they never met you. I ought to go and see them one day.

As for me. Got to thinking I was going to stay single. Looked for other things to do. Went through a phase of reading Blake, even those great long mystical epics. Understood one word in three, but still... Read *Steppenwolf*. Remember that? You made me buy it in Poland. Strange, very strange. Like a letter from you. Was that how you saw me? A grumpy, lonely man, a misanthrope? I don't think I was ever that bad. I read it twice, straight through, thinking about you all the time.

After a few months, I went through all those papers in your crate and found your manuscript. My God, what a mess! And I thought you were so clear-thinking. Not here, you weren't. Pages and pages of stuff, each one scrawled over with corrections and additions, crazy pagination: Version 5(b)—second draft. One evening, I almost threw the whole lot on the fire—it was cold and there was so little coal. Instead, I worked on it, off and on for a year, sorting it out, reading your words and thinking about UNRRA and the DPs and you. Interesting, worth saying. I couldn't have written it. I knew what you meant and loved hearing your voice again. Finally typed a new version myself. (I've got my own typewriter and telephone now.) Spent a year hawking it round publishers. Thought that they would've leapt at it: a memoir about refugees in the post-war world, by a UN aid-worker. Not a chance. *People don't want to hear about refugees.* There wasn't much generosity of spirit around. Still isn't.

I didn't give up. Still had some UNRRA money. Raided my savings, set myself up as a publisher, got your essay printed as a proper booklet, not some grubby pamphlet. Dan gave me the name of a printer. Did 500 copies: they looked beautiful, they really did. Sent copies to the big weeklies and monthlies. Not a single review! In the first year, I sold eight, all to people who knew you. But then—*Peace News* reviewed it. I hadn't thought of them. One or two Quakers got interested, wrote in asking to meet you. Since then—well, it'll never be a best-seller. But each month, a dozen or so people want copies. Often women—you wouldn't be surprised by that, would you? Some of them send me their manuscripts. They're not bad. Might try a second, even a third title one day. There's so much that's never been said, about the war and all that.

As for my epilepsy. When I registered with the National Health Service, a couple of years ago, I saw a new doctor. Told him my symptoms, told him everything. He frowned. Said it didn't sound like epilepsy. Definitely something, of course, but more likely low blood pressure, with migraine. Whatever it was, I haven't had anything since 1946, thank God. So frustrating to think I could have joined up, like everyone else. But then I wouldn't have met you.

We weren't served well by doctors, were we? Pierre saying you had tuberculosis, my false epilepsy.

I finally found the right widow. Or she found me. She turned up in the bookshop one lunchtime, back in February 1948. First thing I thought was how cold she looked. Foreign, obviously. Talked English in a strange way—lively, full of confidence, yet agitated, not quite making sense. She wanted to order books by some writer I'd never heard of and there was a problem spelling his name. Kept looking at me, as if waiting for me to say something. But what? Where was this writer from, I asked. Palestine, she said. I looked at her again. Nafah! She looked different: thinner, colder, maybe unhappier. It wasn't a wild coincidence. She'd renewed her travel visas and finally finished the journey she started in 1938. When she was in London, she found a list of London bookshops and had seen my name.

We talked about that night in the waiting-room in Morocco. I remembered Tawfeek and she remembered you. Sad. Tawfeek went back to Palestine: killed in one of the first skirmishes between Palestinians and Zionists, before the fighting of 1948. By some miracle, the British state granted Nafah temporary asylum.

Meeting Nafah and learning about Palestine made me think of Hanke. I've heard nothing of her, but news of Israel appears regularly in the left-wing press. Generally very positive reports. The *kibbutz* are hailed as a major social experiment and young members of the Labour Party talk of travelling there like going on a pilgrimage. Nafah tells me something else. Mass dispossession and violence: all things we saw in Germany. I'm confused by these two contradictory truths. I suppose time will tell.

But Nafah. Love at first sight? Well, it wasn't *first* sight, was it? Something felt right when I found her in my bookshop. She's not you, I'm not stupid. But it helps that she'd met you.

Things were forced on us. There was a problem with her residence application. She could've been expelled. I didn't want her to go, I really didn't want her to go. So: marriage. My second wedding, her second wedding.

You're happy for me, aren't you? She's very different from you, yet often reminds me of you.

And now—Nafah's in hospital, expecting. There's a problem, not serious they keep telling me, but she's under observation. Two more weeks, they say. It's not easy waiting. I saw her this afternoon, but they don't let you stay long. The evenings drag without her, the flat seems empty.

Nafah asked, if it's a girl, do we call her Eleanor? I was tempted, I really was. But then I thought: no. I want this child to be a new being, who'll find her own way in the world, not someone who has to follow you. Then Nafah surprised me: there are a few names which are common to Arabs and Brits. We'll choose one of them. The same if it's a boy.

The telephone rings. A baby girl! Nafah's fine. I'm a father, I'm a father.

APPENDIX

THE REFUGEE'S LESSON
[Excerpt]
by
ELEANOR JENKINS
(London: Innocence & Experience Press, 1948)

I sit on a stolen chair, facing a stolen type-writer, in a stolen house. My typing-paper, thank goodness, is merely borrowed; my clothes, too, borrowed from the male sex—for reasons I fail to understand, women who seek to help others are required to dress like men. My job? To relieve and rehabilitate, to work with the most cruelly persecuted people in the world. The irony of my position is not lost on me. I sit in a veritable thief's den, and my job entails the promotion of moral standards, which must include the old injunction: *thou shalt not steal*. While I wear a half-sexed uniform, my job requires me to promote the family, to make husbands feel once again they are husbands and wives feel once again they are wives. I am to encourage the return of the Angel in the House, I am to rescue this starved spirit from her hiding-places in the cellars and attics, where she sheltered from the bomber-plane and the cannon.

But as I sip my black-market coffee from my stolen cup, I start to wonder. What right have I to inculcate morality among the unclassified, the undesirable and the uprooted? Have I been looking through the wrong end of the telescope? After all, confusion is rife here. I live and work in a bizarre Alice in Wonderland-world: a devastated half-colony, in which military power, imperial pride and charitable conscience sit at the same bench. Around me is a fragile half-peace, already slipping towards a half-war. Maybe the situation has infected me with its folly, which flatters me by saying that I am the voice of sanity and reason. Maybe the stark reality is that my status—a female aid-worker—is like that of some fantastic creature, to be listed alongside the gryphon and the hippogriff: a being which only exists in the imagination. Maybe, instead, the truth is that it is these infiltrees, these evacuees, these stateless, unassimilable aliens who are real and it is they who can tell me the truth.

What would they teach me?

***

Their first lesson would be the importance of words. Are you a Jewish Pole or a Polish Jew? Are you an evacuee, a deportee, a refugee or merely a Displaced Person? Your livelihood and your future may well depend on producing the right answer. Others will judge your response and then decide for you. For years, you have not been to school, you have not read a newspaper or attended a lecture. For you, news takes the form of rumours: it circulates through gossip at the crossroads, it is demonstrated by the numbers of walkers on a road, by their origins and their destination. These signs revealed to you the progress of the war, not the newspaper headline, the wireless announcement or the cinema newsreel. Yet, even in the devastated conditions of this half-peace, you must quickly learn the language of a modern bureaucracy, you must fit your agony and dispossession into the columns and rows of the printed form.

The second lesson that you could teach would be the importance of being born at the right time. In the seventeenth century, French Huguenot refugees were welcomed by the English state, which calculated that these migrant populations brought wealth with them: they brought their skills and experience. Our modern, civilized, rational twentieth century has propounded more deadly, treacherous arguments and the mass opinion of our peoples has been warped by race-thinking. Governments across the free world have taught their populations to be scared of the ragged figures who traipse along the roads. Britain passed the Aliens Act of 1905, America the Quota Act in 1924. The 'poor, huddled masses yearning to be free' are no longer welcome. Following the most destructive war in history, following mass displacement on a scale unthinkable to past generations, refugees are viewed with suspicion. Democratic governments, liberal newspapers, humanitarian teachers warn that homeless hordes are carriers of disease, rogues seeking to exploit the foolish benevolence of host communities, or subversive revolutionaries bringing their noxious politics into respectable nations. The war against Hitler has not produced any generosity of spirit: instead, it has left populations marked by fear and suspicion.

Victor Serge, a French-Russian writer and a refugee himself, spoke of the 'midnight of the century'. For the refugee, that dark period surely began in June 1938, at the Evian Conference in Switzerland. The world's major powers gathered to discuss the fate of Jews in Nazi Germany. Not a single one was prepared to allow the entry of German Jewish refugees. The situation has barely changed today: midnight's darkness still covers the Continent; we await the dawn. The world fears the Jewish tailor, the Rumanian miner, the Hungarian teacher, the Yugoslav serving-girl and the Polish engineer, and yet in the next breath political leaders talk of reconstruction and call for the revival of great industries.

The third lesson, I think, is the most difficult one: perhaps one which the wise refugee is still in the process of learning. It is about building a home. What could be more important? In the immediate, seize what you can, use it as best you can. Single men and women find each other, cling on to each other, form families and have children. They construct their homes with what is available to them: with packing cases and army blankets, they build walls, make spaces, create rooms. But in the bigger sense? Is home simply the physical space they originated from? Or can the wanderer return to his or her rightful place? But maybe that physical space been so transformed by the military devastation and moral ruin, that it is no longer a berth for wanderer. In that case, where do the wanderers find their home? Do they play the card of ultra-fidelity, and claim that within them there lies the seeds of an ideal homeland, one which transcends the tawdry imitation that occupies the physical space of their homeland? Certainly, one can find in refugees' religious rituals and culinary traditions, in their songs and literature, an ultra-nationalism as dogged and fiery as the official nationalism of the passport, national anthem and school curriculum. Just as James Joyce re-created a Dublin of his imagination while writing in Zurich, so the refugees re-create their homelands in the cabins and open spaces of the refugee camp.

But there may be a different interpretation of this third lesson. If it is possible for a Pole to lose his Polishness, a Greek to lose her Greekness, then maybe this is a lesson about the nature of nationhood. 'All that is solid melts into air' wrote Karl Marx, speaking of the corrosive effects of capitalism on social custom. The refugee may be in a privileged position of lucidity, able to watch the melting of solid matter, able to see through the illusions of nationhood. Is there really some irreducible core at the heart of nationality? Is there some quality which truly makes French-ness different from German-ness, and German-ness from Swedish-ness? Or do we not hear endless variants of the same theme, from green and pleasant land to *la France profonde*, from *Heimat* to *mir*? Each claims to be individual, unique and original, and yet each resembles the other in all important details. The lucid refugee could well think that these are all illusions, pretty and enjoyable in their own way, suitable fairy tales for children in need of diversion, but something that grown men and women should disdain.

Sources for Epigraphs

William Blake, *Proverbs of Hell*

Colin MacInnes, *To the Victors, the Spoils* (London: MacGibbon & Kee, 1950), p. 326

J.B. Priestley, *Postscripts* (London: William Heinemann, 1940), p. 14.

Sir Stafford Cripps, *Democracy Alive: A Selection of Recent Speeches* (London: Sidgwick & Jackson, 1946), p. 11.

W. Arnold-Forster, 'UNRRA's Work for Displaced Persons in Germany,' *International Affairs* 22:1 (Jan 1946), pp. 1—13 (p. 6).

Marvin Klemme, *The Inside Story of UNRRA; An Experience in Internationalism; a First Hand Report on the Displaced People of Europe* (New York: Lifetime Editions, 1949), p. 29.

Francesca M. Wilson, *Aftermath: France, Germany, Austria, Yugoslavia; 1945 and 1946* (West Drayton: Penguin, 1947), p. 18.

Susan T. Pettiss and Lynne Taylor, *After the Shooting Stopped: the Story of an UNRRA Welfare Worker in Germany 1945-1947* (Crewe: Trafford, 2004), p. 65.

Marcus J. Smith, *Dachau: the Harrowing of Hell* (Albany, N.Y.: State University of New York Press, 1995 [1972]), p. 80.

Elsie Thomas Culver, 'A Journey through Post-World War II Europe', http://www.gtuarchives.org/culver/index.html [undated]

Edith Wharton, *In Morocco* (London: I. B. Tauris, 2006 [1920]), p. 21.

Victor Gollancz, *In Darkest Germany* (London: Gollancz, 1947), p. 84.

Abergavenny Small Press.
publishing

Archive Journal Issue #1: Oct 2020

Fiction: Alex Barr, Oliver Barton, Tony Curtis, Andrew Davis, Mike Farrell-Deveau, Steven Glascoe, Karenne Griffin, Tony Lawrence, Martin Locock, Julie Primon.
Poetry: Jackie Biggs, Mark Blayney, Rachel Carney, Tony Curtis, Steven Feeney, Rhiannon Fielder-Hobbs, Alex Hubbard, Suzanne Iuppa,
Niamh Keoghan, Alwyn Marriage, Edmund Morton, Mary Senier.
Art: Louise Burrows, Suzanne Iuppa, David Morgan-Davies.
Available from ASP's online shop, for download. Introductory price: £2.99.
https://www.asppublishing.co.uk/

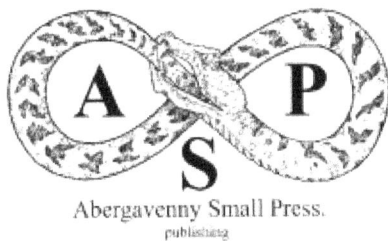

Abergavenny Small Press.
publishing

Archive Journal Issue #2: Jan 2021

Fiction: Clare Babbage, Pat Coates, Lynn Clausen, Andrew Davis, Max Dunbar, Mike Farrell-Deveau, Sharif Gemie, Geoff Gillanders, Robert Mitchell, Gill McEvoy, David Pearce, Diana Powell.
Poetry: Charley Barnes, Rebecca Charles, Helen Cook, Derek Coyle,
John C Lloyd & George Sandifer-Smith, Sheila Jacob, Nicole Lee, Mel Perry, Harriet Truscott, Sue Watling, Helen M Williams, Richard Williams.
Art: Natascha Graham, Melanie Harrison-Gearing, Gareth Owen.
Available from ASP's online shop, for download: £4.99.
https://www.asppublishing.co.uk/

Abergavenny Small Press.
publishing

Archive Journal Issue #3: Apr 2021

Fiction: Bob Baker, Mark Blickley & Inge Dumoulin, Pat Coates, Andrew Davis,
Mike Farrell, Sharif Gemie, Tony Lawrence, J M Curry, Zach Murphy, David Pearce,
Poetry: Ronán P Berry, Sheena Bradley, Lourda Delaney, Natascha Graham,
Ceinwen Haydon, Rhea Johnson, David Pearce, Ceri Savage, Gerry Stewart.
Art: Jantien Powell, Serena Piccoli, Diana Sanders.

Available from ASP's online shop, for download: £4.99.
https://www.asppublishing.co.uk/

Abergavenny Small Press.
publishing

Archive Journal Issue #4: Jul 2021

Fiction: Jack T Canis, J M Curry, Andrew Davis, Sharif Gemie, Martin Locock,
Maddy McEwan, Yash Seyedbagheri, Kate Venables, Richard Williams, Christopher Witty.
Poetry: Clare Fielder, Oz Hardwick, Jennifer A McGowan, Ken Pobo, Damien Posterino,
Stephanie Powell, Diana Saunders, Ruth Taaffe, Kerry Trautman, Susannah Violette.
Art: Fabrice Poussin, Weining Wang, John Winder.

Available from ASP's online shop, for download: £4.99.
https://www.asppublishing.co.uk/

Abergavenny Small Press.
publishing

Archive Journal Issue #5: Oct 2021

Fiction: Will Borger, Jack T Canis, J M Curry, Kimberley Deer, Sharif Gemie,
Ian McNaughton, Nicholas Shroeder, Dave Thomas.
Poetry: Phil Wood (featured poet), Imogen Davies, M Kavin, Kevin McDermott,
Mark J Mitchell, Emma Morgan, John Short.
Art: Steve Patterson, John Winder.

Available from ASP's online shop, for download: £4.99.
https://www.asppublishing.co.uk/

Milton Keynes UK
Ingram Content Group UK Ltd.
UKHW010734300424
441987UK00001B/63

9 781739 652098

Il était
trois petits lapins
qui s'en allaient

Va-t'en, gros loup méchant !

Texte d'Anne-Marie Chapouton
Illustrations d'Annick Bougerolle

Père Castor ● Flammarion

© Flammarion 2010 pour la présente édition
© Flammarion 1992 pour le texte et l'illustration
ISBN : 978-2-0812-3090-3 – ISSN : 0768-3340
Imprimé en Asie par South China Printing – juillet 2012

En chemin, ils chantent :
Hou ! Hou !
Va-t'en loup,
gros loup méchant !
Va-t'en, va-t'en !

au bois
chercher des fraises,
de bonnes fraises des bois.

Mais le loup n'a pas peur.
Il a tout entendu.

Il dit :
« Miam ! miam ! Je suis gourmand !
Le temps de m'habiller, parce qu'il fait frais,
et je m'en vais les croquer tous les trois,
farcis à la fraise des bois. »

Vite, vite, il attrape sa culotte.
Crotte ! l'élastique est craqué.

Alors le loup,
le gros loup méchant,
enfile une aiguille
et se met à raccommoder,
en se disant :
« Pas de panique,
j'ai tout mon temps ! »

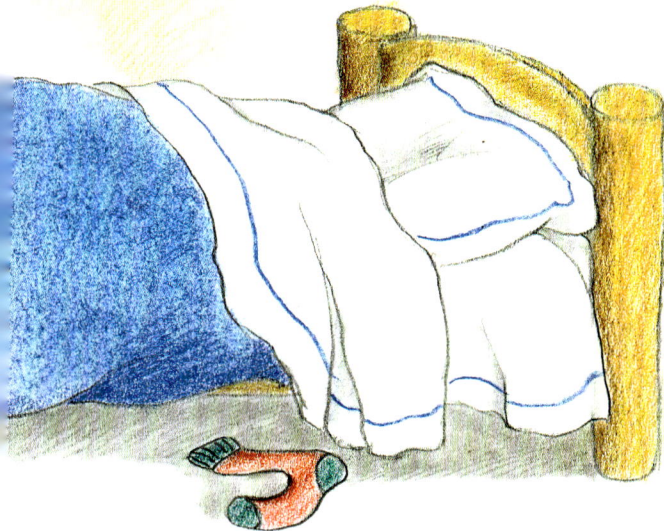

Les lapins sont arrivés.
Ils cueillent des fraises en chantant toujours :

Hou ! Hou !
Va-t'en loup,
gros loup méchant !
Va-t'en, va-t'en !

« Ha ha ! J'arrive »,
pense le loup en enfilant sa chemise.

Mais il lui manque trois boutons.
Ça lui fait un courant d'air
sur l'estomac et des *guili-guili*
sur le nombril.

Alors, il va chercher
une autre chemise.

Les lapins cueillent toujours
en se dépêchant.
Hou ! Hou !
Va-t'en loup,
gros loup méchant !
Va-t'en, va-t'en !

« Minute, minute ! »
dit le loup en glissant la chemise
dans son pantalon.

Ça y est, enfin.
Il est prêt.

Il fait trois pas en courant,
mais, aïe ! Il s'arrête
en se tenant un pied.

« Boudin, crottin !
C'est plein de
piquants par ici ! »

Et il revient en boitillant
pour enfiler ses souliers.
Tant pis si les lacets
sont craqués.

Maintenant, le gros loup
méchant est tout à fait prêt
et il peut enfin crier :
« J'ARRIVE ! »

Mais, *PLAF* !

Il se prend les pieds
dans ses lacets…

… et il s'étale à plat ventre
dans les ronces bien piquantes.

« AILLE ILLE OUILLE ! »
hurle le loup.

« Mon nez !
Mon pauvre nez ! »

Les lapins ont tout entendu
et s'en vont en courant vite, vite,
jusqu'à leur terrier.
Sauvés !

Ce matin, le gros loup des bois
mangera des fraises,
de bonnes fraises des bois
et pas de petits lapins...

23

... et voilà ! Voilà !
Et tant pis s'il n'aime pas ça !

Dépôt légal : avril 2010
Éditions Flammarion (n° L.01EJDN000463.C003) 87, quai Panhard-et-Levassor – 75647 Paris Cedex 13
www.editions.flammarion.com
Loi n° 49-956 du 16 juillet 1949 sur les publications destinées à la jeunesse